About the

Formerly a Video and Radio Producer, Christy McKellen now spends her time writing provocative, passionate, seductive romance. When she's not writing, she can be found enjoying life with her husband and three children, walking for pleasure and researching other people's deepest secrets and desires.

Barbara Wallace can't remember when she wasn't dreaming up love stories in her head, so writing romances for Mills & Boon is a dream come true. Happily married to her own Prince Charming, she lives in New England with a house full of empty-nest animals. Readers can catch up with Barbara through her newsletter. Sign up at barbarawallace.com

Stefanie London is a *USA Today* bestselling author of contemporary romance. Her books have been called 'genuinely entertaining and memorable' by *Booklist*, and her writing praised as 'elegant, descriptive and delectable' by *RT Magazine*. Originally from Australia, she now lives in Toronto with her very own hero and is doing her best to travel the world. She frequently indulges her passions for lipstick, good coffee, books and anything zombie related.

Opposites Attract Collection

March 2025
Love in Paradise

April 2025
Medics in Love

May 2025
Rancher's Attraction

June 2025
Workplace Temptation

July 2025
On Paper

August 2025
Forbidden Love

Opposites Attract: Workplace Temptation

CHRISTY McKELLEN

BARBARA WALLACE

STEFANIE LONDON

MILLS & BOON

All rights reserved including the right of reproduction in whole or in part in any form. This edition is published by arrangement with Harlequin Enterprises ULC.

This is a work of fiction. Names, characters, places, locations and incidents are purely fictional and bear no relationship to any real life individuals, living or dead, or to any actual places, business establishments, locations, events or incidents. Any resemblance is entirely coincidental.

Without limiting the author's and publisher's exclusive rights, any unauthorised use of this publication to train generative artificial intelligence (AI) technologies is expressly prohibited. HarperCollins also exercise their rights under Article 4(3) of the Digital Single Market Directive 2019/790 and expressly reserve this publication from the text and data mining exception.

® and ™ are trademarks owned and used by the trademark owner and/or its licensee. Trademarks marked with ® are registered with the United Kingdom Patent Office and/or the Office for Harmonisation in the Internal Market and in other countries.

First Published in Great Britain 2025
by Mills & Boon, an imprint of HarperCollins*Publishers* Ltd
1 London Bridge Street, London, SE1 9GF

www.harpercollins.co.uk

HarperCollins*Publishers*
Macken House, 39/40 Mayor Street Upper,
Dublin 1, D01 C9W8, Ireland

Opposites Attract: Workplace Temptation © 2025 Harlequin Enterprises ULC.

Unlocking Her Boss's Heart © 2016 Christy McKellen
The Billionaire's Fair Lady © 2013 Barbara Wallace
Hard Deal © 2018 Stefanie Little

ISBN: 978-0-263-41737-1

This book contains FSC™ certified paper and other controlled sources to ensure responsible forest management.

For more information visit: www.harpercollins.co.uk/green

Printed and Bound in the UK using 100% Renewable Electricity
at CPI Group (UK) Ltd, Croydon, CR0 4YY

UNLOCKING HER BOSS'S HEART

CHRISTY McKELLEN

This one is for Babs and Phil, the most generous, loving and supportive parents in the world. You've seen me through all my ups and downs (and there have been a few), and always picked me up, dusted me off and cheered me on.

I love you. I hope you know that.

CHAPTER ONE

CARA WINSTONE CLIMBED the smooth slate steps to the shiny black front door of the town house in South Kensington and tried hard not to be awed by its imposing elegance.

This place was exactly the sort of house she'd dreamed about living in during her naïve but hopeful youth. In her fantasies, the four-storey Victorian house would be alive with happy, mischievous children, whom she and her handsome husband would firmly but lovingly keep in line and laugh about in the evenings once they'd gone to bed. Each room would have a beautiful display of fresh seasonal flowers and light would pour in through the large picture windows, reflecting off the tasteful but comfortable furnishings.

Back in real life, her topsy-turvy one-bed flat in Islington was a million miles away from this grand goddess of a mansion.

Not that it was going to be her flat for much longer if she didn't make good on this opportunity today.

The triple espresso she'd had for breakfast lurched around in her stomach as she thought about how close she was to being evicted from the place she'd called home for the past six years by her greedy landlord. If she didn't find another job soon she was going to have to slink back to Cornwall, to the village that time forgot, and beg to share her parents' box room with the dogs until she got back on her feet.

She loved her parents dearly, but the thought of them all bumping elbows again in their tiny isolated house made her shudder. Especially after they'd been so excited when she'd called six months ago to tell them about landing her dream job as Executive Assistant to the CEO of one of the largest conglomerates in the country. Thanks to her mother's prodigious grapevine, word had quickly spread through both the family and her parents' local community and she'd been inundated with texts and emails of congratulations.

The thought of having to call them again now and explain why she'd been forced to hand in her notice after only three months made her queasy with shame. She couldn't do it. Not after the sacrifices they'd made in order to pay for her expensive private education, so she'd have the opportunities they'd never had. No, she owed them more than that.

But, with any luck, she'd never be forced to have that humiliating conversation because this chance today could be the ideal opportunity to get her feet back under the table. If she could secure this job, she was sure that everything else would fall into place.

Shifting the folder that contained her CV and the glowing references she'd accumulated over the years under her arm, she pressed the shiny brass bell next to the door and waited to be greeted by the owner of the house.

And waited.

Tapping her foot, she smoothed down her hair again, then straightened the skirt of her best suit, wanting to look her most professional and together self when the door finally swung open.

Except that it didn't.

Perhaps the occupier hadn't heard her ring.

Fighting the urge to chew on the nails she'd only just grown out, she rang again, for longer this time and was just about to give up and come back later when the door swung open to reveal a tall, shockingly handsome man with a long-limbed, powerful physique and the kind of self-possessed air that made her heart beat a little faster. His chocolate-brown hair looked as though it could do with a cut, but it fell across his forehead into his striking gold-shot hazel eyes in the most becoming manner. If she had to sum him up in one word it would be *dashing*—an old-fashioned-sounding term, but somehow it suited him down to the ground.

His disgruntled gaze dropped from her face to the folder under her arm.

'Yes?' he barked, his tone so fierce she took a pace backwards and nearly fell off the top step.

'Max Firebrace?' To her chagrin, her voice came out a little wobbly in the face of his unexpected hostility.

His frown deepened. 'I don't donate to charities at the door.'

Taking a deep breath, she plastered an assertive smile

onto her face and said in her most patient voice, 'I'm not working for a charity. I'm here for the job.'

His antagonism seemed to crackle like a brooding lightning storm between them. 'What are you talking about? I'm not hiring for a job.'

Prickly heat rushed across her skin as she blinked at him in panicky confusion. 'Really? But my cousin Poppy said you needed a personal assistant because you're snowed under with work.'

He crossed his arms and shook his head as an expression of beleaguered understanding flashed across his face.

'I only told Poppy I'd look into hiring someone to get her off my back,' he said irritably.

She frowned at him in confusion, fighting the sinking feeling in her gut. 'So you don't need a PA?'

Closing his eyes, he rubbed a hand across his face and let out a short, sharp sigh. 'I'm very busy, yes, but I don't have time to even interview for a PA right now, let alone train them up, so if you'll excuse me—'

He made as if to shut the door, but before he could get it halfway closed she dashed forwards, throwing up both hands in a desperate attempt to stall him and dropping her folder onto the floor with a loud clatter. 'Wait! Please!'

A look of agitated surprise crossed his face at the cacophony, but at least he paused, then opened the door a precious few inches again.

Taking that as a sign from the gods of perseverance, Cara scooped up her folder from the floor, threw back her shoulders and launched into the sales pitch she'd been practising since Poppy's email had landed in her inbox last night, letting her know about this golden opportunity.

'I'm *very* good at what I do and I'm a quick learner—I have six years of experience as a PA so you won't need to show me much at all.' Her voice had taken on an embarrassing squeaky quality, but she soldiered on regardless.

'I'm excellent at working on my own initiative and I'm precise and thorough. You'll see when you hire me,' she said, forcing a confidence she didn't feel any more into her voice.

He continued to scowl at her, his hand still gripping the door as if he was seriously contemplating shutting it in her face, but she was not about to leave this doorstep without a fight. She'd had *enough* of feeling like a failure.

'Give me a chance to show you what I can do, free of charge, today, then if you like what you see I can start properly tomorrow.' Her forced smile was beginning to make her cheeks ache now.

His eyes narrowed as he appeared to consider her proposal.

After a few tense seconds of silence, where she thought her heart might beat its way out of her chest, he nodded towards the folder she was still clutching in her hand.

'Is that your CV?' he asked.

'Yes.' She handed it to him and watched with bated breath as he flipped through it.

'Okay,' he said finally, sighing hard and shoving the

folder back towards her. 'Show me what you can do today, then if I'm satisfied I'll offer you a paid one-month trial period. After *that* I'll decide whether it's going to work out as a full-time position or not.'

'Done.' She stuck out a hand, which he looked at with a bemused expression, before enveloping it in his own large, warm one.

Relief, chased by an unnerving hot tingle, rushed through her as he squeezed her fingers, causing every nerve-ending on her body to spring to life.

'You'd better come in,' he said, dropping the handshake and turning his broad back on her to disappear into the house.

Judging by his abrupt manner, it seemed she had her work cut out if she was going to impress him. Still, she was up for the challenge—even if the man did make her stomach flip in the most disconcerting way.

Shaking off her nerves, she hurried inside after him, closing the heavy door behind her and swivelling back just in time to see him march into a doorway at the end of the hall.

And what a hall. It had more square footage than her entire flat put together. The high, pale cream walls were lined with abstract works of art on real canvases, not clip-framed prints like she had at her place, and the colourful mosaic-tiled floor ran for what must have been a good fifty metres before it joined the bottom of a wide oak staircase which led up to a similarly grand stairwell, where soft light flooded in through a huge stained-glass window.

Stopping by a marble-topped hall table, which, she

noted, was sadly devoid of flowers, she took a deep calming breath before striding down the hallway to the room he'd vanished into.

Okay, she could do this. She could be impressive. Because she *was* impressive.

Right, Cara? *Right?*

The room she entered was just as spacious as the hall, but this time the walls were painted a soft duck-egg blue below the picture rail and a crisp, fresh white above it, which made the corniced ceiling feel as if it was a million miles above her and that she was very small indeed in comparison.

Max was standing in the middle of the polished parquet floor with a look of distracted impatience on his face. Despite her nerves, Cara couldn't help but be aware of how dauntingly charismatic he was. The man seemed to give off waves of pure sexual energy.

'My name's Cara, by the way,' she said, swallowing her apprehension and giving him a friendly smile.

He just nodded and held out a laptop. 'This is a spare. You can use it today. Once you've set it up, you can get started on scanning and filing those documents over there,' he said, pointing to a teetering pile of paper on a table by the window. 'There's the filing cabinet—' he swung his finger to point at it '—there's the scanner.' Another swing of his finger. 'The filing system should be self-explanatory,' he concluded with barely concealed agitation in his voice.

So he wasn't a people person then.

'Okay, thank you,' she said, taking the laptop from him and going to sit on a long, low sofa that was pushed up against the wall on the opposite side of the room to a large oak desk with a computer and huge monitor on top of it.

Tamping down on the nervous tension that had plagued her ever since she'd walked away from her last job, she booted up the laptop, opened the internet browser and set up her email account and a folder called 'Firebrace Management Solutions' in a remote file-saving app. Spotting a stack of business cards on the coffee table next to the sofa, she swiped one and programmed Max's mobile number into her phone, then added his email address to her contacts.

Throughout all this, he sat at his desk with his back to her, deeply absorbed in writing the document she must have stopped him from working on when she'd knocked on his door.

Okay. The first thing she was going to do was make them both a hot drink, then she'd make a start on the mountain of paperwork to be digitally backed up and filed.

Not wanting to speak up and disturb him with questions at this point, she decided to do a bit of investigative work. Placing the laptop carefully onto the sofa, she stood up and made for the door, intent on searching out the kitchen.

He didn't stir from his computer screen as she walked past him.

Well, if nothing else, at least this was going to be a very different experience to her last job. By the end of her time there she could barely move without feeling a set of judging eyes burning into her.

The kitchen was in the room directly opposite and she stood for a moment to survey the lie of it. There was a big glass-topped table in the middle with six chairs pushed in around it and an expanse of cream-coloured marble work surface, which ran the length of two sides of the room. The whole place was sleek and new-looking, with not a thing out of place.

Opening up the dishwasher, she peered inside and saw one mug and one cereal bowl sitting in the rack. *Hmm.* So it was just Max living here? Unless his partner was away at the moment. Glancing round, she scanned the place for photographs, but there weren't any, not even one stuck to the enormous American fridge. In fact, this place was so devoid of personalised knick-knacks it could have been a kitchen in a show home.

Lifting the mug out of the dishwasher, she checked it for remnants of his last drink, noting from the smell that it was coffee, no sugar, and from the colour that he took it without milk. There was a technical-looking coffee maker on the counter which flummoxed her for a moment or two, but she soon figured out how to set it up and went about finding coffee grounds in the sparsely filled fridge and making them both a drink, adding plenty of milk to hers.

Walking back into the room, she saw that Max hadn't budged a centimetre since she'd left and was still busy tapping away on the keyboard.

After placing his drink carefully onto the desk, which he acknowledged with a grunt, she took a look through the filing cabinet till she figured out which system he was using, then squared up to the mountain of paperwork on the sideboard, took a breath and dived in.

Well, she was certainly the most *determined* woman he'd met in a long time.

Max Firebrace watched Cara out of the corner of his eye as she manhandled the pile of documents over to the sofa and heard her put them down with a thump on the floor.

Glancing at the drink she'd brought him, he noticed she'd made him a black coffee without even asking what he wanted.

Huh. He wasn't expecting that. The PAs he'd had in the past had asked a lot of questions when they'd first started working with him, but Cara seemed content to use her initiative and just get on with things.

Perhaps this wasn't going to be as much of a trial as he'd assumed when he'd agreed to their bargain on the doorstep.

It was typical of Poppy to send someone over here without letting him know. His friend was a shrewd operator all right. She'd known he was blowing her off when he promised to get someone in to help him and had clearly taken it upon herself to make it happen anyway.

Irritation made his skin prickle.

He was busy, sure, but, as he'd told Poppy at the time, it wasn't anything he couldn't handle. He'd allow Cara to work her one-month trial period to placate his friend, but then he'd let her go. He wasn't ready to hire someone else full-time yet; there wasn't enough for her to do day-to-day, and he didn't need someone hanging around, distracting him.

Leaning back into the leather swivel chair that had practically become his home in the past few months, he rubbed the heels of his hands across his eyes before picking up the drink and taking a sip.

He'd been working more and more at the weekends now that his management consultancy was starting to grow some roots, and he was beginning to feel it. It had been a slog since he'd set up on his own, but he'd been glad of the distraction and it was finally starting to pay dividends. If things carried on in the same vein, at some point in the future he'd be in a position to rent an office, hire some employees and start expanding. *Then* he could relax a little and things would get back to a more even keel.

The thought buoyed him. After working for other people since graduating from university, he was enjoying having full control over who he worked for and when; it seemed to bring about a modicum of peace—something that had eluded him for the past eighteen months. Ever since Jemima had gone.

No, *died*.

He really needed to allow the word into his interior monologue now. No one else had wanted to say it at the time, so he'd become used to employing all the gentler euphemisms himself, but there was no point pretending it was anything else. She'd died, so suddenly and unexpectedly it had left him reeling for months, and he still wasn't used to living in this great big empty house without her. The house Jemima had inherited from her great-aunt. The home she'd wanted to fill with children—which he'd asked her to wait for—until *he* felt ready.

Pain twisted in his stomach as he thought about all that he'd lost—his beautiful, compassionate wife and their future family. Recently he'd been waking up at night in a cold sweat, reaching out to try and save a phantom child with Jemima's eyes from a fall, or a fire—the shock and anguish of it often staying with him for the rest of the following day.

No wonder he was tired.

A movement in the corner of his eye broke his train of thought and he turned to watch Cara as she opened up the filing cabinet to the right of him and began to deftly slide documents into the manila folders inside.

Now that he looked at her properly, he could see the family resemblance to Poppy. She had the same shiny coal-black hair as his friend, which cascaded over her slim shoulders, and a very short blunt-cut fringe above bright blue almond-shaped eyes.

She was pretty. Very pretty, in fact.

Not that he had any interest in her romantically. It was purely an observation.

Cara looked round and caught him watching her, her cheeks flushing in response to his scrutiny.

Feeling uncomfortable with the atmosphere he'd created by staring at her, he sat up straighter, crossing his arms and adopting a more businesslike posture. 'So, Cara, tell me about the last place you worked. Why did you leave?'

Her rosy cheeks seemed to pale under his direct gaze.

Rocking back on her heels, she cleared her throat, her gaze skittering away from his to stare down at the papers in her hands, as if she was priming herself to give him an answer she thought he'd want to hear.

What was *that* about? The incongruity made him frown.

'Or were you fired?'

Her gaze snapped back to his. 'No, no, I left. At least, I opted for voluntary redundancy. The business I was working for took a big financial hit last year and, because I was the last in, it felt only right that I should be the first out. There were lots of people who worked there with families to support, whereas I'm only me—I mean I don't have anyone depending on me.'

Her voice had risen throughout that little monologue and the colour had returned to her cheeks to the point where she looked uncomfortably flushed. There was something not quite right about the way she'd delivered her answer, but he couldn't put his finger on what it was.

Perhaps she was just nervous? He knew he could come across as fierce sometimes, though usually only when someone did something to displease him.

He didn't suffer fools gladly.

But she'd been fine whilst persuading him to give her a shot at the PA job.

'That's it? You took voluntary redundancy?'

She nodded and gave him a smile that didn't quite reach her eyes. 'That's it.'

'So why come begging for this job? Surely, with your six years of experience, you could snap up a senior position in another blue-chip firm and earn a lot more money.'

Crossing her arms, she pulled her posture up straighter, as if preparing to face off with him. 'I wouldn't say I *begged* you for this job—'

He widened his eyes, taken aback by the defensiveness in her tone.

Noting this, she sank back into her former posture and swept a conciliatory hand towards him. '—but I take your point. To be honest, I've been looking for a change of scene from the corporate workplace and when Poppy mailed me about this opportunity it seemed to fit with exactly what I was looking for. I like the idea of working in a small, dedicated team and being an intrinsic part of the growth of a new business. Poppy says you're brilliant at what you do and I like working for brilliant people.' She flashed him another smile, this time with a lot more warmth in it.

He narrowed his eyes and gave her an approving nod. 'Okay. Good answer. You're an excellent ambassador for yourself and that's a skill I rate highly.'

Her eyes seemed to take on an odd shine in the bright mid-morning light, as if they'd welled up with tears.

Surely not.

Breaking eye contact, she looked down at the papers in her hand and blinked a couple of times, giving the floor a small nod. 'Well, that's good to hear.' When she looked back up, her eyes were clear again and the bravado in her expression made him wonder what was going on in her head.

Not that he should concern himself with such things.

An odd moment passed between them as their gazes caught and he became uncomfortably aware of the silence in the room. He'd been on his own in this house for longer than he wanted to think about, and having her here was evidently messing with his head. Which was exactly what he didn't need.

Cara looked away first, turning to open one of the lower filing cabinet drawers. After dropping the documents into it, she turned back to face him with a bright smile. 'Okay, well, it won't take me too much longer to finish this so I'll nip out in a bit and get us some lunch from the café a couple of streets away. When I walked past earlier there was an amazing smell of fresh bread wafting out of there, and they had a fantastic selection of deli meats and cheeses and some delicious-looking salads.'

Max's stomach rumbled as he pictured the scene she'd so artfully drawn in his mind. He was always too busy to go out and fetch lunch for himself, so ended up eating whatever he could forage from the kitchen, which usually wasn't much.

'Then, if you have a spare minute later on, you can give me access to your online diary,' Cara continued, not waiting for his response. 'I'll take a look through it and organise any transport and overnight stays you need booking.'

'Okay. That would be useful,' he said, giving her a nod. It would be great to have the small daily inconveniences taken care of so he could concentrate on getting this report knocked into shape today.

Hmm. Perhaps it would prove more advantageous than he'd thought to have her around for a while.

He'd have to make sure he fully reaped the benefit of her time here before letting her go.

CHAPTER TWO

She was a terrible liar.

The expression on Max's face had been sceptical at best when she'd reeled out the line about leaving her last job, but Cara thought she'd pulled it off. At least he hadn't told her to sling her hook.

Yet.

She got the impression he was the type of person who wouldn't tolerate any kind of emotional weakness—something she was particularly sensitive to after her last boyfriend, Ewan, left her three months ago because he was fed up with her 'moaning and mood swings'. So she was going to have to be careful not to let any more momentary wobbles show on her face. It was going to be happy, happy, joy, joy! from here on in.

After slipping the last document into the filing cabinet, taking care not to let him see how much her hands were still shaking, she grabbed her coat and bag and, after taking a great gulp of crisp city air into her lungs, went to the café to pick up some lunch for them both, leaving the door off the latch so she wouldn't have to disturb Max by ringing the bell on her return.

Inevitably, she bought a much bigger selection of deli wares than the two of them could possibly eat in one session, but she told herself that Max could finish off whatever remained for his supper. Judging by the emptiness of his cavernous fridge, he'd probably be glad of it later.

This made her wonder again about his personal situation. Poppy had told her very little in the email—which she'd sent in a rare five minutes off from her crazy-sounding filming schedule in the African desert. Cara didn't want to bother her cousin with those kinds of questions when she was so busy, so it was up to her to find out the answers herself. For purely professional reasons, of course. It would make her working life much easier if she knew whether she needed to take a partner's feelings into consideration when making bookings away from the office.

Surprisingly, Max didn't put up much resistance to being dragged away from his computer with the promise of lunch and came into the kitchen just as she'd finished laying out the last small pot of pimento-stuffed olives, which she hadn't been able to resist buying.

'Good timing,' she said as he sat down. 'That deli is incredible. I wasn't sure what you'd prefer so I got just about everything they had—hopefully, there'll be something you like—and there should be plenty left over for tomorrow, or this evening if you don't already have dinner plans.'

Good grief—could she jabber more?

Clearly, this had occurred to Max too because he raised his eyebrows, but didn't say a word.

Trying not to let his silence intimidate her, Cara passed him a plate, which he took with an abrupt nod of thanks, and she watched him load it up with food before tucking in.

'So, Max,' she said, taking a plate for herself and filling it with small triangular-cut sandwiches stuffed with soft cheese and prosciutto and a spoonful of fluffy couscous speckled with herbs and tiny pieces of red pepper. 'How do you know Poppy? She didn't tell me anything about you—other than that you're friends.'

He gave a small shrug. 'We met at university.'

Cara waited for him to elaborate.

He didn't. He just kept on eating.

Okay, so he wasn't the sort to offer up personal details about himself and liked to keep things super professional with colleagues, but perhaps she'd be able to get more out of him once they'd built up a rapport between them.

That was okay. It was early days yet. She could bide her time.

At least she had some company for lunch, even if he wasn't interested in talking much. She'd spent all her lunchtimes at her last place of work alone, either sitting in the local park or eating a sandwich at her desk, forcing the food past her constricted throat, trying not to care about being excluded from the raucous group of PAs who regularly lunched together. The Cobra Clique, she'd called them in her head.

Not to their faces.

Never to their faces.

Because, after making the mistake of assuming she'd

be welcomed into their group when she'd first started working there—still riding on a wave of pride and excitement about landing such a coveted job—she'd soon realised that she'd stepped right into the middle of a viper's nest. Especially after the backlash began to snap its tail a couple of days into her first week.

Fighting the roll of nausea that always assaulted her when she thought about it, she took a large bite of sandwich and chewed hard, forcing herself to swallow, determined not to let what had happened bother her any more. They'd won and she was not going to let them keep on winning.

'It's a beautiful house you have, Max,' she said, to distract herself from the memories still determinedly circling her head. 'Have you been here long?'

His gaze shot to hers and she was alarmed to see him frown. 'Three years,' he said, with a clip of finality to his voice, as if wanting to make it clear he didn't want to discuss the subject any more.

Okay then.

From the atmosphere that now hummed between them, you'd have thought she'd asked him how much cold hard cash he'd laid down for the place. Perhaps people did ask him that regularly and he was fed up with answering it. Or maybe he thought she'd ask for a bigger wage if she thought he was loaded.

Whatever the reason, his frostiness had now totally destroyed her appetite, so she was pushing the couscous around her plate when Max stood up, making her jump in her seat.

'Let me know how much I owe you for lunch and I'll

get it out of petty cash before you leave,' he said, turning abruptly on the spot and heading over to the dishwasher to load his empty plate into it.

His movements were jerky and fast, as if he was really irritated about something now.

It couldn't be her, could it?

No.

Could it?

He must just be keen to get back to work.

As soon as he left the room, she let out the breath she'd been holding, feeling the tension in her neck muscles release a little.

The words *frying pan* and *fire* flitted through her head, but she dismissed them. If he was a friend of Poppy's he couldn't be that bad. She must have just caught him on a bad day. And, as her friend Sarah had pointed out after she'd cried on her shoulder about making a mess of her recent job interviews, she was bound to be prone to paranoia after her last experience.

Once she'd cleared up in the kitchen, Cara got straight back to work, using the link Max gave her to log in to his online diary and work through his travel requirements for the next month. His former ire seemed to have abated somewhat and their interaction from that point onwards was more relaxed, but still very professional. Blessedly, concentrating on the work soothed her and the headache that had started at the end of lunch began to lift as she worked methodically through her tasks.

Mid-afternoon, Max broke off from writing his document for a couple of minutes to outline some research he wanted her to do on a few businesses he was considering targeting. To her frustration, she had to throw every molecule of energy into making scrupulous notes in order to keep focused on the task in hand and not on the way Max's masculine scent made her senses reel and her skin heat with awareness every time he leaned closer to point something out on the computer they were huddled around.

That was something she was going to have to conquer if they continued to work together, which hopefully they would. She definitely couldn't afford a crush on her boss to get in the way of her recuperating future.

After finally being released from the duress of his unnerving presence, she spent the remainder of the day happily surfing the internet and collating the information into a handy crib sheet for him, revelling in the relief of getting back into a mindset she'd taken for granted until about six months ago, before her whole working life had been turned inside out.

At five-thirty she both printed out the document and emailed it to him, then gathered up her coat and bag, feeling as though she'd done her first good day's work in a long time.

Approaching his desk, she cleared her throat and laid the printout onto it, trying not to stare at the way his muscles moved beneath his slim-fitting shirt while she waited for him to finish what he was typing. Tearing her eyes away from his broad back, she took the opportunity to look at his hands instead, noting with a strange satisfaction that he wasn't wearing a wedding ring on his long, strong-looking fingers.

Okay, not married then. But surely he must have a girlfriend. She couldn't imagine someone as attractive as Max being single.

He stopped typing and swivelled round in his chair to face her, startling her out of her musings and triggering a strange throb, low in her body.

'You've done well today; I'm impressed,' he said, giving her a slow nod.

She couldn't stop her mouth from springing up into a full-on grin. It had been a long while since she'd been complimented on her work and it felt ridiculously good.

'Thank you—I've really enjoyed it.'

His raised eyebrow told her she'd been a bit over-effusive with that statement, but he unfolded his arms and dipped his head thoughtfully.

'If you're still interested, I'm willing to go ahead with the one-month trial.'

Her squeak of delight made him blink. 'I can't promise there'll be a full-time job at the end of it, though,' he added quickly.

She nodded. 'Okay, I understand.' She'd just have to make sure she'd made herself indispensable by the end of the month.

He then named a weekly wage that made her heart leap with excitement. With money like that she could afford to stay in London and keep on renting her flat.

'I'll see you here at nine tomorrow then,' he concluded, turning back to his computer screen.

'Great. Nine o'clock tomorrow,' she repeated, smiling at the back of his head and retreating out of the room.

She floated out of the house on a cloud of joy, desperate to get home so she could phone her landlord and tell him she was going to be able to make next month's rent so he didn't need to find a new tenant for her flat.

It was all going to be okay now; she could feel it.

Back in her flat, she dialled her landlord's number and he answered with a brusque, 'Yes.'

'Dominic—it's Cara Winstone. I'm calling with good news. I've just started at a new job so I'll be able to renew my lease on your property in Islington.'

There was a silence at the end of the phone, followed by a long sigh. 'Sorry, Cara, but I've already promised my nephew he can move in at the end of the week. I got the impression you wouldn't be able to afford the rent any more and I've kept it pitifully low for the last couple of years already. I can't afford to sub you any more.'

Fear and anger made her stomach sink and a suffocating heat race over her skin as she fully took in what he'd just said. He was such a liar. He'd been hiking the rent up year on year until she'd felt as if she was being totally fleeced, but she hadn't wanted the hassle of moving out of her comfortable little flat so she'd sucked it up. Until she wasn't able to any more.

'Can't you tell your nephew that your current tenant has changed her mind?' Even as she said it she knew what his answer was going to be.

'No. I can't. You had your chance to renew. I couldn't wait any longer and my nephew was having trouble finding somewhere suitable to live. It's a cut-throat rental market in London at the moment.'

That was something she was about to find out herself, she felt sure of it.

'Do you have anywhere else available to rent at the moment?' she asked, desperately grasping for some glimmer of a solution.

'No. Sorry.'

He didn't sound sorry, she noted with another sting of anger.

'You've got till the end of the week, then I want you out,' he continued. 'Make sure the place is in a good state when you leave or I'll have to withhold your damage deposit.' And, with that, he put the phone down on her.

It took a few minutes of hanging her head between her knees for the dizziness to abate and for her erratic heartbeat to return to normal.

Okay, this was just a setback. She could handle it.

Just because it would be hard to find a decent flat to rent in London at short notice didn't mean she wouldn't find somewhere else. She'd have to be proactive though and make sure to put all her feelers out, then respond quickly to any leads.

That could prove tricky now that she was working so closely with Max and she was going to have to be very careful not to mess up on the job, because it looked as though she was going to need things to work out there more than ever now.

The rest of the week flew by for Max, with Cara turning up exactly when she said she would and working diligently and efficiently through the tasks he gave her.

Whilst it was useful having her around to take care of some of the more mundane jobs that he'd been ignoring for far too long, he also found her presence was disrupting his ability to lose himself in his work, which he'd come to rely on in order to get through the fiercely busy days.

She was just so *jolly* all the time.

And she was making the place smell different. Every morning when he came downstairs for his breakfast he noticed her light floral perfume in the air. It was as though she was beginning to permeate the walls of his house and even the furniture with her scent.

It made him uncomfortable.

He knew he'd been rude during their first lunch together when Cara had asked him about the house and that he'd been unforthcoming about anything of a personal nature ever since—preferring to spend his lunchtimes in companionable silence—but he was concerned that any questions about himself would inevitably lead on to him having to talk about Jemima.

Work was supposed to be sanctuary from thinking about what had happened and he really didn't want to discuss it with Cara.

He also didn't want them to become too sociable because it would only make it harder for him to let her go after the promised month of employment.

Clearly she was very good at her job, so he had no concerns about her finding another position quickly after her time was up, but it might still prove awkward when it came down to saying no to full-time employment if they were on friendly terms. He suspected Cara's story about taking voluntary redundancy wasn't entirely based on truth and that she and Poppy had cooked up the story to play on his sympathy in order to get him to agree to take her on. While he was fine with allowing his errant friend to push him into a temporary arrangement to appease her mollycoddling nature, he wasn't going to allow her to bully him into keeping Cara on full-time.

He didn't need her.

After waking late on Friday morning and having to let an ebullient Cara in whilst still not yet ready to face the day, he had to rush his shower and hustle down to the kitchen with a pounding headache from not sleeping well the night before. Opening the fridge, he found that Cara had stocked it with all sorts of alien-looking food—things he would never have picked out himself. He knew he was bad at getting round to food shopping, but Cara's choices were clearly suggesting he wasn't looking after himself properly. There were superfoods galore in there.

He slammed the fridge door shut in disgust.

The damn woman was taking over the place.

Cara was in the hallway when he came out of the kitchen a few minutes later with a cup of coffee so strong he could have stood his spoon up in it. She waved a cheery hello, then gestured to a vase of brightly coloured flowers that she'd put onto the hall table, giving him a jaunty smile as if to say, *That's better, right?* which really set his teeth on edge. How was it possible for her to be so damn happy all the time? Did the woman live with her head permanently in the clouds?

They'd never had fresh flowers in the house when Jemima was alive because she'd suffered with bad hay fever from the pollen, and he was just about to tell Cara that when he caught himself and clamped his mouth shut. It wasn't a discussion he wanted to have this morning, with a head that felt as if it was about to explode. The very last thing he needed right now was Cara's fervent pity.

'I thought it would be nice to have a bit of colour in here,' she said brightly, oblivious to his displeasure. 'I walked past the most amazing florist's on my way over here and I just couldn't resist popping in. Flowers are so good for lifting your mood.'

'That's fine,' he said through gritted teeth, hoping she wasn't going to be this chipper all day. He didn't think his head could stand it.

'I'll just grab myself a cup of tea, then I'll be in,' she said.

Only managing to summon a grunt in response, he walked into the morning room that he'd turned into an office. He'd chosen it because it was away from the distractions of the street and in the odd moment of pause he found that staring out into the neatly laid garden soothed him. There was a particular brightly coloured bird that came back day after day and hopped about on the lawn, looking for worms, which captivated him. It wasn't there today, though.

After going through his ever-growing inbox and dealing with the quick and easy things, he opened up his diary to check what was going on that day. He had a conference call starting in ten minutes that would probably last till lunchtime, which meant he'd need to brief Cara now about what he wanted her to get on with.

Where was she, anyway?

She'd only been going to make herself a hot drink. Surely she must have done that by now?

Getting up from his chair with a sigh of irritation, he walked through to the kitchen to find her. The last thing he needed was to have to chase his PA down. It was going to be a demanding day which required some intense concentration and he needed her to be on the ball and ready to knuckle down.

She was leaning against the table with her back to the door when he walked into the kitchen, her head cocked to one side as if she was fascinated by something on the other side of the room.

He frowned at her back, wondering what in the heck could be so absorbing, until she spoke in a hushed tone and he realised she was on the phone.

'I don't know whether I'll be able to get away at lunchtime. I have to fetch my boss's lunch and there's a ton of other stuff I have to wade through. His systems are a mess. Unfortunately, Max isn't the type you can ask for a favour either; he's not exactly approachable. I could make it over for about six o'clock, though,' she muttered into the phone.

The hairs rose on the back of his neck. She was making arrangements to see her friends on his time?

He cleared his throat loudly, acutely aware of the rough harshness of his tone in the quiet of the room.

Spinning around at the noise, Cara gave him a look of horror, plainly embarrassed to be caught out.

Definitely a personal call then.

Frustration rattled through him, heating his blood.

How could he have been so gullible as to think it would be easy having her as an employee? Apparently she was going to be just as hard work to manage as all the other PAs he'd had.

'Are you sure you took redundancy at your last place? Or did they let you go for taking liberties on the job?' he said, unable to keep the angry disappointment out of his voice.

She swallowed hard and he found his gaze drawn to the long column of her throat, its smooth elegance distracting him for a second. Shaking off his momentary befuddlement, he snapped his gaze back to hers, annoyed with himself for losing concentration.

'I do not expect behaviour like this from someone with six years of experience as a personal assistant. This isn't the canteen where you waste time gossiping with your mates instead of doing the job you're being paid to do. Things like this make you look stupid and amateurish.'

She nodded jerkily but didn't say anything as her cheeks flushed with colour and a tight little frown appeared in the centre of her forehead.

Fighting a twist of unease, he took another step forwards and pointed a finger at her. 'You do not take personal phone calls on my time. Is that understood? Otherwise, you and I are going to have a problem, and problems are the last thing I need right now. I took a chance on you because you came recommended by Poppy. Do not make a fool out of my friend. Or out of me.'

'I'm sorry—it won't ever happen again. I promise,' she said, her voice barely above a whisper.

The look in her eyes disturbed him. It was such a change from her usual cheery countenance that it sat uncomfortably with him. In fact, to witness her reaction you'd have thought he'd just slapped her around the face, not given her a dressing-down.

'See that it doesn't,' he concluded with a curt nod, an unnerving throb beginning to beat in his throat.

As he walked back into his office, he found he couldn't wipe the haunted expression in her eyes from his mind, his pace faltering as he allowed himself to reflect fully on what had just happened.

Perhaps he'd been a bit too hard on her.

Running a hand over his tired eyes, he shook his head at himself. Who was he kidding—he'd definitely overreacted. For all he knew, it could have been a sick relative on the phone whom she needed to visit urgently.

The trouble was, he'd been so careful to keep her at arm's length and not to let any of his own personal details slip he'd totally failed to ask her anything about herself.

And he was tired. So tired it was making him cranky.

Swivelling on the spot, he went back out of the room to find her, not entirely sure what he was going to say, but knowing he should probably smooth things over between them. He needed her on his side today.

Walking back towards the kitchen, he met her as she was coming out, a cup of tea in her hand.

Instead of the look of sheepish upset he'd expected to see, she gave him a bright smile.

'I know you have a conference call in a couple of

minutes, so if you can walk me through what I need to tackle today I'll get straight on it,' she said, her voice steady and true as if the past few minutes hadn't happened.

He stared at her in surprise, unnerved by the one hundred and eighty degree turn in her demeanour.

Had he imagined the look in her eyes that had disturbed him so much?

No, it had definitely been there; he was sure of it.

Still, at least this showed she wasn't one to hold grudges and let an atmosphere linger after being reprimanded. He appreciated that. He certainly couldn't work with someone who struggled to maintain a professional front when something didn't go their way.

But her level of nonchalance confused him, leaving him a little unsure of where they now stood with each other. Should he mention that he felt he'd been a bit hard on her? Or should he just leave it and sweep it under the carpet as she seemed keen to do?

What was the matter with him? This was ridiculous. He didn't have time for semantics today.

Giving her a firm nod, he turned around and walked back towards the office. 'Good, let's get started then.'

Determined to keep her hand from shaking and not slop hot tea all over herself, Cara followed Max back into the office, ready to be given instructions for the day.

She knew she couldn't afford to show any weakness right now.

Based on her experiences with Max so far, she was pretty damn sure if he thought she wasn't up to the job he'd fire her on the spot and then she'd be left with absolutely nothing.

That was not going to happen to her today.

She needed this job, with its excellent wage and the prospect of a good reference from a well-respected businessman, to be able to stay here in London. All she had to do was keep her head down and stick it out here with him until she found another permanent position somewhere else. She had CVs out at a couple more places and with any luck another opportunity might present itself soon. Until then she'd just have to make sure she didn't allow his blunt manner and sharp tongue to erode her delicate confidence any further.

The trouble was, she'd allowed herself to be lulled into a false sense of security on her first day here after Max's compliment about her being a good ambassador for herself, only for him to pull the rug out from under her regrouping confidence later with his moods and quick temper.

The very last thing she needed was to work with another bully.

Not that she could really blame him for being angry in this instance. It must have looked really bad, her taking a personal phone call at the beginning of the working day. The really frustrating thing was that she'd never done anything like that before in her life. She was a rule follower to the core and very strict with herself about not surfing the Net or making personal calls on her employer's time, even in a big office where those kinds of things could go unnoticed.

Putting her drink down carefully, she wheeled her

chair nearer to Max's desk and prepared to take notes, keeping her chin up and a benign smile fixed firmly on her face.

His own professional manner seemingly restored, Max outlined what he wanted her to do throughout the day, which she jotted down in her notebook. Once he appeared to be satisfied that he'd covered everything he leaned back in his chair and studied her, the intensity of his gaze making the hairs stand up on her arms.

'Listen, Cara, I'm finishing early for the day today,' he said, surprising her with the warmth in his voice. 'I'm meeting a friend in town for an early dinner, so feel free to leave here at four o'clock.'

She blinked at him in shock before pulling herself together. 'That would be great. Thank you.'

There was an uncomfortable pause, where he continued to look at her, his brows drawn together and his lips set in a firm line. He opened his mouth, as if he was about to tell her what was on his mind, but was rudely interrupted by the alarm going off on his phone signalling it was time for his conference call.

To her frustration, he snapped straight back into work mode, turning back to his computer and dialling a number on his phone, launching straight into his business spiel as soon as the person on the other end of the line picked up.

Despite her residual nerves, Cara still experienced the familiar little frisson of exhilaration that swept through her whenever she heard him do that. He'd set up a small desk for her next to his the day after he'd offered her the trial, which meant there was no getting away from the sound of his voice with its smooth, reassuring intonation.

He really was a very impressive businessman, even if he was a bit of a bear to work for.

Forcing her mind away from thinking about how uplifting it would be to have someone as passionate and dedicated as Max for a boyfriend—especially after the demeaning experience of her last relationship—she fired up her laptop and started in on the work he'd given her to take care of today.

After a few minutes, her thoughts drifted back to the fateful phone call she'd taken earlier, before their confrontation, and she felt a twitch of nerves in her stomach. It had been a friend calling to let her know about a possible flat coming onto the rental market—which was why she'd broken her rule and answered the call. If she managed to get there early enough she might just be able to snag it, which was now a real possibility thanks to Max's sudden announcement about leaving work at four o'clock.

Come to think of it, she was a little surprised about him finishing early to meet a friend in town. He'd never done that before, always continuing to work as she packed up for the day and—she strongly suspected—on into the evening. That would certainly account for the dark circles under his eyes. And his irascible mood.

The man appeared to be a workaholic.

After an hour of working through some truly tedious data inputting, Cara got up to make them both a hot drink, aware that Max must be parched by now from having to talk almost continuously since he'd begun his call.

Returning with the drinks, she sat back down at her desk to see she had an email from the friend that had called her earlier about the flat for rent.

Hmm. That couldn't be a good sign; she'd already mailed the details through earlier.

With a sinking feeling, she opened it up and scanned the text, her previously restored mood slipping away.

The flat had already been let.

An irrational impulse to cry gripped her and she got up quickly and made for the bathroom before the tears came, desperate to hide her despondency from Max.

Staring into the mirror, she attempted to talk herself down from her gloom. Her friend Sarah had offered to put her up on her sofa for a few days, so she at least had somewhere to stay in the interim. The only trouble was, her friend lived in a tiny place that she shared with her party animal boyfriend and he wouldn't want her hanging around, playing gooseberry, for too long.

The mere idea of renting with strangers at the ripe old age of twenty-seven horrified her, so she was going to have to be prepared to lower her standards to be in with a chance of finding another one-bedroom flat that she could afford in central London.

That was okay; she could do that. Hopefully, something would come up soon and then she'd be able to make some positive changes and get fully back on her feet.

Surely it was time for things to start going her way now?

CHAPTER THREE

AFTER MAKING UP the excuse about seeing a friend on Friday night in order to let Cara leave early, Max decided that he might as well phone around to see if anyone was available for a pint after work and actually surprised himself by having an enjoyable night out with some friends that he hadn't seen for a while.

He'd spent the rest of the weekend working, only breaking to eat his way through the entire contents of the fridge that Cara had stocked for him. Despite his initial disdain at her choices, he found he actually rather enjoyed trying the things she'd bought. They certainly beat the mediocre takeaways he'd been living on for the past few months.

Perhaps it *was* useful for him to have someone else around the house for a while, as Poppy had suggested the last time they'd seen each other. He'd baulked at her proposal that he should get back out on the dating scene though—he definitely wasn't ready for that, and honestly couldn't imagine ever being ready.

He and Jemima had been a couple since meeting at the beginning of their first year at university, their initial connection so immediate and intense they'd missed lectures for three days running to stay in bed together. They'd moved in with each other directly after graduating, making a home for themselves first in Manchester, then in London. After spending so much of his youth being moved from city to city, school to school, by his bohemian mother—until he finally put his foot down and forced her to send him to boarding school—it had been a huge relief to finally feel in control of his own life. To belong somewhere, with someone who wouldn't ask him to give up the life and friends he'd painstakingly carved out for himself—just *one* more time.

Jemima had understood his need for stability and had put up with his aversion to change with sympathetic acceptance and generous bonhomie. His life had been comfortably settled and he'd been deeply content—until she'd died, leaving him marooned and devastated by grief.

The idea of finding someone he could love as much as Jem seemed ludicrous. No one could ever replace his wife and it wouldn't be fair to let them try.

No, he would be fine on his own; he had his business and his friends and that would be enough for him.

Walking past the flower arrangement that Cara had left on the hall table on his way to sort through yesterday's junk mail, he had a memory flash of the expression on her face when he'd bawled her out in the kitchen the other day.

His chest tightened uncomfortably at the memory.

He needed to stop beating himself up about that now. He'd made amends for what had happened, even if she hadn't seemed entirely back to her happy, bright-eyed self again by the time she'd left on Friday afternoon. But at least he hadn't needed to delve into the murky waters of how they were both *feeling* about what had happened. He'd had enough of that kind of thing after forcing himself through the interminable sessions with grief counsellors after Jemima's death; he certainly didn't need to put himself through that discomfort again for something as inconsequential as a spat with his employee.

Fortunately, Cara seemed as reluctant to talk about it all as he was.

Rubbing a hand over his face, he gave a snort of disbelief about where his thoughts had taken him. Again. Surely it wasn't normal to be spending his weekend thinking about his PA.

Hmm.

His initial concerns about her being an unwanted distraction seemed to be coming to fruition, which was a worry. Still, there were only a few more weeks left of the promised trial period, then he'd be free of her. Until then he was going to have to keep his head in the game, otherwise the business was going to suffer. And that wasn't something he was prepared to let happen.

Monday morning rushed around, bringing with it bright sunshine that flooded the house and warmed the still, cool air, lifting his spirits a little.

Max had just sat down at his desk with his first cup of coffee of the day when there was a ring on the doorbell.

Cara.

Swinging open the door to let her in, he was taken aback to see her looking as if she hadn't slept a wink all night. There were dark circles around her puffy eyes and her skin was pallid and dull-looking. It seemed to pain her to even raise a smile for him.

Was she hung-over?

His earlier positivity vanished, to be replaced by a feeling of disquiet.

'Did you have a good weekend?' he asked as she walked into the house and hung up her coat.

She gave him a wan smile. 'Not bad, thanks. It was certainly a busy one. I didn't get much sleep.'

Hmm. So she had been out partying, by the sound of it.

Despite his concerns, Cara appeared to work hard all day and he only caught her yawning once whilst making them both a strong cup of coffee in the kitchen, mid-afternoon.

At the end of the day, she waved her usual cheery goodbye, though there was less enthusiasm in her smile than she normally displayed at knocking-off time.

To his horror, she turned up in the same state the following day.

And the next.

In fact, on Thursday, when he opened the door, he could have sworn he caught the smell of alcohol on her as she dashed past him into the house. She certainly looked as though she could have been up drinking all night and plainly hadn't taken a shower that morning, her hair hanging greasy and limp in a severely pulled back ponytail.

Her work was beginning to suffer too, in increments. Each day he found he had to pick her up on more and more things she'd missed or got wrong, noticing that her once pristine fingernails were getting shorter and more ragged as time went on.

Clearly she was letting whatever was happening in her personal life get in the way of her work and that was unacceptable.

His previous feelings of magnanimity about having her around had all but vanished by Thursday afternoon and he was seriously considering having a word with her about her performance. The only reason he hadn't done so already was because he'd been so busy with back-to-back conference calls this week and in deference to Poppy he'd decided to give Cara the benefit of the doubt and put her slip-ups down to a couple of off days.

But he decided that enough was enough when he found her with her head propped on her arms, fast asleep, on the kitchen table when she was supposed to be making them both a hot drink.

Resentment bubbled up from his gut as he watched her peaceful form gently rise and fall as she slumbered on, totally oblivious to his incensed presence behind her. He'd been feeling guilty all weekend about how he'd spoken to her on Friday and here she was, only a few days later, turning up unfit for work.

His concern that her presence here would cause more harm than good had just been ratified.

'Wakey, wakey, Sleeping Beauty!' he said loudly, feeling a swell of angry satisfaction as she leapt up from the table and spun around to look at him, her face pink and creased on one side where it had rested against her arm.

'Oh! Whoa! Was I sleeping?' she mumbled, blinking hard.

Crossing his arms, he gave her a hard stare. 'Like a baby.'

She rubbed a hand across her eyes, smudging her make-up across her face. 'I'm so sorry—I only put my head down to rest for a moment while I was waiting for the kettle to boil and I must have drifted off.'

'Perhaps you should start going to bed at a more reasonable time then,' he ground out, his hands starting to shake as adrenaline kicked its way through his veins. 'I didn't hire you as a charity case, Cara. For the money I'm paying, I expected much more from you. You had me convinced you were up to the job in the first couple of days, but it's become clear over the last few that you're not.' He took a breath as he made peace with what he was about to say. 'I'm going to have to let you go. I can't carry someone who's going to get drunk every night and turn up unfit to work.'

Her eyes were wide now and she was mouthing at him as if her response had got stuck in her throat.

Shaking off the stab of conscience that had begun to poke him in the back, he pointed a finger at her. 'And you can hold the "It'll never happen again" routine,' he bit out. 'I'm not an idiot, though I feel like one for letting you take me in like this.'

To his surprise, instead of the tears he was readying himself for, her expression morphed into one of acute fury and she raised her own shaking finger back at him.

'I do not get drunk every night. For your information, I'm homeless at the moment and sleeping on a friend's couch, which doesn't work well for her insomniac boyfriend, who likes to party and play computer games late into the night and who came home drunk and spilled an entire can of beer over me while I was trying to sleep and who then hogged the bathroom this morning so I couldn't get in there for a shower.'

Her face had grown redder and redder throughout this speech and all he could do was stand there and stare at her, paralysed by surprise as she jabbed her finger at him with rage flashing in her eyes.

'I've worked my butt off for you, taking your irascible moods on the chin and getting on with it, but I'm not going to let you treat me like some nonentity waster. I'm a real person with real feelings, Max. I tried to make this work—you have no idea how hard I've been trying—but I guess this is just life's way of telling me that I'm done here in London.' She threw up her hands and took a deep shaky breath. 'After all the work I put into building myself a career here that I was so proud of—'

Taking in the look of utter frustration on her face, he felt his anger begin to drain away, only to be replaced with an uncomfortable twist of shame.

She was right, of course—he had been really unfriendly and probably very difficult to work with, and she was clearly dealing with some testing personal circumstances, which he'd made sure to blithely ignore.

He frowned and sighed heavily, torn about what to do next. While he could do without any extra problems at the moment, he couldn't bring himself to turn her away now he knew what she was dealing with. Because, despite it all, he admired her for standing up for herself.

Cara willed her heart to stop pounding like a pneumatic drill as she waited to see what Max would say next.

Had she really just shouted at him like that?

It was so unlike her to let her anger get the better of her, but something inside her had snapped at the unfairness of it all and she hadn't been able to hold back.

After spending the past few days using every ounce of energy keeping up the fake smile and pretending she could cope with the punishing days with Max on so little sleep, she'd hit a wall.

Hard.

The mix of panic, frustration and chronic tiredness had released something inside her and in those moments after she'd let the words fly she had the strangest sensation of the ground shifting under her feet. She was painfully aware that she'd probably just thrown away any hope of keeping this job, but at the same time she was immensely proud of herself for not allowing him to dismiss her like that. As if she was worth nothing.

Because she *wasn't*.

She deserved to be treated with more respect and she'd learnt by now that she wasn't going to get that from Max by meekly taking the insults he so callously dished out.

At her last place of work, in a fug of naïve disbelief,

she'd allowed those witches to strip her of her pride, but there was no way she was letting Max do that to her, too.

No matter what it cost her.

She could get another job—and she would, eventually—but she'd never be able to respect herself again if she didn't stand up to him now.

Her heart raced as she watched a range of expressions run across Max's face. The fact that he hadn't immediately repeated his dismissal gave her hope that there might be a slim chance he'd reverse his decision to fire her.

Moving her hands behind her back, she crossed her fingers for a miracle, feeling a bead of sweat run down her spine.

Sighing hard, Max ran a hand through the front of his hair, pushing it out of his eyes and looking at her with his usual expression of ill-concealed irritation.

'I'm guessing you became homeless on Friday, which is when the mistakes started to happen?' he asked finally.

She nodded, aware of the tension in her shoulders as she held her nerve. 'I spent all day on Sunday moving my furniture into storage. I've been staying with my friend Sarah and her boyfriend ever since.'

'But that can't carry on,' he said with finality to his voice.

Swallowing hard, she tipped up her chin. 'No. I know. I've tried to view so many places to rent in the last week, but they seem to go the second they're advertised. I can't get to them fast enough.'

He crossed his arms. 'And you have nowhere else to stay in London? No boyfriend? No family?'

Shaking her head, she straightened her posture, determined to hang on to her poise. She wouldn't look away, not now she'd been brave enough to take him on. If she was going to be fired, she was going down with her head held high. 'My parents live in Cornwall and none of my other friends in London have room to put me up.' She shifted uncomfortably on the spot and swallowed back the lingering hurt at the memory of her last disastrous relationship. 'I've been single for a few months now.'

He stared back at her, his eyes hooded and his brow drawn down.

A world of emotions rattled through her as she waited to hear his verdict.

'Okay. You can stay here until you find a flat to rent.'

She gawped at him, wondering whether her brain was playing tricks on her. 'I'm sorry—*what*?'

'I said—you can stay here,' he said slowly, enunciating every word. 'I have plenty of spare rooms. I'm on the top floor so you could have the whole middle floor to yourself.'

'Really?'

He bristled, rolling his eyes up to the ceiling and letting out a frustrated snort. 'Yes, really. I'm not just making this up to see your impression of a goldfish.'

She stared at him even harder. Had he just made a *joke*? That was definitely a first.

Unfolding his arms, he batted a hand through the air. 'I'm sure it won't take you long to find somewhere else and until then I need you turning up to work fully rested and back to your efficient, capable self.'

Her eyes were so wide now she felt sure she must look as if she was wearing a pair of those joke goggle-eye glasses.

He was admitting to her being good at her job too now? Wonders would never cease.

But she was allowing these revelations to distract her from the decision she needed to make. Could she really live in the same house as her boss? Even if it was only for a short time.

Right now, it didn't feel as though she had much of a choice. The thought of spending even one more night in Party Central made her heart sink. If she turned Max down on his offer, that was the only other viable option—save staying in a hotel she couldn't afford or renting a place a long way out and spending her life commuting in. Neither of them were appealing options.

But could she really live here with him? The mere idea of it made her insides flutter and it wasn't just because he was a bit of a difficult character. During the week and a half that she'd known him, she'd become increasingly jittery in his presence, feeling a tickle of excitement run up her spine every time she caught his scent in the air or even just watched him move around his territory like some kind of lean, mean, business machine. Not that he'd ever given her a reason to think she was in any kind of danger being there alone with him. Clearly, he had no interest in her romantically. If anything, she'd felt it had been the total opposite for him, as if he didn't think of her as a woman at all, only a phone-answering, data-sorting robot.

So she was pretty sure he didn't have an ulterior motive behind his suggestion that she should stay in his house.

Unfortunately.

Naughty, naughty Cara.

'Well, if you're sure it won't be too much of an inconvenience to you,' she said slowly.

'No. It's fine,' he answered curtly. 'We'll have to make sure to respect each other's privacy, but it's a big place so that shouldn't be a problem. All the rooms have locks on them, in case you're worried.'

Her pulse picked up as a host of X-rated images rushed through her head.

Slam a lid on that, you maniac.

'I'm not worried,' she squeaked.

He nodded.

'And your girlfriend won't mind me staying here?' she asked carefully.

'I don't have a girlfriend.'

'Or your w—?' she began to ask, just in case.

'I'm single,' he cut in with a curt snap to his voice.

Okay, so the subject of his relationships was out of bounds then.

She was surprised to hear that he wasn't attached in any way, though. Surely someone with his money, looks and smarts would have women lining up around the block for the pleasure of his company. Although, come to think of it, based on her run-ins with him so far, she could see how his acerbic temperament might be a problem for some people.

'Right, I may as well show you your room now,' Max said, snapping her out of her meandering thoughts. 'Clearly, you're not in a fit state to work this afternoon, so you may as well finish for the day.' He turned and walked out of the room, leaving her gaping at the empty space he'd left.

So that was it then—decision made.

'Oh! Okay.' She hustled to catch him up, feeling her joints complain as she moved. *Crikey.* She was tired. Her whole body ached from sleeping on a saggy sofa and performing on so little sleep for the past few days.

She followed him up the sweeping staircase to the next level and along the landing to the third door on the right.

Opening it up, he motioned for her to walk past him into the bedroom.

She tried not to breathe in his fresh, spicy scent as she did so, her nerves already shot from the rigours of the day.

It was, of course, the most beautifully appointed bedroom she'd ever been in.

Light flooded in through the large window, which was framed by long French grey curtains in a heavy silk. The rest of the furnishing was simple and elegant, in a way Cara had never been able to achieve in her own flat. The pieces that had been chosen clearly had heritage and fitted perfectly with the large airy room. His interior designer must have cost a pretty penny.

Tears welled in her eyes as she took in the original

ornate fireplace, which stood proudly opposite a beautiful king-sized iron-framed bed. Fighting the urge to collapse onto it in relief and bury herself in the soft, plump-looking duvet, she blinked hard, then turned to face Max, who was hanging back by the door with a distracted frown on his face.

'This is a beautiful room—thank you,' she said, acutely aware of the tremor in her voice.

Max's frown deepened, but he didn't comment on it. 'You're welcome. You should go over to your friend's house and get your things now, then you'll have time to settle in. We'll start over again tomorrow.'

'Okay, good idea.'

'I'll leave you to it then,' he said, turning to go.

'Max?'

He turned back. 'Yes?'

'I'm really grateful—for letting me stay here.'

'No problem,' he said, turning briskly on the spot and walking away, leaving her staring after him with her heart in her mouth.

Well, she certainly hadn't expected this when she'd woken up this morning reeking of stale beer.

Sinking down gratefully onto the bed, she finally allowed her tense muscles to relax, feeling the tiredness rush back, deep into her bones.

How was she ever going to be able to drag herself away from this beautiful room when she managed to find a place of her own to rent?

More to the point, was she really going to be able to live in the same house as Max without going totally insane?

Steeling herself to make the journey over to Sarah's house and pick up her things, she rocked herself up off the bed of her dreams and onto her feet and took a deep, resolute breath.

There was only one way to find out.

CHAPTER FOUR

If someone had asked Max to explain exactly what had prompted him to suggest that Cara move in, he was pretty sure he'd have been stumped for an answer.

All he knew was that he couldn't let things go on the way they were. Judging by her outburst, she was clearly struggling to cope with all that life had thrown at her recently and it was no skin off his nose to let her stay for a few nights in one of the empty bedrooms.

He had enough of them, after all.

Also, as a good friend of her cousin's he felt a responsibility to make sure that Cara was okay whilst Poppy was away and unable to help her herself. He knew from experience that good friends were essential when life decided to throw its twisted cruelty your way, and he was acutely aware that it was the support and encouragement of his friends that had helped him find his way out of the darkness after Jemima died.

Watching Cara working hard the next day, he was glad she was still around. When she was on good form, she was an asset to the business and, truthfully, it had become comforting for him to have another person around—it stopped him from *thinking* so much in the resounding silence of the house.

They hadn't talked about what had happened again, which was a relief. He just wanted everything to get back to the way it had been with the minimum of fuss. With that in mind, he was a little concerned about what it would be like having her around at the weekend. He'd probably end up working, like he always did, so he wasn't too worried about the daytime, but they'd need to make sure they gave each other enough space in the evenings so they didn't end up biting each other's heads off again.

With any luck, she'd be out a lot of the time anyway, flat-hunting or seeing friends.

At six o'clock he leant back in his chair and stretched his arms above his head, working the kinks out of his tight muscles.

'Time to finish for the day, Cara,' he said to the side of her head.

She glanced round at him, the expression in her eyes far away, as if she was in the middle of a thought.

'Um, okay. I'll just finish this.' She tapped on her keyboard for a few more seconds before closing the laptop with a flourish.

'Okay then. Bring on the weekend.' She flashed him a cheeky smile, which gave him pause.

'You're not thinking of bringing the party to this house, I hope.'

Quickly switching to a solemn expression, she gave a shake of her head. 'Of course not. That's not what I meant.'

'Hmm.'

The corner of her mouth twitched upwards. 'You seem to have a really skewed impression of me. I don't go in for heavy drinking and partying—it's really not my style.'

'Okay.' He held up both hands. 'Not that it's any of my business; you can stay out all night at the weekends, for all I care,' he said, aware of a strange plummeting sensation in his chest as images of what she might get up to out on the town flashed through his head.

Good God, man—you're not her keeper.

'As long as your work doesn't suffer,' he added quickly.

'Actually,' she said, slouching back in her seat and hooking her slender arm over the back of her chair, 'I was thinking about cooking you a meal tonight, to say thank you for letting me stay.'

He wasn't sure why, but the thought of that made him uncomfortable. Perhaps because it would blur the lines between employee and friend too much.

'That's kind, but I have plans tonight,' he lied, racking his brain to remember what his friend Dan had said about his availability this weekend. Even if he was busy he was sure he could rustle up a dinner invitation somewhere else, to let Cara off the hook without any bad feelings.

'And you don't need to thank me for letting you stay here. It's what any decent human being would have done.'

Her face seemed to fall a little and she drew her arm back in towards her body, sliding her hands between her knees so that her shoulders hunched inwards. 'Oh, okay, well, I'm just going to pop out and shop for my own dinner, so I'll see you shortly,' she said, ramping her smile back up again and wheeling her chair away from the desk with her feet.

'Actually, I'm heading out myself in a minute and I'll probably be back late, so I'll see you tomorrow.'

Her smile froze. 'Right. Well, have a good night.'

This was ridiculous. The last thing he'd wanted was for them both to feel awkward about living under the same roof.

He let out a long sigh and pushed his hair away from his face. 'Look, Cara, don't think you have to hang out with me while you're staying here. We don't need to be in each other's pockets the whole time. Feel free to do your own thing.'

Clearly he'd been a bit brusque because she recoiled a little. 'I understand,' she said, getting up and awkwardly pushing her chair back under her desk. 'Have a good night!' she said in that overly chirpy way she had, which he was beginning to learn meant he'd offended her.

Not waiting for his reply, she turned her back on him and walked straight out of the room, her shoulders stiff.

Great. This was exactly what he'd hoped to avoid.

He scrubbed a hand over his face. Maybe it had been a mistake to ask her to stay.

But he couldn't kick her out now.

All he could do was cross his fingers and hope she'd find herself another place to live soon.

***

To his surprise, he didn't see much of Cara over the next couple of days. She'd obviously taken his suggestion about giving each other space to heart and was avoiding being in the house with him as much as possible.

The extremity of her desertion grated on his nerves.

What was it that made it impossible for them to understand each other? They were very different in temperament, of course, which didn't help, but it was more than that. It was as if there was some kind of meaning-altering force field between them.

On Sunday, when the silence in the house got too much for him, he went out for a long walk around Hyde Park. He stopped at the café next to the water for lunch, something he and Jemima had done most Sundays, fighting against the painful undertow of nostalgia that dragged at him as he sat there alone. It was all so intensely familiar.

All except for the empty seat in front of him.

He snorted into his drink, disgusted with himself for being so pathetic. He should consider himself lucky. He was the one who got to have a future, unlike his big-hearted, selfless wife. The woman who everyone had loved. One of the few people, in his opinion, who had truly deserved a long and happy life.

Arriving home mid-afternoon, he walked in to find the undertones of Cara's perfume hanging in the air.

So she was back then.

Closing his eyes, he imagined he could actually sense her presence in the atmosphere, like a low hum of white noise.

Or was he being overly sensitive?

Probably.

From the moment she'd agreed to move in he'd experienced a strange undercurrent of apprehension and it seemed to be affecting his state of mind.

After stowing his shoes and coat in the cloakroom, he went into the living room to find that a large display of flowers had been placed on top of the grand piano. He bristled, remembering the way he'd felt the last time Cara had started to mess with his environment.

Sighing, he rubbed a hand through his hair, attempting to release the tension in his scalp. They were just flowers. He really needed to chill out or he was going to drive himself insane. Jemima would have laughed if she'd seen how strung-out he was over something so inconsequential. He could almost hear her teasing voice ringing in his ears.

A noise startled him and he whipped round to see Cara standing in the doorway to the room, dressed in worn jeans and a sloppy sweater, her face scrubbed of make-up and her bright blue eyes luminous in the soft afternoon light. To his overwrought brain, she seemed to radiate an ethereal kind of beauty, her long hair lying in soft, undulating waves around her face and her creamy skin radiant with health. He experienced a strangely intense moment of confusion, and he realised that somewhere in the depths of his screwed-up consciousness he'd half expected it to be Jemima standing there instead—which was why his, 'Hello,' came out more gruffly than he'd intended.

Her welcoming smile faltered and she glanced down

at her fingernails and frowned, as if fighting an impulse to chew on them, but when she looked back up her smile was firmly back in place.

'Isn't it a beautiful day?' She tipped her head towards the piano behind him. 'I hope you don't mind, but the spring sunshine inspired me to put fresh flowers in most of the rooms—not your bedroom, of course; I didn't go in there,' she added quickly. 'The house seemed to be crying out for a bit of life and colour and I wanted to do something to say thank you for letting me stay, even though you said I didn't need to.'

'Sure. That's fine,' was all he could muster. For some reason his blood was flying through his veins and he felt so hot he thought he might spontaneously combust at any second.

'Oh, and I stripped and remade the bed in the room next to yours,' she added casually. 'It looked like the cleaners had missed it. I gave it a good vacuum, too; it was really dusty.'

The heat was swept away by a flood of icy panic. 'You *what*?'

The ferocity in his tone obviously alarmed her because she flinched and blinked hard.

But hurting Cara's feelings was the least of his worries right then.

Not waiting for her reply, he pushed past her and raced up the stairs, aware of his heart thumping painfully in his chest as he willed it not to be so.

Please don't let her have destroyed that room.

Reaching the landing on the top floor, he flung open the door and stared into the now immaculate bedroom, the stringent scent of cleaning fluid clogging his throat and making his stomach roll.

She'd stripped it bare.

Everything he'd been protecting from the past had been torn off or wiped away. The bed, as she'd said, now had fresh linen on it.

He heard her laboured breath behind him as she made it up to the landing and whipped round to face her.

'Where are the sheets from the bed, Cara?' he demanded, well past the point of being able to conceal his anger.

Her face was drained of all colour. 'What did I do wrong?'

'The *sheets*, Cara—where are the *sheets*?'

'I washed them,' she whispered, unable to meet his eyes. 'They're in the dryer.'

That was it then. Jemima's room was ruined.

Bitterness welled in his gut as he took in her wide-eyed bewilderment. The woman was a walking disaster area and she'd caused nothing but trouble since she got here.

A rage he couldn't contain made him pace towards her.

'Why do you have to meddle with everything? Hmm? What is it with you? This need to please all the time isn't natural. In fact it's downright pathetic. Just keep your hands off my personal stuff, okay? Is that really too much to ask?'

She seemed frozen to the spot as she stared at him with glassy eyes, her jaw clamped so tight he could see the muscle flickering under the pressure, but, instead of shouting back this time, she dragged in a sharp, painful-sounding breath before turning on the spot and walking out of the room.

He listened to her heavy footsteps on the stairs and then the slam of her bedroom door, wincing as the sound reverberated through his aching head. Staring down at the soulless bed, he allowed the heat of his bitterness and anger and shame to wash through him, leaving behind an icy numbness in its wake.

Then he closed his eyes, dropped his chin to his chest and sank down onto the last place he'd been truly happy.

Oh, God, please don't let this be happening to me. Again.

Cara wrapped her arms around her middle and pressed her forehead against the cool wall of her bedroom, waiting for the dizziness and nausea to subside so she could pack up her things and leave.

What was it with her? She seemed destined to put herself in a position of weakness, where the only option left to her was to give up and run away.

Which she really didn't want to do again.

But she had to protect herself. She couldn't be around someone so toxic—someone who clearly thought so little of her. Even Ewan hadn't been that cruel to her when he'd left her after she'd failed to live up to his exacting standards. She'd never seen a look of such pure disgust on anyone's face before. The mere memory of it made the dizziness worse.

There was no way she was staying in a place where she'd be liable to see that look again. She'd rather go home and admit to her parents that she'd failed and deal with their badly concealed disappointment than stay here with Max any longer.

She'd never met anyone with such a quick temper. What was his problem, anyway? He appeared to have everything here: the security of a beautiful house in one of the most sought-after areas of London, a thriving business, friends who invited him out for dinner, and he clearly had pots of cash to cushion his easy, comfortable life. In fact, the more she thought about it, the more incensed she became.

Who was he to speak to her like that? Sure, there had been a couple of little bumps in the road when she'd not exactly been at her best, but she'd worked above and beyond the call of duty for the rest of the time. And she'd been trying to do something nice for him in making the house look good—pretty much the only thing she could think of to offer as a thank you to a man who seemed to have everything. What had been so awful about that? She knew she could be a bit over the top in trying to please people sometimes, but this hadn't been a big thing. It was just an empty guest room that had been overlooked.

Wasn't it?

The extremity of his reaction niggled at her.

Surely just giving it a quick clean didn't deserve that angry reaction.

No.

He was a control freak bully and she needed to get away from him.

As soon as she was sure the dizziness had passed,

she carefully packed up all her things and zipped them into her suitcase, fighting with all her might against the tight pressure in her throat and the itchy heat in her eyes.

She'd known this opportunity had to be too good to be true—the job, working with someone as impressive as Max and definitely being invited to stay in this amazing house.

But she wasn't going to skulk away. If she didn't face up to Max one last time with her head held high she'd regret it for the rest of her life. He wasn't going to run her out of here; she was going to leave in her time and on her terms.

Taking a deep breath, she rolled her shoulders back and fixed the bland look of calm she'd become so practised at onto her face.

Okay. Time for one last confrontation.

She found Max in the guest room where she'd left him, sitting on the bed with his head in his hands, his hunched shoulders stretching his T-shirt tight against his broad back.

As she walked into the room, he looked up at her with an expression of such torment on his face that it made her stop in her tracks.

What was going on? She'd expected him to still be angry, but instead he looked—*beaten*.

Did he regret what he'd said to her?

Giving herself a mental shake, she took another deliberate step towards him. It didn't matter; there wasn't anything he could say to make up for the cruelty of his last statement anyway. This wasn't the first time he'd treated her with such brutal disdain and she wasn't going to put up with it any longer.

Forcing back her shoulders, she took one final step closer to him, feeling her legs shaking with tension.

'This isn't going to work, Max. I can't live in a place where I'm constantly afraid of doing the wrong thing and making you angry. I don't know what I did that was so bad, or what's going on with you to make you react like that, but I'm not going to let you destroy what's left of my confidence. I'm not going to be a victim any more.' She took a deep, shuddering breath. 'So I'm leaving now. And that goes for the job, too.'

Her heart gave a lurch at the flash of contrition in his eyes, but she knew she had to be strong and walk away for her own good.

'Goodbye, Max, and good luck.'

As she turned to go, fighting against the tears that threatened to give her away, she thought she heard the bedsprings creak as if he'd stood up, but didn't turn round to find out.

She was halfway down the stairs when she heard Max's voice behind her. 'Wait, Cara!'

Spinning round, she held up a hand to stop him from coming any closer, intensely aware that, despite her anger with him, there was a small part of her that was desperate to hear him say something nice to her, to persuade her that he wasn't the monster he seemed to be. 'I can't walk on eggshells around you any more, Max; I don't think my heart will stand it.'

In any way, shape or form.

He slumped down onto the top step and put his elbows on his knees, his whole posture defeated. 'Don't go,' he said quietly.

'I have to.'

Looking up, he fixed her with a glassy stare. 'I know I've been a nightmare to be around recently—' He frowned and shook his head. 'It's not you, Cara—it's one hundred per cent me. Please, at least hear me out. I need to tell you what's going on so you don't leave thinking any of this is your fault.' He sighed and rubbed a hand through his hair. 'That's the last thing I want to happen.'

She paused. Even if she still chose to leave after hearing him out, at least she'd know *why* it hadn't worked and be able to make peace with her decision to walk away.

The silence stretched to breaking point between them. 'Okay,' she said.

He nodded. 'Thank you.' Getting up from the step, he gestured down the stairs. 'Let's go into the sitting room.'

Once there, she perched on the edge of the sofa and waited for him to take the chair opposite, but he surprised her by sitting next to her instead, sinking back into the cushions with a long guttural sigh which managed to touch every nerve-ending in her body.

'This is going to make me sound mentally unstable.'

She turned to frown at him. 'Oka-ay...' she said, failing to keep her apprehension out of her voice.

'That bed hasn't been changed since my wife, Jemima, died a year and a half ago.'

Hot horror slid through her, her skin prickling as if

she were being stabbed with a thousand needles. 'But I thought you said—' She shook her suddenly fuzzy head. 'You never said—' Words, it seemed, had totally failed her. Everything she knew about him slipped sickeningly into place: the ever-fluctuating moods, the reluctance to talk about his personal life, his anger at her meddling with things in his house.

His *wife's* house.

Looking away, he stared at the wall opposite, sitting forward with clenched fists as if he was steeling himself to get it all out in the open.

'I couldn't bring myself to change it.' He paused and she saw his shoulders rise then fall as he took a deep breath. 'The bed, I mean. It still smelled faintly like her. I let her mother take all her clothes and other personal effects—what would I have done with them?—but the bed was mine. The last place we'd been together before I lost her—' he took another breath, pushing back his hunched shoulders '—before she died.'

'Oh, God, Max... I'm so, so sorry. I had no idea.'

He huffed out a dry laugh. 'How could you? I did everything I could to avoid talking to you about it.' He grimaced. 'Because, to be honest, I've done enough talking about it to last me a lifetime. I guess, in my twisted imagination, I thought if you didn't know, I could pretend it hadn't happened when you were around. Outside of work, you're the first normal, unconnected thing I've had in my life since I lost her and I guess I was hanging on to that.'

He turned to look at her again. 'I should have told you, Cara, especially after you moved in, but I couldn't find a way to bring it up without—' He paused and swallowed hard, the look in his eyes so wretched that, without thinking, she reached out and laid a hand on his bare forearm.

He frowned down at where their bodies connected and the air seemed to crackle around them.

Disconcerted by the heat of him beneath her fingertips, she withdrew her hand and laid it back on her lap.

'It's kind of you to consider me *normal*,' she said, flipping him a grin, hoping the levity might go some way to smoothing out the sudden weird tension between them.

He gave a gentle snort, as if to acknowledge her pathetic attempt at humour.

Why had she never recognised his behaviour as grief before? Now she knew to look for it, it was starkly discernible in the deep frown lines in his face and the haunted look in his eyes.

But she'd been so caught up in her own private universe of problems she hadn't even considered *why* Max seemed so bitter all the time.

She'd thought he had everything.

How wrong she'd been.

They sat in silence for a while, the only sound in the room the soothing *tick-tock* of the carriage clock on the mantelpiece, like a steady heartbeat in the chaos.

'How did she die?' Cara asked eventually. She was pretty sure he wouldn't be keen to revisit this conversation and she wanted to have all the information from this point onwards so she could avoid any future blunders.

The familiarity of the question seemed to rouse him. 'She had a subarachnoid haemorrhage—it's where a blood vessel in the brain bursts—' he added, when she frowned at him in confusion. 'On our one-year wedding anniversary. It happened totally out of the blue. I was late for our celebration dinner and I got a phone message saying she'd collapsed in the restaurant. By the time I got to the hospital she had such extensive brain damage she didn't even recognise me. She died two weeks later. I never got to say goodbye properly.' He snorted gently. 'The last thing I said to her before it happened was "Stop being such a nag; I won't be late," when I left her in bed that morning and went to work.'

Cara had to swallow past the tightness in her throat before she could speak. 'That's why you didn't want me to leave here with us on bad terms.' She put a hand back onto his arm and gave it an ineffectual rub, feeling completely out of her depth. 'Oh, Max, I'm so sorry. What a horrible thing to happen.'

He leant back against the cushions, breaking the contact of her touch, and stared up at the ceiling. 'I often wonder whether I would have noticed some signs if I'd paid more attention to her. If I hadn't been so caught up with work—'

She couldn't think of a single thing to say to make him feel better—though maybe there wasn't anything she could say. Sometimes you didn't need answers or solutions; you just needed someone to listen and agree with you about how cruel life could be.

He turned to look at her, his mouth drawn into a tight line.

'Look, Cara, I can see that you wanting to help comes from a good place. You're a kind and decent person—much more decent than I am.' He gave her a pained smile, which she returned. 'I've been on my own here for so long I've clearly become very selfish with my personal space.' He rubbed a hand across his brow. 'And this was Jemima's house—she was the one who chose how to decorate it and made it a home for us.' He turned to make full eye contact with her again, his expression apologetic. 'It's taking a bit of adjusting to, having someone else around. Despite evidence to the contrary, I really appreciate the thoughtful gestures you've made.'

His reference to her *gestures* only made the heavy feeling in her stomach worse.

'I'm really sorry, Max. I can totally understand why you'd find it hard to see me meddling with Jemima's things. I think I was so excited by the idea of living in such a beautiful house that I got a bit carried away. I forgot I was just a visitor here and that it's your home. That was selfish of *me*.'

He shook his head. 'I don't want you to feel like that. While you're here it's your home, too.'

She frowned and turned away to stare down at the floor, distracted for a moment by how scratty and out of place her old slippers looked against the rich cream-coloured wool carpet.

That was exactly the problem. It wasn't her home and it never would be. She didn't really *fit* here.

For some reason that made her feel more depressed than she had since the day she'd left her last job.

'Have you had any luck with finding a flat to rent?' he asked, breaking the silence that had fallen like a suffocating layer of dust between them.

'Not yet, but I have an appointment to view somewhere tomorrow and there are new places coming up all the time. I'll find something soon, I'm sure of it,' she said, plastering what must have been the worst fake smile she'd ever mustered onto her face.

He nodded slowly, but didn't say anything.

Twitching with discomfort now, she stood up. 'I should go.'

He frowned at her in confusion. 'What do you mean? Where are you going?'

'Back to Sarah's. I think that would be best.'

Standing up, too, he put out a hand as if to touch her, but stopped himself and shoved it into the back pocket of his jeans instead.

'Look, don't leave. I promise to be less of an ogre. I let my anger get the better of me, which was unfair.'

'I don't know, Max—' She couldn't stay here now. Could she?

Obviously seeing the hesitation on her face, he leant forward and waited until she made eye contact. 'I like having you around.' There was a teasing lightness in his expression that made her feel as if he was finally showing her the real Max. The one who had been hiding inside layers of brusque aloofness and icy calm for the past few weeks.

Warmth pooled, deep in her body. 'Really? I feel like I've made nothing but a nuisance of myself since I got here.'

He gave another snort and the first proper smile she'd seen in a while. It made his whole face light up and the sight of it sent a rush of warm pleasure across her skin. 'It's certainly been *eventful* having you here.'

She couldn't help but return his grin, despite the feeling that she was somehow losing control of herself.

'Stay. Please.'

Her heart turned over at the expression on his face. It was something she'd never seen before. Against all the odds, he looked *hopeful*.

Despite a warning voice in the back of her head, she knew there was no way she could walk out of the door now that he'd laid himself bare. She could see that the extreme mood swings were coming from a place of deep pain and the very last thing he needed was to be left alone with just his tormenting memories for company in this big empty house.

It appeared as though they needed each other.

The levelling of the emotional stakes galvanised her.

'Okay,' she said, giving him a reassuring smile. 'I'll stay. On one condition.'

'And that is?'

'That you *talk* to me when you feel the gloom descending—like a *person*, not just an employee. And let me help if I can.' She crossed her arms and raised a challenging eyebrow.

He huffed out a laugh. 'And how do you propose to help?'

'I don't know. Perhaps I can jolly you out of your moods, if you give me the chance.'

'*Jolly*. That's a fitting word for you.'

'Yeah, well, someone has to raise the positivity levels in this house of doom.' She stilled, wondering whether she'd gone a step too far, but when she dared to peek at him he was smiling, albeit in a rather bemused way.

A sense of relief washed over her. The last thing she wanted to do was read the situation wrong now they'd had a breakthrough. In fact, she really ought to push for a treaty to make things crystal clear between them.

'Look, at the risk of micromanaging the situation, can we agree that from this point on you'll be totally straight with me, and in return I promise to be totally straight with you?'

He gave her a puzzled look. 'Why? Is there something you need to tell me?'

She considered admitting she'd lied about why she'd left her last job and dismissed it immediately. There was no point going over that right now; it had no relevance to this and it would make her sound totally pathetic compared to what he'd been through.

'No, no! Nothing! It was just a turn of phrase.'

He snorted gently, rolling his eyes upward, his mouth lifting at the corner. 'Okay then, Miss Fix-it, total honesty it is. You've got yourself a deal.'

CHAPTER FIVE

Just as Max thought he'd had enough drama to last him a lifetime, things took another alarming turn, only this time it was the business that threatened to walk away from him.

Opening his email first thing on Monday morning, he found a missive from his longest standing and most profitable client, letting him know that they were considering taking their business elsewhere.

Cara walked in with their coffee just as he'd finished reading it and the concern on her face made it clear how rattled he must look.

'Max? What's wrong?'

'Our biggest client is threatening to terminate our contract with them.'

Her eyes grew larger. 'Why?'

'I'm guessing one of our competitors has been sniffing around, making eyes at them and I've been putting off going to the meetings they've been trying to arrange for a while now. I haven't had the time to give them the same level of attention as before, so their head's been turned.'

'Is it salvageable?'

'Yes. If I go up there today and show them exactly why they should stay with me.'

'Okay.' She moved swiftly over to her desk and opened up her internet browser, her nails rattling against her keyboard as she typed in an enquiry. 'There's a train to Manchester in forty minutes. You go and pack some stuff; I'll call a cab and book you a seat. You can speak to me from the train about anything that needs handling today.'

He sighed and rubbed a hand through his hair, feeling the tension mounting in his scalp. 'It's going to take more than an afternoon to get this sorted. I'll probably need to be up there for most of the week.'

'Then stay as long as you need.'

Shaking his head, he batted a hand towards his computer. 'I have that proposal to finish for the end of Thursday, not to mention the monstrous list of things to tackle for all the other clients this week.'

'Leave it with me. If you set me up with a folder of your previous proposals and give me the questions you need answering, I'll put some sections together for you, so you'll only need to check and edit them as we go. And don't worry about the other clients; I can handle the majority of enquiries and rearrange anything that isn't urgent for next week. I'll only contact you with the really important stuff.'

'Are you sure you can handle that? It's a lot to leave you with at such short notice.'

'I'll be fine.' She seemed so eager he didn't have the heart to argue.

In all honesty, it was going to be tough for him to let go of his tight grip on the business and trust that this would work out, but he knew he didn't have a choice—there was no way he was letting this contract slip through his fingers. He really couldn't afford to lose this firm's loyalty at this point in his business's infancy; it would make him look weak to competitors as well as potential new clients, and presenting a confident front was everything in this game.

'Okay.' He stood up and gathered his laptop and charger together before making for the door. 'Thanks, Cara. I'll get my stuff together and call you from the train.'

Turning back, he saw she was standing stiffly with her hands clasped in front of her, her eyes wide and her cheeks flushed.

Pausing for a moment, he wondered whether he was asking too much of her, but quickly dismissed it. She'd chosen to stay and she knew what she was getting herself into.

They were in it together now.

To his relief, Cara successfully held the fort back in London whilst he was away, routinely emailing him sections of completed work to be used in the business proposal that he wrote in the evenings in time to make the deadline. She seemed to have a real flair for picking out relevant information and had made an excellent job of copying his language style.

She also saved his hide by sending flowers and a card in his name to his mother for her birthday, which he was ashamed to discover he'd forgotten all about in his panic about losing the client.

Damaging the precarious cordiality that he and his mother had tentatively built up after working through their differences over the past few years would have been just as bad, and he was immensely grateful to Cara for her forethought and care.

She really was excellent at her job.

In fact, after receiving compliments from clients about how responsive and professional she'd been when they'd contacted her with enquiries and complications to be dealt with, he was beginning to realise that he'd actually been very fortunate to secure her services. He felt sure, if she wanted to, she could walk into a job with a much better salary with her eyes shut.

Which made him wonder again why she hadn't.

Whatever the reason, the idea of losing her excellent skill base now made him uneasy. Even though he'd been certain he'd want to let her go at the end of the trial month, he was now beginning to think that that would be a huge mistake.

He had some serious thinking to do.

If he was honest, he reflected on Thursday evening, sitting alone in the hotel's busy restaurant, having time and space away from Cara and the house had been a relief. He'd been glad of the opportunity to get his head together after their confrontation. She was the first person, outside his close circle of friends, that he'd talked to in any detail about what had happened to Jemima and it had changed the atmosphere between them. To Cara's credit, she hadn't trotted out platitudes to try and make him feel better and he was grateful to her for that, but he felt a little awkward about how much of himself he'd exposed.

Conversely, though, it also felt as though a weight that he'd not noticed carrying had been lifted from his shoulders. Not just because he'd finally told Cara about Jem—which he'd begun to feel weirdly seedy about, as if he was keeping a dirty secret from her—but also because it had got to the point where he'd become irrationally superstitious about clearing out the room, as though all his memories of Jemima would be wiped away if he touched it. Which, of course, they hadn't been—she was still firmly embedded there in his head and his heart. So, even though he'd been angry and upset with Cara at the time, in retrospect, it had been a healthy thing for that decision to be wrenched out of his hands.

It felt as though he'd taken a step further into the light.

Cara was out when he arrived back at Friday lunchtime, still buzzed with elation from keeping the client, so he went to unpack his bags upstairs, return a few phone calls and take a shower before coming back down.

Walking into the kitchen, he spotted her standing by the sink with her back to him, washing a mug. He stopped to watch her for a moment, smiling as he realised she was singing softly to herself, her slim hips swaying in time to the rhythm of the song. She had a beautiful voice, lyrical and sweet, and a strange, intense warmth wound through him as he stood there listening to her. It had been a long time since anyone had sung in this house and there was something so pure and uplifting about it a shiver ran down his spine, inexplicably chased by a deep pull of longing.

Though not for Cara, surely? But for a time when his life had fewer sharp edges. A simpler time. A happier one.

Shaking himself out of this unsettling observation, he moved quickly into the room so she wouldn't think he'd been standing there spying on her.

'Hi, Cara.'

She jumped and gasped, spinning round to face him, her hand pressed to her chest. She looked fresh and well rested, but there was a wary expression in her eyes.

'Max! I didn't hear you come in.'

'I was upstairs, taking a shower and returning some urgent calls. I got back about an hour ago.'

She nodded, her professional face quickly restored. 'How was Manchester?'

'Good. We got them back on board. How have things been here?'

'That's great! Things have been fine here. It's certainly been very quiet without you.'

By 'quiet' he suspected she actually meant less fraught with angry outbursts.

There was an uncomfortable silence while she fussed about with the tea towel, hooking it carefully over the handle of the cooker door and smoothing it until it lay perfectly straight.

Tearing his eyes away from the rather disconcerting sight of her stroking her hands slowly up and down the offending article, he walked over to where the kettle sat on the work surface and flicked it on to boil. He was unsettled to find that things still felt awkward between them when they were face to face—not that he should be surprised that they were. Their last non-work conversation had been a pretty heavy one, after all.

Evidently he needed to make more of an effort to be friendly now if he was going to be in with a chance of persuading her to stay after the month's trial was up.

The thought of going back to being alone in this house certainly wasn't a comforting one any more. If he was honest, it had been heartening to know that Cara would be here when he got back. Now that the black hole of Jemima's room had been destroyed and he'd fully opened the door to Cara, the loneliness he'd previously managed to keep at bay had walked right in.

Turning to face her again, he leant back against the counter and crossed his arms.

'I wanted to talk to you about the quality of the work you've been producing.'

Her face seemed to pale and he realised he could have phrased that better. He'd never been good at letting his colleagues know when he was pleased with their work—or Jemima when he was proud of something she'd achieved, he realised with a stab of pain—but after Cara had given it to him straight about how it affected her, he was determined to get better at it.

'What I mean is—I'm really impressed with the way you've handled the work here this week while I've been away,' he amended.

'Oh! Good. Thank you.' The pride in her wobbly smile made his breath catch.

He nodded and gave a little cough to release the peculiar tension in his throat, turning back to the counter to grab a mug for his drink and give them both a moment to regroup. There was a brightly coloured card propped up next to the mug tree and he picked it up as a distraction while he waited for the kettle to finish boiling and glanced at what was written inside.

'You didn't tell me it was your birthday,' he said, turning to face her again, feeling an unsettling mixture of surprise and dismay at her not mentioning something as important as that to him.

Colour rushed to her cheeks. 'Oh, sorry! I didn't mean to leave that lying around.' She walked over and took the card from his hand, leaning against the worktop next to him and enveloping him in her familiar floral scent. She tapped the corner of the card gently against her palm and he watched, hypnotised by the action. 'It was on Wednesday. As you were away I didn't think it was worth mentioning.' She looked up at him from under her lashes. 'Don't worry—I didn't have a wild house party here while you were away, only a couple of friends over for dinner and we made sure to tidy up afterwards.'

Fighting a strange disquiet, he flapped a dismissive hand at her. 'Cara, it's okay for you to keep some of your things in the communal areas and have friends over for your birthday, for God's sake. I don't expect the place to be pristine the whole time.'

'Still. I meant to put this up in my room with the others.'

Despite their pact to be more open with each other, it was evidently going to take a lot more time and effort to get her to relax around him.

Maybe he should present her with some kind of peace offering. In fact, thinking about it, her birthday could provide the perfect excuse.

He'd seen her reading an article about a new play in a magazine one lunchtime last week, and when he picked it up later he noticed she'd put a ring around the box office number, as if to remind herself to book tickets.

After dispatching her back to the office with a list of clients to chase up about invoices, he called the theatre, only to find the play had sold out weeks ago. Not prepared to be defeated that easily, he placed a call to his friend James, who was a long-time benefactor of the theatre.

'Hey, man, how are things?' his friend asked as soon as he picked up.

'Great. Business is booming. How about you?'

'Life's good. Penny's pregnant again,' James said with pleasure in his voice.

Max ignored the twinge of pain in his chest. 'That's great. Congratulations.'

'Thanks. Let's just hope this one's going to give us less trouble arriving into the world.'

'You're certainly owed an easy birth after the last time.'

'You could say that. Anyway, what can I do for you, my friend?'

'I wanted to get hold of tickets for that new play at the Apollo Theatre for tonight's performance. It's my PA's birthday and I wanted to treat her, but it's sold out. Can you help me with that?'

'Your PA, huh?' There was a twist of wryness in James's voice that shot a prickle straight up his spine.

'Yeah. My PA,' he repeated with added terseness born of discomfort.

His friend chuckled. 'No problem. I'll call and get them to put some tickets aside for you for the VIP box. I saw it last week—it's great—but it starts early, at five, so you'll need to get a move on.' There was a loaded pause. 'It's good to hear you're getting out again.'

Max bristled again. 'I go out.'

'But not with women. Not since Jemima passed away.'

He sighed, beginning to wish he hadn't called now. 'It's not a date. She's my *PA*.'

James chuckled again. 'Well, she's lucky to have you for an *employer*. These tickets are like gold dust.'

'Thanks, I owe you one,' Max said, fighting hard to keep the growl out of his voice. To his annoyance, he felt rattled by what his friend was insinuating. It wasn't stepping over the line to do something like this for Cara, was it?

'Don't worry about it,' James said.

Max wasn't sure for a moment whether he'd voiced his concerns out loud and James was answering that question or whether he was just talking about paying him back the favour.

'Thanks, James, I've got to go,' he muttered, wanting to end the call so he could walk around and loosen off this weird tension in his chest.

'No worries.'

Max put the phone down, wondering again whether this gesture was a step too far.

No. She'd worked hard for him, under some testing circumstances and he wanted her to know that he appreciated it. If he wanted to retain her services—and he was pretty sure now that he did—he was going to have to make sure she knew how much she was valued here so she didn't go looking for another job.

Cara was back at her desk, busily typing away on her laptop, when he walked into the room they used as an office. Leaning against the edge of her desk, he waited until she'd finished and turned to face him.

'I'm nearly done here,' she said, only holding eye contact for a moment before glancing back at her computer.

'Great, because a friend of mine just called to say he has two spare tickets to that new play at the Apollo and I was thinking I could take you as a thank you for holding the fort so effectively whilst I've been away. And for missing your birthday.'

She stared at him as if she thought she might have misheard. 'I'm sorry?'

He smiled at her baffled expression, feeling a kink of pleasure at her reaction. 'We'll need to leave in the next few minutes if we're going to make it into town in time to catch the beginning.' He stood up and she blinked in surprise.

'You and *me*? Right *now*?'

'Yes. You don't have other plans, do you?'

'Um, no.'

He nodded. 'Great.'

Gesturing up and down her body, she frowned, looking a little flustered. 'But I can't go dressed like this.'

He glanced at her jeans and T-shirt, trying not to let his eyes linger on the way they fitted her trim, slender body. 'You're going to have to change quickly then,' he said, pulling his mobile out of his pocket and dialling the number for the taxi.

Cara chattered away in the cab all the way there about how the play had been given rave reviews after its preview performance and how people were already paying crazy money on auction websites for re-sold tickets to see it. Her enthusiasm was contagious and, stepping out of the car, he was surprised to find he was actually looking forward to seeing it.

The theatre was a recently renovated grand art deco building slap-bang in the middle of Soho, a short stroll from the hectic retail circus of Oxford Street.

It had been a while since he'd made it into town on a Friday night and even longer since he'd been to see any kind of live show. When he and Jemima had moved to London they'd been full of enthusiasm about how they'd be living in the heart of the action and would be able to go out every other night to see the most cutting-edge performances and mind-expanding lectures. They were going to become paragons of good taste and spectacularly cultured to boot.

And then real life had taken over and they'd become

increasingly buried under the weight of work stress and life tiredness as the years went by and had barely made it out to anything at all. It had been fine when they'd had each other for company, but he was aware that he needed to make more of an effort to get out and be sociable now he was on his own.

Not that he'd been a total recluse since Jem had died; he'd been out with friends—Poppy being his most regular pub partner—but he'd done it in a cocoon of grief, always feeling slightly detached from what was going on around him.

Doing this with Cara meant he was having to make an effort again. Which was a good thing. It felt healthy. Perhaps that was why he was feeling more upbeat than he had in a while—as if there was life beyond the narrow world he'd been living in for the past year and a half.

After paying the taxi driver, they jogged straight to the box office for their tickets, then through the empty lobby to the auditorium to find their seats in the VIP box, the usher giving them a pointed look as she closed the doors firmly behind them. It seemed they'd only just made it. This theory was borne out by the dimming of the lights and the grand swish of the curtain opening just as they folded themselves into their seats.

Max turned to find Cara with her mouth comically open and an expression that clearly said *I can't believe we've just casually nipped into the best seats in the house.* He flashed her a quick smile, enjoying her pleasure and the sense of satisfaction at doing something good here, before settling back into his plush red velvet chair, his heart beating heavily in his chest.

A waft of her perfume hit his nose as she reached up to adjust her ponytail, which made his heart beat even harder—perhaps from the sudden sensory overload. Taking a deep breath, he concentrated on bringing his breathing back to normal and focused on the action on stage, determined to put all other thoughts aside for the meantime and try to enjoy whatever this turned out to be.

Cara was immensely relieved when the play stood up to her enthusiastic anticipation. It would have been pretty embarrassing if it had been a real flop after all the fuss she'd made about it on the way there. Every time she heard Max chuckle at one of the jokes she experienced a warm flutter of pleasure in her stomach.

Max bringing her here to the theatre had thrown her for a complete loop. Even though he'd finally let her into his head last weekend, she'd expected him to go back to being distant with her again once he came back from Manchester. But instead he'd surprised her by complimenting her, then not only getting tickets to the hottest play in London, but bringing her here himself as a reward for working hard.

Dumbfounded was not the word.

Not that she was complaining.

Sneaking a glance at him, she thought she'd never seen him looking so relaxed. She could hardly believe he was the same man who had opened the door to her on the first day they'd met. He seemed larger now somehow, as if he'd straightened up and filled out in the time since she'd last seen him. That had to be all in her head, of course, but he certainly seemed more *real* now that she knew what drove his rage. In fact it was incredible how differently she felt now she knew what sort of horror he'd been through—losing someone he loved in such a senseless way.

No wonder he was so angry at the world.

Selfishly, it was a massive relief to know that none of his dark moods had been about her performance—apart from when she'd fallen asleep on the kitchen table during business hours, of course.

After he'd left for Manchester, she'd had a minor panic attack about how she was going to cope on her own, terrified of making a mistake that would impact negatively on the business, but, after giving herself a good talking-to in the mirror, she'd pulled it together and got on with the job in hand. And she'd been fine. More than fine. In fact she'd actually started to enjoy her job again as she relaxed into the role and reasserted her working practices.

Truth be told, before she'd started working for Max, she didn't know whether she'd be able to hold her nerve in a business environment any more. He'd been a hard taskmaster but she knew she'd benefited from that, discovering that she had the strength to stand up for herself when it counted. She'd been tested to her limits and she'd come through the other side and that, to her, had been her biggest achievement in a very long time.

She felt proud of herself again.

As the first half drew to a close she became increasingly conscious of the heat radiating from Max's powerful body and his arm that pressed up against hers as he leaned into the armrest. Her skin felt hot and prickly where it touched his, as if he was giving off an electric charge, and it was sending little currents of energy through the most disconcerting places in her body.

It seemed her crush on him had grown right along with her respect and she was agonisingly aware of how easy it would be to fall for him if she let herself.

Which she wasn't going to do. He was clearly still in love with his wife and there was no way she could compete with a ghost.

Only pain and heartache lay that way.

As soon as the curtain swished closed and the lights came on to signal the intermission she sprang up from her seat, eager to break their physical connection as soon as possible.

'Let's grab a drink,' Max said, leaning in close so she could hear him over the noise of audience chatter, his breath tickling the hairs around her ear.

'Good idea.' She was eager to move now to release the pent-up energy that was making her heart race.

Max gestured for her to go first, staying close behind her as they walked down the stairs towards the bar, his dominating presence like a looming shadow at her back.

They joined the rest of the audience at the bottom of the stairs and she pushed her way through the shouty crowd of people towards the shiny black-lacquered bar, which was already six people deep with waiting customers.

'Hmm, this could take a while,' she said to Max as they came to a stop at the outskirts of the throng.

'Don't worry, I'll get the drinks,' he said, walking around the perimeter of the group as if gauging the best place to make a start. 'Glass of wine?' he asked.

'Red please.'

'Okay, I'm going in,' he said, taking an audible breath and turning to the side to shoulder through a small gap between two groups of chatting people with their backs to each other.

Cara watched in fascinated awe as Max made it to the bar in record time, flipping a friendly smile as he sidled through the crowd and charming a group of women into letting him into a small gap at the counter next to them.

After making sure his newly made friends were served first, he placed his order with the barman and was back a few moments later, two glasses of red wine held aloft in a gesture of celebration.

'Wow, nice work,' Cara said, accepting a glass and trying not to grin like a loon. 'I've never seen anyone work a bar crowd like that before.'

Max shrugged and took a sip of wine, pinning a look of exaggerated nonchalance onto his face. 'I have hidden depths.'

She started to laugh, but it dried in her throat as she locked eyes with someone on the other side of the room.

Someone she thought she'd never see again.

Swallowing hard, she dragged her gaze back to Max and dredged up a smile, grasping for cool so she wouldn't have to explain her sudden change in mood.

But it was not to be. The man was too astute for his own good.

'Are you okay? You look like you've seen a ghost,' he said, his intelligent eyes flashing with concern.

Damn and blast. This was the last thing she wanted to have to deal with tonight.

'Fine,' she squeaked, her cheeks growing hot under the intensity of his gaze.

'Cara. I thought we'd agreed to be straight with each other from now on.'

Sighing, she nodded towards the other side of the bar. 'That guy over there is an old friend of mine.'

He frowned as she failed to keep the hurt out of her voice and she internally kicked herself for being so transparent.

'He can't be a very good friend if you're ignoring each other.'

She sighed and tapped at the floor with the toe of her shoe. 'It's complicated.'

He raised his eyebrows, waiting for her to go on.

After pausing for a moment, she decided there was no point in trying to gloss over it. 'The thing is—his fiancée has a problem with me.'

'Really? Why?'

'Because I'm female.'

He folded his arms. 'She's the jealous type, huh?'

'Yeah. And no matter how much Jack's tried to convince her that our friendship is purely platonic, she won't believe him. So I've been confined to the rubbish heap of Friends Lost and Passed Over.' She huffed out a sigh. 'I can't really blame him for making that choice, though. He loves her and I want him to be happy, and if that means we can't be friends any more then so be it.'

The look of bewildered outrage in Max's expression made the breath catch in her throat and she practically stopped breathing altogether as he reached out and stroked his hand down her arm in a show of solidarity, his touch sending tingles of pure pleasure through every nerve in her body.

Staring up into his handsome face, she wondered again what it would feel like to have someone like Max for a partner. To know that he was on her side and that he had her back, no matter what happened.

But she was kidding herself. He was never going to offer her the chance to find out. She was his employee and she'd do well to remember that.

Tearing her gaze away from him, she glanced back across the room to where the fiancée in question had now appeared by Jack's side. From a distance they appeared to be having a heated discussion about something, their heads close together as they gesticulated at each other. As she watched, they suddenly sprang apart and Jack turned to catch her eye again, already moving towards where she and Max were standing.

He was coming over.

Her body tensed with apprehension and she jumped in surprise as Max put his hand on her arm again, then increased his grip, as if readying himself to spirit her away from a painful confrontation.

'Cara! It's been ages,' Jack said as he came to a stop in front of her, looking just as boyishly handsome as ever, with his lopsided grin and great mop of wavy blond hair.

'It has, Jack.'

'How are you?' he asked, looking a little shame-faced now, as well he should. They'd become good friends after meeting at their first jobs after university and had been close once, spending weekends at each other's houses and standing in as 'plus ones' at weddings and parties if either of them were single and in need of support.

There had been a time when she'd wondered whether they'd end up together, but as time had passed it became obvious that wasn't meant to be. He was a great guy, but the chemistry just wasn't there for her—or for him, it seemed. But seeing him here now reminded her just how much she missed his friendship. She could have really done with his support after Ewan sauntered away from their relationship in search of someone with less emotional baggage, but it had been at that point that his fiancée had issued her ultimatum, and Cara had well and truly been the loser in that contest.

Not that she blamed him for choosing Amber. She had to respect his loyalty to the woman he loved.

'I'm great, Jack, thanks. How are you—' she paused and flicked her gaze to his fiancée, who had now appeared at his side '—both?' Somehow she managed to dredge up a smile for the woman. 'Hi, Amber.'

'Hi, Cara, we're great, thanks,' Amber said, acerbity dripping from every word as she pointedly wrapped a possessive arm around Jack's waist. Turning to look at Max, she gave him a subtle, but telling, once-over.

'And who's this?'

'This is Max...' Cara took a breath, about to say *my boss*, when Max cut her off to lean in and shake hands with Amber.

'It's lovely to meet you, Amber,' he said in the same smooth tone she'd heard him use to appease clients.

It worked just as well on Amber because her cheeks flooded with colour and she actually fluttered her lashes at him. Turning back to Cara, she gave her a cool smile, her expression puzzled, as if she was trying to work out how she'd got her hands on someone as impressive as Max.

'Did Jack tell you—our wedding's on Sunday so this evening is our last hurrah before married life?' Amber's eyes twinkled with malice. 'Jack's firm is very well reputed in the City and people practically throw invitations at him every day,' she said, her tone breezy but her eyes hard, as though she was challenging Cara to beat her with something better than that.

Which, of course, she had no hope of doing.

Pushing away the thump of humiliation, Cara forced her mouth into the shape of a smile.

'That's wonderful—congratulations! I had no idea the wedding was so soon.'

Amber leaned in and gave her a pitying smile. 'We've kept it a small affair, which is why we couldn't send you an invitation, Cara.'

Max shifted next to her, pulling her a bit tighter against him in the process and surprising her again by rubbing her arm in support. She wondered whether he could feel how fast her pulse was racing through her body with him holding her so close.

'But we had two spaces open up this week,' Jack said suddenly and a little too loudly, as if he'd finally decided to step out of his fiancée's shadow and take control. 'My cousin and her husband have had to drop out to visit sick family abroad. If you're not busy you could come in their place.'

Judging by the look on Amber's face, she obviously hadn't had this in mind when she'd agreed to be dragged over here.

'It would be great if you could make it,' Jack pressed, his expression open, almost pleading now. It seemed that he genuinely wanted her to be there. Perhaps this was his way of making things up to her after cutting her out of his life so brutally. At least that was something.

But she couldn't say yes when the invitation was for both her and Max and she hated the idea of turning up and spending the day on her own amongst all those happy couples.

Before she could open her mouth to make up an excuse and turn them down, Max leaned in and said, 'Thank you—we'd love to come.'

She swivelled her head to gape at him, almost giving herself whiplash in the process, stunned to find a look of cool certainty on his face.

'Are you sure we're not busy?' she said pointedly, raising both eyebrows at him.

'I'm sure,' he replied with a firm nod.

Turning back to Jack, she gave him what must have

been the weirdest-looking smile. 'Okay—er—' she swallowed '—then we'd love to come. Thanks.'

'That's great,' Jack said, giving her a look that both said *I'm sorry for everything* and *thank you*.

'We'd better go and get a drink before the performance starts again,' Amber said with steel in her voice, her patience clearly used up now.

'I'll text you with the details, Cara,' Jack said as Amber drew him away.

'Okay, see you on Sunday,' Cara said weakly to their disappearing figures.

As soon as they were out of earshot she turned to stare at Max, no doubt doing her impression of a goldfish again.

'He's a brave man,' was all Max said in reply.

'You realise they think we're a couple?'

He nodded, a fierce intensity in his eyes causing a delicious shiver to rush down her spine. 'I know, but I wanted to see the look on that awful woman's face when we said yes, and I have no problem pretending to be your partner if it's going to smooth the way back to a friendship with Jack for you.'

Max as her partner. Just the thought of it made her quiver right down to her toes.

'That's—' she searched for the right words '—game of you.'

'It'll be my pleasure.'

There was an odd moment where the noises around her seemed to get very loud in her ears. Tearing her gaze away from his, she gulped down the last of her wine and wrapped her hands around the glass in order to prevent herself from chewing on her nails.

Okay. Well, that happened.

Who knew that Max would turn out to be her knight in shining armour?

CHAPTER SIX

MAX HAD NO idea where this strange possessiveness towards Cara had sprung from, but he hadn't been about to let that awful woman, Amber, treat her with so little respect. She deserved more than that. Much more. And while she was working for him he was going to make sure she got it.

Which meant he was now going to be escorting her to a wedding—the kind of event he'd sworn to avoid after Jemima died. The thought of being back in a church, watching a couple with their whole lives ahead of them begin their journey together, made his stomach clench with unease.

One year—that was all he'd been allowed with his wife. One lousy year. It made him want to spit with rage at the world. Why her? Why them?

Still, at least he didn't know the happy couple and would be able to keep a low profile at the wedding, hiding his bitterness behind a bland smile. He didn't need to engage. He'd just be there to support Cara; that was all.

After the play finished they travelled home in silence, a stark contrast to their journey there, but he was glad of the quiet. Perversely, it felt as though he and Cara had grown closer during that short time, the confrontation and subsequent solidarity banding them together like teammates.

Which of course they were, he reminded himself as he opened the front door to his house and ushered her inside, at least when it came to the business.

Cara's phone beeped as she shrugged off her coat and she plucked it out of her handbag and read the message, her smile dropping by degrees as she scanned the text.

'Problem?' he asked, an uncomfortable sense of foreboding pricking at the edge of his mind. It had taken him a long time to be able to answer the phone without feeling the crush of anxiety he'd been plagued with after the call telling him his wife had collapsed and had been rushed into hospital.

He took a step closer to her, glad she was here to distract him from the lingering bad memories.

Glancing up, she gave him a sheepish look. 'It's a text from Jack with the details of the wedding.'

'Oh, right.' He stepped back, relief flowing through him, but Cara didn't appear to relax. Instead her grimace only deepened.

'Um. Apparently it's in Leicestershire. Which is a two and a half hour drive from here. So we'll need to stay overnight.' She wrinkled her nose, the apology clear on her face.

Great. Just what had he let himself in for here?

'No problem,' he forced himself to say, holding back

the irritation he felt at the news. It wasn't Cara's fault and he was the one who had pushed for this to happen.

More fool him.

'Really? You don't mind?' she asked, relief clear in her tone.

'No, it's fine,' he lied, trying not to think about all the hours he'd have to spend away from his desk so he could make nice with a bunch of strangers.

'Great, then I'll book us a couple of rooms in the B&B that Jack suggested,' she said, her smile returning.

'You do that.' He gave her a firm nod and hid a yawn behind his hand. 'I'm heading off to bed,' he said, feeling the stress of the week finally catching up with him. 'See you in the morning, Cara. And Happy Birthday.'

Cara disappeared for most of the next day, apparently going to look at potential flats to rent, then retiring to bed early, citing exhaustion from the busy, but fruitless, day.

After the tension of Friday night, Max was glad of the respite and spent most of his time working through the backlog of emails he'd accumulated after his week away.

Sunday finally rolled around and he woke early, staring into the cool empty air next to him and experiencing the usual ache of hollowness in his chest, before pulling himself together and hoisting his carcass out of bed and straight into the shower.

The wedding was at midday so at least he had a couple of hours to psych himself up before they had to head over to the Leicestershire estate where it was being held.

The sun was out and glinting off the polished windows of the houses opposite when he pulled his curtains open, momentarily blinding him with its brightness. It was definitely a day for being outdoors.

He'd barely breathed fresh air in the past week, only moving between office and hotel, and the thought of feeling the warm sun on his skin spurred him into action. He pulled on his running gear, something he'd not done for over a year and a half, and went for a long run, welcoming the numbing pain as he worked his lethargic muscles hard, followed by the rewarding rush of serotonin as it chased its way through his veins. After a while it felt as though he was flying along the pavement, the worries and stresses of the past week pushed to the very back of his mind by the punishing exercise.

For the first time in a long while he felt as if he were truly awake.

Cara appeared to be up and about when he limped back into his kitchen for a long drink of water, his senses perking up as he breathed in the comforting smell of the coffee she'd been drinking, threaded with the flowery scent of her perfume.

Glancing up at the clock as he knocked back his second glass of water, he was shocked to see it was already nearly nine o'clock, which meant he really ought to get a move on if he was going to be ready to leave for the wedding on time.

Turning back from loading his glass into the dishwasher, he was brought up short by the sight of Cara standing in the hallway just outside the kitchen door, watching him. She'd twisted her long hair up into some sort of complicated-looking hairstyle and her dark eyes sparkled with glittery make-up. The elegant silver strapless dress she wore fitted her body perfectly, moulding itself to her gentle curves and making her seem taller and—something else. More mature, perhaps? More sophisticated?

Whatever it was, she looked completely and utterly beautiful.

Realising he was standing there gawping at her like some crass teenage boy, he cleared his suddenly dry throat and dredged up a smile which he hoped didn't look as lascivious as it felt.

'Hey, you look like you're dressed for a wedding,' he said, cringing inside at how pathetic that sounded.

She smiled. 'And you don't. I hope you're not thinking of going like that because I'm pretty sure it didn't say "sports casual" on the invitation.' Her amused gaze raked up and down his body, her eyebrows rising at the sight of his sweat-soaked running gear.

He returned her grin, finding it strangely difficult to keep it natural-looking. His whole face felt as if he'd had his head stuck in the freezer. What was wrong with him? A bit of sunshine and a fancy dress and his mind was in a spin.

'I'd better go and take a shower; otherwise we're going to be late,' he said, already walking towards the door.

'Could you do me a favour before you go?' she asked, colour rising in her cheeks.

'Er…sure. As long as it's not going to cost me anything,' he joked, coming to a stop in front of her. In her heels she was nearly as tall as him, making it easier to directly meet her gaze. She had such amazing eyes: bright and clear with vitality and intellect. The make-up and hair made him think of Audrey Hepburn in *Breakfast at Tiffany's*.

'Could you do up the buttons on the back of my dress?' she asked, her voice sounding unusually breathy, as if it had taken a lot for her to ask for his help.

'Sure,' he said, waiting for her to turn around and present her back to him. His breath caught as he took in the long, elegant line of her spine as it disappeared into the base of her dress. There were three buttons that held the top half of it together, with a large piece cut out at the bottom, which would leave her creamy skin and the gentle swells of muscle at the base of her back exposed.

Heaven help him.

Hands feeling as if they'd been trapped in the freezer, too, he fiddled around with the buttons, feeling the warmth of her skin heat the tips of his fingers. Hot barbs of awareness tracked along his nerves and embedded themselves deep in his body and his breath came out in short ragged gasps, which he'd like to think was an after-effect of the hard exercise, but was more likely to be down to his close proximity to a woman's body, after his had been starved of attention for the past year and a half.

'There you go,' he said, snapping the final button into its hole with a sigh of relief. 'I'll be back down in fifteen.'

And with that he made his escape.

***

Wow. This felt weird, being at Jack's wedding—a friend she thought she'd never see again—with Max—her recalcitrant boss—as her escort. The whole world seemed to have flipped on its head. If someone had told her a week ago that this was going to happen she would have given them a polite smile whilst slowly backing away.

But here she was, swaying unsteadily in the only pair of high heels she owned, with Max at her side. The man who could give Hollywood's top leading men a run for their money in the charisma department.

There had been a moment in the kitchen, after he'd turned around and noticed her, when she thought she'd seen something in his eyes. Something that had never been there before. Something like desire.

And then when he'd helped her with her dress it had felt as though the air had crackled and jumped between them. The bloom of his breath on her neck had made her knees weak and her heart race. She could have sworn his voice had held a rougher undertone than she was used to hearing as he excused himself.

But she knew she was kidding herself if she thought she should read more than friendly interest into his actions.

They had Radio Four on for the entire journey up to Leicestershire, listening in rapt silence to a segment on finance, then chuckling along to a radio play. Cara was surprised by how easy it was to sit beside Max and how relaxed and drawn into their shared enjoyment of the programme she was. So much so, that it was to her great surprise that they pulled into the small car park of the church where the wedding was taking place, seemingly only a short time after leaving London.

The sunshine that had poured in through her bedroom window that morning had decided to stick around for the rest of the day, disposing of the insubstantial candyfloss clouds of the morning to reveal the most intensely blue sky she'd ever seen.

All around her, newly blooming spring flowers bopped their heads in time to the rhythm of the light spring breeze, their gaudy colours a striking counterpoint to the verdant green of the lawns surrounding them.

Taking a deep breath, she drew the sweet, fresh air deep into her lungs. This should mark a new beginning in her life, she decided. The start of the next chapter, where the foundations she'd laid in the past few weeks would hopefully prove strong enough to support her from this point onwards.

'It's nearly twelve o'clock; we should go in,' Max said with regret in his voice as he cast his gaze around their beautiful surroundings.

Attempting to keep her eyes up and off the tantalising view of his rear in the well-cut designer suit he'd chosen to wear today, she tripped into the church after him, shivering slightly at the change in temperature as they walked out of the sunshine and into the nave.

Most of the pews were already full, so they hung back for a moment to be directed to a seat by one of the ushers.

And that was when the day took a definite turn for the worse.

Her world seemed to spin on its axis, rolling her stomach along with it, as her former and current life lined up on a collision course. One of the PAs who had belonged to the Cobra Clique was standing down by the altar, her long blond hair slithering down her back as she threw her head back and laughed at something that the man standing next to her said.

Taking a deep breath, Cara willed herself not to panic, but her distress must have shown plainly on her face because Max turned to glance in the direction she was staring and said, 'Cara? What's wrong?'

'Ah...nothing.' She flapped a dismissive hand at him, feeling her cheeks flame with heat, and took a step backwards, hoping the stone pillar would shield her. But serendipity refused to smile as the woman turned towards them, catching her eye, her pupils flaring in recognition and her gaze moving, as if in slow motion, from Cara to Max and back again. And the look on her face plainly said she wasn't going to miss this golden opportunity to make more trouble for her.

Looking around her wildly, Cara's heart sank as she realised there was nowhere to run, nowhere to hide.

It was usually at this point in a film that the leading lady would pull the guy she was with towards her and kiss him hard to distract him from the oncoming danger, but she knew, as she stared with regret at Max's full, inviting mouth, that there was no way she could do that. He'd probably choke in shock, then fire her on the spot if she even attempted it. It wouldn't just put her job in jeopardy—it would blow it to smithereens.

There was only one thing left to do.

'Max, I need to tell you something.'

He frowned at her, his eyes darkening as he caught on to her worried tone.

'What's wrong?'

'I—er—'

'Cara?' He looked really alarmed now and she shook her head, trying to clear it. She needed to keep her cool or she'd end up looking even more of an idiot.

'I wasn't entirely straight with you about why I left my last job. Truth is—' she took a breath '—I didn't take redundancy.'

He blinked, then frowned. 'So you were fired?'

'No. I—'

'What did you do, Cara? What are you trying to tell me?' His voice held a tinge of the old Max now—the one who didn't suffer fools.

'Okay—' She closed her eyes and held up a hand. 'Look, just give me a minute and I'll explain. The thing is—' Locking her shaking hands together, she took a steadying breath. 'I was bullied by a gang of women there who made my life a living hell and I handed in my notice before my boss could fire me for incompetence as a result of it,' she said, mortified by the tremor in her voice.

When she opened her eyes to look at him, the expression of angry disbelief on his face made her want to melt into a puddle of shame.

'What?'

She swallowed past the tightness in her throat. 'I had no choice but to leave.'

He shook his head in confusion. 'Why didn't you tell me?'

Out of the corner of her eye she saw her nemesis approaching and felt every hair on her body stand to attention. The woman was only ten steps away, at most.

'And why are you telling me this now?' he pressed.

'Because one of the women is here at the wedding and she'll probably tell you a pack of lies to make me look bad. I didn't exactly leave graciously. There was a jug of cold coffee and some very white blouses involved.' She cringed at the desperation in her voice, but Max just turned to glare in the direction she'd been avoiding, then let out a sharp huff of breath.

'Come outside for a minute.'

Wrapping his hand around her arm, he propelled her back out through the doors of the church and down the steps, coming to a sudden halt under the looming shadow of the clock tower, where he released her. Crossing his arms, he looked down at her with an expression of such exasperation it made her quake in her stilettos.

'Why didn't you mention this to me before?' he asked, shoving back the hair that had fallen across his forehead during their short journey, only drawing more attention to his piercing gaze.

Sticking her chin in the air, she crossed her own arms, determined to stand up for herself. 'I really wanted to work with you and I thought you might not hire me if you knew the truth. It didn't exactly look good on my CV that I'd only stuck it out there for three months before admitting defeat.'

'So you thought you had to lie to me to get the job?'

She held up her hands in apology. 'I know I should have told you the truth, but I'd already messed up other job interviews because I was so nervous and ashamed of myself for being so weak.' She hugged her arms around her again. 'I didn't want you to think badly of me. Anyway, at the time you barely wanted to talk to me about the work I had to do, let alone anything of a personal nature, so I thought it best to keep it to myself.' She looked at him steadily, craving his understanding. 'You can be pretty intimidating, you know.'

She was saved from having to further explain herself by one of the ushers loudly asking the stragglers outside to please go into the church and take their seats because the bride had arrived.

From the look on Max's face she wasn't sure whether he was going to walk away and leave her standing there like a total lemon on her own or turn around and punch the wall. She didn't fancy watching either scenario play out.

To her surprise, he let out a long, frustrated sigh and looked towards the gaggle of people filing into the church.

'We can't talk about this now or we'll be walking in with the bridal party, and there's no way I'd pass for a bridesmaid,' he said stiffly.

She stared at him. 'You mean you're not going to leave?'

'No, I'm not going to leave,' he said crossly. 'We'll talk more about this after the ceremony.'

And with that he put his hand firmly against the middle of her back and ushered her inside.

Sliding into the polished wooden pew next to Max and surreptitiously wiping her damp palms on her dress, she glanced at him out of the corner of her eye. From the set of his shoulders she could tell he wasn't likely to let *this* go with a casual wave of his hand.

In fact she'd bet everything she had left that he was really going to fire her this time.

Frustration churned in her stomach. After all the progress she'd made in getting back on her feet, and persuading Max to finally trust her, was it really going to end like this?

Looking along the pews, she saw that her nemesis was sitting on the other side of the church, a wide smile on her face as she watched the ceremony unfold. At least that threat had been neutralised. There wasn't anything left that she could do to hurt her.

She hoped.

Rage unfurled within Cara at the unfairness of it all. Why did this woman get to enjoy herself when she had to sit here worrying about her future?

As she watched Amber make her stately way up the aisle towards a rather nervous-looking Jack, she could barely concentrate for wondering what Max was going to say to her once they were facing each other over their garlic mushrooms at the lunch afterwards. There was no way she was going to be able to force down a bite of food until they'd resolved this.

Oh, get a grip, Cara.

When she dared take a peek at him from the corner of her eye again, he seemed to be grimly staring straight ahead. Forcing herself to relax, she uncrossed her legs, then her arms and sat up straighter, determined not to appear anxious or pitiful. She knew what she had to do. There would be no gratuitous begging or bartering for a reprieve. She would hold her head high throughout it all and calmly state her case.

And until she had that opportunity she was going to damn well enjoy watching her friend get married.

Judging by her rigid posture and ashen complexion, Cara really didn't appear to be enjoying the ceremony, which only increased Max's discomfort at being there, too. Not that he blamed her in any way for it. He'd chosen to come here with her after all. Though, from the sound of it, she must be regretting bringing him along now.

Had he really been so unapproachable that she'd chosen to lie to his face instead of admitting to having a rough time at her last place of work?

He sighed inwardly.

She was absolutely right, though. Again. He could be intimidating. And he'd been at the peak of his remoteness when she'd first arrived on his doorstep and asked him for a job. He also knew that if she'd mentioned the personal issues that had been intrinsic to her leaving her last job when they'd first met it would have given him pause enough to turn her away. He hadn't wanted any kind of complication at that point.

But he was so glad now that he hadn't.

Somehow, in her innocent passive-aggressive way, she'd managed to push his buttons and, even though he'd fought it at the time, that was exactly what he'd needed.

She was what he'd needed.

After the ceremony finished they were immediately ushered out of the church and straight up the sweeping manicured driveway to the front of a grand Georgian house where an enormous canvas marquee had been set up next to the orangery.

A small affair, his foot.

As soon as they stepped inside they had toxic-coloured cocktails thrust upon them and were politely but firmly asked to make their way back outside again to the linen-draped tables on the terrace next to the house.

'This is like a military operation,' he muttered to Cara, who had walked quietly next to him since they'd left the church, her face pale and her expression serious. She gave him a weak smile, her eyes darting from side to side as if she was seriously contemplating making a run for it and scoping out the best means of escape.

He sighed. 'Come and sit down over here where it's quiet,' he said, looping his arm through hers and guiding her towards one of the empty tables nearest the house.

To his frustration she stiffened, then slipped out of his steadying grip and folded her arms across her chest instead, her shoulders rigid and her chin firmly up as they walked. Just as they picked their way over the last bit of gravelled path to reach the table she stumbled and on reflex he quickly moved in to catch her.

'Are you okay?' he asked, placing a hand on the exposed part of her back, feeling the heat of her body warm the palm of his hand and send an echoing sensation through his entire abdomen.

His touch seemed to undo something in her and she collapsed into the nearest chair and gave him such a fearful look his heart jumped into his throat.

'I'm sorry for lying to you, Max. Please don't fire me. If I lose this job I'll have to move back to Cornwall and I really, really don't want to leave London. It's my home and I love it. I can't imagine living anywhere else now. And I really like working for you.' Swallowing hard, she gave him a small quavering smile. 'I swear I will never lie to you again. Believe it or not, I usually have a rock-solid moral compass and if I hadn't felt backed into a corner I never would have twisted the truth. I was on the cusp of losing everything and I was desperate, Max. Totally. Desperate.' She punctuated each of the last words with a slap of her hand on the table.

'Cara, I'm not going to fire you.'

How could she think that he would? Good grief, had he done such a number on her that she'd think he'd be capable of something as heartless as that?

'You're not?' Her eyes shone in the reflected brightness thrown up by the white tablecloth and he looked away while she blinked back threatening tears.

'Of course not.' He shifted forward in his seat, closer to her. 'You well and truly proved your worth to the business last week.' He waited till she looked at him again. 'I have to admit, I'm hurt that you thought I'd fire you for admitting to being bullied.' He leaned back in his chair with a sigh. 'God, you must think I'm a real tool if you seriously believed I'd do something like that.'

'It's just—you can be a bit...fierce...sometimes. And

I didn't want to show any weakness.' She visibly cringed as she said it, and his insides plummeted.

'Tell me more about what happened at your last job,' he said quietly, wanting to get things completely straight between them, but not wanting to spook her further in the process.

Her gaze slid away. 'It's not a happy tale, or something I'm particularly proud of.'

'No. I got that impression.'

'Okay, I'll tell you, but please don't judge me too harshly. Things like this always look so simple and manageable from a distance, but when you're in the thick of it, it's incredibly difficult to think straight without letting your emotions get in the way.'

He held up his hands, palms forward, and affected a non-judgemental expression.

She nodded and sat up straighter. 'I thought I'd hit the jackpot when I was offered that position. Ugh! What an idiot,' she said, her self-conscious grimace making him want to move closer to her, to draw her towards him and smooth out the kinks of her pain. But he couldn't do that. It wasn't his place.

So he just nodded and waited for her to continue.

'When I started as Executive Assistant to the CEO of LED Software I had no idea about the office politics that were going on there. But it didn't take me long to find out. Apparently one of the other PAs had expected to be a shoo-in for my job and was *very* unimpressed when they gave it to me. She made it her mission from my first day to make my life miserable. As one of the longest-standing members of staff—and a very, er, *strong* personality—she had the allegiance of all the other PAs and a lot of the other members of staff and they ganged up on me. At first I thought I was going mad. I'd make diary appointments for my boss with other high-ranking members of staff in the company, which their PAs would claim to have no knowledge of by the time I sent him along for the meeting. Or the notes I'd print out for an important phone call with the Executive Board would go missing from his desk right before it took place and he'd have to take it unbriefed.' She tapped her fingers on the table. 'That did not go down well. My boss was a very proud guy and he expected things to be perfect.'

'I can relate to that,' Max said, forcing compassion into his smile despite the tug of disquiet in his gut. He was just as guilty when it came to perfectionism.

But, instead of admonishing him, she smiled back.

'Lots of other little things like that happened,' she continued, rubbing a hand across her forehead, 'which made me look incompetent, but I couldn't prove that someone was interfering with my work and when I mentioned it to my boss he'd wave away my concerns and suggest I was slipping up on the job and blaming others to cover my back. I let the stress of it get to me and started making real mistakes, things I never would have let slip at the last place I worked. It rattled me, to the point where I started believing I wasn't cut out for the job. I wasn't sleeping properly with the stress of it and I ended up breaking down one day in front of my boss. And that—' she clicked her fingers '—was the end of our working relationship. He seemed to lose all respect for me after that and started giving the other PAs things that were my job to do.'

Max snorted in frustration. 'The guy sounds like an idiot.'

She gave him a wan smile. 'I was the idiot. I only found out what was really going on when I overheard a couple of the PAs laughing about it in the ladies' bathroom.'

Her eyes were dark with an expression he couldn't quite read now. Was it anger? Resentment? It certainly didn't look like self-pity.

'So you left,' he prompted.

She took a sip of her drink and he did the same, grimacing at the claggy sweetness of the cocktail.

'I had to,' she said. 'My professional reputation was at stake, not to mention my sanity. I couldn't afford to be fired; it would have looked awful on my CV. Not to mention how upset my parents would have been. They're desperate for me to have a successful career. They never had the opportunity to get a good education or well-paid job themselves so they scrimped and saved for years to put me through private school. It's a point of pride for my dad in particular. Apparently he never shuts up to his friends about me working with "the movers and shakers in the Big Smoke".' She shot him an embarrassed grimace.

He smiled. 'You're lucky—my mother couldn't give two hoots whether I'm successful or not. She's not what you'd call an engaged parent.'

Her brow furrowed in sympathy. 'And your father?'

'I never met him.' He leant back with a sigh. 'My

mother fell pregnant with me when she was sixteen and still maintains that she doesn't know who he was. She was pretty wild in her youth and constantly moved us around the country. Barely a term at school would go by before she had us packing up and moving on. She couldn't bear to stay in the same place for long. Not that she's exactly settled now.'

Her gaze was sympathetic. 'That must have been tough when you were young.'

He shrugged. 'It was a bit. I never got to keep the friends I made for very long.'

He thought about how his unsettled youth had impacted on the way he liked to live now. He still didn't like change, even all these years later; it made him tetchy and short-tempered. Which was something Cara had got to know all about recently.

Keen to pull his mind away from his own shortcomings, he leaned forward in his seat and recaptured eye contact with her. 'So what happened when you handed in your notice?'

She started at the sudden flip in subject back to her and twisted the stem of her glass in her fingers, looking away from his gaze and focusing on the garish liquid as it swirled up towards the rim. 'My boss didn't even bat an eyelid, just tossed my letter of resignation onto his desk and went back to the email he was typing, which confirmed just how insignificant I was to him. I took a couple of weeks to get my head straight after that, but I needed another job. I've never earned enough to build up any savings and my landlord chose that moment to hoick my rent up. I sent my CV out everywhere and got a few interviews, but every one I attended was a washout. It was as if they could sense the cloud of failure that hung around me like a bad smell.'

'And that's when Poppy sent you to me.'

Wrinkling her nose, she gave him a rueful smile. 'I told her a bit about what had happened before she went off to shoot her latest project and she must have thought the two of us could help each other out because she emailed me to suggest I try you for a job. She made it sound as if you were desperate for help and it seemed like fate that I should work for you.'

'Desperate, huh?' He leant back in his seat and raised an eyebrow, feeling amusement tug at his mouth. That was textbook Poppy. 'Well, I have to admit it's been good for me, having you around. It's certainly kept me on my toes.'

'Yeah, there's never a dull moment when I'm around, huh?'

The air seemed to grow thick between them as their eyes met and he watched in arrested fascination as her cheeks flamed with colour.

Sliding her gaze away, she stared down at the table, clutching her glass, her chewed nails in plain view. He'd known it the whole time, of course, that she was fighting against some inner trauma, as her nerve and buoyancy deteriorated in the face of his brittle moods. Her increasingly ragged nails had been the indicator he'd been determined to ignore.

But not any more.

A string quartet suddenly started up on the terrace behind them and he winced as the sound assaulted his ears. He'd never liked the sound of violins and an instrument such as that should never be used to play soft rock covers. It was a crime against humanity.

'Come on, let's take a walk around the grounds and clear our heads,' he said, standing up and holding out his hand to help her up from the chair.

She looked at it with that little frown that always made something twist in his chest, before giving a firm nod and putting her hand in his.

CHAPTER SEVEN

A WALK WAS exactly what Cara needed to clear her head.

She couldn't quite believe she'd just spilled her guts to Max like that, but it was a massive relief to have it all out in the open, even if she did still feel shaky with the effort of holding herself together.

Of course, seeing the concern on his handsome face had only made her ridiculous crush on him deepen, and she was beginning to worry about how she was going to cope with seeing him every day, knowing that they'd never be anything more than colleagues or, at the very most, friends.

A twinkling light in the distance danced in her peripheral vision and she stopped and turned to see what it was, feeling her heels sink into the soft earth beneath her feet. Pulling her shoes off, she hooked her fingers into the straps before running to catch up with Max, who was now a few paces ahead of her, seemingly caught up in his own world, his head dipped as a frown played across his brow.

'Hey, do you fancy walking to that lake over there?' she asked him.

'Hmm?' His eyes looked unfocused, as if his thoughts were miles away. 'Yes, okay.'

The sudden detachment worried her. 'Is everything okay?' Perhaps, now he'd had more time to reflect on what she'd told him, he was starting to regret getting involved in her messed up life.

She took a breath. 'Do you want to head back to London? I wouldn't blame you if you did.'

Turning to look her in the eye again, he blinked, as though casting away whatever was bothering him. 'No, no. I'm fine.' His gaze flicked towards the lake, then back to her again and he gave her a tense smile. 'Yeah, let's walk that way.'

It only took them a couple of minutes to get there, now that she was in bare feet, and they stopped at the lakeshore and looked out across the water to the dark, impenetrable-looking forest on the other side.

'It's a beautiful setting they've chosen,' Cara said, to fill the heavy silence that had fallen between them.

'Yes, it's lovely.' Max bent down and picked up a smooth flat stone, running his fingertips across its surface. 'This looks like a good skimmer.' He shrugged off his jacket and rolled up the sleeves of his shirt, revealing his muscular forearms.

Cara stared at them, her mouth drying at the sight. There was something so real, so virile about the image of his tanned skin, with its smattering of dark hair, in stark contrast to the crisp white cotton of his formal shirt. As if he was revealing the *man* inside the businessman.

Supressing a powerful desire to reach out and trace

her fingers across the dips and swells of his muscles, she took a step away to give him plenty of room as he drew his elbow back and bent low, then flung the stone hard across the water.

A deep, satisfied chuckle rumbled from his chest as the stone bounced three times across the still surface, spinning out rings of gentle ripples in its wake, before sinking without a trace into the middle of the lake.

He turned to face her with a grin, his eyes alive with glee, and she couldn't help but smile back.

'Impressive.'

He blew on his fingers and pretended to polish them on his shirt. 'I'm a natural. What can I say?'

Seeing his delight at the achievement, she had a strong desire to get in on the fun. Perhaps it would help distract her from thinking about how alone they were out here on the edge of the lake. 'Does your natural talent stretch to teaching me how to do that?'

'You've never skimmed a stone?' He looked so over-the-top incredulous she couldn't help but laugh.

'Never.'

'Didn't you say your parents live in Cornwall? Surely there's plenty of opportunities to be near water there.'

She snorted and took a step backwards, staring down at the muddy grass at their feet. 'Yeah, if you live near the coast, which they don't. I never learnt to drive when I was living there and my parents didn't take me to the beach that much when I was young. My dad's always suffered with a bad back from the heavy lifting he has to do at work, so he never got involved in anything of a physical nature. And my mum's a real homebody. She's suffered with agoraphobia for years.'

She heard him let out a low exhalation of breath and glanced up to find an expression of real sympathy in his eyes. 'I'm sorry to hear that. That must have been hard for you as a kid,' he said softly.

Shrugging one shoulder, she gave a nod to acknowledge his concern, remembering the feeling of being trapped inside four small walls when she was living at home, with nowhere to escape to. Going to school every day had actually been a welcome escape from it and as soon as she'd finished her studies she'd hightailed it to London.

'Yeah, it was a bit. My parents are good people, though. They threw all their energy into raising me. And they made sure to let me know how loved I was.' Which was the absolute truth, she realised with a sting of shame, because she'd distanced herself from them since leaving home in an attempt to leave her stultifying life there behind her. But she'd left them behind, too. They didn't deserve that. A visit was well overdue and she made a pact with herself to call them and arrange a date to see them as soon as she got back to London.

Max nodded, seemingly satisfied that she didn't need any more consoling, and broke eye contact to lean down and pick up another flat pebble.

She watched him weigh it in his palm, as if checking it was worth the effort of throwing it. Everything he did was measured and thorough like that, which was probably why he was such a successful businessman.

'Here, this looks like a good one. It's nice and flat

with a decent weight to it so it'll fly and not sink immediately.' He turned it over in his hand. 'You need to get it to ride the air for a while before it comes down and maintain enough lift to jump.'

He held it out to her and she took it and looked at it with a frown. 'Is there a proper way to hold it?'

'I find the best way is to pinch it between my first finger and thumb. Like this.' He picked up another stone and demonstrated.

She copied the positioning in her own hand then gave him a confident nod, drew back her arm and threw it as hard as she could.

It landed in the lake with a *plop* and sank immediately.

'Darn it! What did I do wrong?' she asked, annoyed with herself for failing so badly.

'Don't worry; it can take a bit of practice to get your technique right. You need to get lower to the ground and swing your arm in a horizontal arc. When it feels like the stone could fly straight forward and parallel with the water, loosen the grip with your thumb and let it roll, snapping your finger forwards hard.'

'Huh. You make it sound so easy.'

He grinned and raised his eyebrows. 'Try again.'

Picking up a good-looking candidate, she positioned the stone between her finger and thumb and was just about to throw it when Max said, 'Stop!'

Glancing round at him with a grimace of frustration, she saw he was frowning and shaking his head.

'You need to swing your arm at a lower angle. Like this.'

Before she could react, he'd moved to stand directly behind her, putting his left hand on her hip and wrapping his right hand around the hand she was holding the stone in. Her heart nearly leapt out of her chest at the firmness of his touch and started hammering away, forcing the blood through her body at a much higher rate than was reasonable for such low-level exercise.

As he drew their arms backwards the movement made her shoulder press against the hard wall of his chest and she was mightily glad that he couldn't see her face at that precise moment. She was pretty sure it must look a real picture.

'Okay, on three we'll throw it together.' His mouth was so close to her ear she felt his breath tickle the downy little hairs on the outer whorl.

'One...two...three!'

They moved their linked hands in a sweeping arc, Cara feeling the power of Max's body push against her as the momentum of the move forced them forwards. She was so distracted by being engulfed in his arms she nearly didn't see the stone bounce a couple of times before it sank beneath the water.

'Woo-hoo!' Max shouted, releasing her to take a step back and raise his hand, waiting for her to give him a high five.

The sudden loss of his touch left her feeling strangely light and disorientated—but now was not the time to go to pieces. Mentally pulling herself together, she swung her hand up to meet his, their palms slapping loudly as they connected, then bent down straight away, pretending to search the ground for another missile.

'Who taught you to skim stones? A brother?' she asked casually, grimacing at the quaver in her voice, before grabbing another good-looking pebble and righting herself.

He'd stooped to pick up his own stone and glanced round at her as he straightened up. 'No. I'm an only child. I think once my mother realised how much hard work it was raising me she was determined not to have any more kids.' He raised a disparaging eyebrow then turned away to fling the stone across the lake, managing five bounces this time. He nodded with satisfaction. 'I used to mountain bike over to a nearby reservoir with a friend from boarding school at the weekends and we'd have competitions to see who could get their stone the furthest,' he said, already searching the ground for another likely skimmer, his movements surprisingly lithe considering the size of his powerful body.

A sudden need to get this right overwhelmed her.

She wasn't usually a superstitious person, but she imagined she could sense the power in this one simple challenge. If she got this stone to bounce by herself, maybe, just maybe, everything would be okay.

She was throwing this for her pride and the return of her strength. To prove to Max—but mostly to herself—that she was resilient and capable and—dare she even suggest it?—brave enough to try something new, even if there was a good chance she'd fail spectacularly and end up looking foolish again.

Harnessing the power of positive thought, she drew back her hand, took a second to centre herself, then flung the stone hard across the water, snapping her finger like he'd taught her and holding her breath as she watched it sail through the air.

It dropped low about fifteen feet out and for a second she thought she'd messed it up, but her spirits soared as she saw it bounce twice before disappearing.

Spinning round to make a celebratory face at Max, she was gratified to see him nod in exaggerated approval, a smile playing about his lips.

'Good job! You're a quick study; but then we already knew that about you.'

The compliment made her insides flare with warmth and she let out a laugh of delight, elation twisting through her as she saw him grin back.

Their gazes snagged and held, his pupils dilating till his eyes looked nearly black in the bright afternoon light.

A wave of electric heat spread through her at the sight of it, but the laughter died in her throat as he turned abruptly away and stared off towards the house instead, folding his arms so tightly against his chest she could make out the shape of his muscles under his shirt.

He cleared his throat. 'You know, this place is just like the venue where Jemima and I got married,' he said, so casually she wondered how much emotion he'd had to rein in, in order to say it.

Ugh. What a selfish dolt she was. Here she'd been worrying about what he thought of her and her tales of woe, when he was doing battle with his own demons.

It had occurred to her earlier that morning, as she'd struggled to do up her dress, that attending a wedding could be problematic for him, but she'd forgotten all about it after the incident in the kitchen, her thoughts distracted by the unnerving tension that had crackled between them ever since.

Or what she'd thought was tension.

Perhaps it had been apprehension on his part.

And then, when he'd mentioned how transient and lonely his youth had been over drinks earlier, it had brought it home to her why Jemima's death had hit him so hard. It sounded as if she'd been the person anchoring his life after years of feeling adrift and insecure. And this place reminded him of everything he'd lost.

No wonder he seemed so unsettled.

He'd still come here to help her out, though, despite his discomfort at being at this kind of event, which was a decent and kind thing for him to do and way beyond the call of duty as her boss. Her heart did a slow flip in her chest as she realised exactly what it must have cost him to agree to come.

'I'm sorry for dragging you here today. I didn't think about how hard it would be for you. After losing Jemima.'

He put his hand on her arm and waited for her to look at him before speaking. 'You have nothing to apologise for. *Nothing*. I wanted to come here to support you because you've done nothing but support me for the last few weeks. It's my turn to look after you today.' He was looking directly at her now and the fierce intensity in his eyes made a delicious shiver zip down her spine.

'Honestly, I thought it would be awful coming here,' he said, casting his gaze back towards the house again, 'but it's not been the trial I thought it'd be. In fact—'

he ran a hand over his hair and let out a low breath '—it's been good for me to confront a situation like this. I've been missing out on so much life since Jem died and it's time I pulled my head out of the sand and faced the world again.'

Cara swallowed hard, ensnared in the emotion of the moment, her heart thudding against her chest and her breath rasping in her dry throat. Looking at Max now, she realised that the ever-present frown was nowhere to be seen for once. Instead, there was light in his eyes and something else...

They stood, frozen in the moment, as the gentle spring wind wrapped around them and the birds sang enthusiastically above their heads.

It would be so easy to push up onto tiptoe and slide her hands around his neck. To press her lips against his and feel the heat and masculine strength of him, to slide her tongue into his mouth and taste him. She ached to feel his breath against her skin and his hands in her hair, her whole body tingling with the sensory expectation of it.

She wanted to be the one to remind him what living could be like, if only he'd let her.

To her disappointment, Max broke eye contact with her and nodded towards the marquee behind them. 'We should probably get back before they send out a search party. We don't want to find ourselves in trouble for messing with Amber's schedule of events and being frogmarched to our seats,' he said lightly, though his voice sounded gruffer than normal.

Had he seen it in her face? The longing. She hoped

not. The thought of her infatuation putting their fragile relationship under any more strain made her insides squirm.

Anyway, that tension-filled moment had probably been him thinking about Jemima again.

Not her.

They walked in silence back to the marquee, the bright sun pleasantly warm on the back of her neck and bare shoulders, but her insides icy cold.

Despite their little detour, they weren't the last to sit down. It was with a sigh of relief that Cara slumped into her seat and reached for the bottle of white wine on the table, more than ready to blot out the ache of disappointment that had been present ever since he'd suggested they give up their truancy from the festivities and head back into the fray.

It wasn't that she didn't want to be here exactly; it was just that it had been so much fun hanging out with him. Just the two of them together, like friends. Or something.

Knocking back half a glass of wine in one go, she refilled it before offering the bottle to Max.

He was looking at her with bemusement, one eyebrow raised. 'Thirsty?'

Heat flared across her cheeks. 'Just getting in the party mood,' she said, forcing a nonchalant smile. 'It looks like we have some catching up to do.'

The raucous chatter and laughter in the room suggested that people were already pretty tiddly on the cocktails they'd been served.

'Okay, well, I'm going to stick to water if I have to

drive to the bed and breakfast place later. I think one of us should stay sober enough to find our way there at the end of the night. I don't fancy kipping in the car.'

She gave him an awkward grin as the thought of sleeping in such close proximity to him made more heat rush to her face.

Picking up her glass, she took another long sip of wine to cover her distress.

Oh, good grief. It was going to be a long night.

The meal was surprisingly tasty, considering how many people were being catered for, and Cara began to relax as the wine did its work. She quickly found herself in a conversation with the lady to her right, who turned out to be Amber's second cousin and an estate agent in Angel, about the dearth of affordable housing to rent in London. By the end of dessert, the woman had promised to give Cara first dibs on a lovely-sounding one-bedroom flat that was just about to come onto her books. And that proved to Cara, without a shadow of a doubt, that you just had to be in the right place at the right time to get lucky.

Turning to say this exact thing to Max, she was disturbed to find he'd finished his conversation with the man next to him and was frowning down at the tablecloth.

'Sorry for ignoring you,' she said, worried he was getting sucked down into dark thoughts again with all the celebrating going on around him.

He gave her a tense smile and pushed his chair away from the table. 'You weren't. I overheard your conversation about finding a flat; that's great news—you should definitely get her number and follow that up,' he said, standing and tapping the back of his chair. 'I'm going to find the bathrooms. I'll be back in a minute.'

She watched him stride away with a lump in her throat. Was he upset about the prospect of her moving out? She dismissed the notion immediately. No, he couldn't be. He must be craving his space again by now. Even though she'd loved living there, she knew it was time to move out. Especially now that her feelings for him had twisted themselves into something new. Something dangerous.

'That's a good one you've got there—very sexy,' Amber's second cousin muttered into her ear, pulling back to waggle her eyebrows suggestively, only making the lump in Cara's throat grow in size.

Unable to speak, she gave the woman what she hoped looked like a gracious smile.

'Hi, Cara.'

The voice behind her made her jump in her seat and she swivelled round, only to find herself staring into the eyes of the woman she'd been trying to avoid since spotting her in the church earlier.

Her meal rolled uncomfortably in her stomach.

'Hi, Lucy.'

Instead of the look of cool disdain Cara was expecting, she was surprised to see Lucy bite her lip, her expression wary.

'How are you?' Lucy asked falteringly, as if afraid to hear the answer.

'Fine, thank you.' Cara kept her voice deliberately

neutral, just in case this was an opening gambit to get her to admit to something she really didn't want to say.

'Can I talk to you for a moment?'

Cara swallowed her anxiety and gestured towards the chair Max had vacated, wondering what on earth this woman could have to say to her. Whatever it was, it was better to get it over with now so she didn't spend the rest of the night looking over her shoulder. Straightening her back, she steeled herself to deal with anything she could throw at her.

Lucy sat on the edge of the seat, as close as she could get to Cara without touching her, and laid her hands on her lap before taking a deep breath. 'I wanted to come over and apologise as soon as I could so there wasn't any kind of atmosphere between us today.'

Cara stared at her. 'I'm sorry? Did you say *apologise*?'

Lucy crossed her legs, then uncrossed them again, her cheeks flooding with colour. 'Yes... I'm really sorry about the way you were treated at LED. I feel awful about it. I let Michelle bully me into taking her side—because I knew she'd turn on me, too, if I stood up for you—and I was pathetic enough to let her. I want you to know that I didn't do any of those awful things to you, but I didn't stop it either.' She shook her head and let out a low sigh. 'I feel awful about it, Cara, truly.'

At that moment Cara felt a pair of hands land lightly on her shoulders. Twisting her head round, she saw that Max had returned and was standing over her like some kind of dark guardian angel.

'Everything okay, Cara?' From the cool tone in his

voice she suspected he'd be more than willing to step in and eject Lucy from her seat if she asked him to.

'Fine, thanks, Max. This is Lucy. She came over to apologise for her *unfriendliness* at the last place I worked.'

'Is that so?'

Cara couldn't see the expression on his face from that angle but, from the sound of his voice and the way Lucy seemed to shrink back in her chair, she guessed it wasn't a very friendly one.

Lucy cleared her throat awkwardly. 'Yes, I feel dreadful about the whole thing. It was horrible working there. In fact, I left the week after you did. I couldn't stand the smug look on Michelle's face any more. Although—' she leaned forward in a conspiratorial manner '—I heard from one of the other girls that she only lasted a month before he got rid of her. She couldn't hack it, apparently.' She snorted. 'That's karma in action, right there.' Clearly feeling she'd said her piece, Lucy stood up so that Max could have his chair back and took a small step away from them. 'Anyway, I'd better get back to my table; apparently there's coffee on the way and I'm desperate for some. Those cocktails were evil, weren't they?'

'Why are you here today?' Cara asked before she could turn and leave, intrigued by the coincidence.

'I'm Jack's—the groom's—new PA.'

Cara couldn't help but laugh at life's weird little twist. 'Really?'

'Yeah, he's a great boss, really lovely to work for.' She leant forward again and said in a quiet voice, 'I don't think Amber likes me very much, though; she didn't seem very pleased to see me here.'

'I wouldn't take that too personally,' Cara said, giving her a reassuring smile. 'She's an intensely protective person.' She put a hand on Lucy's arm. 'Thanks for being brave enough to come over and apologise, Lucy; I really appreciate the gesture.'

Lucy gave her one last smile, and Max a slightly terrified grimace, before retreating to her table.

Max sat back down in his chair, giving her an impressed nod. 'Nicely handled.'

Warm pleasure coursed through her as she took in the look of approval in his eyes. Feeling a little flustered by it, she picked up her glass of wine to take a big gulp, but judged the tilt badly and some escaped from the side of the rim and dribbled down her chin. Before she had time to react, Max whipped his napkin under her jaw and caught the rogue droplets with it, stopping them from splashing onto her dress.

'Smooth!' she said, laughing in surprise.

'I have moves,' he replied, his eyes twinkling and his mouth twitching into a warm smile.

A wave of heat engulfed her and her stomach did a full-on somersault.

Oh, no, what was *happening* to her?

Heart racing, she finally allowed the truth to filter through to her consciousness.

It was, of course, the very last thing she needed to happen.

She was falling in love with him.

CHAPTER EIGHT

AFTER THE MEAL and speeches, all the guests were encouraged to go through to the house, where a bar had been set up under the sweeping staircase in the hall and a DJ in the ballroom was playing ambient tunes in the hope of drawing the guests in there to sit around the tables that surrounded the dance floor.

Waiting at the bar to grab them both a caffeinated soft drink to give them some energy for the rest of the evening's events, Max allowed his thoughts to jump back over the day.

He'd had fun at the lake with Cara, which had taken him by surprise, because the last thing he'd expected when he'd got up that morning was that he would enjoy himself today.

But Cara had a way of finding the joy in things.

In fact, he'd been so caught up in the pleasure of showing her how to skim stones, he hadn't thought about what he was doing until his hand was on the soft curve of her hip and his body was pressed up close to hers, the familiar floral scent of her perfume in his nose and the heat of her warming his skin. He'd hidden his instinctive response to it well enough, he thought, using the excessive rush of adrenaline to hurl more stones across the water.

And then she'd been so delighted when she'd managed to skim that stone by herself he'd felt a mad urge to wrap his arms around her again in celebration and experience the moment with her.

But that time he'd managed to rein himself in, randomly talking about his own wedding to break the tension, only to feel a different kind of self-reproach when Cara assumed his indiscriminate jump to the subject was down to him feeling gloomy about his situation.

Which it really hadn't been.

Returning with the drinks to where he'd left Cara standing just inside the ballroom, he handed one to her and smiled when she received it with a grimace of relieved thanks. The main lights in the room were set low and a large glitter ball revolved slowly from the ceiling, scattering the floor and walls with shards of silver light. Max watched them dance over Cara's face in fascination, thinking that she looked like some kind of ethereal seraph, with her bright eyes and pale creamy skin against the glowing silver of her dress.

A strange elation twisted through him, triggering a lifting sensation throughout his whole body—as if all the things that had dragged him down in the past eighteen months were losing their weight and slowly drifting upwards. The sadness he'd expected to keep on hitting him throughout the day was still notably absent, and instead there was a weird sense of rightness about being here.

With her.

Catching her giving him a quizzical look, he was just about to ask if she wanted to take another walk outside so they could hear each other speak when Jack and Amber walked past them and onto the empty dance floor. Noticing their presence, the DJ cued up a new track as a surge of guests crowded into the room, evidently following the happy couple in to watch their first dance as husband and wife.

Max found himself jostled closer to Cara as the edges of the dance floor filled up and he instinctively put an arm around her to stop her from being shoved around, too. She turned to look at him, the expression in her eyes startled at first, but then sparking with understanding when he nodded towards a gap in the crowd a little along from them.

He guided them towards it, feeling her hips sway against his as they moved, and had to will his attention-starved body not to respond.

Once in the space, he let her go, relaxing his arm to his side, and could have sworn he saw her shoulders drop a little as if she'd been holding herself rigid.

Feeling a little disconcerted by her obvious discomfort at him touching her again, he watched the happy couple blindly as they twirled around the dance floor, going through the motions of the ballroom dance they'd plainly been practising for the past few months.

Had he overstepped the mark by manhandling her like that? He'd not meant to make her uncomfortable but they were supposed to be there as a couple, so it wasn't as though it wasn't within his remit to act that way around her.

Ugh. There was no point in beating himself up about it. He'd just have to be more careful about the way he touched her, or not, for the rest of the evening.

As soon as the dance finished, other couples joined the newlyweds on the dance floor and, spotting Cara, Jack broke away from Amber and made his way over to them.

'Cara, I'm so glad you made it!' he said, stooping down to pull her into a bear hug, making her squeal with laughter as he spun her around before placing her back down again.

Cara pulled away from him, her cheeks flushed, and rubbed his arm affectionately. 'Congratulations. And thank you for inviting us. It's a beautiful wedding.'

'I'm glad you're having a good time,' Jack replied, smiling into her eyes. 'Want to dance with me, for old times' sake?' he said, already taking her arm and leading her away from Max onto the dance floor. 'You don't mind if I steal her away for a minute, do you, Max?' he tossed over his shoulder, plainly not at all interested in Max's real opinion on the matter.

Not that Max *should* mind.

Watching Cara laugh at something that Jack whispered into her ear as he began to move her around the dance floor, Max was hit by an unreasonable surge of irritation and had to force himself to relax his arms and let them hang by his sides instead of balling them into tight fists. What the heck was going on with him today? How messed up was he to be jealous of a new groom, who was clearly infatuated with his wife, just because he was dancing with Cara? It must be because the guy seemed to have everything—a wife who loved him, a successful career with colleagues who respected him, Cara as a friend...

The track came to a close and a new, slower one started up. Before he could check himself, Max strode across to where Jack and Cara were just breaking apart.

'You don't mind if I cut in now, do you?' he said to Jack, intensely conscious that his words had come out as more of a statement than a question.

Jack's eyebrows rose infinitesimally at Max's less than gracious tone, but he smiled at Cara and swept a hand to encompass them both. 'Be my guest.' Leaning forward, he kissed Cara on the cheek before moving away from her. 'It's great to see you so happy. You know, you're actually glowing.' He slapped Max on the back. 'You're obviously good for her, Max. Look after her, okay? She's a good one,' he said. 'But watch your feet; she's a bit of a toe-stamper,' he added, ducking out of the way as Cara swiped a hand at him and walked off laughing.

Turning back, Cara fixed Max with an awkward smile, then leaned in to speak into his ear. 'Sorry about that. I didn't want to admit to the truth about us and break the mood.'

Max nodded, his shoulders suddenly stiff, surprised to find he was disappointed to hear her say that her glow was nothing to do with him.

Don't be ridiculous, you fool—how could it be?

His feelings must have shown on his face because she

took a small step away from him and said, 'You don't really need to dance with me, but thanks for the gesture.'

He shrugged. 'It's no problem. You seemed to be enjoying yourself and I was anticipating Jack being commandeered at any second by Amber or another relative wanting his attention so I thought I'd jump in,' he replied, feeling the hairs that had escaped from her up-do tickle his nose as he leaned in close to her.

She looked at him for the longest moment, something flickering behind her eyes, before giving him a small nod and a smile. 'Okay then, I'd love to dance.'

Holding her as loosely as he could in his arms, he guided her around the dance floor, leading her in a basic waltz and finding pleasure in the way she responded to his lead, copying his movements with a real sense that she trusted him not to make a false step. His blood roared through his veins as his heart worked overtime to keep him cool in the accumulated heat of the bodies that surrounded them. Or was it the feeling of her in his arms that was doing that to him?

He felt her back shift against his palm and turned to see she was waving to Lucy, the woman who had come over to apologise to her at dinner.

A sense of admiration swept thorough him as he reflected on how well she'd handled that situation. When he'd returned to the table, after needing to take a breath of air and talk himself down from a strange feeling of despondency when he heard she was likely to find a new place to live soon, and seen them talking, he'd feared the worst. An intense urge to step in and protect her had grabbed him by the throat, making him move fast and put his hands on her, to let her know he had her back if she needed him.

She hadn't, though. In fact she'd shown real strength and finesse with her response. Another example of why she was so good at her job. And why he respected her so much as a person. Why he liked her—

Halting his thoughts right there, he guided her over to the side of the dance floor as the music changed into retro pop and drew away from her, feeling oddly bereft at the loss of her warm body so close to his own.

The room was spinning.

And it wasn't from the alcohol she'd consumed earlier or even the overwhelming heat and noise—it was because of Max. Being so close to him, feeling the strength of his will as he whirled her around the dance floor had sent her senses into a nosedive.

'Max, do you mind if we go outside for a minute? I need some air.'

The look her gave her was one of pure alarm. 'Are you all right?'

'I'm fine, just a bit hot,' she said, flapping a hand ineffectually in front of her face.

Giving her a curt nod, he motioned for her to walk out of the ballroom in front of him, shadowing her closely as she pushed her way through the crowd of people in the hallway and out into the blissfully cool evening air.

Slumping down onto a cold stone bench pushed up against the front of the house, she let out a deep sigh of relief as the fresh air pricked at her hot skin.

'I'm going to fetch you a drink of water,' Max said, standing over her, his face a picture of concern. 'Stay here.'

She watched him go, her stomach sinking with embarrassment, wondering how she was ever going to explain herself if she didn't manage to pull it together.

Putting her head in her hands, she breathed in the echo of Max's scent on her skin, its musky undertones making her heart trip over itself.

'Are you okay there?'

The deep voice made her start and she looked up to see one of the male guests looking down at her, his brow creased in worry. She seemed to remember Amber's second cousin pointing him out as Amber's youngest brother and the black sheep of the family. *Womaniser* was the word she'd used.

Sitting up straighter in her seat, she gave him a friendly but dispassionate smile. 'I'm fine, thanks, just a bit hot from dancing.'

Instead of nodding and walking away, he sat down next to her and held out his hand. 'I'm Frank, Amber's black sheep of a brother,' he said with a twinkle in his eye.

She couldn't help but laugh as she shook his hand. 'I'm Cara.'

'I don't know whether anyone's told you this today, Cara, but you look beautiful in that dress,' he said, his voice smooth like melted chocolate. He wanted her. She could see it in his face.

Cara was just about to open her mouth to politely brush him off when a shadow fell across them. Looking up, she saw that Max had returned with her glass of water and was standing over them with a strange look on his face.

'Here's your drink, Cara,' he said, handing it over and giving Frank a curt nod.

Frank must have seen something in Max's expression because he got up quickly and took a step away from them both. 'Okay, well, it looks like your boyfriend's got this, so I'll say good evening. Have a good one, Cara,' he said, flashing her a disappointed smile as he backed away, then turning on his heel to disappear into the dark garden.

'Sorry,' Max said gruffly, 'I didn't mean to scare him off.' He didn't look particularly sorry, though, she noted as he sat down next to her and laid his arm across the back of the bench. In fact, if anything, he seemed pleased that the guy had gone. Turning to look him directly in the eye, her stomach gave a flutter of nerves as something flickered in his eyes. Something fierce and disconcerting.

Telling herself she must be seeing things, she forced a composed smile onto her face. 'It's okay; he wasn't my type anyway.'

Not like you.

Pushing the rogue thought away, she took a long sip of the water he'd fetched to cover her nerves. What was she doing, letting herself imagine there was something developing between them?

'Thanks for the water. I didn't mean to worry you. I'm feeling better now I'm in the fresh air.'

Despite her claims, he was still looking at her with that strange expression in his eyes.

'Why are you single?' he asked suddenly, making her blink at him in surprise.

'Oh, you know...'

He frowned. 'It's not because I've been working you too hard, is it?'

'No, no!' She shook her head. 'It's through personal choice.'

His frown deepened, as if he didn't quite believe her.

She swallowed before expanding on her answer, linking her fingers tightly together around the glass. 'I decided to take a break from dating for a while. My last relationship was a bit of a disaster.'

He relaxed back against the bench. 'How so?'

'The whole fiasco at LED pretty much ruined it. After I started having trouble coping with what was going on at work I got a bit down and it made me withdraw into myself. My ex-boyfriend, Ewan, got fed up with me being so...er...*unresponsive*.' She cringed. 'That's why I've been trying so hard to stay positive. I know how it can get boring, having people around who feel sorry for themselves all the time.'

He ran his hand through his hair, letting out a long, low sigh.

Heat rushed through her as she realised how Max might have interpreted what she'd just said. 'I didn't mean... I wasn't talking about you.'

He snorted gently and flashed her a smile. 'I didn't think you were. I was frustrated on your behalf. I can't believe the guy was stupid enough to treat you like that.'

'Yeah, well, it's in the past now. To be honest, that relationship was always doomed to fail. He was a little too self-centred for my liking. He made it pretty obvious he thought I wasn't good enough for him.'

'Not good enough! That's the most ridiculous thing I ever heard,' he snapped out, the ferocity in his tone telling her he had a lot more he wanted to say on the matter, but for the sake of propriety was keeping it to himself.

She smiled at him, her heart rising to her throat. 'It's okay. It doesn't bother me any more.' And it really didn't, she realised with a sense of satisfaction. Her experiences since breaking up with Ewan had taught her that her real self-worth came from her own actions and achievements, not pleasing someone else.

Putting the empty glass onto the ground by the bench, she tried to hide a yawn of tiredness behind her hand. It had been a long and intense day.

'Do you want to get out of here?' Max asked quietly.

Clearly she hadn't been able to hide her exhaustion from him.

Looking at him with a smile of gratitude, she nodded her head. 'I wouldn't mind. I don't think I've got the energy for any more dancing.'

He stood up. 'Okay, I'll go and fetch the car.'

'I'll just pop back in and say goodbye to Jack and Amber and I'll meet you back here,' she said, gesturing to the pull-in place at the end of the sweeping driveway.

He nodded, before turning on his heel and heading off towards where they'd left the car parked by the estate's church.

She watched him disappear into the darkness, with his

jacket slung over his arm and the white shirt stretched across his broad shoulders glowing in the moonlight, before he dipped out of sight.

After saying a hurried goodbye to the now rather inebriated newlyweds, she came out to find Max waiting for her in the car and jumped in gratefully, sinking back into the soft leather seat with a sigh. Now she knew that bed wasn't far away, she was desperate to escape to her room and finally be able to relax away from Max's unsettling presence.

It only took them five minutes to drive to the B&B she'd booked them into and as luck would have it there was a convenient parking space right outside the pretty thatched cottage.

'We're in the annexe at the back,' she said to Max as he hauled their overnight bags out of the boot. 'They gave me a key code to open the door so we won't need to disturb them.'

'Great,' Max said, hoisting the bags onto his back and following her down the path of the colourful country cottage garden towards the rear of the house. The air smelled sweetly of the honeysuckle that wound itself around a large wooden arch leading through to the back garden where their accommodation was housed, and Cara breathed it in with a great sense of pleasure. The place felt almost magical, shrouded as it was in the velvety darkness of the night.

Cara tapped the code into the keypad next to the small oak door that led directly into the annexe and flipped on the lights as soon as they were inside, illuminating a beautifully presented hallway with its simple country-style furniture and heritage-coloured décor. Two open bedroom doors stood opposite each other and there was a small bathroom at the back, which they would share.

'I hope this is okay. All the local hotels were fully booked and Jack said this was the place his cousin and her family were going to stay in, so the owners were pleased to swap the booking to us, considering it was such a last-minute cancellation.'

Max nodded, looking around at the layout, his expression neutral. 'It's great.'

The hallway was so small they were standing much closer to each other than Cara was entirely comfortable with. Max moved past her to drop his bag into one of the rooms and his musky scent hit her senses, making her whole body quiver with longing. The thought of him being just a few feet away from her was going to make it very difficult to sleep, despite how tired she was.

After dropping her bag into the other room, Max walked back into the hallway and stood in front of her, a small frown playing across his face. 'Are you feeling okay now?'

She smiled, the effort making her cheeks ache. 'I'm fine.' She took a nervous step backwards, and jumped a little as her back hit the wall behind her. 'Thank you so much for coming with me. I really appreciate it.'

He was looking at her with that fierce expression in his eyes again and a heavy, tingly heat slid from her throat, deep into her belly, sending electric currents of need to every nerve-ending in her body. For some reason she was finding it hard to breathe.

'It was my pleasure, Cara,' he said, his voice gruff as if he was having trouble with his own airways. 'You know, that guy you were talking to earlier was right. You do look beautiful in that dress.'

She stared at him, a disorientating mixture of excitement and confusion swirling around her head.

His gaze flicked away from hers for a second and when his eyes returned to hers the fierce look had gone and was replaced with a friendly twinkle. 'It occurred to me that you might have a bit of trouble getting out it—after needing my help to do it up this morning. Want me to undo the buttons for you?'

What was this?

Cara knew what she wanted it to be: for Max to want the same thing that she did—to alleviate this unbearable need to touch and kiss and hold him. To slide off all their clothes and lose themselves in each other's body.

To love him.

Did he want that, too?

Could he?

Her heart was beating so hard and fast, all she could hear and feel was the hot pulse of her blood through her body.

'That would be great. Thank you,' she managed to force past her dry throat.

She rotated on the spot until her back was to him, her whole body vibrating with tension as she felt his fingers graze her skin as he released each of the buttons in turn.

As soon as the last one popped free, she trapped the now loose dress against her body and turned to face him again, trying to summon an expression that wouldn't give her feelings away.

He looked at her for the longest time, his eyes wide and dark and his breathing shallow.

She watched him flick his tongue between his lips and something snapped inside her. Unable to stand the tension any longer, she rocked forward on her toes and tipped her head up, pressing her mouth to his. His lips were firm under hers and his scent enveloped her, wrapping round her senses, only adding to her violent pull of need to deepen the kiss.

Until she realised he wasn't kissing her back.

He hadn't moved away from her, but she could feel how tense he was under her touch. As if he was holding himself rigid.

She stilled, one hand anchoring herself against his broad shoulder, the other still holding her dress tightly against her body, and pulled away, eyes screwed shut, her stomach plummeting to her shoes at his lack of response.

What had she *done*?

When she dared open her eyes, he was looking at her with such an expression of torment that she had to close them again

'I'm sorry. So, so sorry,' she whispered, her throat locking up and her face burning with mortification.

'Cara—' He sounded troubled. Aggrieved. Exasperated.

Stumbling away from him, her back hit the wall again and she felt her way blindly into her bedroom and slammed the door shut, leaning back on it as if it would keep out the horror of the past few seconds.

Which, of course, it wouldn't.

What must he think of her? All he'd done was offer to help her with her dress and she'd thrown herself at him. What had possessed her to do that when she knew he wasn't over losing his wife? How could she have thought he wanted anything more to develop between them?

She was a fool.

And she couldn't even blame it on alcohol because she'd been drinking soft drinks for the past couple of hours.

She jumped in fright as she felt Max knock on the door, the vibration of it echoing through her tightly strung body. She knew she had to face him. To apologise and try to find some way to make things right again.

Struggling to get her breathing under control, she stepped away from the door and opened it, forcing herself to look up into Max's face with as much cool confidence as she could muster.

Before he could say anything, she held up a hand. 'I really am sorry... I don't know what happened. It won't ever happen ag—'

But, before she could finish the sentence, he took a step towards her, the expression in his eyes wild and intense as he slid his hand into her hair, drawing her forward and pressing his lips against hers.

They stumbled into the room, off balance, as their mouths crashed together. Electric heat exploded deep within her and she heard him groan with pleasure when she pressed her body hard into his. She could feel the urgency in him as he pushed her back against the wall, his hard body trapping her there as he fervently explored her mouth with his own, his tongue sliding firmly against hers. Taking a step back, he pulled his shirt over his head in one swift movement and dropped it onto the floor next to them.

'Are you sure you want this, Cara?' he asked, his voice guttural and low as she feverishly ran her hands over the dips and swells of his chest in dazed wonder.

'Yes.'

She smiled as he exhaled in relief and brought his mouth back down to hers, sliding his hands down to her thighs so he could pick her up and carry her over to the bed.

Then there was no more talking, just the feel of his solid body pressed hard against hers and the slide and twist of his muscles under his soft skin and—sensation—a riot of sensation that she sunk into and lost herself in. Her body had craved this for so long it was a sweet, beautiful relief to finally have what she wanted.

What she needed.

In those moments there was no past and no future; they were purely living for the moment.

And it was absolutely perfect.

CHAPTER NINE

MAX AWOKE FROM such a deep sleep it took him a while to realise that he wasn't in his own bed.

And that he wasn't alone.

Cara's warm body was pressed up against his back, her arm draped heavily over his hip and her head tucked in between his shoulder blades. He could feel her breath against his skin and hear her gentle exhalations.

Memories from the night they'd just spent together flitted through his head like a film on fast-forward, the intensity of them making his skin tingle and his blood pound through his body. It had been amazing. More than amazing. It had rocked his world.

It had felt so good holding her in his arms, feeling her respond so willingly to his demands and clearly enjoying making her own on him.

But, lying here now, he knew it had been a mistake.

It was too soon after losing his wife to be feeling like that. It felt wrong—somehow seedy and inappropriate. Greedy.

He'd had his shot at love and it wasn't right that he should get another one. Especially not so soon after losing Jemima. In the cold light of day it seemed tasteless somehow, as if he hadn't paid his dues.

He'd been in such a fog of need all day yesterday that he'd pushed all the rational arguments to the back of his head and just taken what he'd wanted, which had been totally unfair on Cara.

He wasn't ready to give himself over to a relationship again. And he knew that Cara would need more from him than he was able to give. She'd want the fairy tale, and he was no Prince Charming.

The worst thing was: he'd known that this was going to happen. From the moment he'd set eyes on her. He'd been attracted to her, even though he'd pretended to himself that he wasn't. And he'd only made things worse for himself by keeping her at arm's length. The more he'd told himself *no*, the more he'd wanted her. That was why he'd really thought it best to get rid of her quickly, before anything could happen between them. And then, once it became clear there was no hiding from the fact she was a positive force in his life, he'd pretended to himself that he wanted her to stay purely for her skills as a PA.

Idiot.

It had well and truly backfired on him.

This was precisely why he'd stopped himself from becoming friends with her at the beginning. He'd known it would guide them down a dangerous path.

His concerns hadn't stopped him from knocking on her door after she'd run away from him last night, though. Even after it had taken everything he'd had not to respond to that first kiss. But she'd looked so hurt, so devastatingly bereft that he'd found himself chasing after her to try and put it right. And, judging by her reaction when he'd been unable to hold back a second time and stop himself from kissing her, she'd been just as desperate as him for it to happen. In fact, the small, encouraging noises that had driven him wild made him think she'd wanted it for a while.

And, as his penance, he was now going to have to explain to her why it could never happen again.

Drawing away from her as gently as he could so as not to wake her, he swung his legs out of bed and sat on the edge, putting his head in his hands, trying to figure out what to do next. He wasn't going to just leave her here in the middle of rural Leicestershire with no transport, but the thought of having to sit through the whole car journey home with her after explaining why last night had been a mistake filled him with dread.

He jumped as a slender arm snaked round his middle and Cara kissed down the length of his spine, before pulling herself up to sit behind him with her legs on either side of his body, her breasts pressing into his back.

'Good morning,' she said, her voice guttural with sleep.

Fighting to keep his body from responding to her, he put his hand on the arm that was wrapped around his middle and gently prised it away.

'Are you okay?' she asked, her tone sounding worried now.

'Fine.' He stood up and grabbed his trousers, pulling them on roughly before turning back to her.

She'd tugged the sheet around her and was looking

up at him with such an expression of concern he nearly reached for her.

Steeling himself against the impulse, he shoved his hands in his pockets and looked at her with as much cool determination as he could muster.

'This was wrong, Cara. Us, doing this.'

'What?' Her eyes widened in confused surprise.

'I'm sorry. I shouldn't have let it happen. I got caught up in the moment, which was selfish of me.'

Her expression changed in an instant to one of panic. 'No.' She held out her hands beseechingly. 'Please don't be sorry about it. I wanted it to happen, too.'

He swallowed hard, tearing his eyes away from her worried gaze. 'I can't give you what you want long-term, Cara.'

Pulling the sheet tighter around her body, she frowned at him. 'You don't know what I want.'

He smiled sadly. 'Yes, I do. You want this to turn into something serious, but I don't. I'm happy with my life the way it is.'

'You're *happy*?' She looked incredulous.

He rubbed his hand over his face in irritation. 'Yes, Cara, I'm happy,' he said, but he felt the lie land heavily in his gut.

'But what we had last night—and all day yesterday— I didn't imagine it.' She shook her head as if trying to throw off any niggling doubts. 'It was so good. It felt right between us, Max. Surely you felt that, too.'

He looked at her steadily, already hating himself for what he was about to say. 'No. Sorry.' He scrubbed a hand through his hair. 'Look, I was feeling lonely and you happened to be there. I feel awful about it and I won't blame you for being angry.'

She didn't believe him; he could see it in her eyes.

'I understand why you're panicking,' she said, holding out her hands in a pleading gesture, 'because we've just changed the nature of our relationship and it's a scary thing, taking things a step further, especially after what happened to Jemima…'

'See, that's the thing, Cara. I've been through that once and I'm not prepared to put myself through something like that again.'

'But it was so random—'

'The type of illness isn't the point here. It's the idea of pouring all your love into one person, only to lose them in the blink of an eye. I can go through that again.'

'But you can't cut yourself off from the world, Max. It'll drive you insane.'

He took a pace forward and folded his arms across his chest. 'You want to know what really drives me insane—that my wife was lying there in hospital with the life draining out of her and there wasn't a thing I could do about it. Not one damn thing. I promised her I'd look after her through thick and thin. I failed, Cara.' His throat felt tight with emotion he didn't want to feel any more.

'You didn't fail.'

He rubbed a hand over his eyes, taking a deep breath to loosen off the tension in his chest. 'I'm a fixer, Cara, but I couldn't fix that.'

'There wasn't anything you could have done.'

'I could have paid her more attention.'

'I'm sure she knew how much you loved her.'

And there was the rub. He did love Jemima. Too much to have room for anyone else in his heart.

'Yes, I think she did. But that doesn't change anything between you and me. I don't want this, Cara,' he said, waggling a finger between the two of them.

She stared at him in disbelief. 'So that's it? You've made up your mind and there's nothing I can do to change it?'

'Yes.'

Tipping up her chin, she looked him dead in the eye. 'Do you still want me to work for you?' she asked, her voice breaking with emotion.

Did he? His working life had been a lot less stressful since she'd been around, but what had just happened between them would make his personal life a lot more complicated. They were between a rock and a hard place. 'Yes. But I'll understand if it's too uncomfortable for you to stay.'

'So you'd let me just walk away?'

He sighed. 'If that's what you want.'

The look she gave him chilled him to the bone. 'You know, I don't believe for a second that Jemima would have wanted you to mourn her for the rest of your life. I think she'd have wanted you to be happy. You need to stop hiding behind her death and face the world again. Like you said you were going to yesterday. What happened to that, Max? Hmm? What happened to *you*? Jemima might not be alive any more, but *you* are and you need to stop punishing yourself for that and start living again.'

'I'm not ready—'

'You know, I love you, Max,' she broke in loudly, her eyes shining with tears.

He took a sharp intake of breath as the words cut through him. No. He didn't want to hear that from her right now. She was trying to emotionally manipulate him into doing something he didn't want to do.

'How can you love me?' Anger made his voice shake. 'We barely know each other.'

'I know you, Max,' she said calmly, her voice rich with emotion.

'You might think you do because I've told you a few personal things about myself recently, but that doesn't mean you get who I am and what I want.'

'Do you know what you want? Because it seems to me you're stopping yourself from being happy on purpose. You enjoyed being with me yesterday, Max, I know it.'

'I did enjoy it, but not in the way you think. It was good to get out of the house and have some fun, but that's all it was, Cara, *fun*.'

She shook her head, her body visibly shaking now. 'I don't believe you.'

'Fine. Don't believe me. Keep living in your perfect little imaginary world where everything is jolly and works out for the best, but don't expect me to show up.'

She reacted as if his words had physically hurt her, jolting back and hugging her arms around herself. 'How can you say that to me?'

Guilt wrapped around him and squeezed hard. She was right; it was a low blow after what he'd already put her through, but he was being cruel to be kind. Sinking onto the edge of the bed, he held up a pacifying hand. 'You see, I'm messed up, Cara. It's too soon for me. I'm not ready for another serious relationship. Maybe I'll never be ready. And it's not fair to ask you to wait for me.'

Her shoulders stiffened, as if she was fighting to keep them from slumping. 'Okay. If that's the way you feel,' she clipped out.

'It is, Cara. I'm sorry.'

The look she gave him was one of such disappointed disdain he recoiled a little.

'Well, then, I guess it's time for me to leave.' She shuffled to the edge of the bed. 'I'm not going to stick around here and let you treat me like I mean nothing to you. I'm worth more than that, Max, and if you can't appreciate that, then that's your loss.' With the sheet still wrapped firmly around her, she stood up and faced him, her eyes dark with anger. 'You can give me a lift to the nearest train station and I'll make my own way back to London.' Turning away from him, she walked over to where her overnight bag sat on the floor.

'Cara, don't be ridiculous—' he started to say, his tone sounding so insincere he cringed inwardly.

Swivelling on the spot, she pointed a shaking finger at him. 'Don't you dare say I'm the one being ridiculous. I'm catching the train. Please go and get changed in your own room. I'll meet you by the car in fifteen minutes.'

'Cara—' He tried to protest, moving towards her, but it was useless. He had nothing left to say.

There was no way to make this better.

'Okay,' he said quietly.

He watched her grab her wash kit from her bag, his gut twisting with unease.

Turning back, she gave him a jerky nod and then, staring resolutely ahead, went to stride past him to the bathroom.

Acting on pure impulse, he put out a hand to stop her, wrapping his fingers around her arm to prevent her from going any further. He could feel her shaking under his grip and he rubbed her arm gently, trying to imbue how sorry he was through the power of his touch.

She put her hand over his and for a second he thought she was going to squeeze his hand with understanding, but instead she pulled his fingers away from her arm and, without giving him another look, walked away.

Cara waited until Max's car had pulled away from the train station before sinking onto the bench next to the ticket office and putting her head in her hands, finally letting the tears stream down her face.

She'd spent the whole car journey there—which had only taken about ten minutes but had felt like ten painful hours—holding her head high and fighting back the hot pressure in her throat and behind her eyes.

They hadn't uttered one word to each other since he'd started the engine and she was grateful for that, because she knew if she'd had to speak there was no way she'd be able to hold it together.

It seemed they'd come full circle, with him withdrawing so far into himself he might as well have been a machine and her not wanting to show him any weakness.

What a mess.

And she'd told him she loved him.

Her chest cramped hard at the memory. When the words left her mouth, she hadn't known what sort of reaction to expect; in fact she hadn't even known she was going to say them until they'd rolled off her tongue, but she was still shocked by the flare of anger she'd seen in his eyes.

He'd thought she was trying to manipulate him, when that had been the last thing on her mind at the time. She'd wanted him to know he was loved and there could be a future for them if he wanted it.

Thinking about it now, though, she realised she had been trying to shock him into action. To reach something deep inside him that he'd been fiercely protecting ever since Jemima had died. It wasn't surprising he'd reacted the way he had, though. She couldn't begin to imagine the pain of losing a spouse, but she understood the pain of losing someone you loved in the blink of an eye or, in this case, in the time it took to say three small words.

Fury and frustration swirled in her gut, her empty stomach on the edge of nausea. How could she have let herself fall for a man who was still grieving for his wife and had no space left in his heart for her?

Clearly she was a glutton for punishment. And, because of that, she'd now not only lost her heart, she'd lost her home and her job, as well.

* * *

Back in London three hours later, she let herself wearily into Max's house, her nerves prickling at the thought of him being there.

Part of her wanted to see him—some mad voice in the back of her head had been whispering about him changing his mind after having time to reflect on what she'd said—but the other, sane part told her she was being naïve.

Walking into the kitchen, she saw that a note had been left in the middle of the table with her name written on it in Max's neat handwriting.

Picking it up with a trembling hand, she read the words, her stomach twisting with pain and her sight blurring with tears as she took in the news that he'd gone to Ireland a couple of days early for his meeting there, to give them a bit of space.

He wasn't interested in giving them another chance.

It was over.

Slumping into the nearest chair, she willed herself not to cry again. There was no point; she wasn't going to solve anything by sitting here feeling sorry for herself.

She had to look after herself now.

Her life had no foundations any more; it was listing at a dangerous angle and at some point in the near future it could crash to the ground if she didn't do something drastic to shore it up.

She'd *so* wanted to belong here with him, but this house wasn't her home and Max wasn't her husband.

His heart belonged to someone else.

She hated the fact she was jealous of a ghost, and not

just because Jemima had been beautiful and talented, but because Max loved her with a fierceness she could barely comprehend.

How could she ever compete with that?

The stone-cold truth was: she couldn't.

And she couldn't stay here a moment longer either.

After carefully folding her clothes into her suitcase, she phoned Sarah to ask whether she could sleep on her couch again, just until she'd moved into the flat that Amber's cousin had promised to let to her.

'Sure, you'd be welcome to stay with us again,' Sarah said, after finally coaxing out the reason for her needing a place to escape to so soon after moving into Max's house. 'But you might want to try Anna. She's going to be away in the States for a couple of weeks from tomorrow and I bet she'd love you to housesit for her.'

One phone call to their friend Anna later and she had a new place to live for the next couple of weeks. So that was her accommodation sorted. Now it was just the small matter of finding a new job.

She'd received an email last week from one of the firms that she'd sent a job application to, offering her an interview, but hadn't had time to respond to it, being so busy keeping the business afloat while Max was in Manchester. After firing off an email accepting an interview for the Tuesday of that week, she turned her thoughts to her current job.

Even though she was angry and upset with Max, there was no way she was just going to abandon the business without finding someone to take over the role she'd carved out for herself. Max might not want her around, but he was still going to need a PA. The meeting he had with a large corporation in Ireland later this week was an exciting prospect and if he managed to land their business he was going to need to hire more staff, pronto.

So this week it looked as if she was going to be both interviewer and interviewee.

The thought of it both exhausted and saddened her.

But she'd made her bed when she'd shared hers with Max, and now she was going to have to lie in it.

CHAPTER TEN

Max had thought he was okay with the decision to walk away from a relationship with Cara, but his subconscious seemed to have other ideas when he woke up in a cold sweat for the third day running after dreaming that Cara was locked in the house whilst it burnt to the ground and he couldn't find any way to get her out.

Even after he'd been up for a while and looked through his emails, he still couldn't get rid of the haunting image of Cara's face contorted with terror as the flames licked around her. Despite the rational part of his brain telling him it wasn't real, he couldn't shake the feeling that he'd failed her.

Because, of course, he had, he finally accepted, as he sat down to eat his breakfast in the hotel restaurant before his meeting. She'd laid herself bare for him, both figuratively and literally, and he'd abused her trust by treating her as if she meant nothing to him.

Which wasn't the case at all.

He sighed and rubbed a hand over his tired eyes. The last thing he should be doing right now was worrying about how he'd treated Cara when he was about to walk into one of the biggest corporations in Ireland and convince them to give him their business. This was exactly what he'd feared would happen when he'd first agreed to let her work for him—that the business might suffer. Though, to be fair to Cara, this mess was of his own making.

Feeling his phone vibrate, he lifted it out of his pocket and tapped on the icon to open his text messages. It was from Cara.

With his pulse thumping hard in his throat, he read what she'd written. It simply said:

Good luck today. I'll be thinking of you.

A heavy pressure built in his chest as he read the words through for a second time.

She was thinking about him.

Those few simple words undid something in him and a wave of pure anguish crashed through his body, stealing his breath and making his vision blur. Despite how he'd treated her, she was still looking out for him.

She wanted him to know that he wasn't alone.

That was so like Cara. She was such a good person: selfless and kind, but also brave and honourable. Jemima would have loved her.

Taking a deep breath, he mentally pulled himself together. Now was not the time to lose the plot. He had some serious business to attend to and he wasn't about to let all the work that he and Cara had put into making this opportunity happen go to waste.

* * *

Fourteen hours later Max flopped onto his hotel bed, totally exhausted after spending the whole day selling himself to the prospective clients, then taking them out for a celebratory dinner to mark their partnership when they signed on the dotted line to buy his company's services.

He'd done it; he'd closed the deal—and a very profitable deal it was, too—which meant he could now comfortably grow the business and hire a team of people to work for him.

His life was moving on.

A strong urge to call Cara and let her know he'd been successful had him sitting up and reaching for his phone, but he stopped himself from tapping on her name at the last second. He couldn't call her this late at night without it *meaning* something.

Frustration rattled through him, swiftly followed by such an intense wave of despondency it took his breath away. He needed to talk to someone. Right now.

Scrolling through his contacts, he found the name he wanted and pressed *call*, his hands twitching with impatience as he listened to the long drones of the dialling tone.

'Max? Is everything okay?' said a sleepy voice on the other end of the line.

'Hi, Poppy, sorry—I forgot it'd be so late where you are,' he lied.

'No problem,' his friend replied, her voice strained as if she was struggling to sit up in bed. 'What's up? Is everything okay?'

'Yes. Fine. Everything's fine. I won a pivotal contract for the business today so I'm really happy,' he said, acutely aware of how flat his voice sounded despite his best efforts to sound upbeat.

Apparently it didn't fool Poppy either. 'You don't *sound* really happy, Max. Are you sure there isn't something else bothering you?'

His friend was too astute for her own good. But then she'd seen him at his lowest after Jemima died and had taken many a late night call from him throughout that dark time. He hadn't called her in a while though, so it wasn't entirely surprising that she thought something was wrong now.

'Er—' He ran a hand through his hair and sighed, feeling exhaustion drag at him. 'No, I'm—' But he couldn't say it. He wasn't fine. In fact he was far from it.

A blast of rage came out of nowhere and he gripped his phone hard, fighting for control.

It was a losing battle.

'You did it on purpose, didn't you? Sent Cara to me so I'd fall in love with her,' he said angrily, blood pumping hard through his body, and he leapt up from the bed and started to pace the room.

His heart gave an extra hard thump as the stunned silence at the other end of the line penetrated through his anger, bringing home to him exactly what he'd just said.

'Are you in love with her?' Poppy asked quietly, as if not wanting to break the spell.

He slapped the wall hard, feeling a sick satisfaction at the sting of pain in the palm of his hand. 'Jemima's only been dead for a year and a half.'

'That has nothing to do with it, and it wasn't what I asked you.'

He sighed and slumped back down onto the bed, battling to deal with the disorientating mass of emotions swirling though his head. 'I don't know, Poppy,' he said finally. 'I don't know.'

'If you don't know, that probably means that you are but you're too pig-headed to admit it to yourself.'

He couldn't help but laugh. His friend knew him so well.

'Is she in love with you?' Poppy asked.

'She says she is.'

He could almost feel his friend smiling on the other end of the phone.

Damn her.

'Look, I've got to go,' he said, 'I've had a very long day and my flight back to London leaves at six o'clock in the morning,' he finished, not wanting to protract this uncomfortable conversation any longer. 'I'll call you tomorrow after I've had some sleep and got my head straight, okay?'

'Okay.' There was a pause. 'You deserve to be happy though, Max, you know that, don't you? It's what Jemima would have wanted.'

He cut the call and threw the phone onto the bed, staring sightlessly at the blank wall in front of him.

Did he deserve to be happy, after the way he'd acted? Was he worthy of a second chance?

There was only one person who could answer that question.

* * *

The house was quiet when he arrived home at eight-thirty the next morning. Eerily so.

Cara should have been up by now, having breakfast and getting ready for the day—if she was there.

His stomach sank with dread as he considered the possibility that she wasn't. That she'd taken him at his word and walked away. Not that he could blame her.

Racing up the stairs, he came to an abrupt halt in front of her open bedroom door and peered inside. It was immaculate. And empty. As if she'd never been there.

Uncomfortable heat swamped him as he made his way slowly back down to the kitchen. Perhaps she hadn't gone. Perhaps she'd had a tidying spree in her room, then gone out early to grab some breakfast or something.

But he knew that none of these guesses were right when he spotted her keys to the house and the company mobile he'd given her to use for all their communications sitting in the middle of the kitchen table.

The silence of the house seemed to press in on him, crushing his chest, and he slumped onto the nearest chair and put his head in his hands.

This was all wrong. *All* of it.

He didn't want to stay in this house any longer; it was like living in a tomb. Or a shrine. Whatever it was, it felt wrong for him to be here now. Memories of the life he'd had here with Jemima were holding him back, preventing him from moving on and finding happiness again. Deep down, he knew Jem wouldn't have wanted that for him. He certainly wouldn't have wanted her to mourn him for the rest of her life.

She'd want him to be happy.

Like he had been on Sunday night.

He was in love with Cara.

Groaning loudly into his hands, he shook his head, unable to believe what a total idiot he'd been.

Memories of Cara flashed through his mind: her generous smile and kind gestures. Her standing up to him when it mattered to her most. Telling him she loved him.

His heart swelled with emotion, sending his blood coursing through his body and making it sing in his ears.

So this was living. How he'd missed it.

A loud ring on the doorbell made him jump.

Cara.

It had to be Cara, arriving promptly at nine o'clock for work like she always did.

Please, let it be her.

Tension tightened his muscles as he paced towards the door and flung it open, ready to say what he needed to say to her now. To be honest with her. To let her know how much he loved her and wanted her in his life.

'Max Firebrace?'

Instead of Cara standing on his doorstep, there was a tall, red-haired woman in a suit giving him a broad smile.

'Yes. Who are you?' he said impatiently, not wanting to deal with anything but his need to speak to Cara right then.

She held out a hand. 'I'm Donna, your new PA.'

The air seemed to freeze around him. *'What?'*

The smile she gave him was one of tolerant fortitude. 'Cara said you might be surprised to see me because you've been in Ireland all week.'

'Cara sent you here?'

'Yes, she interviewed me yesterday and said I should start today.'

He stared at her, stunned. 'Where is Cara?'

Donna looked confused. 'Er... I don't know. I wasn't expecting her to be here. She said something about starting a new job for a firm in the City next week. We spent all of yesterday afternoon getting me up to speed with the things I need to do to fulfil the role and went through the systems you use here, so I assumed she'd already served her notice.'

So that was it then. He was too late to save the situation. She was gone.

'You'd better come in,' he muttered, frustration tugging hard at his insides.

'So will we be working here the whole time? It's a beautiful house,' Donna said brightly, looking around the hall.

'No. I'm going to rent an office soon,' he said distractedly, his voice rough with panic.

How was he going to find her? He didn't have any contact details for her friends or her personal mobile number; she'd always used the company one to call or text him. He could try Poppy, but she'd probably be out filming in the middle of the desert right now and wouldn't want to be disturbed with phone calls.

A thought suddenly occurred to him. 'Donna? Did Cara interview you here?'

'No. I went to her flat.' She frowned. 'Although, come to think of it, I don't think it was her place; she didn't know which cupboard the sugar for my drink was kept in.'

He paced towards her, startling her with a rather manic smile.

'Okay, Donna. Your first job as my PA is to give me the address where you met Cara.'

At first Cara thought that the loud banging was part of her dream, but she started awake as the noise thundered through the flat again, seeming to shake the walls. Whoever was knocking really wanted to get her attention.

Pulling her big towelling dressing gown on over her sleep shorts and vest top, she stumbled to the door, still half-asleep. Perhaps the postman had a delivery for one of the other flats and they weren't in to receive it.

But it wasn't the postman.

It was Max.

Her vision tilted as she stumbled against the door in surprise and she hung on to the handle for dear life in an attempt to stop herself from falling towards him.

'Max! How did you find me?' she croaked, her voice completely useless in the face of his shocking presence.

She'd told herself that giving them both some space to breathe was the best thing she could do. After leaving his house on Monday she'd tried to push him out of her mind in an attempt to get through the dark, lonely days without him, but always, in the back of her mind, was the hope that he'd think about what she'd said and maybe, at some point in the future, want to look her up again.

But she hadn't expected it to happen so soon.

'My new PA, Donna, gave me the address,' he said, raising an eyebrow in chastisement, though the sparkle in his eyes told her he wasn't seriously angry with her for going ahead and hiring someone to take her place without his approval.

Telling herself not to get too excited in case he was only popping round to drop off something she'd accidentally left at the house, she motioned for him to come inside and led him through to the kitchen diner, turning to lean against the counter for support.

'You did say you'd understand if I couldn't work with you any more. After what happened,' she said.

He came to a stop a few feet away from her and propped himself against the table. 'I did.'

She took a breath and tipped up her chin. 'I'm not made of stone, Max. As much as I'd like to sweep what happened on Sunday under the carpet, I can't do that. I'm sorry.'

Letting out a long sigh, he shifted against the table. 'Don't be sorry. It wasn't your fault. It was mine. I was the one who knocked on your door when you had the strength to walk away.'

She snorted gently. 'That wasn't strength; it was cowardice.'

'You're not a coward, Cara; you just have a strong sense of self-preservation. You should consider it a gift.'

She stared down at the floor, aware of the heat of her humiliation rising to her face, not wanting him to see how weak and out of control she was right now.

'So you start a new job next week?' he asked quietly.

Forcing herself to look at him again, she gave him the most assertive smile she could muster. 'Yes, at a place in the City. It's a good company and the people were very friendly when they showed me around.'

'I bet you could handle just about anything after having to work for me.' He smiled, but she couldn't return it this time. The muscles in her face wouldn't move. They seemed to be frozen in place.

Gosh, this was awkward.

'You've been good for my confidence.' She flapped a hand at him and added, 'Work-wise,' when he raised his eyebrows in dispute. 'You were great at letting me know when I'd done a good job.'

'Only because you were brave enough to point out how bad I was at it.'

She managed a smile this time, albeit a rather wonky one. 'Well, whatever. I really appreciated it.'

There was a tense silence where they both looked away, as if psyching themselves up to tackle the real issues.

'Look, I'm not here to ask you to come back and work for me again,' Max said finally, running a hand over his hair.

'Oh. Okay,' she whispered, fighting back the tears. She would not break down in front of him. She *wouldn't*.

He frowned, as if worried about the way she'd reacted, and sighed loudly. 'Argh! I'm so bad at this.' He moved towards her but stopped a couple of feet away, holding up his hands. 'I wanted to tell you that I think I've finally made peace with what happened to Jemima. Despite my best efforts to remain a reclusive, twisted misery guts, I think I'm going to be okay now.' He took another step towards her, giving her a tentative smile. 'Thanks to you.'

Forcing down the lump in her throat, she smiled back. 'That's good to hear, Max. Really good. I'm happy that you're happy. And I do understand why you don't want me to come back and work for you. It must have been hard having me hanging around your house so much.'

'I'm going to sell the house, Cara.'

She stared at him in shock, her heart racing. 'What? But—how can you stand to leave it? That beautiful house.'

'I don't care about the house. I care about us.' This time he walked right up to her, so close she could feel the heat radiating from his body, and looked her directly in the eye. 'I'm ready to live again and I want to do it with you.'

'You—?'

'Want *you*, Cara.' His voice shook with emotion and she could see now that he was trembling.

'But—? I thought you said—when did you...?' Her voice petered out as her brain shut down in shock.

He half smiled, half frowned. 'Clearly I need to explain some things.' He took her hand and led her gently over to the sofa in the living area, guiding her to sit down next to him, keeping his fingers tightly locked with hers and capturing her gaze before speaking.

'When we slept together I felt like I'd betrayed a promise to Jemima.' He swallowed hard. 'After what happened to her I thought I had no right to be happy and start again when she couldn't do that. I truly thought I'd never love someone else the way I loved her, but then I realised I didn't need to. The love I feel for you is different—just as strong, but a different flavour. Does that make sense?'

He waited for her to nod shakily before continuing. 'I don't want to replicate Jemima or the way it was with her. I want to experience it all afresh with you. I'll always love Jem because she was a big part of my life for many years, but I can compartmentalise that now as part of my past.' He squeezed her fingers hard. 'You're my future.'

'Really?' Her throat was so tense with emotion she could hardly form the word.

'Yes. I love you, Cara.'

And she knew from the look on his face that he meant every word. He'd never given up anything of an emotional nature lightly and she understood what a superhuman effort it must have taken for him to come here and say all that to her.

Reaching out a hand, she ran her fingers across his cheek, desperate to smooth away any fears he might have. 'I love you, too.'

He closed his eyes and breathed out hard in relief before opening them again, looking more at peace than she'd ever seen him before. Lifting his own hand, he slid his fingers into her hair and drew her towards him, pressing his mouth to hers and kissing her long and hard.

She felt it right down to her toes.

Drawing away for a moment, he touched his forehead to hers and whispered, 'You make me so happy.'

And then, once again, there was no more talking. Just passion and joy and excitement for their bright new future together.

EPILOGUE

One year later

THE HOUSE THEY'D chosen to buy together was just the sort of place Cara had dreamed of owning during her romantic but practical twenties. It wasn't as grand or impressive as the house in South Kensington, but it felt exactly right for the two of them. And perhaps for any future family that chose to come along.

Not that having children was on the cards *right* now. Max was focusing hard on maintaining the expansion of his Management Solutions business, which had been flying ever since the Irish company awarded him their contract, and Cara was happy in her new position as Executive Assistant to the CEO of the company she'd joined in the City. But they'd talked about the possibility of it happening in the near future and had both agreed it was something they wanted.

Life was good. And so was their relationship.

After worrying for the first few months that, despite his assurances to the contrary, Max might still be in the grip of grief and that they had some struggles ahead of them, her fears had been assuaged as their partnership flourished and grew into something so strong and authentic she could barely breathe with happiness some days.

Max's anger had faded but his fierceness remained, which she now experienced as both a protective and supportive force in her life. Being a party to his sad past had taught her to count her blessings, and she did. Every single day.

Arriving home late after enjoying a quick Friday night drink with her colleagues, she let herself into their golden-bricked Victorian town house—which they'd chosen for the views of Victoria Park and its close location to the thriving bustle and buzz of Columbia Road with its weekly flower market and kitschy independent furniture shops—and stopped dead in the doorway, staring down at the floor.

It was covered in flowers, of all colours and varieties. Frowning at them in bewilderment, she realised they were arranged into the shape of a sweeping arrow pointing towards the living room.

'Max? I'm home. What's going on? It looks like spring has exploded in our hallway!'

Tiptoeing carefully over the flowers so as not to crush too many of them, she made her way towards the living room and peered nervously through the doorway, her heart skittering at the mystery of it.

What she saw inside took her breath away.

Every surface was covered in vibrantly coloured bouquets of spring flowers, displayed in all manner of receptacles: from antique vases to the measuring jug she used to make her porridge in the mornings. Even the light fitting had a large cutting of honeysuckle spiralling down from it, its sweet fragrance permeating the air. It reminded her of their first night together after Jack's wedding. Which quickly led her to memories of all the wonderful nights that had come after it, where she'd lain in Max's arms, breathing in the scent of his skin, barely able to believe how loved and cherished she felt.

And she was loved, as Max constantly reminded her, and her support and love for him had enabled him to finally say goodbye to Jemima and the past that had kept him ensnared for so long.

She'd unlocked his heart.

She was the key, he'd told her as he carried her, giggling, over the threshold into their house six months ago.

She'd finally found her home.

Their home.

He was standing next to the rose-strewn piano in the bay, looking at her with the same expression of fierce love and desire that always made her blood rush with heat.

'Hello, beautiful, did you have a good night?' he asked, walking towards where she stood, his smile bringing a mesmerising twinkle to his eyes.

'I did, thank you.' She swept a hand around the room, unable to stop herself from blurting, 'Max, what is this?'

The reverent expression on his face made her heart leap into her throat. 'This is me asking you to marry me,' he said, dropping to one knee in front of her and taking her hand in his, smiling at her gasp of surprise.

'This time last year I thought I'd never want to be married again—that I didn't deserve to be happy—but meeting you changed all that. You saved me, Cara.' Reaching into his pocket, he withdrew a small black velvet-covered box and flipped it open to reveal a beautiful flower-shaped diamond ring.

'I love you, and I want to spend the rest of my life loving you.' His eyes were alive with passion and hope. 'So what do you say—will you marry me?'

Heart pounding and her whole body shaking with excitement, she dropped onto her knees in front of him and gazed into his face, hardly able to believe the intensity of the love she felt for him.

'Yes,' she said simply, smiling into his eyes, letting him know how much she loved him back. 'Yes. I will.'

* * * * *

THE BILLIONAIRE'S FAIR LADY

BARBARA WALLACE

To the fabulous Donna Alward, who talked me off ledges and pushed me to get this story on paper. You're the best!

To Flo, the best editor a woman could ask for.

To the real Fran and Alice for providing the legal background information. Thanks for the help.

And, as always, to my boys Pete and Andrew, who put up with an awful lot so I can live my dream of writing stories for a living.

CHAPTER ONE

HE DIDN'T believe her.

Color her not surprised. *You've got to go uptown to fight uptown.* Minute the thought entered her brain, she should have shoved it aside. After all, bad ideas were a Roxy O'Brien specialty. But no, she opened the phone directory and picked the first uptown law firm whose ad mentioned wills. Which was why she now sat in her best imitation business outfit—really her waitress uniform with a new plaid blazer—waiting for Michael Templeton, attorney at law, to deliver his verdict.

"Where did you say you found these letters?" he asked. His gold-rimmed reading glasses couldn't mask the skeptical glint in his brown eyes. "Your mother's closet?"

"Yes," she replied. "In a shoe box." Tucked under a collection of seasonal sweaters.

"And you didn't know they existed before then?"

"I didn't know anything until last month."

That was putting it mildly. Her head was still reeling.

The attorney didn't reply. Again, not surprising. He'd done very little talking the entire meeting. In fact, Roxy got the distinct impression he found the whole appointment something of a trial. Something to get through so he could move on to more important, more believable business.

To his credit, disbelief or not, he didn't rush her out the

door. He let her lay out her story without interruption, and was now carefully reading the letter in his hand. The first of what was a collection of thirty, all lovingly preserved in chronological order. Her mother's secret.

You have his eyes.

The memory rolled through her. Four words. Fourteen letters. With the power to change her life. One minute she was Roxanne O'Brien, daughter of Fiona and Connor O'Brien, the next she was… Who? The daughter of some man she'd never met. A lover her mother never—ever— mentioned. That's why she came to Mike Templeton. To find answers.

Well, maybe a little bit more than answers. After all, if her mother told the truth, then she, Roxy O'Brien whoever, could be entitled to a far different life. A far better life.

You have his eyes.

Speaking of eyes, Mike Templeton had set down the letter and sat studying her. Roxy'd been stared at before. Customers figured ogling the waitress came with the bar tab. And they were the polite ones. So she'd grown immune to looks long ago. Or so she'd thought. For some reason, Mike Templeton's stare made her want to squirm. Maybe because he'd removed his glasses, giving her an unobstructed view of what were really very intense brown eyes. It felt like he wasn't so much looking at her as trying to see inside. Read her mind, or gauge her intentions. A self-conscious flutter found its way to her stomach. She recrossed her legs, wishing her skirt wasn't so damn short, and forced herself to maintain eye contact. A visual Mexican standoff.

To her relief, he broke first, sitting back in his leather chair. Roxy found her eyes drawn to the black lacquered pen he twirled between his long, elegant fingers.

Everything about him was elegant, she thought to herself. His fingers, his "bearing" as her high school drama teacher would say. He fit the surroundings, that's for sure, right down to the tailored suit and crisp white shirt. Roxy wasn't sure, but she thought she'd seen a similar look on the pages of a men's fashion magazine. Simply sitting across from him made her feel every inch the downtown girl.

Except, if what her mother said was true, she wasn't so downtown after all, was she?"

"Are all the letters this...intimate?" he asked.

Cheeks warming, Roxy nodded. "I think so. I skimmed most of them." Like the man said, the letters were intimate. Reading them closely felt too much like reading a stranger's diary.

A stranger who was her father. Come to think of it, the woman described on those pages didn't sound very much like her mother, either.

"You'll notice the dates, though," she told him. "The last letter is postmarked. Nine months before I was born."

"As well as a couple of weeks before his accident."

The car accident that killed him. Roxy had read a brief account when doing her internet research.

The attorney frowned. Somehow he managed to make even that expression look sophisticated. "You're positive your mother never said anything before last month?"

He was kidding, right? Roxy shot him a long look. What was with all these repetitive questions anyway? She'd already laid out her whole story. If he planned on dismissing her, then dismiss her. Why waste time? "I think I would have remembered if she did."

"And she didn't explain why?"

"Unfortunately she was too busy dying."

The words were out before Roxy could pull them back, causing the lawyer's eyebrows to arch. Clearly not the best way to impress the man.

Seriously though, how did he expect her to answer? That while on her deathbed, her mother laid out a detailed and concise explanation of her affair with Wentworth Sinclair? "She was pretty out of things," Roxy said, doing her best to choke back the sarcasm. "At first I thought it was the painkillers talking." Until her mother's eyes had cleared for that one, brief instant. *You have his eyes....*

"Now you think otherwise."

"Based on what I read in those letters, yes."

"Hmmm."

That was it. Just hmmm. He'd begun twirling the pen again. Roxy didn't like the silence. Reminded her too much of the expectant pause that followed an audition speech while the casting director made notes. Here the expectation felt even thicker. Probably because the stakes were so much higher.

"So let me see if I have this straight," he said finally, drawing out his words. "Your mother just happens to tell you on her deathbed that you're the daughter of Wentworth Sinclair, the dead son of one of New York's wealthiest families. Then, when cleaning out her belongings, you just happen to find a stack of love letters that not only corroborates your claim, but lays out a timeline that ends right before his death." He gave the pen another couple of twirls. "Ties up pretty conveniently, wouldn't you say? The fact both parties are dead and unable to dispute your story?"

"Why would they dispute anything? I'm telling the truth." Roxy didn't like where this conversation was heading one little bit. "If you're suggesting I'm making the story up—" She *knew* he didn't believe her.

"I'm not suggesting anything. I'm simply pointing out the facts, which are convenient." He leaned forward, fingers folded in front of him. "Do you know how many people claim to be long-lost heirs?"

"No." Nor did she care about any claim but hers, which happened to be true.

"More than you'd realize. Just last week, for example, a man came in saying he'd traced his family tree back to Henry Hudson. He wanted to know if he was eligible for reparation from the city of New York for his share of the Hudson River."

"And your point?" Anger ticking upward, she gritted her teeth.

"My point," he replied, leaning closer, "is that he had more paperwork than you."

Son of a— The man all but called her a fraud. No, worse. He was implying she made up the story like it was some kind of scam. As if she hadn't spent the past month questioning everything she'd known about her life. How dare he? "You think I'm lying about being Wentworth Sinclair's daughter?"

"People have done more for less."

"I— You—" It took every ounce of restraint not to grab the nameplate off his desk and smash it over his head. "This isn't about money," she spat at him.

"Really?" He sat back. "So you have no interest at all in gaining a share of the Sinclair millions?"

Roxy opened her mouth, then shut it. She'd like nothing better than to say absolutely not and make him feel like a condescending heel, but they both knew she'd be lying. If it were only her, or if she lived in a perfect world, she could afford to be virtuous, but it wasn't only about her. And Lord knows her world was far from perfect. That was the point. Being Wentworth Sinclair's daughter could be her only shot at not screwing up the one worthwhile thing in her miserable life.

Try explaining that to someone like Mike Templeton, however. What would he know about mistakes and imperfect worlds? He'd probably spent his whole life watching everything he'd touched turn to gold.

Right now, he was smirking at her reaction. "That's what I thought. Sorry, but if you're looking for a payout, you'll have to do better than a stack of thirty-year-old love letters."

"Twenty-nine," Roxy corrected, although really, why bother? He'd already made up his mind she was some lying money-grabber.

"Twenty-nine then. Either way, next time I suggest you try bringing a document that's more useful, like a birth certificate perhaps."

"You mean the one naming Wentworth Sinclair as my father?" The battle against sarcasm failed, badly, and she mockingly slapped her forehead. "Silly me, I left it at home." When he gave her a pointed look, she returned it with an equally pointed expression of her own. He wasn't the only one who could do judgmental. "Don't you think if I had something like that, I would have brought it with me?"

"One would think, but then one would think your mother would have named the correct father thirty years ago, too." He was folding the letter and placing it back in its envelope. Roxy wanted to grab his long fingers and squeeze them until he yelped. *One would think*. Maybe her mother had been afraid no one would believe her either.

"You know what," she said, reaching for the stack of letters, "forget this."

What made her think uptown would want to help her? Uptown didn't care about people like her, period, and she'd be damned if she was going to sit here and let some stuffed-shirt lawyer look down his nose at her. "The only reason I came here was that your directory ad said you handled wills and estates, and I *thought* you could help me. Apparently I was wrong."

She snatched her leather coat off the back of her chair. If Mike Templeton didn't think her problems were worth his time, then he wasn't worth hers. "I'm sure another law firm will be willing to listen."

"Miss O'Brien, I think you misunderstood. Please sit down."

No, Roxy didn't feel like sitting down. Or listening to any kind of explanation. Why? Rejection was rejection regardless of how many pretty words you attached to it. She should know. She'd heard enough "thanks but no thanks" in her lifetime. And they felt like kicks to the stomach.

She jammed her arm into her coat sleeve. Emotion clogged her throat, and she absolutely refused to let him see her eyes water.

"By the way," she said, adjusting her collar. "Your ad said you welcomed all types of cases. If you don't mean it, then don't say so in the headline."

An unnecessary jab, but she was tired of playing polite and classy. Besides, being called a gold-digging fraud should entitle her to at least one parting shot.

"Miss O'Brien—"

She strode from the office without turning around, proud that she got as far as street level before her vision grew blurry.

Dammit. She'd have thought she'd be cried out by now. When would she stop feeling so raw and exposed?

You have his eyes...

"Why didn't you say anything, Mom?" she railed silently. "Why did you wait till it was too late to tell me?"

Was she that ashamed of her daughter?

Not cool, Templeton, Not cool at all.

Mike had to admit, though, as indignant exits went,

Roxy O'Brien's was among the best. Ten years of estate law had shown him his share of scam artists and gold diggers, but she was the first who'd truly teared up upon storming out. She probably didn't think he noticed, but he had. There was no mistaking the overly bright sheen in those green eyes of hers, in spite of her attempts to blink them dry.

Pen twirling between his fingers, he rocked back and forth in his chair. Couldn't blame her for being upset. Like a lot of people, she must have thought she'd stumbled across the legal equivalent of a winning lottery ticket. If she'd stuck around instead of stomping off like a redheaded windstorm he'd have explained that making a claim against the Sinclairs wasn't that simple, even if her story was true. There were legal precedents and statutes of limitations to consider.

Of course, he thought, stilling his pen, she didn't have to completely prove paternity for her claim to work. Simply put forth a believable argument.

He couldn't believe he was contemplating the thought. Had he fallen so low he'd take on an audacious case simply for the potential settlement money?

One look at the meager pile of case files on his desk answered his question. At this point, he'd take Henry Hudson's nephew's case.

This was what failure felt like. The constant hollow feeling in his stomach. The weight on his shoulders. The tick, tick, tick in the back of his head reminding him another day was passing without clients knocking on his door.

It wasn't supposed to be like this. Templetons, as had been drilled in his head, didn't fail. They blazed trails. They excelled. They were leaders in their field. Doubly so if you were named Michael Templeton III and had two generations of namesakes to live up to.

You're letting us down, Michael. We raised you to be better than this. A dozen years after he first heard them, his father's words rose up to repeat themselves, reminding him he had no choice. Succeed or else. He took on the challenge of starting his own practice. He had to make it work, by hook or by crook.

Or audacious case, as it were. Unfortunately his best opportunity stormed out the door in a huff. So how did he get the little hothead to come back?

A patch of gray caught the corner of his eye. Realizing what he was looking at, Mike smiled. Perhaps his luck hadn't run out after all. He picked up the grey envelope Roxanne O'Brien had left behind.

God bless indignant exits.

Thursday nights were always busy at the Elderion Lounge. The customers, businessmen mostly, their out-of-town visits winding down, tended to cut loose. Bar tabs got bigger, rounds more frequent, tables more boisterous. Normally Roxy didn't mind the extra action since it meant more money in her pocket. Tonight, though, she wasn't in the mood for salesmen knocking back vodka tonics.

"Six vodka tonics, one house pinot and two pom martinis," she ordered. Despite being cold outside, the air was stifling and hot. She grabbed a cocktail napkin and blotted her neckline. This afternoon's business jacket disappeared long ago and she was back to a black camisole and skirt.

The bartender, a beefy guy named Dion, looked her up and down. "You look frazzled. Table six isn't giving you trouble, are they?"

"Nothing I can't handle. Bad day is all."

Who did Mike Templeton think he was anyway? Arrogant, condescending… Just because he was lucky enough to be born on the right side of town, what made him think he had the right to judge her or her mother or anyone else for that matter?

Wadding the napkin into a ball, she tossed it neatly into the basket behind the bar. "You'd think by this point I'd be immune to rejection."

"I thought you gave up acting," Dion said.

"I did. This was something else." And the rejection stung worse. "You don't know a good lawyer, do you?"

The bartender immediately frowned. "You in trouble?"

"Nothing like that. I need a business lawyer."

"Oh." He shook his head. "Sorry."

"'S'all right." Who's to say the next guy wouldn't be as condescending as Mike Templeton?

"Oh, my God!" Jackie, one of the other waitresses rushed up, earrings and bangle bracelets jangling. "Please let this guy sit at my table."

Busy stacking her tray, Roxy didn't bother looking up. At least once a week, the man of Jackie's dreams walked in. "What's the deal this time? He look like someone famous?"

"Try rich."

Here? Hardly. Unless the guy was lost and needed directions. Rich men hung at far better clubs. "I suppose he's gorgeous, too."

"Put it this way. If he was poor, I'd still make a move. He's that sexy."

Roxy had to see this male specimen for herself. Craning her neck, she surveyed the crowd. "I seriously doubt anyone with that much to offer—"

Mike Templeton stood by table eight, peeling the gloves off his hands one finger at a time. His eyes scanned the room with a heavy-lidded scrutiny. Roxy's stomach dropped. Jackie was right, he was the best-looking man in the room. Stood out like a pro in a field of amateurs. What on earth was he doing here?

"Told you he was breathtaking," she heard Jackie say. Before she could reply, he turned and their eyes locked. She stood rooted to the spot as he shrugged off his camel hair coat and draped it over the back of his chair. His actions were slow, deliberate, all the while holding her gaze. Goose bumps danced up her bare arms. It felt like she was the one removing layers.

"I don't suppose I can convince you to switch tables, can I? You're not interested in dating anyway. I'll give you both my twelve and fifteen."

Eyes still glued to the lawyer, Roxy shook her head. "Sorry, Jackie, no can do. Not this time."

Grabbing her tray, she purposely served her other tables before making her way toward him. With her back to that stare, his pull diminished a little, though she could still feel him watching her with every move she made. Reminding her of his existence. As if she could forget.

Finally she had no choice—or customers—left and sauntered her way to his table.

"You're a difficult person to pin down, Miss O'Brien," he greeted. "I went by your apartment first and some guy told me you were 'at the bar.' I took a chance and assumed he meant here." He smiled, as though being there was the most natural thing in the world, which it was decidedly not. "We never finished our conversation from earlier."

The guy had to be joking. "What was there to finish? I pretty much heard everything I needed to hear when you insulted me and my mother."

"You misunderstood. I wasn't trying to insult you. Had you stuck around, you would have realized I was merely pointing out your story has some very questionable holes in it."

"My mistake." Misunderstood her foot. If that was his idea of a misunderstanding, then she was the Queen of New York. "Next time my life is turned upside down by a deathbed confession, I'll try to make sure the story is more complete."

She tucked her tray under her arm. "Is there anything else? I've got customers to wait on." He wasn't the only one who could be dismissive.

"I'll have a Scotch. Neat."

Great. He planned to stick around. Maybe she would let Jackie have the table. "Anything else?"

"Yes, there is. You forgot this." Reaching into his briefcase, he pulled out a gray envelope. Seeing it, Roxy nearly groaned out loud. "Your mother took so much effort to preserve the collection. Seemed a shame to break up the set."

She felt like an idiot. Figures she'd mess up her grand exit. She never was good at stage directions. "Thank you. But you didn't have to drive all the way here to return it. You could have mailed it back to me."

"No problem at all. I didn't want to risk the envelope being damaged. Besides…"

Roxy had been reaching for the stack, when his hand came down to cover hers. "I figured this would buy me a few more minutes of your time," he finished, his eyes catching hers.

Warmth spread through Roxy's body, starting with her arm and moving upward. Glancing down at the table, she saw his hand still covered hers. The tapered fingers were almost twice the size of hers. If he wanted, he would wrap her hand right up in a strong, tight embrace. Feeling the warmth seeping into her cheeks, she pulled free.

"For what?" she asked, gripping her tray tightly. Squeezing the hard plastic helped chase away the sensation his hand left behind.

"I told you. You left before we could finish our conversation."

"Given what I stuck around for, can you blame me? I'll go get your drink."

"Tsk, tsk, tsk," he said as soon as she'd spun around. "You're going to need a lot thicker skin than that if you want to go after the Sinclairs."

Roxy froze. What did he say?

"That is why you came by to see me, isn't it?" he continued. "Because you want to make a claim against Wentworth Sinclair's estate?"

She was afraid to say yes, in case the other shoe dropped on her head. Slowly she turned around to find the lawyer looking more than a little pleased with himself for having caught her off guard. Was he trying to tell her she had a case after all?

So help him, if he was playing with her....

"Look, here's the deal." He leaned forward, gold cuff links catching the light. "Your case is a long shot. Both parties have passed away, and the only proof you have is a pile of love letters. Not to mention thirty years have gone by. The courts aren't exactly generous when it comes to claims that old. Truth is, scaling Mount Everest would be easier."

"Thanks for the recap." And here she thought there was something to his comment. "If that's what you came all the way over here to tell me, you wasted the gas."

"You're not letting me finish again."

Roxy stopped. Although hearing him out seemed like a waste of time to her. How many times did she need to hear him say her case wasn't good enough for him? "Okay," she said, waiting. "Finish. My case is harder than climbing Mount Everest. What else do you need to tell me?"

A slow smile broke out across his face. A confident smile that stilled everything in her body. "Only that I happen to really enjoy mountain climbing."

CHAPTER TWO

"I'll, um, go get your drink." Spinning around, Roxy made a beeline to the bar. It was the only response she could think of. Did he say what she thought he said? He was taking her case?

"You look like a truck hit you," Jackie remarked when she reached the bar rail. "What happened? Richie Rich turn out to be a creep?"

If she weren't still in a daze, Roxy would comment on the hopeful expectancy in the other woman's voice. "Not a creep. My lawyer," she corrected.

"I thought you said you didn't have one," Dion said.

"I didn't think I did." She still wasn't sure. She didn't trust her ears. For that matter, she wasn't entirely sure she trusted Mike Templeton. There had to be a catch.

Quickly she looked over her shoulder. There he sat, stiff and formal, arranging what looked like paperwork on the table. He certainly didn't seem the type to lead someone on.

"If you're serious," she said, when her rounds finally brought him back to his table, "then what was all that business about Henry Hudson and not having proof?"

"Had to figure out how loyal you were to your story somehow, didn't I?" he remarked, raising the glass to his lips.

"Un-freaking-believable." It was a *test*. If it weren't such an amazingly bad idea, she'd pour Scotch in his lap. She still might. "Do you have any idea how pis— How upset I was?"

"From the way you stormed out, I could hazard a guess. But that also tipped the scale in your favor. Either you truly believed your story or you were a damn good actress."

She could give him a long list of directors and casting agents who could refute the latter. Still, a *test?* She had half a mind to tell him he could stuff himself regardless of whether he wanted to take on her claim or not. "I can't believe you. Are you like this with everyone who tries to hire you?"

"Only the ones claiming to be heirs to multimillion-dollar fortunes."

Millions? Was he joking? Roxy checked his expression. His face was deadly serious.

Oh, my. She dropped into the seat across from him. "Millions?" she repeated.

"What were you expecting?"

"I don't know." She swiped the hair from her face, trying to focus. "I knew they were rich, but... Wow."

His test was beginning to make a bit of sense. Millions. A tingle ran up her spine.

"There's no guarantee, mind you. Like I said, the courts seldom rule in favor of claims like yours."

Mind still reeling, Roxy nodded.

"Plus, the Sinclairs' lawyers will put up a heck of a fight. This isn't the first time someone's challenged their estate, I'm sure. Nevertheless, if we play our cards right, and there's no reason to believe I won't, we'll both be looking at a nice little payday."

Again, Roxy nodded. She didn't know what else to do. His proclamation had stunned her to silence.

"Yo, Roxy! Table four!" Dion called. "Get your butt in gear."

A few feet away, a trio of women with empty martini glasses were looking in her direction, visibly annoyed.

"You better get to your customers," Mike noted.

He watched with amusement as the waitress half stumbled, half rushed away. Funny how her expression went from annoyed to dazed in literally the blink of an eye. The prospect of money could do that to a person. Made him jump in his car and drive to this place, didn't it?

For a moment he'd been afraid he'd laid it on a little too heavy with that "test" stuff, but she accepted his behavior. All he needed to do now was get her to cooperate with the rest of the case. Shouldn't be too hard. Especially given her alternative.

Leaning back in his chair, he sipped his drink and looked around the bar. As bars went, the Elderion was in the upper-lower half. Below average, but far enough up to avoid being a dive. Both the tables and the clientele had mileage.

Wentworth's letter lay where Roxanne dropped it. He ran his finger along the edge of the gray envelope. The contents had long been committed to memory. *"I can still smell your scent on my skin,"* Wentworth had written for the opening line. College passion. He knew it well. That heady reckless feeling. The blind confidence the days would last forever. Until reality barged in with its expectations and traditions waiting to be fulfilled and impractical dreams had to be shoved aside.

Look at you. We raised you to be better than this, Michael.

A hollow feeling lodged in his stomach. He blamed the surroundings. Ever since walking in to the Elderion, he'd been possessed by the strangest feeling of déjà vu.

Memories of another bar with dim lights and warm beer came floating back. When quality and atmosphere took a backseat to political debates and slow dancing in the dark.

His semester of ill-spent youth. He hadn't thought about those days in years. They'd been jettisoned to the past when he took his first law internship.

A few feet away, his new client—least he hoped she was his new client—negotiated her way through the narrow tables with the grace of a dancer. Amazing she could navigate anything in that scrap of cloth she called a uniform. Without the pink-and-gray blazer for coverage, he had a perfect view of how the spandex skirt molded to her curves. An open invitation to check out the assets. As she bent over, the skirt pulled tighter. Forget invitation, Mike decided, try full-blown neon sign. Feeling an uncomfortable tightness, he shifted his legs. Definitely not what his usual client would wear.

But then, this case wasn't his usual case. In fact, it was everything he'd been taught to avoid—splashy, risky, generating more notoriety than respect. Beggars couldn't be choosers could they? Beat closing his doors and telling his family he wasn't the Templeton they'd groomed him to be. Watching Roxanne dodge the palm of a customer right before it caressed her bottom, he retrieved his pen and made a quick note: smooth out the rough edges.

It was an hour later before Roxanne returned to his table, carrying with her a bottle of water. Mike tried not to stare at her legs as she approached. Given her outfit, it was a Herculean task at best. "You're still here," she said.

"Seemed silly to drive all the way back to the office when I could work here." He'd stacked what little legal work he did have in piles on the desk.

"It's eight o'clock. Most people have stopped working by now."

"Maybe in this place, but I'm not most people." He should know. It'd been drilled into his head enough growing up. "I also figured you'd have questions."

"You're right. I do." She pointed to the empty chair. "Do you mind?"

"Your big bad boss won't care?"

"I'm on my ten."

"Then be my guest. What's your question?"

"Well, first…" She picked at the label on her water bottle, obviously searching for the right words. "Are you sure you weren't kidding? About it being a million-dollar claim? That wasn't another one of your tests, was it?"

Ah, straight to the money. "I told you, I don't kid. Not about case value. Although keep in mind, I'm not making any promises, either. I'm saying there's potential. Nothing more."

"I appreciate the honesty. I don't like being misled."

"Me, neither," he replied. Seemed the hothead had a bit of a cautious streak after all. A good sign.

He watched as she peeled off a strip of label. "So what's the next step?" she asked. "Do I take a DNA test or something?"

If it were so easy. "Easy there, Cowboy. Don't get ahead of yourself. It's a little more complicated. You got any Sinclair DNA lying around?" he asked her.

Immediately her eyes went to the envelope. Cautious *and* quick. "I'm afraid you've watched too many crime shows. Getting anything off letters that old would be a miracle." Besides, he'd already had a similar thought and checked online. "You're going to need a more recent sample."

"How do we get one?"

Now they were getting to the complicated part. "Best

way would be for one of the Sinclair sisters to agree to a test. They are Wentworth's closest living relatives."

"But you said they would put up a fight."

"Doesn't mean we don't ask," he told her. "We give them enough evidence, and they'll have to comply."

"You mean, prove I'm a Sinclair, and they'll let me have proof."

Mike couldn't help smiling. Definitely quick. He liked that. If he had to take a case like this, he preferred to work with a client who understood what they were doing. Made his job easier. "Never fear. We'll make enough noise that they'll have to pay attention. The squeaky wheel and that sort of thing."

Frowning, she tore another strip. Some of the eagerness had left her face. Without it, she looked tired and, dare he say, a bit vulnerable. "You make it sound like I'm out to get them."

"The Sinclairs would argue you are."

"Why? I didn't go looking for this. My mother dropped the story in my lap."

"A story you promptly took to a lawyer to see if you have a claim to his estate."

That silenced her. "I didn't look at it that way." Another strip peeled away. "I'm just trying to make my life better. If this guy—Wentworth Sinclair—was my father, he'd want that, too, wouldn't he?"

Mike had to admit, if the relationship painted in the letter he read carried forward, she might be right. "Which is why we're pursuing the claim. To help you get that better life."

"What if they refuse to listen?"

"Then we'll keep fighting," Mike answered simply. Sooner or later, the Sinclairs would have to pay attention if only to make them disappear. He wasn't kidding about the squeaky wheel; it always yielded some kind of result.

Roxy was looking down at the table. Following her gaze, Mike saw that at some point while talking, he'd once again covered her hand. When had he reached across? When the dimness hit her eyes? That wasn't like him. He always kept an invisible wall between himself and his clients. For good reason. Getting too close led to making mistakes.

He studied the hand beneath his. She had skin the color of eggshells, pale and off-white. There was a small tattoo on the inside of her wrist as well. A yellow butterfly. The wings called out for a thumb to brush across them.

Mike realized he was about to do just that when she pulled her hand free and balled it into a fist. He found himself doing the same.

"Why?" she asked aloud.

Distracted by his reaction to the butterfly, it took a moment for her question to register. "Why what?"

"Why would you fight for me? If it's such a long shot, why are you taking this case?"

Somehow he didn't think she'd appreciate the truth, that he needed the money from this case as badly as she wanted it. "Told you, I like a challenge. As for fighting, I don't believe in quitting. Or losing. So you can be assured, I'll stick around to the bloody end."

"Colorful term."

"I also don't believe in mincing words."

"That so? Never would have guessed from your gentle desk side manner." She smiled as she delivered the comment. Mike fought the urge to smile back, taking a sip of his drink instead.

"You can have hand-holding or you can have results." Unfortunate choice of words given his behavior a moment earlier. "Up to you."

"Results are fine," she replied. "In my book, hand-holding is overrated. Sympathy just leads to a whole lot of unwanted problems."

Add practical to her list of attributes. Maybe this case would go smoother than he thought, in spite of this morning's dramatics. "I agree."

"Still…"

Mike's senses went on alert. Any sentence beginning with the word "still" never ended well. "What is it?"

"Don't get me wrong. I'm not looking for reassurance, but I'm wondering. When you say the word bloody, just how bloody do you mean?"

"The Sinclair legal team won't hold back, if that's what you're asking. They'll have no qualms about digging into your life." Her expression fell, followed quickly by his stomach. She had a skeleton, didn't she? "If you've got secrets, you best start sharing."

"No secrets." She shook her head, a little too vehemently if you asked him.

"Then what?"

"I've got a kid. A little girl. Her name is Steffi."

Wentworth Sinclair's granddaughter. That wasn't what he expected to hear. "No problem," he replied. His enthusiasm started building. Alice and Frances Sinclair would no doubt be very interested in the little girl's existence. "In fact, this might actually make the case—"

"Whoa!" She held up her hand, cutting him off. "I don't want her involved. She's only four years old. She won't understand what's going on."

Mike took a deep breath. "I don't think you understand. The fact that Wentworth might have a granddaughter could go a long way in convincing the sisters to comply with our requests."

She shook her head. "I don't care. I'm not going to have

her being upset. She can't be involved. You'll have to find a different way."

"I don't think—"

"Promise."

What was he going to do? He wanted to tell her she was in no position to issue conditions, that as her lawyer, it was his job to do everything he could to win her case, meaning he was the one who would decide what tactics he could or couldn't use. He also wanted to tell her there was no way he could keep such a promise. Sooner or later the Sinclair sisters would discover the child's existence. Her fiercely determined expression stopped him from saying so. There was no way he'd get her to budge on the issue tonight. Push and he ran the risk of her walking away again.

"Fine." He'd agree to her condition for now, and renegotiate their position later.

"Thank you." Satisfied, she opened her now naked water bottle and took a long drink. "When do we start?"

The spark had returned to her eyes, turning them brilliantly green. She was leaning forward, too, enough to remind him her tank top was extremely low cut. His legal mind definitely did not appreciate the male awareness the sight caused. Definitely had to smooth out the rough edges.

"Soon," he told her. "Very soon."

He stayed the rest of the evening. Nursing his drink and scribbling notes on his yellow legal pad. Damn unnerving it was, too. His existence filled the entire room making it impossible to ignore him. Three times she messed up an order because he distracted her, mistakes Dion made clear he planned to take out of her check.

Why was he sticking around anyway? He'd returned her letter, they'd talked. Shouldn't he be at his uptown apartment, drinking expensive Scotch by a fireplace? Surely he wasn't sticking around for the ambience. No one came to the Elderion for the ambiance.

"Maybe he wants to negotiate payment," Jackie teased. Ever since Roxy had mentioned the fact Mike was working on a legal problem for her the other waitress wouldn't stop with the innuendos.

"Very funny," she shot back, though the comment did make her hair stand on edge. They hadn't talked about payment. How did he expect her to pay for his services?

His presence continued to dog her as she delivered a round to the table next to his. Thank goodness the patrons all ordered bottled beer. She wasn't sure she could handle anything more complicated while standing in such close proximity.

Funny thing was the guy hadn't looked in her direction. Not once, and she'd been checking fairly frequently. Staring she could handle. She got looks every night. So why couldn't she shake Mike Templeton? Why did she feel that same penetrating scrutiny she felt back at his office every time she walked in his line of sight? All night long, it felt like he was right behind her, staring at her soul.

Another thing. He insisted on looking good. By this point in the night, the rest of the men in the place had long shed their jackets and ties. Heck, some were close to shedding their shirts. The room smelled of damp skin and aftershave.

Mike, however, barely looked bothered. His tie remained tightly knotted, and he still wore his suit jacket. Roxy didn't even think there were wrinkles in his shirt. If he was going to stick around, the least he could do was try to blend in with the rest of the drunken businessmen.

"Why are you still here?" she finally asked, when her rounds brought her to his table.

He looked up from the chicken scratches he'd been making on his notepad. "I'd like to think the answer's apparent. I'm working."

"I can see that. Why are you still working?"

She expected him to say something equally obvious such as "I'm not done yet" but he didn't. Instead he got an unusually faraway look in his eye. "I have to."

No, Roxy thought. *She* had to. A guy like Mike Templeton chose to. In the interest of good relations, she kept the difference to herself, and instead tried to decipher the notes in front of her. "Smooth out the rough edges? What does that mean?"

"Part of my overall strategy. I'm still fleshing it out."

"You planning to share it with me?"

"Eventually." The vague answer didn't sit well. Too much like information being kept from her, and she'd had enough of that this month. "Why can't I see now?"

"Because it's not fleshed out yet."

"Uh-huh." Uncertain she believed him, she bounced her tray off her thigh, and tried to see if she could find further explanation hidden in his expression. "In other words, trust you."

"Yes." He paused. "You can do that, can't you?"

Roxy didn't answer. "You want another Scotch?" she asked instead.

"Should I take that as a no?"

"Should I take that as you don't want another drink?" she countered.

"Diet cola. And when the idea is fully formed, you'll know. You don't share your order pad before bringing the drinks do you?"

The two analogies had absolutely nothing to do with one another as far as she could see. "I would if the customer asked. If they didn't like being kept in the dark."

"Fine," he said, giving an exasperated sigh. "Here."

He angled his pad so she could read better. All she saw were a bunch of half sentences and notations she didn't understand.

"Satisfied?" he asked when she turned the notepad around.

Yes. Along with embarrassed. "You have terrible handwriting."

"I wasn't planning on my notes being studied. Are you always this mistrustful?"

"Can you blame me?" she replied. "I just found out my mother lied to me for thirty years."

"Twenty-nine," he corrected, earning a smirk.

"Twenty-nine. Plus, I work here. This place hardly inspires trust."

"What do you mean?"

He wanted examples? "See that table over there?" She pointed to table two where a quartet of tipsy businessmen were laughing and nuzzling with an equally tipsy pair of women. "Half those guys wear wedding bands. So does one of the women.

"You see it all the time," she continued. "Men telling women how beautiful and special they are while the entire time keeping their left hands stuffed in a pocket so no one sees the tan line." Or promising comfort when all they really wanted was a roll in the sack.

"Interesting point," Mike replied. "One difference, though. I'm not one of your bar customers."

No, she thought, looking him over. He wasn't. "I don't know you much better," she pointed out.

"You will."

Something about the way he said those two words made her stomach flutter, and made the already close atmosphere even closer. All evening long, she'd been battling a stirring awareness, and now it threatened to blossom. She didn't like the feeling one bit.

Jackie's innuendos popped into her head.

"How do you expect me to pay out?" she blurted. He frowned, clearly confused, but to her the change in topic made perfect sense. "We never talked, and last time I checked you guys don't work for free. How exactly do you expect to collect payment?"

Realization crested across his face, followed quickly by his mouth drawing into a tight line. "It's called a contingency fee," he said tersely.

"Like those personal injury lawyers that advertise on television? The ones that say you don't have to pay them until you win?"

"Exactly. What else did you expect?"

He already knew, and she felt her skin begin to color. What could she say? She was paranoid. Life made her that way. "I didn't. Why else would I ask?"

"If you don't like that plan, you can pay hourly." He looked around the bar. "If doing so fits your budget."

Doubtful, and he knew that, too. "Your plan is fine."

"Good. Glad you approve."

"Do you still want your diet soda?"

"Please."

Shoot. She'd been hoping he'd say no, so she wouldn't have to visit his table again. "Coming right up. I'll drop it off before I cash out."

"You're done for the evening?" He straightened in his seat at the news.

Roxy nodded. The ability to clock out earlier than other bars was one of the reasons she continued working at the place. She could get home at a decent hour and be awake enough to get up with Steffi.

Reaching for his wallet, Mike pulled out a trio of bills. "This should cover my tab and tip. I'll meet you out front."

"For what?"

"To drive you home of course."

Drive her home. Maybe Jackie's comment wasn't so far off. She fingered the bills, noting his tip was beyond generous for one drink. "What's the catch?"

"No catch."

"Really?" She may have made her share of bad calls, but she wasn't stupid. Uptown lawyers didn't hang out at the Elderion and offer waitresses rides for no reason. She hadn't forgotten what he implied about her mother. "You drive all your clients home in the middle of the night?"

"If they're dressed like that, I do."

What was wrong with the way she was dressed?

"For one thing, you're not," he replied when she asked.

A comment like that was supposed to make her want to get into a car with him? "I'll have you know I've been riding the same bus for years without a single incident."

"Well, aren't you lucky."

"Luck has nothing to do with it. After a while you develop a kind of invisible armor and no one bothers you."

He frowned. "Invisible armor?"

"Street smarts, you know? People see you and realize straight off they can't hassle you. You blend in." It was outsiders like him that had to worry. Unfortunately, from the way he was already packing his things, Roxy had the distinct feeling he wasn't interested in her argument or in taking no for an answer.

What the heck. Wouldn't kill her to ride in a warm car for a change.

"I'll meet you in five," she told him.

Did she really think she was safe riding the bus wearing

that outfit? Watching her sashay off, Mike rolled his eyes. For crying out loud, she wasn't even his type.

In this lifetime anyway. A memory danced on the edge of his mind. Of other late-night bus rides and willing partners. He shook it away.

"You make this commute every night?" he asked when they finally met up. She'd slipped a leather jacket over her uniform. The waist-length jacket covered her bare shoulders, but still left the legs exposed.

"Five nights a week."

They rounded the corner and headed to the pay lot, walking past the bus stop in time to see a drunken patron relieving himself on the wall. Did her invisible armor protect her from that, too? he wondered as the splash narrowly missed his shoe.

"I thought about adding a sixth," Roxy was saying, "but that would mean less time with Steffi. I hardly see her much as it is. She sees more of her babysitter."

"When you win this case, you'll have all the time in the world."

"At this point in my life I'd settle for not having to schlep drinks for a living. I don't care what they say, the smell of stale beer doesn't go away."

"You never thought of doing something else?"

"Oh, sure. I was going to be a doctor but the Elderion was too awesome to give up.

"Sorry," she quickly added. "Couldn't help myself. I could have found a day job, but originally I wanted my days free for auditions."

"Auditions? You're an actress?" A strange emotion stirred inside him. He should be concerned her career aspirations made her more interested in grabbing fifteen minutes of fame than in seeing the case through. Instead the tug felt more like envy. He chalked it up to being in the bar. The night had him thinking of old times and old aspirations.

The driver had brought out his sedan from the back of the lot. As Roxy slid into the passenger seat, her skirt bunched higher, almost to the juncture of her thighs. Mike averted his eyes while she adjusted herself. Yeah, she blended in.

"I'm impressed," he said when he settled into his driver's seat.

"Don't be. It was eight years of nothing."

"Couldn't have been that bad."

"Try worse. Turns out you need one of two things to make it in show business. Talent or cleavage. I was saving up for the latter when I had Steffi."

"So you quit for motherhood."

"Couldn't very well work all night, run around to auditions all day and take care of her, too. Since the whole acting thing wasn't working out anyway, I figured I'd cut my losses and do one thing halfway decently."

"Halfway?"

Her shrug failed to hide her embarrassment. Clearly she hadn't expected him to pick up on the modifier. "The whole 'wish I could spend more time with her' thing. Not that I have a choice, right?"

"No." He stared at the brake lights ahead of him. The city that never sleeps. Even after midnight, gridlock could snag you. "But then a lot of choices aren't really in our control."

"What do you mean?"

This time he was the one who shrugged as a way of covering up. He didn't know what he meant. The words sort of bubbled up on their own. "That a lot of the time life makes the decisions for us."

"You mean like how getting knocked up put my acting

career out of its misery?" Her nonchalant expression was poorly crafted. No wonder she failed as an actress.

"She's why I'm doing all this now," she continued after a beat. "Partly anyway. I want her to have more choices than I can give her now."

This time she wasn't acting. The desperate determination in her voice was very real.

A thought suddenly occurred to him. "What about her father?"

"What about him?"

He'd hit a sore spot. He could feel her stiffen. "Is he still in the picture?"

"No."

Interesting. "Any chance he'll pop back in?"

"No."

"You sure?" Wouldn't be the first time an ex reappeared at the scent of a payday. From his point of view, the fewer complications the better.

"He's not in our lives," she repeated, her voice a little terse.

Her clenched jaw said there was more to the story. "Because he's not…?" He left the end of his sentence hoping she'd fill in the blank.

"Because he's not," she repeated. "Why are you asking anyway? I thought this case was about *my* paternity."

"It's my job to know as many details as possible about my clients."

"Even things that aren't your business?

"Everything about you is my business."

"I don't think so," she scoffed.

This was the second time tonight she'd tried to dictate what he could and couldn't discuss. Time he explained how this relationship would work. Yanking the steering wheel, he cut off the car in the next lane and pulled to the curb. "Let's get a few things straight right now. You came to me asking for help. I can't do that without your cooperation. Your. Full. Cooperation. That means if I need to know what you had for dinner last Saturday night, you need to tell me. Do you understand? Because if you can't, then this—" he waved his hand in the space between them "—isn't going to work.

"Are we clear?" he asked, looking her in the eye. Although the lecture was necessary, she could very well tell him to go to blazes. He held his breath, hoping he hadn't pushed her—and his luck—too far.

From her seat, she glared, her eyes bright in the flash of passing headlights. "Crystal."

"Good. Now I suggest you learn to deal with tough questions, because we've only scratched the surface." They were definitely revisiting her daughter's paternity, too. There was way too much emotion behind her reaction.

They drove the rest of the distance in silence, eventually pulling up in front of a nondescript building, on a street lined with them. Tall towers with squares of light, the kind of buildings his architect brother would call void of personality. At this hour of night, with the green landscaping unlit, Mike thought they had an eerie futuristic quality.

He stole a look at his companion. She hadn't moved since his lecture, her face locked on the view outside the windshield. With the shadows hiding her makeup and her hair tumbling down her back, he was surprised how classical her profile looked. Reminding him of one of those Greek busts in a museum, strong and delicate at the same time. If, that is, the pieces in the museum were gritting their teeth.

Her fingers were already wrapped around the door handle. "Want to wait till I come to a full stop or will slowing down to a crawl be good enough?" he asked her.

"Either will be fine." Her voice was tight to match her jaw. Still upset over his lecture. He added the discussion to his mental revisit list. Thing was getting pretty long. "I'll stop at the front walkway if you don't mind. Road burn never looks good on a client."

Without so much as cracking a smile, she pointed to the crosswalk a few feet ahead. "Here is fine. I'll walk the rest of the way." She pushed open the door the moment the wheels stopped spinning. Eager to get away.

"Roxanne!" Call it guilt or anxiety over his harshness earlier, but he needed to call her back and make sure they were truly on the same page. "Do we understand each other?"

"We do." From her resignation, however, she wasn't happy about it. Never mind, she'd be happy enough with him when they settled her case.

"You still want to proceed then?" he double-checked.

She nodded, again with resignation. "I do."

"I have an opening at nine-thirty tomorrow. I'll see you then."

Resignation quickly switched to surprise. "You want to meet tomorrow?"

"Unless you'd rather meet tonight. We have a lot to go over, and you're my only source of information. Sooner we get started, the better."

Seeing her widening eyes, he added, "Is that a problem?"

"No," she replied. "No problem."

There was, but to her credit, she seemed resolved to solving whatever it was. "I'll see you at nine-thirty."

"Sharp," he added. As if he had anything better to do. "Oh, and Roxanne? You might as well get used to spending time with me. In fact, you could say I'm about to become your new best friend."

"Great." Thrilled, she was not; he could tell by the smirk.

Surprisingly, however, he found the annoyance almost amusing. There was mettle underneath her attitude that would come in handy. Smiling, he watched her walk away, waiting till she disappeared behind the frosted front door before shifting his car into Drive. For the first time in weeks, he looked forward to a new workday. Roxanne O'Brien didn't know it yet, but she'd just become his newest and biggest priority.

He had a feeling both their futures would be better for it.

CHAPTER THREE

Roxy could feel Mike all the way to her front door and this time the sensation had nothing to do with his "presence." He was watching her.

Her new best friend. The idea was beyond laughable. She wasn't entirely sure she even liked the guy with his bossy, arrogant, elegant attitude. Add nosy, too. What business was it of his whether Steffi's father was around or not? *Everything about you is my business.* Recalling the authority in his voice, she got a hot flash. Men who could truly take charge were few and far between in her world. Most of them simply took off.

Bringing her back to Steffi's father. What a nice big bitter circle. She really did have to stop overreacting when people mentioned him. Not every remark was a reference to her bad judgment.

No, those would come later, when the Sinclairs got involved. Maybe chasing down the truth wasn't such a good idea.

Then she thought about Steffi, and her resolve returned.

Mrs. Ortega's apartment was on the third floor. The older woman met her at the door. "She give you any problems?" Roxy asked.

"Nada. Went down during her movie, same as always. She had a busy day. I had all three grandchildren."

"Sounds like a houseful."

Steffi was curled up sound asleep on the sofa, the late-night news acting as a night-light. In her hand she clutched a purple-haired plastic pony. Roxy smiled. Her daughter was in the middle of a pony fascination, the purple-haired animal not having left her hand in a month.

Carefully she scooped her up. The little girl immediately stirred. "Dusty's thirsty," she murmured, half swatting at her amber curls. Roxy wasn't quite sure she was awake.

"We'll get him some water upstairs."

"Okay." The little girl nodded and tucked her head into the crook of Roxy's neck. Her skin smelled of sleep and baby shampoo. Roxy inhaled a noseful and the scent tugged at her heart. Her little angel. Steffi might have started as a mistake, but she was the one decent accomplishment in Roxy's life. She'd do anything not to screw it up.

After making arrangements with Mrs. Ortega for the next morning, she carried Steffi to the elevator. Stepping off onto the eleventh floor, she could hear the screech of a high speed chase playing on a television. Would it be too much to ask for it not to be her apartment?

Yes. Fumbling to balance her keys and her daughter, she opened the door to find the volume blasting. A thin, acne-prone stain wearing an orange-and-blue throwback jersey lay sprawled on the sofa. Roxy cringed. Wayne. When she first decided to take on a roommate, she figured an extra person would allow her to afford a better apartment and Alexis had been one of the few decent applicants who didn't mind living with a four-year-old. Roxy didn't realize till they signed the lease that the woman's loser brother came along with the package. He showed up at all times of the night, offering some lame excuse as to why he needed to sponge off them for the night. If she didn't need Alexis's share of the rent money, she'd kick them both to the curb.

Another reason to hope Mike Templeton was as good as he said. "Can you turn the TV down?" she whispered harshly.

"Why? The kid's asleep."

She shot him a glare. Not for long. "Because you can hear it at the elevator."

"Turn it down, Wayne." Carrying a laundry basket on her hip, his sister, Alexis, came down the hallway. "No one wants to hear that noise."

With a roll of his eyes, Wayne reached for his remote.

Alexis greeted her with a nod and dropped the basket on the dining room table. "Some guy came by looking for you. He find you?"

"Dude wouldn't stop buzzing," Wayne said. "Woke me up."

Poor baby. "Yeah, he found me," she told Alexis.

"New boyfriend?"

"No. Business. He's a lawyer who's going to be helping me with some stuff of my mother's." She flashed back to five minutes earlier, in the close confines of his car. *Better get used to my company. You and I are going to be spending a lot of time together.* Against her will, a low shiver worked its way to the base of her spine. Immediately she kicked herself. You know, Roxy, your outbursts of moral outrage might carry a little more weight if you didn't find the man attractive.

"What kind of business?" Wayne asked. "You getting money?"

"I thought you said your mother didn't leave you anything?" Alexis said. She paused. "Is this about that stuff your mother said?"

"What stuff?" Wayne asked.

Roxy ignored him. In a moment of extreme loneliness and needing someone to talk to, Roxy had shared her mother's last words to her roommate. In fact, it was Alexis who first suggested she might have money coming to her.

"Yeah."

"He going to help you?" Her roommate's eyes became big brown saucers. Roxy swore the pupils were dollar signs. It made her reluctant to answer.

"Maybe."

She could have answered no and it wouldn't matter. Alexis had already boarded the money train and was running at high speed. "Get out. We're talking Kardashian kind of money, right? I read those Sinclairs are loaded."

"We aren't talking any kind of money." She especially wasn't talking money with the two of them. "He said he'd look into things. That's all. I have to put Steffi down before she wakes up."

It was a wonder the little girl hadn't woken up already with all the noise going on. She really must have had a busy day. Knowing her daughter had fun should have been a relief. Instead she felt a stab of guilt. She should have been the one providing the fun, not the elderly grandmother downstairs. The one who read her stories and fed her dinner. So many things she should be doing. What happened if she couldn't? Would she fade into the background like her mother, there but not there, a virtual stranger in a work uniform?

She lay her daughter in the plastic princess bed and pulled the blankets over her. Almost immediately Steffi burrowed into the mattress, Dusty the horse still gripped in her fist. Roxy brushed a curl from her cheek, and marveled at the innocence. Mike Templeton better realize how much she had riding on his ability to climb legal mountains.

* * *

"Tell me everything you can about your mother."

It was the next morning, and Roxy was sitting with her new best friend for their nine-thirty meeting. She half expected another lecture about her overreaction the night before, but he behaved as if it never happened. He even provided breakfast. Muffins and coffee, arranged neatly on his office conference table. Like they were having an indoor picnic.

"Standard client procedure?" she'd asked.

The question earned her an odd, almost evasive look that triggered her curiosity meter. "Figured you could use breakfast," he'd replied when she remarked on it.

Now he sat, legal pad at the ready, asking her about her mother. "There's not much to tell." Her mother had always been an enigma. Thanks to those letters, she was now a total stranger. "She wasn't what you'd call an open book, in case you couldn't guess." More like a locked diary.

"Let's start at the beginning. When did your parents get married?"

"June 18. They eloped."

She watched as he wrote down the date. It was barely legible. How could a man who moved his pen so fluidly have such horrendous penmanship?

"Seven months before you were born."

"Yup. To the day. I always figured I was the reason they got married."

"And you were their only child."

"One and only. I used to wish I had brothers and sisters, though. Being the only one could be lonely sometimes. Now that I think about it, that's probably one of the reasons I became an actress. I did a lot of pretending."

"Trust me, siblings aren't always great to have around," he replied.

"You have brothers and sisters?"

"One of each. And before you ask, I'm the oldest."

She wasn't sure why, but the idea he had a family intrigued her. Were they all as smooth and refined as he was? She pictured a trio of perfection all in navy blue blazers. "Are they lawyers, too?"

"No, I'm the only one."

"Tough act to follow, huh?"

Voice flat, he replied, "So I'm told." Another unreadable expression crossed his face. Sounded like she'd touched a nerve. Sibling rivalry or something else?

She wanted to ask more, but he steered the conversation back to being one-sided. "Your father—the one you grew up with—is he still alive?"

"Looked alive at the funeral."

Like she figured he would, he stopped writing and looked up, just in time to witness the shame creeping into her cheeks. "He took off for Florida when I was little. Guess he figured once he made a legal woman out of my mother, his job was done."

"They're divorced then."

"Good Lord, no. They were Irish Catholic. They stayed married." Instead they lived separate lives in separate states. Chained to one another by a mistake. Her.

Wonder what he'd think when he learned that he might not have had to marry her mother at all.

Mike scribbled on his notepad. "Interesting."

"What is?"

"That neither sought an annulment. If your father knew about Wentworth, he'd certainly have grounds."

"Oh." She popped a piece of muffin into her mouth, swallowing it along with the familiar defensiveness that had risen with the conversation. Her mother's story always cut so close to home. Reminded her too much of choices she did or didn't make. She always wondered which path would have been better. Hers or her mother's?

"Maybe he didn't care," she said, as much to herself as aloud. "I always figured he wanted out as easily as possible. My mother was— I'm not sure what word I'd use."

"Quiet?"

Too simple. "Absent."

"Because she was working?"

"No. I mean, yes, she worked, but absent in a different way." She thought of all the nights she spent alone with her babysitter, nights followed by mornings where her mother would sit wordlessly with coffee and cigarettes while Roxy ate her cereal. "She was there, but not there. Like that guy in the musical, *Chicago*. Mr. Cellophane. Invisible. Only instead of being Roxy's husband, she was Roxy's mother."

She laughed at her own joke before sobering. "I always felt like part of her was missing. Guess there was."

She broke off a piece of muffin, ate it, broke off another. "She must have really loved him."

"Who?"

"Wentworth, obviously." What else would explain the change from the woman described in those letters to the ineffectual, worn-down woman Roxy grew up with? "I have no idea how much she loved my father."

"Enough to marry him."

Roxy gave him a long look. He wasn't serious, was he? "We both know there were a lot of reasons to get married that had nothing to do with being in love. First and foremost the fact she was pregnant."

With another man's child. "Think that's why he left?"

"There's only one person who knows that answer."

"I know."

Looking down, Roxy saw that while talking, she'd broken the rest of her muffin into small pieces. If ever there was a conversation worth avoiding, this was the one. Hey, Dad, I was wondering, did Mom ever mention whether you biologically deserved the title? She wasn't sure which response would be better. Him knowing, meaning yet another person kept the truth from her, or him not knowing. Which meant he really had taken off because he didn't care.

Appetite gone, she rose from the table and walked toward the window. The conference room looked across to the building next door. In one window, she could see the back of a woman as she spoke on the phone. A large potted plant sat in another. If she leaned closer to the glass and looked left, she could just see the street below.

Behind her, she heard the crinkle of leather, and a moment later the air grew warm and thick. Mike stood behind her.

Odd. At work she spent her time weaving in and out of a crowd, bodies often pressing against her. The human swarm didn't feel half as overpowering as the body heat coming from her lawyer. It was like she could feel him breathing.

He didn't say a word. He merely stood there offering silent camaraderie. Feeling him—his presence—Roxy suddenly became acutely aware they were alone and behind closed doors. Why that mattered, she wasn't sure, but it did. Maybe it was the strange urge she had to lean back and let him hold her.

"Are you close to your family?" she asked him.

"I don't see why that's relevant."

Despite not seeing his face, she could easily imagine his raised brow.

"I'm curious," she told him. And talking about her family was depressing. "Besides, I thought we were going to be each other's new best friend. Isn't that what you said last night?"

"An expression. I didn't mean we were going to start getting our nails done and telling each other secrets."

"You have secrets?"

"No." But his answer came out stiff. She'd poked the nerve again.

Turning around, she found him standing far closer than she'd expected. No wonder she'd felt his body heat so keenly. "You don't sound very convincing."

"This meeting is about you. Not me." Again, the words and expression didn't go hand in hand. In this case, the shameful look in his copper eyes belied the stern dictate. Instead of the desired effect, it only made her more curious.

"Do they live in New York?"

"Who?"

"Your parents. Do they live in the city?"

He let out a frustrated breath, catching on that she would keep pressing until he answered. "Part of the year. They're very busy with their careers."

"They're successful like you then."

"Success is taken for granted in my family."

"Kind of like how screwing up is in mine."

"At least you have the choice."

He looked…distressed; she couldn't come up with a better word. She only knew the look didn't suit him.

He was frowning again. Never one to pay much attention to men's mouths, she hadn't noticed before, but he had a great-looking one. Lips not too full, not too thin, with a sharply defined Cupid's bow. They weren't suited for frowning.

She raised her eyes to study the rest of his face and connected with his gaze. In that second, a spark ignited. A feeling she couldn't define but felt all the way to her toes. She found herself mesmerized by the cloudiness in his eyes, the way the brown darkened the copper-colored flecks, making them almost invisible. "You didn't have a choice?"

Her question flipped a switch, and the moment ended. The flecks returned, and he was back once again to lawyer mode. "Don't know. I make a practice of succeeding."

Roxy got the hint. Sharing time had ended. "Let's hope you don't break the streak with my case."

"I don't intend to."

He spoke with savage determination. And yet, in the back of her mind, Roxy found herself wondering exactly who the determination was meant to convince. Her?

Or himself?

CHAPTER FOUR

Dear Fiona,
I can't believe it's only been two days. Feels like two years. You must think I'm crazy writing you again, especially after we talked half the night, but I can't stop thinking about you. This morning in English class, while the professor was going over the syllabus, all I could think of was your voice. I love your accent. I could listen to it for hours. You don't even have to say much. The grocery list would work....

TAKING off his glasses, Mike rubbed his eyes. He'd been reading since Roxanne's departure, hoping to get a feel of Wentworth's state of mind. He found out. The guy had it bad. Four letters into the pile and it was already obvious. Wonder if his parents knew he was infatuated with one of their housekeepers. Did they care? Was he going to find a letter later in the stack telling Fiona goodbye?

He hoped not. It would completely kill his case. Roxanne, too, since she was clearly counting on the money. Couldn't be easy waiting tables and raising a kid on your own. Taking the bus home in a skimpy uniform night after night. He didn't care how invisible she thought she was; when you showed that much leg, you weren't invisible.

Once again, a memory danced around his head. Grace

Reynolds. Wow, he hadn't thought about her in years. How often did they snuggle in the last row of a bus, doing things buses weren't meant for? They almost got caught more than once. The thrill of discovery was half the fun.

Roxanne reminded him of Grace. Or rather of that time. Of course, there was a big difference between an Ivy League philosophy student and a cocktail waitress. Big difference. Must be the acting thing. The idea Roxanne chased her dream. Sure, she failed, but she still chased.

Mike couldn't remember the last time he had a dream. Least one that wasn't ordained from birth and piled heavy with expectations. Except for that one crazy semester. But that had been childish fantasy. He'd let those days go. Why were the memories coming back?

I don't know, Mike. Why did you have those thoughts this morning?

They were definitely not childish fantasies. He didn't know what they were. One second he's talking about his family—which was none of her business—next he's looking in her eyes and thinking about how the light crowned her hair, and noting how her eyes were more a merger of earthy colors rather than simple green.

Things he had no business noticing about a client.

He'd felt this inexplicable pull the moment their eyes met.

Oh, God, listen to him. Who did he think he was, Wentworth Sinclair? His days of sparks and pulls were long gone.

Setting Wentworth's letter aside, he turned his attention to a different pile. The pile he'd been avoiding for days.

When he broke off from Ashby Gannon, everything seemed so straightforward. Templetons make things happen. They go for what they want. Wasn't that what he'd been drilled to do? Failure never entered his mind. After all, he had contacts, a proven reputation. He did all the right research. Created a business plan. Talk about arrogant overconfidence. Business plans and contacts didn't mean squat when the economy was tanking.

The first six months had been all right, but then the referrals dried up as his colleagues began keeping the work in-house. Doing "all right" became a luxury. Last month he didn't clear enough to make expenses. This month looked worse.

Which was why he needed Roxanne's case to succeed—and settle—quickly. If he could keep himself afloat until the Sinclairs made an offer, he might be all right. Otherwise...

We raised you to be better than this.

"I know, Dad," he muttered to the voice in his head. Dear Lord, did he know.

The phone rang, drowning out the thoughts. "Knew you'd be burning the midnight oil," his baby brother, Grant, said when he answered the phone. "No rest for the wicked, huh?"

Or the soon to be bankrupt. "What do you want?"

"Everything's great," Grant replied. "Thanks for asking."

"Precisely why I didn't bother asking. Everything's always going great lately." His brother was high on life at the moment.

"Can't argue with you there," Grant replied. "I'm calling to see what you're doing tomorrow night. Sophie and I thought we could all grab dinner."

Mike stilled. "Tomorrow?"

"Yeah. We thought it'd be great to talk to you in person for a change."

No, it wouldn't. Keeping up appearances was so much easier over the phone. "I can't."

He searched his brain for an excuse, the guilt hitting him before he even got the words out. "The Bar's hosting an event."

His stomach churned at the lie. This was his brother, after all. Family. He shouldn't feel the need to pretend anything with him.

Other than the fact he spent the better part of two years lecturing Grant on living up to his potential. It was getting harder and harder to pretend he had life under control in the face of his brother's newfound happiness. The reminder of his hypocrisy was too loud.

"Another one? I swear, you're a worse workaholic than my Sophie, and we know how bad she can be."

"Not everyone can afford to lounge around," he remarked, eyes falling to the stack of bills."

"I'm sure you can."

If only it were that easy. He opened his mouth to say as much, then quickly shut it. His problems were his; he'd deal with them. "I've already committed to this thing. Bought my ticket."

"Say no more. Heaven forbid you back out on an RSVP."

"Not my fault I believe in keeping my commitments." Nonexistent or otherwise.

"How about next week then?"

Again, Mike paused. The right answer was yes, of course. He had no plans. Couldn't afford them. He washed a hand over his face. "I don't know." He hated putting his brother off. "I just took on this big case and it's going to take up a lot of time...."

"Big case, hey? Anything interesting?"

Mike gave him the short version, causing the man to whistle. "Long-lost heirs. Impressive. Not your usual kind of client."

Definitely not, Mike replied in his head. "I'm branching out."

"Can't wait to hear more."

"Not much more to tell yet. I'm just drafting the initial DNA request this afternoon."

"I meant when we see you on Saturday. You can give us an update."

Closing his eyes, Mike shook his head. He wasn't going to dodge this one. "All right," he said, "I'll come by next Saturday."

"Great. I'll take care of the reservations," Grant answered. "It'll be great to catch up."

"Yeah, it will," Mike replied in a quiet voice.

They spoke a little longer, mostly about Grant's latest architectural project, which was going spectacularly. As he listened, Mike tried to remind himself Grant had floundered for two whole years, and his returning to architecture was to be celebrated. He hated the part of him that twisted with envy. He was happy for him. Truly.

After promising for a second—and third—time he would keep their next date, he hung up. No sooner did the phone line click dead than he found his thoughts right back to Roxanne. When she left this morning, she'd promised to make a phone call of her own. To Florida to ask her father about Wentworth. He didn't envy the task. *Are you close to your parents?* Her question came floating back, along with the note in her voice that made her sound so very small and vulnerable. The memory alone was enough to tug at him. He'd never had a client get to him like this before. Then again, he'd never had a client this important before, either. Grant was right: she wasn't his usual client.

She was way, way more.

"Don't look now, but your lawyer's back."

Hearing Jackie's announcement, Roxy nearly dropped her tray. "Mike's here?" Sure enough, he sat at the same table as before in the same blue blazer as this morning.

Recalling how closely she'd stood to those buttons, Roxy felt a shiver go through her. "What does he want?"

"Better be a drink," Dion replied. "We aren't here so he can set up shop and take the table away from paying customers."

Roxy ignored him. She was too busy watching Mike as he folded his coat over the back of a chair. Why on earth would he drive across town for a second night in a row?

Only one way to find out. Soon as she unloaded the drinks on her tray, she made her way to his table. Just like last night, he was scribbling away on a yellow legal pad. "Is there a problem?"

He looked up, so unsuited for a bar like this it wasn't funny. It caused her breath to catch. "Why would there be a problem?" he asked.

"Because you're here."

"Felt like a Scotch."

An incomplete answer if ever she heard one. "Don't they serve liquor in your neck of the woods?"

"They do, but I like this place. It reminds me of somewhere I used to spend time."

Really? The idea of Mike Templeton anywhere near a bar like the Elderion on a regular basis boggled her mind. She covered her surprise with a shrug. "It's a free country." Though she had to wonder.

"Wait." She paused midturn. "This isn't about my taking the bus home is it? Because I told you already—"

"You take the bus all the time. Don't worry, I got that message loud and clear."

"Good. I hate having to repeat myself."

"Wouldn't want that, would we." He was looking over the rim of his glasses at her. The way the light reflected off the lenses made reading his eyes impossible so she couldn't tell if his tone was sarcastic or not.

"Although I have to ask," he continued. "Would it be so awful if I did bring you home?"

No, her mind immediately answered. Wow, talk about old mistakes rearing their ugly head. As if she'd let anyone take her home again. "I'll go get your Scotch."

"I did come by for a reason."

Ah, she knew there was something. She waited for him to explain.

"I wanted to let you know I plan to submit the DNA request on Monday."

"So soon?" Her heart stopped. The crowd around them receded, drowned out by the wind tunnel sounding in her ears. She hadn't expected things to move so quickly. "I haven't reached my father yet." A sinking sensation erupted in her stomach. Could she still call him her father?

"You'll reach him soon enough. The Sinclairs will reject this request out of hand anyway giving you plenty of time. We're really filing so they know we exist. Once we make our position clear, we can force an offer."

"Offer?" She was confused. "I thought we were asking for a DNA test."

"We are."

He motioned for her to sit down. After glancing over to make sure Dion wasn't paying attention, Roxy complied.

"This is our opening move. They'll react. We'll counteract, and so on, till we get what we want."

"You're talking about the money."

"Exactly."

"Where does the DNA test come in?"

"It doesn't."

"But—" She was lost. "Are you saying there won't be a DNA test?"

Mike looked up from his paperwork. "Not if we accept a settlement offer first."

"Wait a second. Without a test, how will I know for certain whether Wentworth is my father?"

"Does it matter?"

Yes, it mattered. She didn't realize until this moment but it mattered a lot. "Did you think I only wanted the money?"

"Basically, yes."

In other words, his opinion from the other day hadn't changed at all. He still thought her a gold-digging fraud. Worst part of it was she'd gone to him about the money. She had no one to blame for his opinion but herself.

"I've got tables to wait on." She couldn't deal with this right now. Not at work. Blindly she headed into the crowd, colliding with the first body that crossed her path.

"Hey," a nasal-voiced brunette whined. "Watch where you're going."

"Sorry," Roxy muttered.

"Look what you did. You made me spill my drink!"

"I'll get you a new one." More charges against her paycheck.

"Damn right, you're getting me a free drink." Based on the way her words slurred, she didn't need one, either. "And a new blouse. Did you see what you did?" She gave a wobbly wave across her torso. A blue splash, about waist-high, marred the orange silk. "This is designer! Do you know how much it cost?"

Full price or discount? Roxy would bet she didn't pay retail. She knew the woman's type.

Still, the customer was always right. "Send the bill to the guy in the blue blazer," she told the woman. "He's the money man."

The brunette squinted in confusion. "What?"

"Just send us the bill." More charges for Dion to deduct from her paycheck. At this rate, she might as well be working for free. Trying to move on, she attempted to sidestep the woman, but unfortunately, the brunette wasn't ready to let the topic drop. "I want to talk to a manager," she slurred. Came out more like *I wannatalkamanger*. "Someone's going to pay for my blouse."

"Like I said, send us the dry-cleaning bill, and we'll gladly take care of it."

"Dry cleaners? What's a dry cleaner going to do? This shirt's ruined."

Pul-leeze. The stain wasn't that big. Dion would tell the woman the same exact answer. She turned around, planning to head to the bar and get him. The brunette, thinking she was walking away, grabbed her arm. "Don't you walk away from me."

She attempted to yank Roxy around. Stopping short on her heels, Roxy instead stumbled backward, bumping shoulders with the woman and causing more cocktail to splash.

"You stupid idiot!" the woman shrieked. Blue liquid stained her bare arm. "Look at what you did now! How would you like it if I spilled a drink all over you?"

There was maybe a half an inch left in her martini glass. Rearing back, the woman tossed the liquid at Roxy's face. An arm appeared out of nowhere and grabbed Roxy's waist, pulling her safely out of the line of fire.

She didn't need to look to see who the arm belonged to. The way her insides reacted was identification enough.

"Come on, Roxy," Mike murmured in her ear, "let's go get you some air."

"Why are you pulling me away?" she protested as he dragged her toward the front door. "I didn't start the fight."

"No, but I didn't want to take the chance of you sticking around and letting the situation escalate. Last thing we need is an article in the *Daily Post* about you getting into a bar fight."

"News flash, I work in a bar." She yanked her arm free. What did a news article matter anyway?

Oh, right. The lawsuit. He didn't want bad publicity impacting his "settlement."

A blast of cold air hit her, a harsh reminder spring was still a few weeks away. "Here." Before she could say a word, she found herself enveloped in a blue worsted-wool cocoon. Despite her annoyance, she wrapped the blazer around her with gratitude.

"She started it," she muttered.

"Technically you started it when you stormed into the crowd. You've got to stop overreacting to everything I say. Or—" he adjusted the jacket on her shoulders "—at least stop storming off before we're done talking. Do you want to explain what I said this time that was so wrong?"

"Isn't it obvious?"

"Honestly, not really. The other night you talked about wanting to make a better life for your daughter. I assumed you meant financially."

"I did." After all, it was the Sinclair money that would help her help Steffi, not the bloodline. Truth be told, she didn't understand her reaction completely herself except that as soon as he talked about not going through with the DNA test, her blood ran cold. She didn't realize until that moment how badly she wanted—she needed to know the truth. Needed to know how and why she was brought into this world. If she was created out of love or simply created.

She hugged the jacket tighter. The cloth smelled of bar soap and musk-scented aftershave, exactly how she expected his clothes to smell.

Meanwhile, Mike had moved over to the curb where he stood studying the traffic. Realizing she was seeing him in shirtsleeves for the first time, she took a good look. Without the extra layer he looked different. More exposed, more human. The broadcloth pulled taut across his shoulders and back, revealing a body that was lean and muscular. Bet if she touched him, it would feel like chiseled rock. She doubted a man like him, with so many assets, could understand her desire. "I can't explain why, but knowing makes a difference."

"You know that makes the case a whole lot more difficult," he said.

"I know."

Joining him, she touched his shoulder. "Not knowing for certain would haunt me. I want to be able to tell Steffi where she came from." She wanted to know herself.

"You're the client." He washed a hand across his features. "If you want a DNA test, then we push for a DNA test."

Roxy smiled. She knew his acquiescence had everything to do with her wishes as his client and not for her personally, but at the moment she didn't care. It just felt good to have her wishes heard.

The bar door opened, and Jackie's ponytailed head peered around the corner. "Hey, Rox, you comin' back in or what? We're swamped here."

"I'll be right there," Roxy replied. To Mike, she said, "Your idea of disaster is bad publicity, but mine is getting fired. Bills still need to be paid."

He half nodded in response. "I know what you mean."

Doubtful, but she appreciated the attempt at commiseration. There was another gust of wind and musk teased her nostrils, reminded her that the warmth around her shoulders belonged to him. Reluctantly she moved to shed his jacket.

"Keep it on till you get inside," Mike told her.

"You sure? A drink might come flying in my direction when I walk through the door."

"I'll take my chances," he replied, flashing a smile.

"Thank—" Her answer drifted off as she found herself caught in his coppery eyes. The gentle reassurance swirling in the brown depths caught her breath. All of a sudden her lungs felt too big for her chest, as if some giant balloon had expanded. The air hummed with energy and the sound of their breathing. What happened to the traffic? Surely the world hadn't disappeared leaving only the two of them.

Or had it? The spark, that inexplicable connecting spark from this morning resurrected itself. Her gaze dropped to his mouth. She heard a hitch and realized, without having to look, that his gaze had dropped, too. He was studying her mouth. Did he like what he saw? She did. Her body swayed a little bit closer. Close enough to put them both in a very dangerous position.

CHAPTER FIVE

What are you doing, Templeton? Mike didn't know. In front of him, Roxanne's lips glistened invitingly. He couldn't tear his eyes away. The strong connection he felt this morning had returned, and he was trapped in its pull. Thoughts raced through his head. Wild, crazy thoughts like pressing her against the brick wall and kissing her until their lungs ran out of air. And more.

He didn't have these kinds of thoughts. Not anymore. He certainly shouldn't be having them now.

"This is a mistake." He delivered his verdict in a whisper, part of him wondering if he was speaking quietly on purpose. To avoid hearing his own warning. Roxanne heard, though, and relief filled her face. Clearly she agreed.

Whether the tightness in his gut was relief or disappointment, he refused to say.

He was pretty sure he knew the answer when she looked away and the tightness grew. "I better get inside before Dion has my head," she said in a soft voice. She shrugged off his jacket and handed it to him. "You should take this back," she said. "I can't afford the dry-cleaning bill."

"Yet," he corrected, hoping the teasing would bring back some of the connection.

"Yet," she repeated.

That was another thing. Agreeing to push for the DNA

test. All he did was postpone any settlement offers, delaying payment. He couldn't afford to delay. Like the lady said, you still got to pay the bills.

But listening to her, the way she was trying so hard to keep her voice from quivering, he knew he had to say yes. He wanted her to have her answers.

Why was he suddenly feeling so invested in her results? What happened to the invisible wall between lawyer and client? To focusing on using this case to regain his financial footing? Was nostalgia getting to him?

Or a set of soft red curls, he asked himself, fingers twitching to touch them.

He pulled himself back to business. "Hopefully no one took my paperwork while we were outside talking," he said. "I can see your boss tossing them out so someone else could sit down."

"Me, too," Roxanne replied, rewarding him with a smile. Mike felt a wave of something rolling over him, settling dangerously near his chest. Whatever had him acting out of character—nostalgia or the curls—it was getting stronger.

Maybe instead of worrying about paperwork, he should worry about that instead.

Roxy clicked off her cell phone and let it drop to her lap. Just her luck. Her father had taken off for a fishing trip in the Bahamas, and no one was sure when he would return. So much for getting answers from him. He wasn't even available by cell; she had to leave a message with his lady "friend".

And she'd been worried about blindsiding him so soon after her mother's death. She should have realized. After all, this was the man who, when she told him about being pregnant said, "What do you want me to do?"

Her fingers played with the edge of her phone case. She'd told Mike she'd give him an update after she called. Updating, however, meant talking to each other, which she'd been avoiding doing the past three days. She'd even gone so far as to ignore his phone calls.

"A mistake." His words floated back. Actually they never left. She'd been hearing them loud and clear since he whispered them Friday night. A mistake. Story of her life.

He was right, of course. They had been teetering on the brink of a very bad idea. She had absolutely no business kissing the man, no matter how compassionate he seemed or how drawn she was to him. Seeking reassurance in a man's arms was a dangerous idea with ramifications that lasted a lifetime. She should know. Assuming, of course, things had gone further than a kiss. What made her think he was remotely interested? Why would he be?

Desire and loneliness. The worst combination in the world. Made a person make stupid decisions. Like reaching out for the wrong person or seeking solace in the wrong places. Problem was desire only killed loneliness for a short time. Then the sun came up leaving you to deal with the fallout. She'd learned that lesson the hard way four years ago.

Clearly Mike's resolution saved them both a lot of potential problems. Now if she could only shake the needy, lonely ache in her chest.

A purple-and-white blur danced before her face. Blinking back to earth, she smiled at her little girl, who was making her pony dance through the air.

"Can I have a cookie?" Steffi asked.

"After dinner," Roxy replied. The answer earned her a pout. "If you're really hungry, you can have orange chips." Orange chips were her way of selling sliced carrots as a snack. Sometimes the trick worked; sometimes it didn't.

Today looked to be a hard sell. "Wayne bought potato chips."

"I don't think Wayne would want us touching his things without asking," she replied. Talk about irony. Wayne sure didn't have a problem with touching others' stuff. "We have orange chips. Would you like some?"

"Okay." Enthusiastic, the response was not. "Can Dusty have some, too?"

"Sure." If it would help her daughter eat better. "We'll give him his own bowl so he can share with the other ponies. And," she added, "if you're both good and eat them all up, we can have macaroni and cheese for supper."

"Yay!" Satisfied she'd won something—in her little mind, mac and cheese was boxed gold—her daughter went back to her farm set. A half dozen ponies lay on their sides on the floor in front of the red plastic barn. "The horses are having a sleepover," she explained in an important voice.

"I better get the chips then. They might get hungry."

"Chips, chips, chips," Steffi chanted, pretending the cheer came from the horses.

While she watched her daughter chatter and play, a lump worked its way into Roxy's throat. Today was the way every day should be. Filled with mommy-daughter time and pretend pony games. If it were up to her, Steffi would never go a day unhappy. Or feeling unwanted. She'd wake up every day knowing the world was glad she existed.

If she had one regret in this world it was that Steffi didn't have a father who knew what a joy the little girl was. At the moment her daughter was too young to wonder too much about her dad. Eventually, though, she would, and Roxy would be forced to tell her the truth. Then what?

Hopefully she could at least give her a grandfather.

In her chest, the lonely feeling grew. She squeezed her phone. Go on, call him. You know you want to.

That was the problem. In spite of her avoidance, she wanted to talk with him. Worse, she wanted to feel his body close to hers again, and lose herself in the coppery concern of his eyes. She wanted to carry through on that kiss. So much for hard lessons learned, eh?

The front door buzzed while she was putting the bag of sliced carrots back in the fridge.

"Roxanne?" called the voice on the other end.

Her insides took a pathetic little tumble. She cursed herself. "Mike?" she repeated, as if she really needed to identify him. "What are you doing here?"

"Hoping to talk with you obviously. I've been trying to reach you all day."

"My phone's been off," she lied.

There was a pause. "Oh. May I come up?"

Did she have a choice? She buzzed him in.

Soon as she did, all her mental berating went out the window. Her heart sped up at the prospect of seeing him. Quickly she scanned the apartment. The place looked terrible. Folded laundry sat in a basket in the hall waiting to be put away. Steffi's toys littered the floor—the farm took up a lot of real estate. A half-drunk juice box and bowls of carrots on the floor. Picture books on the couch. How fast could she straighten up? Or did she straighten herself up instead? Change the yoga pants and T-shirt she'd tossed on this morning. And makeup! She wasn't wearing a stitch! She was a bigger mess than the apartment. Get a grip, Roxy. Bad idea, remember?

He knocked. She jumped.

"Mommy, someone's at the door," Steffi announced, not moving from the floor.

"I know, baby." Stupid elevator would be fast for once. Combing her fingers through her hair, she prayed whatever brought him here was important enough to make him oblivious to his surroundings.

Opening the door, she realized instantly it wouldn't matter if he was oblivious or not. No amount of sprucing would make her or the apartment worthy. He'd still outclass the place.

"What's up?" she asked, forcing a casual note into her voice. She could at least act unaffected, right?"

A challenge as he strode inside the same way he entered the bar. Like he owned the place. "I met with Jim Brassard today," he said.

"Who's Jim Brassard?"

"Managing partner at—" He stopped short when he saw Steffi. Her daughter was squatting in front of her farm, staring up at him with Dusty clutched protectively in her fist.

"Baby, this is Michael," Roxy said. "He's a...friend... of Mommy's."

Mike arched a brow at the word friend, but made no correction. "Hello, Steffi."

For a second, Roxy thought he might stick out his hand to go along with his formal greeting. Instead the two of them had a mini stare-off. Steffi won. Mike looked back up at her, with a silent "What now?"

"Mike and I have some business we need to talk about at the table. Can you play with your ponies while we talk?"

Wordlessly Steffi went back to her farm, but not before casting another look in Mike's direction from over her shoulder.

"She looks like you," Mike remarked, shedding his overcoat. He'd given up the winter camel hair in favor of a trench coat that hung unbuttoned over a different shade gray suit. Eyeing the peach-colored shirt, Roxy did her best not to think about the body she glimpsed the other night. Naturally she failed.

"Can I get you some coffee or something?" she asked, still acting unaffected. It felt weird watching him settle in as if this were his home. He so clearly didn't fit.

"We're not at the bar," he replied. "You don't have to serve me." He moved to sit down only to shoot back up. Reaching down, he held up a plastic duck.

Roxy's cheeks warmed. "Sorry. The chair doubles as the farm pond. Steffi, can you come get Mr. Quack Quack? I think he's done swimming."

Wordlessly Steffi trotted over and plucked the critter from Mike's fingers before settling back in front of her farmhouse. Mr. Quack Quack, Roxy noticed, found a home on her lap where he couldn't be touched.

"We don't get a lot of visitors," she whispered to Mike, feeling the need to explain. "Make's her a little shy. So long as you don't mess up her farm animals you should be fine."

"Don't worry. I think the farm is safe."

Seeing he'd settled in and had his briefcase on the table, Roxy switched to business mode. "So you talked to this Jim person," she prodded.

"Jim Brassard from Brassard, Lester. He manages the Sinclair sisters' legal affairs. I remember him from when I was at Ashby Gannon. He's sharp. Very old school, too."

Roxy wasn't sure she liked the term "old school." "What did he say?"

"About what I expected. I presented our evidence and requested a test. He said no."

Roxy's heart sank. He told her to expect a denial, but a part of her still hoped the news would be welcomed with open arms. Foolish, she knew, but wouldn't it have been nice?

The end of the table's veneer edging had come unglued, so she picked at it nervously. "What now?"

"We wait and see," he replied. "I laid some solid groundwork today. Plus, Brassard recognizing me from Ashby Gannon helped. Helped him realize he's not dealing with some ambulance-chasing creep."

"To fight uptown, you gotta go uptown," she mumbled.

"What?"

"Nothing. Something I told myself once."

"Keep in mind," he said, "we've only just started. This was our preliminary salvo. If you want your DNA test, we need to show them we aren't going away.

"You still want to push for the test, right?" he asked.

Roxy looked to the little girl playing nearby. Playing Mike's way—for the money—would ensure her little girl's future. But she deserved to know something about where she came from. "Yes," she answered without doubt. "I want to know. Steffi needs to know her mother wasn't…" She paused, the thought too painful to say aloud. "I want to know."

Returning to playing with the veneer, she kept her eyes more focused on the chipped plastic than on the man across from her. His scrutiny felt more intense than ever. Who knew what looking into his eyes would make her feel. "I—" she heard him start.

Roxy gave in and looked up. "Yes?"

"Never mind. Back to Jim's response. His refusal means we'll need to step things up on our own end."

"How?" Her attention was aroused.

"Legally he can refuse our request until the cows come home. The law is very specific about the amount of time you have to bring a claim against an estate, and you're well past the deadline."

Story of her life. Too little. Too late. "What can we do then?"

He clicked his black lacquer pen. "Way I see things,

our best approach is to mount a two-prong approach. We file the appropriate legal challenges and wait for them to wend their way through court—which could take years, by the way."

"What's the other prong?"

"We increase public pressure. Force the Sinclairs to act in the interest of good public relations."

She waited while he rummaged through his briefcase, coming up with his yellow legal pad. The pages were half-filled by this point and he had to flip several over until he reached a blank sheet. When he did, he folded his hands and leaned forward.

Roxy leaned forward, too. There was a cautiousness to his movements that made her wary. She wanted to make sure she didn't miss a word. "What exactly do you want to do?"

Those coppery eyes sparkled, completely not helping her cause. Making matters worse, he slowly raised the left corner of his mouth, creating a lopsided, sexy smile.

"We talk to the press."

Mike had hoped the fact she'd been an actress would mean Roxanne would be fairly receptive to his idea. He'd hoped wrong. Immediately her attention went to the little girl playing nearby. "Won't talking to the press tick them off?"

"There is a risk," he conceded. "But going public also lets us tell our side of the story."

"You mean mine," she corrected. "*My* side of the story. You're not going to be the one sharing your life history."

"No, I'm not." She was right about that.

He watched her chew the inside of her cheek, an action that turned her mouth into an uneven, yet still amazingly appealing, pout. Without makeup she looked a lot younger than twenty-nine. Sure, there were circles under her eyes from keeping late hours, but the fatigue was offset by a newly acquired innocence. The vulnerability he always sensed lurking had risen to the surface. She looked softer. Sweeter. Dangerous words to use when describing a client, especially when he spent the better part of the past couple of days reminding himself a good lawyer did not pursue his clients. They did not kiss them. And they especially didn't fantasize about taking late-night bus rides and reliving college age exploits.

So of course, when she didn't return his calls, he went across town for a face-to-face meeting so he could battle those thoughts all over again. As if he couldn't be more distracted.

"It's a good strategy." For the case's sake, he forced himself to stay on topic. "Going public prevents them from sweeping you or your request under the rug."

No sale. He could tell by the way her eyes went from mostly green to mottled brown.

Seriously, did he really know her mood based on eye color?

Why was she so against the idea anyhow? She'd wanted to be an actress, for crying out loud. This was her shot to be in the limelight.

There was a rattle of plastic behind him. Her daughter fixing a plastic fence, mumbling something to the plastic purple-and-white pony about not getting lost.

Of course. He bet her reaction went back to their conversation the other night regarding Steffi's father. "You know," he said, "another benefit to talking to the press is that you get to be proactive. You can control the message." He indicated Steffi with a flicker of his eyes.

Picking up on his point immediately, she crossed her arms. "You promised to leave her out of this."

Now her eyes were green. A very angry shade of green.

Her whisper was equally harsh. "I told you I didn't want her involved."

"What I said was I'd do my best." He decided not to point out her wish had been completely unrealistic.

"Well, if this is your best, then you suck." Shoving her chair so hard it nearly tipped over, she marched into the kitchen. From behind the dividing wall, Mike heard the sound of pots and cupboards being slammed about.

Feeling scrutinized, he looked over to find Steffi staring at him with wide, accusing eyes. Great. The kid was mad at him, too. What was he supposed to do?

"Your mother is… Um, that is, she and I…" The girl continued to stare.

Dammit. He'd have an easier time getting through to Roxanne.

"You've got to stop the storming off," he said, joining her in the kitchen. "It makes having a conversation very difficult."

She stood at the kitchen sink filling a saucepan with water. "I promised Steffi macaroni and cheese."

"At this exact moment?"

"Better than making her wait. Not like we had anything more to talk about."

Mike rolled his eyes. "I thought you were past arguing with me about everything I want to do?"

"You thought wrong." She slapped off the faucet and lifted the pan from the sink. The motion caused her T-shirt skimming the waistband of her pants to rise, too, creating yet another invitation to look at her behind. Damn if he wasn't developing a fixation for studying the woman's body.

He fanned his fingers in his hair, tugging the roots as a way of forcing his eyes upward. "Look, I get it. You want to protect your child. But surely you realized you couldn't keep her existence a secret forever. Brassard's investigators would find her in two seconds."

"Of course I didn't think I could keep her a secret."

"Then what?" There was a small space of countertop between the stove and sink. He leaned against it, fingers curling around the Formica lip, and waited while she adjusted the burner. "Is it because you're embarrassed?"

"What? No! How can you even say that? Steffi's the best thing I ever accomplished. I could never be embarrassed of her."

Not of her, maybe. But of something else? Her angry reaction the other night came home to roost. "Is it her father then?"

Roxanne slapped the lid on the saucepan with a clank so loud he wondered if she wanted the water to boil faster or let off steam. "I told you, Steffi's father's out of the picture."

Out, but not forgotten. "Wouldn't be the first time an absentee parent crawled out of the woodwork at the scent of money."

"He wouldn't."

So she said the other night. "You can't be certain."

"Yes, I can. In order to crawl anywhere he'd have to know she exists."

"He doesn't know?"

"No." She'd crossed the room and was manically moving boxes around an upper cabinet. "I couldn't tell him."

Mike couldn't see her face, but he could hear the tension in her voice. She was literally gritting her teeth. "What do you mean you couldn't tell him?" Didn't she mean wouldn't? "Is he dead? Married?"

She laughed at his suggestions, hollow and without humor, but didn't answer. It was like pulling teeth.

"I need to know," he pushed. "If there's any chance

the Sinclairs can dig up the information, then you need to tell me."

"I couldn't tell him because I don't know his last name." She choked on the answer, the words barely getting out. "I'm not a hundred percent sure of his first name, either."

It took a moment for him to process her reply. When he finally did, he was shocked at how viscerally he reacted. His chest burned with anger against the man. "You're saying—"

"I got drunk and knocked up by a total stranger? Yeah, that pretty much sums up the story." She was trying to sound indifferent, as though it was no big deal, and having no luck. Hearing the same in her voice, his anger toward this faceless stranger rose. He hurt for her. If he could take away her embarrassment and shame he would.

His hand barely closed over her shoulder when she shrugged him away. "Like mother like daughter, right?" she said bitterly.

"What happened?" Much as he didn't want to ask, he had to know. For the case, he told himself.

"What do you think happened? I'd had a really lousy day so I went to the lounge to drown my sorrows. This guy offered a shoulder and free drinks. He was gone when I woke up."

Mike balled his fist. What kind of man wouldn't want to be there when she woke up?

"Least I got Steffi out of the deal." Again, she failed at nonchalance. Mike blamed the unshed tears brimming in her eyes.

"She doesn't know obviously. When she asks about her father, I can usually distract her."

Sniffing back the emotion, she reached up with a shaky hand and closed the cabinet door. "Don't know what I'll tell her when she gets older."

Finally the pieces were coming together. "You're afraid she'll learn the truth."

"What if I embarrass her?" she asked in a voice so small it kicked him square in the gut.

Unlikely, given the girl was four years old and could be kept sheltered, but he understood the fear nonetheless. More than she realized. "No one wants to let down the people they love. To think you failed them."

"You must think you picked a real winner of a client."

He had to hold back the urge to cup her chin and force her to meet his eyes. "Actually I think I picked just fine. Way I see it, you're simply a woman who made a mistake. Hardly the first."

"The second in my family alone," she remarked. "Least my mother and Wentworth could say they were in love. I can pretend he would have been happy about the news."

Whereas her other father what? Wasn't?

That's why the DNA test was so important to her. She needed context. A better legacy to give her daughter.

Emotions that had been shoved to the background years before began to unfurl, and in that moment he found himself looking not at a client or even a physically attractive woman, but a person, alone and hurting. He understood her fear. She was afraid of letting her daughter down, because doing so might mean losing her as well.

Yeah, he understood that fear all too well. Suddenly winning her case became doubly important, becoming as much about helping her as it did about saving his own failing hide. He would do anything in his power to make sure she got everything she deserved.

Halfway across the kitchen, he stopped. The strength of his conviction frightened him. She was a client, for goodness' sake. She shouldn't be so damn important. She shouldn't be anything more than the means to an end.

Yet, here he was closing the space between them with the singular thought of taking her in his arms.

"Mommy?" There was the sound of small feet approaching the doorway. Mike immediately stiffened and moved away. Roxy did the same.

Steffi appeared in the doorway. "Dusty and I finished our chips," she announced. "Can we have our macaroni cheese now?"

"Sure, baby," Roxy replied. She still hadn't turned around. Mike saw her swiping at her cheek. "I'm making it right now. How about you go wash your hands, okay?"

"Okay." The little girl shot a look in his direction before turning around. He didn't think four-year-olds had accusing glares, but he'd been wrong. She clearly blamed him for her mother's unusual behavior.

On the stove, the saucepan cover rattled. "Don't know why I bother to tell her to wash her hands," Roxy said, giving a large sniff. "She's going to grab that horse again, and goodness knows how many germs are on that thing."

She was grasping at normalcy, pretending the earlier conversation didn't happen. Needing the reprieve himself, he let her. He returned to his spot next to the stove. "I take it she loves horses."

"What gave you your first clue?" Macaroni cascaded from the box into boiling water. "Right before the holidays I took her to Central Park and she saw the carriages. Since that moment it's been all horses all the time. I'm not sure, but I think she wants to move into that farm."

"Has she been to the stables in the park yet?"

"No. I'd like to, but I'm concerned she'll want to sign up for riding lessons and I'm not sure when I'll be able to afford them. I hate saying 'maybe…we'll see.' Feels like such a cop-out."

"My sister, Nicole, took lessons," he told her. "Did the whole jumping and riding around the circle thing."

"Was she any good? Wait, let me guess." She cast him a look from over her shoulder. "She was excellent."

"Made the junior Olympic team in high school."

"Impressive."

Not really. Not when you stopped to think there hadn't been any other choice but to excel. A hobby's not worth doing, unless done right, his parents always said.

He followed her back to the dining room table and watched as she lay down the plates in a neat triangle. "How about you? What activity did you dominate?" she asked. "Football? Debate team?"

"Swimming. I was fourth in the all-city eight-hundred meter butterfly my senior year."

He didn't tell her how disappointed his parents had been at the results or how much he hated the sport. Mike had actually wanted to take fencing. A late-night swashbuckler movie had him convinced sword fighting would be the best hobby ever. But his father had been on the swim team in college. Besides, he'd been clumsy in fencing class, enthusiastic but uncoordinated, where as the swimming instructor noted he had natural ability. Unable to fit both in his schedule, fencing class got dropped in favor of the sport with more potential.

He probably wouldn't have enjoyed fencing all that much anyway.

"We're ready, Mommy." Steffi returned. As predicted, the purple-and-white pony was clutched firmly in her hand.

"Dusty wash his hands, too?"

"Uh-huh." The little girl nodded and placed her pony next to one of the plates. Then and only then did Mike realize the table was set for three. Roxanne must have noticed, too, because she suddenly became quite interested in tucking her hair behind her ear. "I wasn't thinking. Would you like to stay for dinner?"

"He can't," Steffi piped in. "He didn't eat any orange chips."

Mimicking the stance her mother had held a few minutes earlier, the little girl crossed her arms in front of her chest.

"Mike and I are going to eat ours with dinner," Roxy replied. Then, as if realizing she'd made an assumption again, her cheeks grew pink. "That is, if you want..."

"Sure." After all his thoughts in the kitchen, he'd probably be better off going home, but he needed to finish their conversation about talking to the press. "Although..." He leaned toward her. "Orange chips?"

"Don't worry," Roxanne replied. "You'll be fine."

Considering the fact his hand still twitched to touch her, Mike wondered.

Orange chips, it turned out thankfully, were nothing more than presliced carrots, which Roxanne thoughtfully steamed.

The meal itself was fairly quiet. Still in judgment mode, Steffi kept a close eye on whether or not he ate his carrots. Mike made a point of eating several forkfuls quickly. Wasn't much choice if he wanted to eat his meal without continual scrutiny. The gesture seemed to mollify her, and she soon focused on her own food.

Her mother on the other hand... Out of the corner of his eye, he stole a look at the woman poking at the pasta on her plate. Although the dinner invitation had been her idea, she had been strangely withdrawn since serving the food. Mike couldn't blame her. He felt a little awkward himself, the realizations from the kitchen still churning up his insides.

Across the table, Steffi dipped her pony's nose in the yellow sauce.

"Don't put your toys in your food," Roxanne told her.

"Dusty's drinking the cheese."

"Steffi."

"Okay." She dragged the word out to two syllables before turning her scrutiny back on him. "You're not eating your macaroni."

"I, um…" How did he tell the girl he didn't like her favorite meal? Especially when he already felt dangerously close to her bad side.

Roxanne saved the day. "Stop worrying about what Mike's doing, and focus on your own meal. Do you want some more?"

Mouth slick with bright yellow cheese, Steffi nodded. "Wayne ate two boxes of macaroni cheese."

"Wayne?" Mike asked, perking up.

"My roommate's brother. He's the one who answered the buzzer when you came by the other evening. And when did you see Wayne eat macaroni and cheese?"

"This morning. When you were taking a shower."

Mike remembered Wayne now. Mr. Personality. "He's here in the morning?"

"He's here all the time," Roxanne replied, scraping half her plate's contents onto her daughter's.

"He uses bad words," Steffi piped in.

"Yes, he does, and don't talk with your mouth full. Bad words are the least of his sins," Roxanne told him. "I thought sharing costs with a roommate would be a good idea, but…" She shrugged, letting him fill in the rest of the sentence.

The woman was entirely too hard on herself, Mike decided. Although, Wayne might serve one good purpose.

"That's another reason to go public. Could get you out of this arrangement that much faster."

She sat back in her chair, fork twisting between her fingers. At least she was considering the point. Meant he was making some headway.

Dinner finished. Mike was just standing to help clear the dishes when a key jingled in the lock. The door opened, and a young couple walked in, one a chunky, unnatural blonde, the other a bony punk wearing a zippered sweater and oversize plaid baseball cap. Both zeroed in on him straight away.

The infamous Wayne and his sister he presumed.

Alexis was the first to greet him, coming around to lean against his side of the table. "Hey," she said, flipping her hair over her shoulder.

Meanwhile Wayne made a beeline for the couch where he immediately threw himself down and turned on the television set. The sound of a reality TV argument filled the apartment.

"Ignore him," the roommate—Alexis he remembered her name being—said. "He's ticked off because he lost money."

From the couch Wayne issued an obscene-laden complaint against spring baseball, proving Roxanne's comment about bad language.

"Told you not to bet on them, idiot," Alexis shot back. She smiled and leaned backward a little more. The change in position caused her back to arch, and her breasts, both ample and on display, to thrust upward. "You must be Roxy's lawyer. The one who's going to make her rich."

From the corner of his eye he saw Roxanne wince, and his sympathy went out to her. "You mean, am I trying to help her prove Wentworth Sinclair is her father? Yes, I am."

"And how is that going?" the blonde asked.

"I'm afraid I can't talk about cases with anyone but my clients."

"Not even with your client's roommate?"

"Not even with her."

"How—" she flipped her hair again "—considerate of you."

"It's the law, idiot," Wayne said. "He can't talk about his cases. Don't you watch television?"

"Doesn't mean he can't be considerate, too," Alexis shot back. She smiled. "Right?"

Mike glanced around the table. Still in her chair, Steffi had gone back to watching him, as if waiting for his response. Meanwhile, Roxanne was nowhere to be seen. A noise in the kitchen told him that's where she escaped. Quickly he snatched up his plate and Steffi's now empty one. "Roxanne is waiting for these," he said following suit.

"So that's the infamous Wayne and his sister, hey?"

She stood at the sink, again filling the saucepan, this time with soapy water. "I hate that Sophie is growing up around people like him," she muttered. Him, meaning Wayne. "I can't wait until I can afford to get out of here."

"You know how you can speed up the process," he replied as he set the dirty plates in the sink.

The remark earned him a sigh. "I know."

"Mommy, Wayne wants a beer," Steffi called out from the dining room table. "And can I have a cookie?"

"Absolutely you can have a cookie, baby. Come on in here and I'll give you one." Reaching into the cabinet, she took down a bag of chocolate frosted cookies and took out two.

"Tell Wayne I said he could get his own drinks," she told the girl after handing the treats over.

"Okay, Mommy."

"Honest to God," Roxanne said after Steffi skipped

back into the other room. "Asking a four-year-old to pick him up a drink. What kind of idiot does that?"

Mike waited while Roxanne watched Steffi leave the room. He could sense the wheels turning inside his head. Wayne's sudden appearance had, in a weird way, helped his cause.

"Going to the press," she said. "You really think it'll help?"

"Keep the Sinclairs from burying the case under a mound of legal paperwork."

"And you're sure we can control the message?"

Translation, he was certain they could protect Steffi. "You know what they say. Best defense is a good offense."

"What's the big deal? It's only a beer." Wayne shuffled his way to the fridge, grabbed a can, paused and grabbed a second. "Wasn't like the kid was doing anything."

"Do it," she said as soon as Wayne shuffled back.

Mike tried to keep his enthusiasm at a minimum so he didn't scare her off. "You sure?"

"I'm sure," she said, eyes finding Steffi. "I want to speed this case along."

"Great. I'll start drafting a plan right way. Find a marketing consultant who will be able to help us out." He worked with a good one back at Ashby Gannon. Expensive but good.

Roxanne continued to look off in Steffi's direction. Her hands twisted in the hem of her T-shirt, rolling and unrolling the material. "Hey," he said, catching hold of one. "You made the right call."

The doubt in her eyes as she looked at him stung. "I won't let anything go wrong. I promise."

It frightened him how much he meant his words.

CHAPTER SIX

"Shoot, shoot, shoot."

"Mommy you're saying bad words."

"I know, baby. I'm sorry. Mom's just really late for an appointment." Really, really late.

It was Saturday morning. Last night Mike showed up at the lounge requesting—make that insisting—she show up to his office this morning. Why he couldn't make the request over the phone she didn't know; he seemed to have this thing for coming by her workplace.

For that matter, she didn't know why she had to show up on a Saturday morning. "We need to get you ready for next week's interview," he'd said. Roxy kinda thought she was ready. They'd spent the whole week working with some fancy consultant he knew who liked picking apart how she pronounced words. "Going with a g, not an a, Miss O'Brien. And don't slouch." If it weren't for Mike and his soothing "You're doing great, Roxanne," she'd have walked out.

Doubt there'd be too much praise being tossed around this morning. She was over a half hour late. Nothing had gone right. First she woke to find Wayne and some complete stranger sleeping the night off in her living room. Then Mrs. Ortega called to say she couldn't babysit forcing her to drag Steffi along. Finally, to top it all off, she missed her scheduled bus meaning she had to hike half a block to the subway station. One more lousy piece of luck and she'd lose it.

"I know, I know, I'm late," she said in a rush when she finally found her way into Mike's office. "This morning has been absolutely—"

The most stunning-looking woman Roxy had ever seen sat on the edge of Mike's desk, Jimmy Choo dangling from her toe. She had blond glossy hair that she wore clipped at the base of her neck and the type of lips women spent thousands of dollars in collagen to achieve. Only hers looked natural. She wore a duster-style sweater and camel hair slacks. Another consultant?

If so, she looked mighty at home around Mike.

Roxy shifted Steffi, who she'd scooped up upon leaving the elevator, from one hip to the other. Mike could have at least warned her there'd be someone joining them so she could have worn something a little better than jeans and a turtleneck.

"Finally!" Mike said. "I was concerned something had happened."

His attention went to Steffi. "Or maybe something did. Hello, Steffi."

Steffi stared.

"Babysitting issues," Roxy explained. "Mrs. Ortega canceled. I didn't have anyone else to watch her."

"No worries. Happens to the best of us," the blonde remarked.

Mike gave the woman a look. "Since when did you grow tolerant of child care issues?"

"Since I became a parent."

"You're not a parent. You're a dog owner," Mike replied.

"She's still a responsibility."

"One you can carry in your purse."

The banter was nauseatingly good-humored. If the woman was another consultant, she was one Mike obviously knew very well. It dawned on Roxy that the blonde was exactly the kind of woman she pictured with Mike, too.

She moved with the same kind of fluid grace, rising to her feet and extending a perfectly manicured hand. "Mike's apparently too busy hassling me about my dog to be polite. I'm Sophie Messina," she said. "It's nice to meet you, Roxanne."

"Sophie is here to help you get ready for your public debut," Mike explained.

Get ready, how? She'd already worked with the media guy. Her skepticism started to kick in. Calling upon what few acting skills she had, Roxy pretended a smile. "Really?"

"Don't worry, I won't push you to do anything drastic," the blonde—Sophie—replied. "Alfredo is going to love your hair by the way."

Roxy narrowed her eyes. "Who's Alfredo?"

"You don't know?" Wearing a frown, Sophie spun around to face Mike. "You did tell her what we were doing today, didn't you?"

"I planned to explain once we were all together."

"Explain once—? You're kidding me."

"Explain what?" Roxy looked at the two of them.

Oh, my God. Smooth out the rough edges. That's what he wrote while in the bar that first night. Part of the overall plan, he'd said. He'd share when he was ready.

He'd been talking about *her* rough edges. "This is a makeover?" she asked them.

Why didn't he come right out and say she wasn't suitable for talking to the press? Too "rough" as it were.

"You son of a—" She caught herself before Steffi heard the next word.

"Roxanne, wait."

"For what? For you to insult me more?"

Forget it.

"What do you mean, insult?"

"When you said this was to prepare for next week's interview, I thought you meant working on my interview skills. Not my appearance."

"I told you you should have said something beforehand," Sophie said, leaning against the desk. "If it were me, I'd be mad, too."

"No one asked your opinion, Sophie," Mike snapped.

"Maybe you should because she's right. What's wrong with the way I look? I've been looking this way for thirty years and it's worked for me just fine."

In the back of her mind, she feared her reaction was over the top as usual. But, dammit, he hurt her feelings. How dare he get his blonde friend to clean her up. She'd thought…

Thought he might think she measured up.

"You misunderstand what I'm trying to do," he said.

"Do I? Because the term makeover sounds pretty clear-cut."

Letting out a long breath, Mike jammed his fingers through his hair. In spite of it being Saturday, he wore a tweed jacket over his lamb's wool sweater. More proof of her inadequacy, Roxy supposed, that she underdressed for a weekend meeting. "Sophie, would you mind taking Steffi to the big conference room and showing her the TV set? I need to talk with Roxanne alone."

To her credit, the blonde silently asked permission before moving. Nodding, Roxy set her daughter on the floor and nudged her toward the door. "It's okay, Steffi. I'll be there in a minute."

"I thought you understood how important it is to put your best foot forward when speaking to the press," Mike said after the door shut.

"Oh, I understand." All too well. "Apparently you don't consider my foot good enough."

"Not true. Your foot is fine."

"Just not good enough to show the world."

"Oh, come on, Roxy, use your head. This isn't about whether or not you look good. It's about selling you as Wentworth Sinclair's daughter. You're an actress. Think of this as playing a role. Roxanne O'Brien, heiress."

"I am Roxanne O'Brien, heiress."

"The public will expect you to look different."

"You mean better." Not like Roxanne O'Brien, cocktail waitress. When was plain old Roxy going to be good enough?

"I mean different," Mike repeated. He stepped forward closing the difference between them until it was no more than a few inches. "They are two vastly difference things, and you know it."

Unfortunately the man had a point. To win over the folks uptown, she had to look like she belonged.

"You still should have told me. You know I don't like secrets."

"I know, but if I told you I risked you not showing up.

"Or having a drink dumped in my lap," he added, offering a slow, charm-laden smile. Roxy decided he was taking up far too much of her personal space than normal. The edge of his tweed blazer abutted her rib cage. Every breath he took caused the wool to gently caress her sweater.

"What about your friend?" she asked. "She doesn't mind doing this?"

"Who, Sophie? Are you kidding? I only had to promise my firstborn. Seriously..." He raised a hand when she opened her mouth to say something. "After she was done lecturing me for blowing her and my brother off for dinner this weekend, she jumped right aboard."

His brother. To her surprise, relief circulated through her.

"So," Mike was saying. Was it her imagination or had he moved another step closer? "Are you on board?"

"What about Steffi? I can't very well take her with me, can I?"

"Now that you say it that might be a problem. I hadn't counted on her showing up."

"I don't suppose—" Roxy shook her head. The idea was ludicrous.

"What?" Mike pressed.

"Well, I was wondering if you'd be, well, if you'd watch Steffi. But then I realized what a bad idea that was."

"It's not bad at all," he replied. "I wasn't going to go on this excursion of yours anyway."

"You weren't?"

"Get in the way of two women and shopping? I'm not sure it's worth the risk. I'd be glad to watch Steffi."

"You?" Him? The two barely spoke to one another. What would they do, spend the afternoon staring at each other? She chewed her lower lip.

"I'm not sure."

"Trust me," Mike said, his voice transforming soft and silky.

Maybe now would be a good idea to remind him about her theory on promises and the men who made and broke them. Or rather it might have been if Mike hadn't moved close enough she could feel his breath on her neck. "Have I lied to you yet?" he asked.

"I—" Roxy had to think. No, he hadn't. There had been misunderstandings and some poor behavior but he never lied. "You promise to help me keep on top of information," she said. "Good, bad or otherwise. Deal?"

The smile gracing his features was so slow and sexy her knees practically buckled. "Everything," Mike reassured her, and darn if his face wasn't so sincere her stomach tumbled a little. To save herself, she stepped backward.

"All right," she said, "let's get this makeup party started."

"Believe me, I had no idea Mike planned to spring today on you like this," Sophie said a short while later. "I thought for sure he'd explain himself. I swear sometimes he's worse than his brother. Grant lives to keep me off balance."

Roxy listened, but didn't answer. She still wasn't happy about this whole makeover project, even if she could see Mike's point. Partly out of anger, partly because she had no idea what the end product would look like.

"I have to admit, though," the blond woman continued, "it was fun watching you give him the what-for."

She held a silver-and-white jacket next to Roxy's face, then shook her head. "You ask me, he needs someone to do that more often. Might loosen him up a little—the man makes me look low-key." A stretch since the woman had already checked her email a dozen times since leaving the office. "Lord knows Grant's been trying to get him to loosen that tie of his for a while."

"I like how formal he looks," Roxy replied.

"No wonder he likes you."

Roxy hated how her stomach somersaulted at Sophie's comment. Same way she hated trying not to relive the moment in his office or any of the other times he'd come close to touching her. Reminding herself theirs was a temporary relationship helped. "Winning this case seems to be important to him."

"Winning, huh?" A pair of skeptical blue eyes stared at her from over the clothes rack. "That why he practically leaped over his desk when you walked in the door? And offered to watch your daughter while we shopped?"

Another flutter found its way to Roxy's stomach. "He probably figured we'd get more done without having to entertain a four-year-old."

"If you say so."

Roxy said so. For once she planned to use her head rather than blindly acting out. She shook her head at the cashmere blazer Sophie had held up. "Too high a cost."

"Sometimes you need to break out of your comfort mold," Sophie replied. "Grant taught me that. In this case, you might find this to be a good investment."

They were talking about the jacket, right?

"I have to admit," Sophie continued. "I've never seen Mike so invested in a case before. Or maybe it seems that way because we haven't seen him much. He's too busy building his super firm."

"Super firm?" Roxy had to ask.

"It's what we prefer to call it because he's always out drumming up business. Grant figures he's on a quest to create the biggest, bestest law firm in the city. That would certainly make my future in-laws happy."

Least you have a choice. "Mike mentioned being from a family of high achievers."

"You can say that again." Turning around from the rack to the shelves behind her, Sophie began looking through a collection of turtleneck sweaters. "Normally I would agree with the philosophy."

"But?" Roxy heard the unspoken word quite clearly.

The blonde shrugged. "Something about the Templetons.

They demand a lot of their kids, even as adults. But what do I know? My parents didn't demand a damn thing from me."

"Me, neither."

"I knew I liked you for some reason," Sophie said with a grin.

As Roxy fingered the leather piping that trimmed a red blazer, a sadness settled over her. *Least you had the choice.* Mike's remark kept coming back to her. Was this the nerve she kept hitting with her questions about his family? The one that made him fold into himself whenever the topic came up?

"Funny," Sophie said. "I expected more clutter."

"Where?" Her remark brought Roxy back to the present.

"At Mike's firm. Today was the first time I visited. I was surprised how little clutter there was. My firm went paperless a while back, and we're still buried in the stuff."

"You're surprised Mike is neat?" Picturing her formal-looking attorney, she couldn't imagine anything about him being cluttered.

"Mike, no. The rest of the staff, yes, I mean, I know it's a co-op office space and they share resources, but he must have at least one paralegal or secretary. I can't believe he managed to find one as neat as he is."

She touched Roxy's shoulder. "Ready to try a few outfits on? I can't wait to see how the wrap dress fits. I have a feeling Mike's eyes will bug out of his head when he sees you in it."

Roxy looked to the ground. The remark was meant to be a compliment. Too bad she didn't feel flattered. It only reminded her she was here because Mike thought she needed "smoothing."

"I thought the point was to impress the Sinclairs," she said.

"It is," Sophie replied. "But would it hurt to impress your lawyer, too?"

"No." She only wished she'd been impressive enough from the start.

My Dearest Fiona:
I miss you, too. When you're not with me, it feels as though the life has been sucked right out of the room. You're my sunshine, my light. Outside my window, I can see the last few leaves of fall. A living O. Henry painting. Their color is nothing compared to yours. Because without you the world feels dead. When I get home, I'm going to take you in my arms and...

Nice dream, pal. Mike set Wentworth's letter down. It was the next to last one in the pile. Twenty-eight letters in looking for information that might prove Wentworth and Fiona fathered a child and he hadn't unearthed a thing. Nothing but a rapidly growing unsettled feeling. Almost like a yearning. And memories of his own college affair. One semester. He'd crammed a lifetime in, though, hadn't he? Enough, he'd assumed, to last.

Odd thing was, it wasn't those days or even those people he missed. Grace, for all the feelings she evoked in him, wasn't what had him feeling empty. It was more. A large, indefinable emotion that he couldn't escape. Same way he couldn't shake how whenever he thought of those days now, Grace's fuzzy dark-haired image morphed into a less fuzzy, decided red-haired one.

"You tap your pen a lot."

At the far end of the conference table, Steffi sat munching on carrot slices. She was staring at him with those big eyes of hers.

"Nervous habit," he answered.

"Why are you nervous?"

"I'm wondering why your mom and Sophie aren't back yet, is all." The pair had been gone for almost four hours. What was taking so long? Making matters worse, Sophie refused to answer his last two texts. "You'll have to wait and see" she'd written before signing off.

"Are they lost?" Steffi's eyes got wide and her lower lip started to jut out.

Great. He didn't mean to make the girl worry. "No, no, nothing like that. When I say nervous I mean eager."

"What's eager?"

You dug yourself into a hole on that one. Mike set down his pen. "Eager is a good thing. It means I'm looking forward to seeing your mother again."

"Because you miss her?"

Talk about a loaded question. "Because she was going shopping, and I want to see what she bought."

He was beginning to wonder if asking Sophie to help had been a good idea. Along with having expensive tastes, his brother's girlfriend was used to talking charge. Combine her control freakiness with Roxanne's quick temper and you were talking incendiary. Visions of two strong-willed women coming to verbal blows popped into his head. Wouldn't that be an excellent headline? Would-Be Heiress Throws Left Hook in Salon.

If he wanted to be brutally honest with himself, the more pressing reason he wanted to talk with Roxanne was to make sure she'd truly forgiven him. It wasn't as if he truly meant to keep his plans a secret. He'd merely been concerned how she would react to his suggestion. He figured if he waited till the last minute, the process would go smoother. A bad plan, as it turned out.

Then again, when it came to Roxy, he seemed to travel down Bad Plan road a lot. If he was going to make this so-called media tour work, he needed to remember to keep his priorities straight.

"I miss Mommy," Steffi said as she stuffed a carrot slice in her mouth. "I don't like it when I have babysitters."

"You don't like the lady who watches you?"

He'd just gotten burned by a four-year-old. "Mrs. Ortega smells like cold medicine."

Lucky Mrs. Ortega. Wonder what the girl thought of him.

"I'm sure your mom will be back soon. I know she doesn't like to leave you with babysitters longer than she has to." He got a warm feeling thinking about Roxy's dedication. One of many things he was starting to appreciate. Along with her green eyes and shapely behind and the vulnerability that never seemed far from her surface.

"You like Mommy?"

Steffi's question startled him. How'd the little dickens manage to read his thoughts?

His answer, he realized, had to be well thought out. He didn't want to give the girl the wrong impression. Finally he decided on the very benign. "Your mother is a very nice woman."

"Wayne says she's stuck up."

Wayne was a jerk. He could tell from their first meeting. "Do you think Mommy's stuck up?"

"What?" If he'd been drinking he'd have choked. "No. I don't think she's stuck up at all."

"'Cause you like her?"

Mike sighed. Like Roxanne? Hell, yeah, he liked her. Way too much. "It's complicated," he told the little girl.

Wrong answer.

"What's complicated?" she immediately asked.

"Complicated means hard." For crying out loud, how many more questions was this little girl going to ask? She was worse than opposing counsel. "Do you need more juice?"

She didn't fall for his diversion attempt. "Why is it hard?"

Because she's my client. Because there are rules and ethical considerations. Because she wasn't part of the plan. He had a whole list of reasons, none of which would make sense to a girl her age. Hell, at the moment none of them made sense to him. "Your mommy and I are friends," he told her.

"Oh." Whether she found the answer satisfying or disappointing, Mike couldn't tell. Her attention had returned to the plastic bag of carrots and the hair tumbling in front of her face that rendered her expression invisible. He should be relieved she was no longer asking difficult questions, only he wasn't. He felt bad she'd grown so quiet.

Looking up, he swore the second hand had gone backward. In a few minutes, she would be done with her snack and then what? More television? There wasn't anything on to interest her. He knew because she'd already made that pronouncement before getting out her snack. Too bad she couldn't read well yet. He'd teach her to file.

A spotted white-and-purple pony caught his eye, giving him an idea. *Thank you, Dusty.*

"Did you know there's a merry-go-round carousel a few blocks from here?"

Steffi's jaw dropped midchew. She was staring again. "You interested in going?" he asked.

A spark of excitement lit up her face, but she still didn't answer. At some point Roxy probably told her to never go anywhere without Roxy's permission and he could see that her four-year-old brain was trying to determine a loophole. Her pensive expression looked so much like her mother's he felt a tug in his chest.

Things were definitely becoming complicated if a child's expression could affect him.

Before a decision could be made, they heard the sound of female laughter coming from the hallway.

"Mommy's back!" Steffi jumped from her seat and ran toward the door. Mike followed behind. At this point, he wasn't sure who was happier to see them return. That is, he was eager to see how his investment paid off.

The main office door opened and wow! Mike had to grab hold of the reception desk to keep his balance. The woman walking through the door with Sophie was… Was…

He'd lost his ability to speak. It was as if Alfredo and Sophie had conspired to take Roxy's natural beauty and softness and shove them under a magnifying glass. Her red mane had been tamed into thick, strawberry-blond locks that tumbled about her shoulders. The skinny jeans and sweater were gone, too. Tossed in favor of a black-and-white wraparound dress and cardigan sweater that subtly showed off her curves. The hint of flesh dipping to a V between her breasts was as enticing as any low-cut camisole. And her legs… Discreetly he stole a look at her bottom half.

"You look different, Mommy," Steffi said.

"Think so?" Roxy asked.

"Uh-huh. Your hair is straight."

Her eyes found his, looking for his reaction. Had her skin always looked this luminescent or was it the expertly applied makeup? "You look amazing," he replied.

"Then I guess the transformation is complete."

A shadow flickered across her face, and had he been less distracted, he might have questioned what it meant. As it was, though, he was too busy absorbing the change.

Other than the straight hair and different clothes, she

didn't look *drastically* different. Not when he had a chance to study her. It was like everything good and attractive about her appearance had been given a polish. Gone was the fatigue, in favor of brighter cheeks and eyes. She looked…softer, less worn down. The way she was meant to look had life not kicked her around.

"Exactly how an heiress should look," he said softly. How she deserved to look.

Her lashes were thick half-moons as she looked down. "Thank you." There was an odd tone to her voice he couldn't quite place. But then, his listening skills had taken a backseat in favor of other senses.

Somewhere in the background, a throat cleared.

Finding his senses, Mike looked to Sophie who had positioned herself against the coat closet door, arms folded, like a proud artist displaying her work. "Thank you for your help," he said.

"My pleasure. It was fun having someone to shop with for a change. I was right about Alfredo, too. Soon as he saw her hair, he was in heaven. What'd he call you, his 'Strawberry-haired goddess'?"

Roxanne's voice was no more than a notch above a whisper. "Something like that."

"He never gushes over me like that," Sophie said. "He loved her. Absolutely loved her."

Who wouldn't, Mike caught himself thinking.

"More likely he loved the check you wrote at the end of the appointment." With a smile, Roxanne squatted down so she was eye to eye with Steffi. Not for the first time, Mike was impressed by the way she lit up when talking to the little girl. It was obvious to anyone watching Steffi meant everything to her mother.

"We bought you a present, too." She handed the little

girl a pink polka-dotted gift bag, which Steffi immediately dived into.

Her responding squeal could be heard across the street. "It's a pony sweater!" She held up the purple knit top.

"I thought he looked like Dusty. Don't worry, I paid for it myself," she said to Mike. "So it won't get mixed in with your business expenses."

"I wouldn't have minded," he replied, surprised at how much he meant the statement. He watched Steffi struggling to pull the sweater over her head and decided, again to his surprise, that her enthusiasm would have been worth the cost.

"Would you like some help with that?" Sophie asked. "There's a mirror in the ladies' room so you can see what you look like."

"I'll take her," Roxy said.

"No, you stay and finish your conversation with Mike. The two of us will be fine." Sophie rescued both the sweater and the girl and took her by the hand. "So you like horses?" she asked as she led her away.

"Uh-huh." Steffi chattered all the way to the door and into the hall, where the door shut behind her, muffling her running commentary.

"Guess she liked the sweater," Roxy said as she watched her go.

Something was off, Mike realized all of a sudden. A note missing from her voice. A light from her eyes. No sooner did Steffi disappear behind closed doors than the one illuminating her faded. "What is it?" he heard himself ask.

"Nothing important. Did the two of you have a good afternoon?"

He thought about his and Steffi's conversation. "We survived. I learned she doesn't like her babysitters." As he held out a hand and helped her back to her feet, he explained what she had said about Mrs. Ortega.

"Arthritis rub," Roxy replied. "Has a lot of menthol. Makes for a pretty pungent smell."

"Hopefully she doesn't have an equally distasteful description of my aroma."

"Doubt it. You smell pretty good."

Not as good as you, he said to himself. Seduced by the new Roxanne, he leaned farther into her space and breathed deep. Thank God the makeover process hadn't erased the uniqueness of her scent. Underneath the hair spray, he could still detect the faint odor he found intoxicating. Suddenly the office felt very empty. He still had his hand resting beneath her elbow. Quickly he removed it, fingers tensing in revolt. They wanted to stay in contact, tighten their grip even, and pull her closer.

"I can't get over how different you look," he said.

Emotion passed across her face, unreadable and uncertain. "Different good or different bad?"

Her real question was unspoken, but he understood just the same. As if she could ever look bad, he wanted to say. "Different," he said instead, hoping his failure to deliver a solid verdict would make his point. He scanned her face. "I think it's the lack of curls. I miss them."

"You do?" She looked surprised.

"Yeah." There had been an untamed quality to her curls that appealed to him. This look was far more reined in, far more controlled. He caught a strand between his thumb and index finger, the back of his hand brushing her temple as he did so. Her sharp intake of breath was unmistakable. Searching her face, he saw her eyes were shifting from hazel to dark green. That was one thing the makeover could never change. The ever-changing color of her gaze. So damn gorgeous.

"Mommy! Mommy! I love my new sweater!"

At the sound of Steffi's voice, both of them stepped backward, breaking the closeness and the moment. Though, not before Mike swore he saw another shadow crossing Roxanne's face.

The little girl raced up to them, Sophie trailing behind. "Whoa! Slow down so I can see if it fits," Roxanne said. Immediately the four-year-old skidded to a stop, a reverse one-eighty in speed.

"She's very excited," Sophie said, stating the obvious. Watching her rush to regain control was kind of amusing. Sophie was nothing, if not order obsessed.

"Can I wear my sweater when we go to the library?" Steffi asked. Having endured her mother's inspection, she was, at the moment, spinning airplane circles.

"The library?"

Steffi stopped her running. "To see the carousel," Steffi replied. If four-year-olds were capable of verbal eye rolls, Steffi had just accomplished one. She stated the destination as if it was a fact out of *Encyclopedia Britannica* and they were all foolish for forgetting. "Mike said we could go."

"Did he now?"

"You're kidding me," Sophie drawled.

Roxy looked over, the surprise causing the green in her eyes to deepen. Heated discomfort rolled through him. He grabbed hold of the reception desk again, pretending to lean. "I may have mentioned the carousel in Bryant Park. I told her we could take a ride over there," he said to Sophie.

"Can I wear my sweater?" Steffi asked. "Please, please!"

"Wait," Sophie interrupted. "You were going to go ride a merry-go-round? You."

He should have known Sophie would have a comment. "No need to sound so surprised. It's a nice day…the kid's been cooped up in my office. Why not take her for some fresh air?"

"Because you don't…" She waved off the sentence, going for her handbag instead. "I've got to call Grant. He won't believe this."

Triumphantly she brandished her cell phone before casting a smile in Roxanne's direction. "I'd take him up on it. Who knows when he'll make an offer like this again."

Sophie was a fine one to talk. She probably emptied her in-box while waiting at the salon. In reality, he'd forgotten his offer the second Roxanne returned, but now that Steffi reminded him, the afternoon didn't sound all that awful.

From her expression, Roxy didn't share his enthusiasm. "I don't know, baby," she started to say. "It's getting late and—"

"*Pul-leeze.* One ride?"

"I did promise," Mike said, figuring that would push the odds in his favor.

He figured right. The woman was a pushover in terms of her daughter. "All right," she said, adding a sigh to show she wasn't completely one hundred percent on board. "We'll go. But only one ride. Then we head home."

"Yay!" Steffi clasped her hands.

From his spot near the reception desk, Mike smiled at the mother and daughter team. He wasn't sure if he'd stepped back on Bad Idea road or not, but watching the two of them smiling, he couldn't help feeling like he'd just had a major win.

Now if he could only figure out what the shadow that kept showing up on Roxanne's face meant.

CHAPTER SEVEN

"Merry-go-round, merry-go-round."

Steffi singsonged the words under her breath as they waited in line at the ticket stand. Her body bounced with excitement.

Roxy was happy for her. She loved watching her daughter having a good time. She just couldn't believe it was at Mike Templeton's suggestion.

"You really planned to take her here on your own?"

Maybe it was the unseasonably warm weather but the park was crowded with families, in spite it being off-season. Some waited in line to ride the custom-made carousel while more milled around a makeshift stage waiting for the next public event. A sign told people Frogiere the French Frog would be arriving in an hour. Several children carried picture books bearing the same name.

"I admit, I wasn't expecting the park to be this crowded," he replied. "It's a good thing you arrived when you did to save us."

Roxy pretended not to catch his grin. She was still annoyed with him over the whole makeover business. Although taking Steffi to a carousel did thaw her a little.

A hand brushed the back of her legs. Looking over her shoulder, she saw a boy a couple years younger than Steffi weaving his way around his mother's legs letting his fingers drift across everything within reach.

The woman immediately apologized. Roxy saw she was wearing a sweater similar to Sophie's, and sported a loudly large diamond. A second child, a little girl, held her right hand and stole looks at Steffi. Both children looked impeccable.

Self-consciousness washed over her from head to toe. "It's all right," she said. "No harm done."

"That's because we washed off the ice cream before getting in line," the woman said smiling. "This is your daughter's first time on the carousel?"

"Yes, it is."

"Jacob's, too. Though, I try to take Samantha once a month when the weather is decent."

The two women began chatting about entertaining children during the winter. Maybe it was her imagination, but Roxy had to ask herself whether the woman would have chatted with her had she been wearing her old clothes. Possibly not. Certainly felt to her she'd been treated differently since the makeover. People who would never speak to her or show her the slightest bit of deference seemed to be extra friendly all of a sudden.

She wished she knew how she felt about the whole thing.

On one hand, when she first looked in the mirror after Alfredo worked his magic, as he put it, she'd loved what she saw. The woman in the reflection looked sleek and sophisticated. A second later, she grew upset with herself. Wasn't approving of her new look a betrayal? A passive agreement that Mike had been right—she needed smoothing out?

Then there was Mike himself. She definitely didn't imagine his expression when she returned to his office. He hadn't been able to take his eyes off her. And when his hand brushed her skin… Even the memory caused excitement and she absentmindedly pressed a fist to her stomach to prevent the emotion from taking hold. Disappointment quickly followed in its tracks anyway. Because Mike's attraction was for the made-over Roxy. It wasn't any more real or substantive than the makeup and clothes.

What killed her the most was how happy she'd been at his reaction, no matter what the reason. She was becoming way too attached to the man's approval for her own good.

"You're so lucky your husband is willing to go with you. Mine is busy with paperwork."

Roxy whipped her head toward Mike. "Oh, he's not—"

"Making this a regular visit?" Mike answered. "You're right. Did you see those ticket prices? Highway robbery."

"The things we do for our kids, huh?" the woman remarked.

He was reaching into his back pocket for his wallet, but his attention had dropped to the bouncing Steffi. "You can say that again."

He couldn't say it once. Steffi wasn't his kid. "Why did you let that woman think we were married?" Roxy asked once they'd moved from the ticket line to the carousel line.

"Why not? Easier than launching into a long explanation about our relationship."

That was just it. They didn't have a relationship beyond lawyer and client. His pretending otherwise was just another layer of fantasy on a day thick with it.

Though smaller than the one in Central Park, the Bryant Park carousel was bright and cheery with beautiful hand-carved animals. Roxy spotted not only horses but a tiger and a whimsical white rabbit. The sounds of foreign music could be barely made out over the noise of kids and conversation. A sign on the fence said that the song was in French, and that the carousel was based on one in France.

Roxy looked around the crowd. Her ticket line acquaintance with her two children were a few people back. She pushed an empty double stroller while her kids were creeping along the barrier fence, something Steffi and half the other kids were doing as well. The mother saw her and offered a commiserating shrug. In front of her, there was a pair of teenage mothers dressed decidedly non-motherly with their children balanced on their hips. Roxy smiled hello, but got nothing but cold blank stares in return.

A few yards from the gate, Steffi squealed in excitement. "Look! It's Dusty!"

Not quite, but there was a brilliant white horse with gold and red trim. "I want to ride him!"

"You'll have to wait and see, baby. There are other kids in line, too. Someone else might get on him first."

As she pretty much expected, her warning fell on deaf ears. Steffi was too busy showing Dusty his "twin." "Dusty wants to ride him, too." She grinned and held the pony over her head for a better look.

Their turn came and the crowd filed onto the wooden platform, where the other kids immediately started running to snag their favorite animal. Steffi was no different. She took off like a shot for her treasured white stallion only to be beat out by a boy in a green puffy coat.

Instantly her daughter's lower lip jutted out. "Sorry, baby. Let's see if there's another horse." Though she would certainly live with the disappointment, Roxy knew Steffi would be let down if she had to ride a different animal or, heaven forbid, one of the sleighs with bench seats. Unfortunately, as they made their way around the circle, it looked more and more like that would be the case.

Nice to see the new look hadn't changed everything.

"Look!" Steffi pulled at her arm, practically removing it from its socket as they rounded the first turn. Soon enough Roxy saw why, and when she did, her chest grew too full for her body. There stood Mike in all his tweeded splendor, leaning against a second white pony. "I saw there was a mate, and figured while you tried to snag the first one, I'd lock in a backup."

It was stupid, but Roxy wanted to throw her arms around him. "Will this pony work?" she asked Steffi.

The little girl nodded, and Roxy moved to lift her up. "You have to hold on with both hands," she said. "Dusty will have to ride with us, okay?" She put her hand out ready to collect the precious plastic horse.

That's when it happened.

The little girl turned to Mike and held out the toy. The lawyer looked like he'd been struck. He stared at the toy for a couple seconds before gently wrapping his long fingers around its plastic middle. "I'll let him ride with me, okay?"

Her daughter nodded.

The fullness in Roxy's chest tripled. Such a simple exchange, and it made her heart ache. The merry-go-round resumed with a jerk, the calliope playing loudly in the center. She barely heard. Nor did she notice the noise and families crowding around her. All her attention was focused on the man and little girl in her orbit. Standing on this wooden platform, she found herself wishing the fantasy could continue. That Saturday afternoons in the park with carousels and giant story-reading frogs was the norm. Not barroom drunks or Wayne passed out in her living room.

Of course, Mike would tell her that once the Sinclairs recognized her existence, this could be her regular life. She could spoil Steffi rotten with merry-go-rounds and ponies and all the giant frogs she wanted.

Only one problem. She wasn't sure that even then the fantasy would be complete. She had a very bad feeling it could never be complete without a certain tweed-wearing ingredient. But he'll have moved on. To the next case, the next challenge. Why wouldn't he? Underneath it all, she'd still be the same old Roxy. He thought her lacking before; eventually the gloss would wear off and he'd find her lacking again.

When the ride was over and Frogiere had made his appearance, they headed to a small café at the rear of the library. Roxy gazed out over the space and the people milling about. "Twenty-nine years living in New York, and not once have I been in this park. Closest I ever came was walking past it on my way to an audition."

"Don't feel bad. It's my first time, too. Too much else going on during the weekends," he added.

Horseback riding, swimming and all those other accomplishments. How could she forget?

"Though now that I think about it," he said, frowning, "the carousel might not have been here when I was really little. I don't remember. I'll have to ask Grant."

"Oh, that reminds me. Sophie said to tell you this is the last time you're allowed to cancel plans."

After checking over at Steffi, who was engrossed in playing with Dusty, Roxy continued, "She's nice. I feel bad for acting like such a brat in front of her." Rightful reason or not, she had to rein in her reactions.

"I wouldn't worry too much. From the tirade I received from her, she considers everything my fault anyway. She doesn't mince words, that's for certain. Probably why Grant likes her so much."

Which reminded her of another comment she was supposed to pass on. "She also thinks the reason you're avoiding the two of them so much is that you feel like the odd man out."

Mike flipped over his menu. "When did she say that to you?"

"At the salon."

"Well, she's being ridiculous."

"Was she?" Then why was he hiding behind his menu while answering? And he was hiding because he wasn't wearing his glasses and therefore couldn't read the type.

"I couldn't be happier for her and Grant. She's good for him. Really good."

"Then why do you keep canceling?"

"I've been busy," he replied, flipping the two-page menu back to its top page. "I've got a law firm to attend to."

The megafirm Grant thought he was trying to build up. The one without clutter, as Sophie put it. Then again, who was she to judge what an office was supposed to look like? "Are you glad you opened your own practice?"

He set the menu down. "What makes you ask?" His tone was harsher than she expected. Way more than the question warranted.

"No real reason. I've been thinking about choices lately is all. The ones my mother made, the ones I made, and wondered, seeing all the time you have to work at it, if you're sorry you didn't stay at your old firm." She wondered even more now, following his reaction.

Mike sipped his water. He retrieved a fork Steffi dropped on the ground. He placed their orders with the waitress. The one thing he didn't do was give her an answer. When the waitress was gone and he leaned forward in his chair, Roxy thought he might but he asked, "Do you regret quitting acting?"

Was this answering a question with a question some kind of tactic or simply changing the topic?

"Wasn't like I had much to give up." One of them should

answer. "Kind of like asking a punching bag if he misses getting hit."

"Couldn't have been so bad."

"I once got told I was too stiff to point at tile samples in a cable access commercial. Trust me, when I say I was terrible, I was terrible."

"Then why…?"

"Did I try?" She shrugged. "I loved pretending to be someone else." Sort of what you're doing now, a voice in her head said. Ignoring it, she reached over and brushed the curls from Steffi's eyes. "I like to think I ended up with the better end of the bargain, although sometimes I wonder if the next audition would have been *the* audition. The one that pushed me into the big-time. It would have been awesome seeing my name in lights."

Their conversation was interrupted by the waitress bringing their order and Steffi expressing wonder at the slab of chocolate cake put in front of her. Roxy immediately earned a brief pout by cutting the piece into two uneven pieces.

"Success isn't all it's cracked up to be," Mike said once the waitress was out of earshot. "It comes with responsibility." His eyes faded a million miles away. "You're expected to always measure up, be an example to others." His finger traced the rim of his glasses. Sad, deliberate circles. "It's not as easy as it looks."

"You've done all right so far."

So far. His tone was hollow. Was he trying to tell her that while not knowing failure, Mike's life had had costs? What kind? she wondered. How deep did the marks go?

"Do you have regrets?"

He didn't answer right away, automatically giving her what she wanted to know. "Regret implies having a choice."

A cop-out answer. Well acquainted with them she recognized the dodge immediately. Never dodge a dodger. There was regret, the evidence lay in the nerve she so consistently pushed whenever she mentioned his family.

She decided to take a chance and push for more. "Who was she?"

"Who?"

"Your regret. I'm guessing it's either a person or a career choice, and since you said you always wanted to be a lawyer..."

Actually if she remembered, he said he couldn't remember a time when he wasn't planning to be a lawyer, but wording wasn't important. Her shot in the dark worked. "Neither," he replied. "Or maybe the answer would be both."

He carved off a piece of apple tart. "Spring of my junior year my adviser told me I was short humanities credits. The number fell through the cracks while I was trying to get in all my major coursework. Anyway, since it was late in the registration process, the only class I could fit in my schedule was philosophy. I had to spend twelve weeks arguing the meaning of life and existentialism."

"Somehow I have trouble picturing you." Steffi carved a bite off her cake and waited for more. Was his regret that he had to take the class?

Apparently not. "Best semester of my life," he told her. "Our study group used to meet Thursday nights at this dive of a bar on the edge of campus where we'd go for hours, and on weekends we'd crash at one of the member's off campus apartment. Grace Reynolds was her name."

Hearing the wistfulness in his voice, Roxy felt a pang of jealousy. Clearly Grace was the female part of the regret.

"We were going to spend the summer backpacking

around Europe—our grand scheme to study political cultures up close. You wouldn't have recognized me."

Based on the man he just described, Roxy agreed. The life was so far removed from the starched, formal man she'd come to know. "What happened?"

"My parents arrived with word I'd gotten an internship at Ashby Gannon. Backpacking or career." He shrugged and reached for a sugar packet. "I chose career."

But had he wanted to? He was trying to act as if the answer was a given, but she wasn't so sure. "What happened with Grace?" Of all the questions she had, the aftermath of his love affair came out first. She needed to know.

"Pretty much what you'd expect. She went backpacking—I went to work. When I returned to school in the fall she was living with someone else. I was studying for the LSATs. We both moved on with our lives."

But the price had been paid, hadn't it? No wonder she'd felt such a connection that day in his office. She was sensing the loneliness he kept so very carefully hidden. Her chest once again squeezed with emotion. Its force scared the hell out of her and called her closer at the same time.

Ever since she'd hired Mike Templeton, she'd sworn she'd use her head instead of her heart. Heaven help her, doing so just got a lot harder.

It was three hours later when the taxicab pulled in front of her building, and Mike climbed out with a sleepy Steffi propped against his shoulder.

After Bryant Park, they'd gone back to Mike's office where Roxy practiced interview questions.

"You didn't have to ride all the way here with us," she told him when they reached her front door. She would have been content with saying goodbye at the office, but Mike insisted.

"Didn't feel right. You had your hands pretty full." He tipped his head toward the packages draped over his wrist along with Steffi, whose legs were wrapped tightly around his chest.

"But now my hands are empty."

"Good. Then you can fish your key out faster. This little pony is getting heavy."

"I'm not a pony, I'm a girl," Steffi muttered.

A tired girl at that. Fresh air and excitement had worn her out. She would be asleep before her head hit the pillow.

Roxy unlocked the door and pushed open the glass with her foot. The greeting smell of greasy food told her she was back in her world. "I'll take her from here," she told Mike.

"I don't mind carrying her upstairs."

"I know, but your cab's waiting, and if you don't get back, the driver's likely to leave. I don't want you stuck standing on the street corner."

She reached out and lifted Steffi from his arms. The little girl's body was warm with his body heat. Roxy shivered a little at the sudden onslaught.

"Thanks again for the merry-go-round. Steffi had a fantastic time."

He leaned in, his breath cool and welcome against her cheek. "How about her mother? Did she enjoy herself?"

Roxy smiled. "Yeah, she did."

"Good. Especially since it appears I hurt her feelings this morning."

"Let's forget this morning happened." She didn't want to think about shortcomings, or makeovers or what any of it meant. Not after such a wonderful afternoon. She wanted to keep the fantasy going a little longer.

"Consider it forgotten." He stayed in her space, eyes veiled and searching. Dark half-moons marked his cheeks, shadows caused by the security light shining down on his lashes. Roxy watched as his tongue wet his lower lip, leaving a trail of shine. Those same lips opened as though to speak, and for a moment, her heart stopped, thinking it might not be conversation he wanted.

"See you Monday," he whispered. He meant for her interview, but with his breath on her skin and his hand squeezing hers, the words sounded like a promise of more.

"Monday," she repeated.

She watched him wait by the taxi door while she waited for the elevator, indulging in the contentment his concern created.

"Look at you," Alexis said when she and Steffi walked through the door.

Her roommate sat on the couch watching television, wedged between Wayne, of course, and some large Irish-looking guy she didn't recognize. Both men followed her directions with slow, leering looks that turned Roxy's stomach.

"Whatcha do?" her roomate asked. "Rob a store on Fifth Avenue?"

"Yeah. I thought you said you didn't get any money yet," Wayne added.

"It's part of Mike's strategy. For when I talk to the press. He wanted me to look more like an 'heiress.'"

"He bought you all this?" Alexis had wriggled her way out of the space and made her way to the shopping bags Roxy set down on the chair. "There's a ton of clothes in here. I can't even afford to walk by this store. Wish I had me a lawyer."

"Only way you're getting a lawyer is if that fat butt of yours gets arrested," Wayne shot at her. He cocked another leering smile in Roxy's direction. "So what you have to do to pay him back?"

"Nothing. It's a business expense."

He raised a beer can to his lips. "Uh-huh."

"Mike likes Mommy," Steffi chose that moment to volunteer.

"I bet he does, kid," Wayne replied, elbowing his friend. They both snickered.

Roxy wasn't in the mood. Because she'd spent the day with a gentleman, Wayne's antics were more repulsive to her than ever. Just the sound of his voice made her skin crawl.

She also needed to correct her daughter before impressions got out of hand. "Mike and I are working together, baby. Remember all the practicing we did back in his office?"

Again, Wayne and his friend sniggered.

"For when Mommy has her big meeting Monday," she finished pointedly. All these comments were turning what had been a wonderful day into something cheap and dirty sounding.

"What big meeting?" Alexis asked. She was holding a pale blue turtleneck to her chest, as if she had a hope of fitting her frame into it.

"Mike has a friend who writes for the *Daily Press*. She's going to write a story about me."

"That mean you're getting your money soon?"

"I don't know," Roxy replied. Her roommate didn't need to know the interview was supposed to speed up the process.

"I hope it's soon." Setting the turtleneck down, Alexis began rummaging through another bag. "I'm sick of this dump. Hey, next time you go shopping, you got to take me with you. I want to see if they got anything I would wear."

Roxy's insides stilled. It never dawned on her Alexis planned on moving *with* her. They'd never once discussed plans like that. She'd always assumed the move would be her and Steffi. She never stopped to think Alexis would consider herself part of the plan—or one of the beneficiaries of her inheritance.

"I told you," she said, not sure what else she could say, "the clothes were a business expense. I won't be going back."

"Oh." There was no disguising the disappointment in her roommate's voice.

"Ha, ha," Wayne said. "Looks like you're out of luck, sis."

The stranger on her couch finally spoke. "I didn't come here to sit around all night talking to your snotty roommate. We gonna party or what?"

"Mama, he said—"

Roxy cut her daughter off. "I know, baby. Just ignore him."

"Yeah, kid. Just ignore us," Wayne said. He was already on his feet and stretching, T-shirt rising up to show his scrawny white stomach. "You comin', Alexis?"

"PJ's friend's throwing an afterhours party on his roof. You wanna join us?"

PJ, she assumed, was the stranger, and he looked less than thrilled at the idea. *Don't worry, pal. Even if I didn't have a kid, I wouldn't join you.* She nodded toward Steffi.

"Oh, yeah, right. Forgot," Alexis replied. "Later then."

"Yeah, later."

Wayne's voice sounded from behind her. "You know, I buy my women things, too, if you're interested."

"Not in your dreams." She flinched as his hot breath dampened her skin. Disgust ran down her spine and turned her stomach.

He replied by muttering one of the vilest words she'd ever heard.

And just like that, the fantasy of the day disappeared, and she found herself back in reality.

Mike's cell phone buzzed the second the cab door closed. Grant had been calling him all night. He'd been told about the carousel from Sophie and eager to give him a hard time, no doubt. He'd probably keep calling all night.

He fished the phone from his pocket and immediately his insides knotted when he saw the caller ID. "Hi, Dad," he greeted. "You're back in the country. How was your trip?"

A few months ago, his mother had been bitten by the urge to see France and dragged his father on a bucket list tour of the country. Naturally, being his parents, they couldn't simply play tourist and they ended up investing in a vineyard they discovered in Bordeaux. They recently went back to check on their investment.

"Terrific. Looks like the initial batch will be top-notch. They're talking about possible medals at the upcoming festivals."

Of course they were. His parents wouldn't invest in anything less than a winning project.

"And you should see your mother. While we were over there, she made friends with one of the local shopkeepers. The woman's teaching her French cooking. I swear, she's going to be the Julia Child of pastry before we're finished. She's gotten so good we've had to take up running to keep the extra pounds off."

Again, not a surprise. They'd probably be doing triathlons next. Cosponsored by their vineyard and the bakery his mother would no doubt start.

"How are things going with you?"

The dreaded question. "Terrific." The lie flowed off his tongue so easily no one would ever guess his stomach had knotted a second time. "I took on a new case last week. Very exciting."

"I know." He did? "I ran into Jim Brassard at Troika yesterday afternoon. He told me you're representing some woman who's going after the Sinclairs?"

Roxy was right. The phrase was unattractive. "I didn't know you and Jim were friends."

"The Bar Association's a small world, Michael. You know that. Is it true?"

"I represent a client with a claim to the estate, if that's what you mean," he replied, not liking the way he referred to Roxanne as some woman.

"Isn't that a little out of character? Since when do you take on flashy cases?"

You think this is flashy, wait till the press interviews start hitting. "I've always handled estate cases. Haven't you always said it takes all kinds to build a practice?"

"Within reason. I also taught you to adhere to some standards. Please tell me I don't have to worry about you passing your business card out at accidents."

Because he was raised better. Mike rolled his eyes. "This is a good case. The woman has a viable claim."

"I hope so. Don't let us down, Michael. Remember, your reputation doesn't just reflect on you in the legal community. You bear my name."

And, as his namesake, had an obligation to not only uphold the Templeton tradition but surpass it. Mike heard the lecture his entire life. Bought it his entire life as well. Placed the lessons before everything else.

He let his mind drift back to a few moments earlier and the way Roxy's face had shimmered oh-so-temptingly under the fluorescent light. What would dear old Dad say about reputation if he knew his namesake was fantasizing about a client?

Not wanting to lose the fantasy, he clicked off the phone, figuring he could always blame a dropped call. He really wasn't in the mood to listen to his father's reminders about family obligations right now. They could come back to haunt him another time.

Right now he wanted to think about his client.

CHAPTER EIGHT

"WILL you stop fidgeting?" Mike reached over and took the fork from Roxanne's hand before she could tap it against the tablecloth again. "It makes you look nervous."

"I *am* nervous," she shot back.

"Doesn't mean you have to let the whole restaurant know."

They were seated in the dining room of the Landmark. He'd selected the stately hotel because its old-money feel made for a good backdrop. Not to mention, it kept the reporter from seeing how slow work was back at his office.

"Shouldn't you have learned how to pretend in acting school?" he asked her.

"I was a lousy actress, remember?" She'd moved to fiddling with her napkin, smoothing and resmoothing the cloth across her lap.

"I remember." Sadly he also completely understood the nerves. His own stomach was doing the Mexican hat dance. They both had a lot riding on this interview. Done right, and Julie's column would spawn other articles. TV coverage. Enough notoriety the Sinclairs would have to act. Screw up, and the Sinclairs could write her off as another crackpot looking for fifteen minutes of fame.

Lord, but it had to work. Under the table, he felt his own knee start to jiggle. He squeezed his thigh.

"You'll be fine," he told Roxy. Taking a page from his own advice, he refused to let her see his agitation. "Just don't say things like 'I can't believe they charge seventeen dollars for a fruit plate.'"

"But I can't believe it."

"I know." The price didn't exactly sit well with him, either. He was beginning to worry about how much money the case was costing him. Not that he'd say so to Roxy. After all, like everyone else, she saw him as a big, uptown lawyer.

"How much longer before she gets here?" she asked.

Mike checked his watch. She was five minutes late. "Soon. Any minute probably."

"Great." He felt the floor jiggling. It was her knee bouncing now.

"Relax. You remember all the answers we rehearsed, don't you?"

"I do."

"Then you have nothing to worry about."

"And you're sure I look all right?"

"I promise, you look fine." More than fine, actually. To his immense pleasure, her hair was less straight, the curls framing her face while a clasp held the rest at the base of her neck. She wore a pale blue cashmere turtleneck and camel hair slacks, with a brown suede jacket. Around her neck she wore a strand of pearls. Her mother's. A far cry from the woman who'd walked into his office a few weeks earlier.

He couldn't help himself. He had to reach over and give her fingers a reassuring squeeze, regardless of whether Julie walked in. The smile Roxanne beamed at him made the gesture worth it. "Thank you."

Before the moment could go any further he spotted the reporter approaching the dining room. He slipped his hand from Roxy's, trying not to feel the chill the absence of contact brought, and waved her over. "Ready?" he asked, rising.

"Ready as I'll ever be."

Julie greeted him with a kiss on the cheek, then extended her hand. "Roxanne O'Brien? Julie Kinogawa from the *Daily Press*. Mike tells me you've got an interesting story to share."

Mike sat back and watched as Roxy took over and told her story the way they rehearsed it. Plainly and honestly. When she got to the part about Steffi, she didn't flinch, admitting her mistakes with the same brutal frankness she used when telling him. It wasn't easy for her. And it wasn't easy to hear. When Mike saw the telltell brown that signaled her eyes were about to moisten, he felt that overwhelming urge to stop the interview and take her in his arms. He didn't, but dammit, it took a lot of effort. When she finished, he didn't know if Julie bought a word. But he was charmed out of his ever loving mind.

"Oh, my God! I can't believe I got through that without making a complete fool of myself!" They were in the Landmark Lobby, having said goodbye to Julie a few minutes earlier. Roxy wanted to fly, she was so hyped up. The interview couldn't have gone better. Soon as Julie started asking questions, the answers flowed out of her. It was as though she became the part she was supposed to be playing—Roxanne O'Brien, long-lost heiress. Then again, she was Roxanne O'Brien, long-lost heiress, wasn't she? She wanted to giggle, the thought seemed so fantastic.

"I was afraid I'd break down when I started to talk about Steffi, but I kept it together. I think because Julie seemed so understanding. I think she knew why I wanted to keep my daughter out of the spotlight. Is she a mother? Oh, God, listen to me. I'm talking a mile a minute."

Mike laughed. Lord, but she never noticed how lyrical a laugh he had before. Why hadn't she noticed? "It's nice to see you excited," he said.

"Oh, I'm excited all right." Excited like she'd downed a half dozen energy drinks.

Turning to face him, she walked backward, relying on her energy to guide her through the space. "She seemed really interested in what I had to say, don't you think? I mean, like really, really interested." She paused. "Or am I being naive?"

"Well, it wouldn't be the first time a reporter feigned friendliness, then did a hatchet job," Mike said.

Roxy's insides froze. Crap. That would be so like her luck.

"But—" coppery reassurance lit up his eyes "—I don't think this is the case."

"I hope you're right." His approval shouldn't feel so good, but it did. It washed through her like a wave, leaving behind a radiant glow that made her feel like the most special woman alive. "I was afraid I'd screw it up."

"All you had to do was tell the truth. How could you screw that up?"

"You'd be surprised."

"Well, you better get used to telling it. If all goes according to plan, this time next week, you'll be flooded with interview offers from around the city. The Sinclair sisters won't have a choice but to acknowledge your existence."

Acknowledge her existence. Hearing those three words, the magnitude of what was about to happen hit her full-on. For once, luck was breaking her way. Life was breaking her way.

"Oh, my God! This is really happening, isn't it?" With

a giddy squeal that was worthy of Steffi, she spun around on her toes. Finally her mother's dying words were going to actually have a legacy besides confusion. She was going to become an heiress! "I can't believe it!"

"I hate to say I told you so, but..."

"You can say it all you want." Far as Roxy was concerned, he was the fairy godmother who made this all come true. "If it weren't for your ad in the directory, none of this would be happening."

Aw, hell. She felt way too magnanimous for simple words. She flung her arms around his neck. "Thank you for everything," she murmured against his shoulder.

His jacket smelled like him, the invitingly masculine scent wrapping around her as surely as his arms. She pressed her cheek to his lapel. Not for long. A second or two. Just long enough for the moment for the aroma to reach inside her. When she pulled back, his arms stayed locked, keeping her trapped in his cocoon. The rest of the world faded away. Looking up, all Roxy could see was the burned copper of his gaze and that perfect shaped mouth.

Who leaned in first didn't matter. Their mouths collided, the kiss desperate and long overdue. Roxy tightened her grip. She couldn't get enough. Couldn't get close enough. Her body was pressed to the length of him, and she still wanted closer—wanted more—with an intensity that she knew would scare the hell out of her once the moment ended.

When the kiss did break, they stood foreheads pressed together, breathless. Roxy wondered if the earth had tipped over. She felt off balance, shaken. She had to clutch Mike's forearms to keep from falling over. "I—I—"

"That—" Mike sounded as shaken as her. His hands were wrapped around her arms; the blood pulsing in his fingertips, discernible through her sweater.

"That was—"

"Definitely a mistake."

Mike's words struck her, hard, recalling the intensity she'd found so frightening a few seconds before. A mistake. He was right.

"Yes," she said, stepping backward. "It was." Right? There was no reason for his words to sound so disheartening.

"I'm your lawyer. You're a client. It's wrong."

"Right. I mean, of course."

"I mean, it's unethical. It's a violation of my legal oath."

She moved farther away, to a railing near the marble steps. Gripping the cold polished brass helped to cool her thoughts if not her insides. "I understand."

But he seemed intent on adding further arguments anyway. "Plus, now you've talked with the press. If Julie or someone else were to see us…"

"I understand. Really, I do." Despite the hollow feeling in the pit of her stomach. "There's Steffi, too. If she were to think we were…you know…then she might get the wrong impression, and I don't want her getting hurt."

The look passing across his face had to be relief. She refused to think it was anything else because that would only put the thought in her head as well. And she didn't want to think anything but relief. "So we agree."

"One hundred percent," Roxy told him. "I let this morning's excitement get me carried away."

"Me, too." He tried a smile. "Guess we chalk it up to gratitude and adrenaline were a dangerous combination."

"Absolutely. It won't happen again."

"No," he agreed. "It won't."

Good, Roxy thought to herself. Better yet, now that the itch was out of her system, maybe she wouldn't be so strangely drawn to every little thing he did or said. Or want to study every expression that crossed his face.

Maybe the longing his presence produced, and that, at the moment, ached stronger than ever, would fade away as well.

CHAPTER NINE

MIKE slapped the lease notice on his desk with a frustrated sigh. It had been two weeks since Julie's column ran in the *Daily Press*. *Modern Day Anastasia Wants Answers; To Claim Her Role in Sinclair Legacy.* The *Press* believed in over-the-top headlines. Still, the piece worked. Roxy had been asked for interviews from several radio stations, two local affiliates and a national lifestyle magazine. As expected a few unsolicited pieces ran, too. A couple reporters found their way to the Elderion and one poked around Roxy's apartment building writing about her "dubious" roommates. Roxy's candid rebuttal to that piece ran in Julie's column today. Pieces also appeared.

And yet, despite all this media activity, silence from Jim Brassard and the Sinclairs. Even he was beginning to be concerned. Of course, when Roxy asked, he made a point of dodging the answer. He didn't want to upset her while she was meeting with the media.

Or rather upset her more than he already had. Like it had all week, his blood shot straight to his groin as the memory of their kiss came flooding forward. In fact, *kiss* was far too benign a word. All-out assault on his senses? Better.

He told her they should blame the rush of the moment.

If that was true, then why was his brain still screaming *More! More! More!*

Way to blur the lines, Templeton. He spun around his chair to stare at the building behind him. Fifteen years ago he made a call. Career and expectations first, personal desires and interests second. It was the only way he'd be able to achieve the level of success his family wanted from him, and thus far, it had served him well. Now was not the time to back off.

He swiveled back around, accidentally scattering Wentworth's letters with his arm. Bending over, he retrieved the trio that fell to the floor. In his final letter, Wentworth had been full of promises and decisions. He was coming home and telling his parents he was leaving Harvard and marrying Fiona, damn the consequences. Wonder what would have happened if Wentworth had made the trip home safely? Would he have carried through with his plans?

The question made him think, with more than a little guilt, about Grace. Fifteen years ago, coward that he was, he took the exact opposite track from Wentworth. Chose the route mapped out for him. That he did so easily told him Grace wasn't as great a passion as he remembered. Backing away from Roxanne yesterday had been harder.

Wonder what he'd do if he had to make the same decision today?

He didn't have time to ponder the thought for long. The phone rang. Soon as the caller identified himself, everything else became unimportant.

"Steffi, please. Hurry up and finish your dinner so we can get to Mrs. Ortega's. I have to get to work." High-heeled toe tapping on the carpeting, Roxy gave her daughter a stern look. Why was it kids were always their slowest when you needed them to move quickly?

At the dining room table, Steffi poked her meat loaf with her fork. "I don't like it," she said.

"You said you liked it when we had it two nights ago."

"Now it's old."

Roxy took a deep breath. She would not lose her patience. No matter if the clock over the stove told her she had about ten minutes to catch her bus.

Truth was, she couldn't completely blame her daughter for being cranky. With all these interviews and meetings, she'd had to spend more and more time at the babysitter's. What was the alternative? Leaving her here to hang with Wayne?

"Can I have more milk?" Steffi asked.

"When you've finished your meat loaf." Nice try, kid, but she was hip to that game; fill up on milk so you were too full to eat. The little girl whined. After giving another quick look at the clock, Roxy squatted so she was at eye level. Her spandex skirt rose distressingly high on her thighs. Since she'd changed up her wardrobe, she found the waitress uniform increasingly uncomfortable. The skirt was too tight and the camisole showed way too much cleavage.

Actually, it was more than the uniform. Simply going to work at the club had become more difficult too. Each day spent meeting with reporters and being treated like she was somebody, made hauling vodka tonics in a pair of high heels worse. It was like she'd finally gotten a tiny glimpse of what the world could possibly become. Except despite the interviews, they still hadn't heard from the Sinclairs. Mike told her not to worry. Then again, he also never answered her questions about the Sinclairs directly anymore, either, preferring to reassure her instead. His way of avoiding having to give her bad news.

Mike. Thinking of the mind-blowing kiss they shared wasn't doing her mood any favors. All it did was create a hot, needy sensation in the pit of her stomach. It stunk that the worst ideas were always the ones that nagged you.

Steffi still wasn't eating her meat loaf. "Baby, if you don't finish your dinner, you and Dusty won't get any dessert."

"Leave the kid alone. I wouldn't eat that warmed-up stuff, either."

"You're not helping, Alexis," Roxy said.

"Just sayin', I'd take her to that fast food burger place."

"Can we, Mommy?"

"No, Steffi."

"But I want chicken nuggets."

"Stephanie Rose O'Brien, finish your meat loaf."

Still swearing to keep her patience, she followed her roommate into the kitchen. Alexis had been as bad as Steffi lately. Worse ever since the *Daily Press* article appeared, though really Roxy thought the article was only part of a bigger issue.

"By the way," she said, "why didn't you tell me the package from AM America arrived?"

"Excuse me," the heavier woman replied, as she grabbed a bag of cheese curls from the pantry. "I didn't know I was your secretary now."

"You're not," Roxy replied. Her patience at treading lightly was wearing thin. "But I told you I was waiting for it. Would it hurt to say something?"

"Sorry. Must be my susceptible side."

"Disreputable," Roxy said. A correction that earned her an eye roll. "I cleared all that up. Didn't you read Julie's column today?

"You mean your big speech about how people shouldn't judge you because of where you live or who you hang out with?"

"People. I said *people* shouldn't be judged by who they associate with. I was lumping you in with me."

"Gee, thanks. Did your boyfriend suggest you say something like that?"

"Mike isn't my boyfriend." Damn, if she didn't feel an ache clear through to her heart at the mention of his name.

"Whatever."

Oh, for crying out loud. She was getting pretty sick and tired of the comments. Roxy stepped over to the countertop. "What's really bugging you? You've been copping an attitude for two weeks."

"Maybe I don't like being dissed."

"I corrected that in Julie's column."

"Oh, right. You say a few snotty things to your new BFF Julie and that's supposed to make it all better?"

Snotty? It was a correction for crying out loud. She didn't have to do anything. "So what would make it better then?"

Alexis shrugged. "You tell me. You're the one with all the fancy uptown friends now. Why don't you ask your sugar daddy next time he takes you shopping or to one of your fancy lunches?"

Is that what this was all about? Her new wardrobe? Going out to eat?

"Get over yourself," her roommate replied at the suggestion. "All I'm saying is while you're running around with reporters and going to fancy restaurants, Wayne and I are still back here waiting for ours."

"Maybe if Wayne stopped sitting..." Roxy muttered.

Alexis slammed the cabinet door, making Roxy jump.

"I'm getting pretty sick of you trashing my baby brother every time you turn around."

"Then we're even because I'm sick of him living on my couch." She hadn't forgotten the disgusting word he muttered to her the other day. A word his sister had to have heard and said nothing about. "I've told you before I don't like him around Steffi. And you're stupid if you think I don't know what kind of 'business' he's doing in this neighborhood."

"Oh, now you're calling me stupid? Excuse me, but not everyone's lucky enough to have a mother get knocked up by a millionaire.

"But you know that," she added, her mouth full of orange cheese.

Roxy squeezed her fists. "You leave Steffi out of this."

"I wasn't talking about Steffi. I was talking about you, acting like you're all better than us. And don't forget," she said, slicing the air with an orange index finger, "I pay half the rent here. You don't want your kid around my brother, then go live with your boyfriend."

"He's not my—" Roxy didn't have time to argue. She'd deal with this after work. Provided she still had a job. Dion was ticked off at her about reporters, too. "Come on, Steffi. Go get your coat."

"But you said I could have dessert."

"You'll have to have dessert at Mrs. Ortega's. Mommy's really late."

"I don't want to go to Mrs. Ortega's. You promised. I want ice cream!" The four-year-old began to cry, the loud, unreasonable gulps of a tantrum.

Naturally. Roxy lifted the little girl from her chair, wincing as her squirming legs banged her exposed thighs. The pain hurt less than the guilt.

"You promised!" Steffi chanted over and over. She

might as well have been saying "You're the worst mother in the world. I hate you", and even though she knew the world wouldn't end because of one missed dessert, Roxy couldn't help feeling like her daughter was right.

Adding insult to injury, as the door shut behind her and a still crying Steffi, she could hear Wayne and Alexis laughing.

"Well, look who decided to grace us with her presence," Jackie drawled when she finally managed to rush in, twenty minutes late.

So not what she needed right now. "Sorry I'm late, Dion," she said, tying on her apron. "Steffi gave me a hard time about going to the sitter's."

"So glad you could fit us in your schedule," he replied. "I gave Jackie your tables one through four."

"What?" He was cutting down her groups? "Why?"

"Because I needed someone to cover them, and she showed up on time."

Great. Just great. First Steffi, then Alexis, now she'd have to make do with half her tip money. Was the whole world conspiring against her tonight?

"Not like you need the money anyway, seeing how you're an heiress now."

"I'm not an heiress yet." Soon as she said it, Roxy realized how off-putting the comment sounded.

"Reminds me," Dion said. "I caught another one of those reporters poking around, asking the customers questions."

"I'm sorry." The articles that appeared earlier in the week ticked him off. "Least it's free publicity."

"Oh, yeah, the owner's thrilled with the place being called shabby."

"Maybe he'll spring for an upgrade." The place certainly needed it.

The bartender didn't appreciate the suggestion. "Maybe you should get your butt in gear and wait on customers before I give Jackie more of your tables."

Without another word, Roxy grabbed her pad and tray, making sure she moved quick enough that neither Dion nor Jackie saw her eyes getting wet. Why was the whole world so angry with her? She didn't ask for her mother to have an affair with Wentworth Sinclair. Why were they all out to punish her now?

If Mike were here, he'd understand.

Soon as the thought formed in her brain, she froze in her tracks. What the heck? A few weeks ago, her insides ran screaming at the idea of leaning on anyone, let alone him. Now here she was desperate to cry on his shoulder. What the heck happened to her?

Mike happened, that's what. Mike and his coppery, reassuring gaze and his day at the park.

This, she thought, was why kissing him had been a bad idea. Why she agreed with him it couldn't happen again, despite being the most mind-blowing kiss she'd ever had. She was getting too attached, too reliant on the man. Seeing him as more than a lawyer. A useless point since the other day, while standing in the Landmark, he made it quite clear that his being a lawyer came first.

Her first table ordered bottled beer. Same with the second. Dion not only reassigned her tables, but he left her with the ones who weren't going to spend any money. The night was getting better and better. Only one thing would make this disaster complete and that was…

"Hello, Roxy."

Mike was sitting at table eight. Karma really felt like kicking her in the butt today, didn't it?

Definitely. Why else would he look absolutely spectacular, in a beige suit she'd never seen before and a striped shirt? Shadows danced across his cheekbones, creating hollows and highlighting planes. Roxy's insides melted upon sight. Knowing her reaction wasn't merely physical was making it worse. She'd felt her spirits lift as soon as she heard his voice.

Suddenly she realized the problem with Mike wasn't a matter of becoming too attached; she *was* attached. Very, very attached. Oh, man, but she was in trouble, wasn't she?

She tucked nonexistent hair behind her ears. "Fancy meeting you here. Got tired of your office?"

"What can I say? There's something about this place that keeps drawing me back." He smiled, and the rest of the club receded. "You got a minute?"

"Not right now. Dion's upset because I was late. Problem with Steffi."

"Nothing serious, I hope."

Seeing his expression change and become serious did nothing to stop the emotion weaving its way through her. In fact, her heart grew. "No. She's tired of going to the babysitter is all."

"Well, Mrs. Ortega does smell like arthritis rub."

"True." *And you smell like wool and Dial soap and have arms that make a woman feel secure and safe.*

She had to shake these thoughts from her head. They weren't doing either of them any good. "Can you stick around till my break?"

"Of course."

"I'll get you the usual then."

Making her way to the bar, she tried to decide if his sticking around was good or not. For the past couple weeks, since the kiss, they'd managed to keep their dealings businesslike and short, involving a third party as often as possible. But tonight, with her working the crowd and wearing this skimpy outfit, knowing his eyes were going to be on her... Maybe risking Dion's anger was the better decision after all.

She purposely waited until she'd served all her other tables before bringing him his drink. She wasn't sure why, except that having an empty tray made it less likely she'd become distracted and ignore her customers. Make that more distracted. His looming presence would be permanently stuck in the front of her brain from now until her break.

It took like what seemed most of the night, but Dion finally gave her a break. "We'll have to be quick," she told Mike, slipping into the chair across from him. "Dion made it very clear I couldn't take a second more than ten minutes." *He wants more, he can meet you at his office,* the bartender had snarked.

"Still angry about the articles, huh."

"Everybody's mad," Roxy replied. "Alexis and Wayne are mad, Steffi's mad, Jackie and Dion are mad. They all think I've gone uptown and think I'm too good for them."

"They're right."

Mike's answer surprised her. Wasn't this the same man who insisted on a makeover? "You sure you didn't have a few pops before you got here?" she asked.

"Not a drop. You're better than all this, Roxanne. If the rest of the world can't see that, then the world's full of idiots."

The moisture returned to her eyes forcing her to blink. Dammit. How was she supposed to unattach herself if he was going to behave so nicely?

Along with reaching across the table to brush a tear from her cheek the way he was doing now. His touch was soft and sweet. She had to fight not to lean into his palm.

"Thank you for the pep talk," she said, managing a bit of a smile.

"You're welcome. I have something else that might cheer you up more."

"Really?" She started to ask when she saw his grin. Only one thing would make him smile that wide and look that confident. Her heart stopped beating. "Don't tell me…"

"Jim Brassard called me earlier this evening."

"Are you saying…?"

His wide grin grew wider. "The Sinclair sisters want to meet you."

CHAPTER TEN

IN NEW YORK society circles, Alice and Frances Sinclair were considered eccentric icons. Both twice divorced, they lived together in the Gramercy Park brownstone where they grew up while their children lived in more modern penthouses nearby. Between the two of them, the Sinclair name was part of almost every charitable board in the city.

Roxy's knees shook as they stood in front of the iron gate. "What if they don't like me?" she whispered in Mike's ear.

"You asked the same thing about Julie. Be yourself and everything will be fine."

Roxy wished she shared his confidence, but she couldn't shake the feeling of anxiety crawling along the back of her neck. For all she knew, the Sinclairs wanted to see her so they could tell her to her face to buzz off.

"Remember, you're their family." As usual Mike seemed to read her thoughts and say the words she needed to hear. What would she do when she didn't have him standing by her side anymore?

She couldn't bear to think about it.

A metallic-sounding voice came on the gate speaker to greet them. Mike introduced themselves and a moment later, the gate clicked open.

"Promising sign."

"Unless there are dogs about to run at us."

"That's my girl. Mistrustful as ever."

Because she'd never been this close to good fortune before. Sixty minutes from now she could be...

Dear God, she was too afraid to form the words.

The ornately carved main entrance sat back from the curb, a short cement walkway protecting the sisters from the noise of the street. No more than six feet, it felt like six hundred. Two steps in, Roxy felt a reassuring pressure at the curve of her elbow. "Making sure you don't trip in those shoes," he said in a soft voice.

"I'm wearing flats."

"You still never know." He gave her elbow a squeeze, sending waves of reassurance up her arm. Roxy felt so cherished in that one moment, she swore her heart grew too big for her heart. *Oh, how she loved this man.*

Before she could argue with herself about her choice of words, they reached the front door and a suited servant opened it. A middle-age woman in a crisp black suit came walking up just behind. "I'm Millicent Webster, the sisters' secretary," she greeted, in a polite and formal voice. "They're waiting for you in the solarium. If you follow me, I'll take you."

Roxy wasn't sure what a solarium was, but she quickly surmised it was another name for sunroom as they were led down a corridor to a large, window-filled room in the rear of the house. When they arrived, they found the two elderly women seated side by side in matching Queen Anne chairs. They were chatting with a gray-haired man sitting on the sofa. The man immediately stood up. "Good afternoon, Mike. Thank you for coming." He looked straight at Roxy. "And you must be Roxanne O'Brien."

Roxy cleared her throat. "Yes," she whispered. Over in

their chairs, the Sinclair sisters were staring intently; she could feel the scrutiny.

The gasp when she walked in didn't help, either.

"I'm Jim Brassard, the Sinclair family attorney. May I introduce Frances and Alice Sinclair."

Frances, the taller of the two motioned for them to take a seat. "We're so glad you could meet with us. Aren't we, Alice?"

"Yes, we are." Alice was a few inches smaller, with bright black eyes that matched her sister's. Both had short-cropped hair and strong features. For the first time Roxy noticed the giant Newfoundland sprawled between the chairs. She just knew there would be dogs. Though this one didn't look too threatening.

"This is Bunty," Frances said, following her line of sight. "He's been with us forever. My second husband bought him as a puppy. Turns out he was the only thing worth salvaging about the relationship. Don't worry. He won't bite. Poor creature hasn't moved fast in years."

Mike chuckled. Roxy managed a wan smile. Her pulse was racing, making breathing, let alone making noise, difficult. Smoothing the front of her slacks, she perched on the edge of the sofa, where Frances had indicated.

"Thank you for being willing to talk with us," she heard Mike say. "I know this must be awkward for you."

"Our family, by nature, is very private," Frances replied. "We aren't one to seek publicity." She cocked her head. "But you already knew that, didn't you, Mr. Templeton."

Roxy looked up in time to see his cheeks blush a sheepish tinge. "I might have heard something to that effect. We weren't trying to embarrass the family, I assure you. Simply get your attention."

"Well, you did. Get our attention," Jim said.

Meanwhile, Alice was still studying her. The probing

made Roxy want to squirm her way behind the sofa cushions. Nervously she tucked her hair behind her ear.

"Alice, stop," Frances snapped, realizing. "You're making the girl uncomfortable."

"I'm sorry. I don't mean to. It's just…that hair and your eyes. I knew as soon as I saw your photograph in the newspaper."

"Knew?" Roxy asked.

"How much you resemble your mother."

They knew her mother. Roxy couldn't believe it.

"We didn't know her name," Frances continued. "Both Alice and I were married and living elsewhere at the time. But she worked for us. As a weekend maid."

"It was the hair," Alice said. "You couldn't forget the hair. Long, strawberry curls. I was so jealous. She had an accent, too, I believe."

"Irish," Roxy supplied. "She came from County Cork as a little girl. I'm confused, though. Are you sure it was my mother? I thought she worked for a hotel."

"She might have. Father let the whole staff go one summer. At the time, we wondered what set him off."

"Then again something was always setting father off," Frances said. "He had a very short temper."

"Finding out his son was involved with one of the staff could certainly anger a man," Mike said.

"I certainly remember how upset Wenty was when he found out. I had stopped by and he was pacing back and forth fuming. Told me he didn't want to talk about it. It was a couple weeks before he left for Cambridge, I believe."

"We didn't talk to him nearly enough that semester," Frances said softly.

"No, we didn't."

Sisterly regret hung in the air. No matter what happened regarding her, she suspected Alice and Frances loved their baby brother, and wanted to do right for him. She looked to her lap, trying to imagine how events unfolded. Her mother, fresh out of high school, coming to work for the Sinclairs, meeting a young Wentworth. The two of them growing closer, then intimate. Powell Sinclair finding out and firing the entire staff.

"You never saw her again after that?" Mike asked.

"Why would we? Shortly after, Wenty left for Cambridge. He was at Harvard. We were both trying to build marriages."

"Fat lot that did," Alice muttered.

And the redhead was nothing more than a former, fired staff member. No reason to follow up. Why indeed? Her mother's failure to talk with the Sinclairs was starting to make sense now. She must have feared what Powell would do.

"Then before we knew it, Wenty died. He should never have been driving so fast."

"He was eager to get home," Jim Brassard said.

"He was rushing home for a reason," Mike told him. He reached into his back pocket and dropped the stack of letters in Roxy's lap. Still looking down, Roxy ran her finger over the velvet ribbon. Mike had told her what Wentworth's final few letters said. His final promises to the woman he loved. She'd given the press a brief overview of the stack's content, but only the broadest of strokes. These pages were the couple's final intimate moments.

"My mother held on to these for thirty years," she told the sisters, holding out the stack.

"Wentworth's final letters," Frances declared. "You mentioned them in your interviews."

The older woman withdrew the top letter. "May we?"

"Please."

Time ticked off on a nearby floor clock. Roxy and Mike waited while the sisters and Jim Brassard read the letters in silence. At some point, a staff member brought in a tea service. Watching the woman set down the tray, Roxy wondered what her mother would think, her sitting as a guest in the solarium thirty years after she got tossed out. Was this what she wanted? *I hope so, Mom.*

She stole a glance to her left. Mike looked right at home. His suit, his bearing—they fit in. No surprise. What did surprise her was how comfortable she felt. This was her father's home. Her family's home. The notion made her smile. Over the rim of his teacup, Mike gave her a wink. Her heart thumped a little harder. Once again, a familiar four-letter word filled her heart. A troublesome four-letter word if true. Love wasn't on the agenda. Not with a man who considered kissing her a mistake.

Examining her feelings for her lawyer, though, would have to wait. Having read enough, the sisters set the letters down and offered a pair of polite coughs.

"Wentworth was always dramatic," Alice remarked. "Whatever his interest, he threw himself in with a passion for as long as he was involved."

"I think his relationship with Roxanne's mother was more than a casual interest," Mike said.

"Oh, I have no doubt they were in love and that he intended to issue an ultimatum to our father," Frances said.

"He was always issuing ultimatums," Alice added. "It was part of his passionate nature. Once, when he discovered our father was investing in a Japanese venture, he went on a hunger strike. Said he wouldn't eat until he had proof the company wasn't involved in harming dolphins."

Her older sister nodded and reverently slid the letter back into the envelope. "That was one of his more over-the-top demonstrations."

Roxy listened to them in disbelief. They weren't seriously equating his love affair with her mother with dolphin-safe fishing? "Forgive me, but those letters—"

"Oh, I know," Alice cut her off. "They are amazingly detailed."

"To say the least," Jim Brassard muttered. "You weren't kidding, Mike."

"And, I have no doubt that he believed every word at the time," Frances said. "Whether he was serious about his threats is something we'll never know."

"He gave up the hunger strike after thirty-six hours," Alice said in a soft voice.

"Still." Frances squared her shoulders. "Fact remains that when he wrote these letters, he was in love, and I think, given your story, your mother loved him. If there were consequences to their love affair, it's our responsibility to see to them."

"Are you saying what I think you're saying?" Mike asked.

Roxy held her breath for the answer. If she heard right, Frances and Alice were willing to... No, she wouldn't believe until she heard the words straight from one of the sister's mouths.

"The Sinclairs place a high value on responsibility and on family. If our brother fathered a child, then that child is part of our family. We won't turn our backs on her existence."

Oh, my goodness, she was saying what Roxy thought she said.

"The question is," the woman continued, showing marks of the shrewdness that made her father a scion of business. "What are your motives, Miss O'Brien?"

"I want the truth." Roxy had been thinking about this for a while now. "More than anything, I want to know the truth. I want to know who I am."

Both women smiled and gave slight nods of their heads. Her answer apparently pleased them. "That's what we'd like as well," Frances replied. "We'll be glad to cooperate with your DNA test, Miss O'Brien."

Pop! Champagne foamed up and down the side of the bottle. Roxy laughed as Mike held it up to keep it from running onto his desk. "Not my neatest opening," he said. "But what's the point of splurging on champagne if you can't be messy?"

"Good point."

They picked up the bottle on the way back from Gramercy Park, feeling the need to cap off the meeting with a celebration. Tomorrow they would go to a local lab so Roxy could have her cheek swabbed for DNA. If lucky, they'd have the results within a week.

Best part of everything had been the sisters themselves. After they agreed to the test, the pair shared with her the family photo albums. She saw pictures of Wentworth as a child and as he looked a few months before he died. Call her crazy, but she could see a little of Steffi in his face. Around the jaw and the chin.

She watched Mike pour champagne into the two ceramic mugs on his desk. "Pretty big drinks," she said, noting they were three-quarters full.

"Big celebrations call for big drinks," he replied, handing her one. "Why, you got somewhere to be?"

Actually she did. Work. "I'm supposed to be at the Lounge in—" She looked at her watch. Shoot! Was it really that late? "I was supposed to be at work fifteen minutes ago."

In a flash, Mike set down his cup, and was on his feet. "I'll drive you."

"It's okay."

"You sure?"

"There's no need." She'd only be rushing to a job that no longer existed. Dion made it very clear at the end of last night's shift, he wouldn't tolerate any more missed time. "I'm pretty sure I'm now unemployed."

"I'm sorry."

"Yeah, me, too." Surprised her how casual she sounded. You'd think she'd be more upset about becoming unemployed. She simply couldn't work up the angst right now.

"What about Steffi? Do we need to get her?"

"She's at Mrs. Ortega's till midnight, and given Alexis's mood lately, it's the best place for her. The less time we're in the apartment, the better."

"Still giving you a hard time, hey?"

"Worse this morning than last night. I didn't dare tell her about our meeting."

She sighed. When Alexis first moved in, the relationship seemed like it had such potential. "I can't wait to get Steffi out of that environment."

"If things go well, you'll be able to move anywhere you'd like," he said, handing her a cup. "To positive DNA tests."

Roxy clinked her mug against his. "To scaling Mt. Everest barefoot. And having a kick-ass attorney."

She took a sip and grimaced at the dry flavor. Guess it was an acquired taste.

Mike set down his drink.

"I wouldn't start patting ourselves on the back too soon. We passed a big hurdle getting them to agree to the DNA test, but we haven't scaled the peak yet. After the results are in, we still have to prove you deserve a share of the estate. I know the sisters said they wanted to do right by their brother's family, but Jim Brassard is going to do whatever he can to protect their assets. He can make it a hell of a fight if he wants to."

"But I've got you." Roxy wasn't worried. She had faith Mike would succeed. He'd gotten her this far, hadn't he?"

Imagine that. Roxy O'Brien having faith. Who'd have thought that a month ago. She took another drink, this time finding the champagne a little more appealing.

"What?" she asked, catching him watching. There was so much tender curiosity in his eyes. Shivers danced along her skin, matching the bubbles in her cup.

"You look very pensive all of a sudden," he said.

"I was thinking how much things can change in a month. Four weeks ago I stormed out of this office thinking you were a condescending, arrogant jerk."

"And now?"

Now I can't imagine a day without you in it. "Now I'm sitting here drinking champagne." To punctuate her point, she took a sip. "I'm glad I left one of my letters behind."

"Me, too."

Coming around to her side of the desk, he sat down next to her. His hip brushed against hers causing the air between them to crackle. Roxy thought about shifting, but the contact felt too nice. She liked the warmth spreading though her body.

"I have a confession to make," he said.

"What's that?"

"I would have tracked you down anyway. I wanted the case."

For the moment, Roxy pretended he didn't say the second line, and focused on him tracking her down. "Well, if this is going to be honesty time, I suppose I owe you an apology."

"You mean for something other than thinking I was arrogant and condescending?"

"Yes," she replied, bumping his shoulder. Wow, had she really already drank half her cup? The stuff grew on you. "When you said you would win this case, you told me you never said anything you couldn't back up. I didn't believe you."

"You might want to hold off on that. Like I said, we haven't won yet."

"But I was wrong to doubt you, your abilities." She stared at the bubbles rising from the golden liquid and popping, creating tiny little sprays in her mug. "Your sincerity. Your confidence. I shouldn't have.

"To Mike Templeton," she said, raising her glass. "The winner he said he was."

"Don't."

What'd she say? He stood up, taking his warmth and his contact with him as he headed to the picture window. The air grew cold. "I thought you wanted me to believe in you."

"Believe your case had a chance, yes. But—" He looked out to some place far away. "I'm not a winner, Roxy."

"Don't be silly." Of course he was. He'd been a winner his whole life. He told her so. "We won today, didn't we?"

He opened his mouth to protest, but she waved it off. He could talk about waiting until the case was over and all that, but as far as she was concerned, he had won today. He'd won her faith.

And maybe a little more? Maybe her heart?

She slipped off the desk, surprised when the floor swayed a little. Stupid floor.

For the third time today, she wondered if her feelings ran deeper than simple gratitude. "Third time's a charm, isn't it?" a voice in her head asked. Possibly. Romance so wasn't on her agenda. He was the wrong man, the wrong person to fall for. And yet, here she was.

She joined him at the window. Between the night outside, and the fluorescent office lights, his face was cast in shadows. He looked sad. Regretful. Slipping in front of him, she sat on the window heater. "What's with the modesty all of a sudden?"

"Speaking the truth is all," he replied. "I don't like to take credit for something that isn't my accomplishment."

"Whose accomplishment is it?"

He blinked, and looked at her with surprise. "Yours, of course. If you win, if you prove you're a Sinclair and get your share of the inheritance, you'll be the reason why."

"Well, sure." She took another long drink. Silly man. "It's my DNA. Still, I couldn't have done anything without you. Don't sell yourself short, Counselor." She giggled the last word because the bubbles chose that moment to tickle her nose.

"I am a good lawyer, aren't I?"

He said it like discovering a new fact. "Okay," he said, "how about we agree we did this together. To us."

She watched as he tipped back his drink. "We make a good team, Roxanne O'Brien," he said, topping off his mug.

At the word team, Roxy's heart did a little dance. "You shouldn't say stuff like that unless you mean it," she told him.

"What makes you think I don't?"

Because if she believed him, she'd fall completely under his spell, that's why. As it was, she'd already dropped three-quarters of the way, maybe more.

God, but she felt so good being here with him.

He was topping off her mug again. She didn't mind. The mellow, happy feeling in her limbs felt amazing. She wanted the whole world to feel the same way. The man standing next to her most of all.

"Do you ever loosen your tie?" she asked, swaying toward him.

He laughed. Such an attractive laugh, thought Roxy, taking another drink. Her cup was emptying way too fast, and her head suddenly felt very heavy. So heavy she had to rest her forehead on his chest. Mike's fingers threaded through her hair.

"That's better," she murmured.

"You've had too much champagne," he said. The unnatural lilt in his voice made her giggle.

"S'your fault. Told you the cup was filled too high." She tried looking up and the room shifted. "I probably should have had something to eat."

"Probably," he replied with a broad smile. With one hand still cradling the back of her head, he used his other to lift his mug and take a long drink. "Same here."

Wow, but he smiled pretty. Could men's smiles be pretty? Never mind, his was. "You haven't answered my question. Do you ever loosen your tie?"

"Haven't since college," he said, giving another one of those adorable laughs. "Got to dress like a Templeton, you know. Can't be seen looking like a bum. Might reflect badly on the family name." Another sip and he leaned in close. "Want to know a secret?"

"Sure." He could tell her anything in that sexy whisper. "What?"

"Sometimes I take my tie off at the end of the day."

"What do you do with it?"

"Depends." He grinned, his eyes shiny like two copper pennies. "On whether or not I've got company."

Oh, my. Roxy's insides turned hot and needy. "It's the end of the day now," she whispered. "And I'm company."

"So you are."

She touched the Windsor knot at his neck. Mike was

right about the alcohol. Her fingers felt thick and clumsy as she undid the silk. Every fumble had her brushing the underside of his chin and caressing his throat. Finally she tugged the cloth loose. "There," she said with a smile. "You're loosened."

"Better?"

"Much." Her smile turned serious as another question came to mind. "Do you really regret kissing me the other day?"

"I never said I regretted it."

"Yes, you did."

"No. I said kissing you was a *mistake*."

"Isn't that the same thing?" Suddenly it was incredibly important for her to know the truth.

"No. A mistake says I shouldn't have done it. Regret implies I was sorry, and I'm not sorry in the least."

Awareness pulsed deep inside her, a low, throbbing need to feel his touch again. Slowly she let her fingers slide from the knot in his tie to the plains of his chest. His hard, chiseled chest. When she reached his heart, her palm flattened and she could feel his heartbeat reaching her through the cloth. The need intensified knowing the rapid beat was because of her. "Would it be a mistake to kiss me again?" she asked, searching his face.

Black eyes, their pupils blown so wide from desire, searched back. Their heat bore into her. "Yes," he whispered.

Yet he didn't move. "Because I'm your client?"

"No. Because you're tipsy." He cradled her face, his thumbs fanning warm arcs across her cheek. "A gentleman doesn't take advantage of a woman who's been drinking."

He smoothed her eyebrows. "No matter how beautiful and tempting she is."

Roxy leaned closer. "What if I kissed you? Would that be a mistake, too?"

A thrill passed through her seeing his Adam's apple bob hard in his throat. He nodded. "Yes."

"Would you regret it?"

"Question is, would you?"

"Guess we'll have to see, won't we?" Pulling herself on her tiptoes, she pressed her lips to his. The kiss was softer, slower than last time. Roxy's eyes fluttered closed. She concentrated on the feel of Mike's mouth on hers, his taste, the texture of his lips as they massaged hers. She was right; his mouth was perfect. She heard a soft moan escape his throat, and felt his hand cup the back of her skull. Fingers tangled in her hair, angling her face upward. Her lips parted, and for a moment, the kiss became more intimate, a dance of tongues.

The soft caress of his breath on his cheek signaled the dance's end.

"Do you regret that?" she asked, coming down to earth.

He shook his head. "Not one second."

"Good. Because neither do I." If anything, tonight felt right. So very, very right. "What would you do then, if I kissed you a second time?"

"Oh, now, that could be a problem."

"Why?"

Lips, soft and eager, nibbled her jawline. "Because I can't guarantee I'll be able to stop at a simple kiss." To prove his point, he slid his hands down to her bottom and pulled her close so she could feel his arousal.

Smiling, Roxy hooked one leg around his calves and merged their bodies even closer. "Who says I want you to?"

CHAPTER ELEVEN

"For goodness' sake, Michael, you really need to check your voice mail. This is my third message in three days. What on earth are you thinking running around doing press interviews with that woman? You are a lawyer, not a—"

Mike switched off the phone midmessage. The woman buttoning her slacks was far more interesting. "Those looked better on the floor," he said with a lazy smile.

Roxanne smiled back. "Wouldn't that make a pretty headline. *Heiress Caught Commuting with Her Pants Down.*"

"I don't know about a headline, but it would definitely make a pretty sight." He ran his hand along the inner thigh he now had intimate knowledge of until she slapped it away.

"Listen to you. The guy who thought my work skirt was too short."

"It was. Doesn't mean I didn't like what I saw." He frowned. "Why are you talking like you're taking the bus?"

"Well, Mr. Half a Bottle of Champagne, I don't think you're capable of driving, do you?"

"Stay here, then." He pulled her into a deep kiss, grinning when her arms found their way around his neck. "I love how you smell," he murmured, burying his face in the crook of her neck. "I could smell you all night. And taste, and..." He kissed the hollow below her collarbone and was rewarded with a whimper.

Maybe they should take the bus, find an empty backseat....

"I have to go," she said when he finally let her up for air. "I told Mrs. Ortega I'd pick up Steffi at midnight."

"Blast Mrs. Ortega." Much as he wanted to argue the point, he knew she was right. They couldn't leave Steffi at the sitter's indefinitely. Eventually this little celebratory rendezvous would have to end. "Let me put on my shirt and I'll get us a cab."

"Us?" She pulled back. "You know you can't stay, right? I can't have Steffi waking up and getting the wrong impression."

He could argue that, given the environment Roxy and her daughter lived in, his sleeping over was the least detrimental, but he wouldn't. He respected Roxy's protectiveness.

However, she never said he couldn't see her first thing in the morning.

"Breakfast?" she said when he told her.

"When I come get you for the DNA test. I'll bring muffins. Then, after the test is over, if Steffi's still at preschool and there's time..." He ran an index finger down the front of her shirt and hooked the waistband of her pants.

"I'll keep my fingers crossed the lab's running on time," Roxy said.

Catching the mischievous glint in her eyes, Mike couldn't help himself. He kissed her again. Deep and hard. "Down, Counselor," Roxy teased. "Save it for tomorrow.

"By the way," she added, tossing him his shirt, "make sure you bring extra muffins."

"For what?" *Please don't say Wayne and Alexis.*

To his immense pleasure, she didn't. She did, however, give him a quick peck on the cheek. "To keep up your strength, of course."

She slipped out of his arms.

Was he wrong? Mike asked himself while waiting by his reception desk for Roxy to return from the washroom. In the back of his mind, he knew he was supposed to feel guilty. She was a client for crying out loud. How many times over the past few weeks had he reminded himself of the ethical and professional repercussions or lectured himself he had a job to do and that his personal desires meant nothing. Because they'd never mattered before.

Except for tonight. Tonight he'd wanted and he'd taken—for three hours he'd taken—and damn if he wasn't glad. For the first time in a very long time, Mike felt one hundred percent alive.

Was this how Wentworth felt when he was with Fiona? No wonder the guy was planning to fight.

"Ready?"

Roxanne stood at the lobby door, her hair still wild from their lovemaking. "Sorry to keep you waiting," she said.

Looking at her, Mike's heart hitched. Amazing how easily tides could turn. A little over a month ago he sat on the edge of failure and judging Roxanne for being rough around the edges. Four and a half weeks later, she was on the cusp of becoming Manhattan's latest socialite and his future was set.

No wonder he felt alive.

He moved toward her, slipping an arm around her waist to lead her toward the door. "No need to apologize," he told her. "You were worth the wait."

"What's a lab tree?" From her perch on top of the counter, Steffi drank her juice from a plastic cup while Roxy moved around the kitchen looking for her coffee mug.

"Laboratory," she corrected. Where was the darn thing? She'd had it a minute ago. "It's a place where people go to get their blood tested."

"Are you sick?"

"Oh, no, baby, I'm not sick." She'd never felt better. To remind herself, she stretched her arms over her head, reveling in the burn of sore muscles from the night before. A soft sigh escaped her lips.

This was the train of thought that caused her to misplace her coffee in the first place.

"Your mama's taking a test to prove she's better than the rest of us." Alexis ambled in, still wearing her nightshirt, and took two mugs from the cabinet.

"Are you better than me?" Steffi asked.

"No one's better than anybody," Roxy replied. "Alexis is making a joke."

From behind the refrigerator door, her roommate coughed. Roxy ignored her. No one was going to ruin her mood, not Alexis. Not even Wayne. In a short while, Mike would be here. Together they'd drop Steffi off at the preschool, go to the lab for her DNA test, and hopefully, if there was time, come back to repeat last night.

For the first time in her life, things were perfect. And, in a few days, when the test results returned, life would become better! She and Steffi would have a full-fledged family tree and the money to build a brand-new life.

She found her coffee. On the dining room table. Cold, but Roxy drank it anyway. Or rather she started to. The phone stopped her.

"Mommy, your phone's ringing." Steffi pointed to the cell on the counter.

Alexis, who'd been standing right next to the phone, looked down and shrugged. "I wouldn't want to mess up one of your interviews," she sneered.

"Never mind, I've got it." Resisting the temptation to get in a snark contest, Roxy simply crossed the room and picked it up. The caller ID said Unknown, but the area code looked familiar.

"Hello?"

"Christina said you're trying to reach me. Said it was important."

Her father. Her other father, that is. Talk about timing. "Yeah, Dad, I wanted to talk to you. It's about Mom."

"There a problem? I thought she had insurance to bury her."

"She did. This is about something else." Taking a deep breath, she asked the multimillion-dollar question. "Did you ever hear of a man named Wentworth Sinclair?"

Mike drove straight to Roxanne's apartment from his. He'd be early but who cared? Early meant a few extra minutes to say hello. The thought made his body wake up better than any alarm clock.

Fortune continued to smile on him as he snagged a parking spot right in front of the building and stepped onto the sidewalk the same time an elderly man exited the building.

"Someone's getting breakfast delivered," the man said as he held open the front door. He nodded at the wax pastry bag and tray of coffee.

"You can say that again." Mike grinned.

To his surprise, it took three rounds of knocking for Roxanne to open the door. He'd have thought she'd be awake by now, this lab appointment being the apex of everything she wanted. Then again, she did earn the right to be a little tired after last night.

His fist was about to start round four when he finally heard the scrape and jingle of security locks. A second later, Roxanne's face appeared in the doorway. And Mike's insides froze.

One look at the pale skin, the colorless lips, the puffy red eyes, told him she'd been crying. "What's wrong?" he asked, dropping the coffee and muffins on the table. "Is it Steffi?"

"Steffi's fine." She wiped at her cheeks. "My father called."

"Oh, I'm so sorry." He didn't know what else to say. Her distress made sense now. "I wish I'd been here earlier. He didn't take the news well."

"Actually he took the news fine," she said with a sniff. "In fact he knew all about Wentworth and my mom."

What? He did? "And he never said anything after all this time?"

Roxy shook her head. "Didn't see the point. He also told me not to bother taking the test. Because there's absolutely no way I can be Wentworth's daughter."

CHAPTER TWELVE

He didn't believe her.

"What are you talking about?" he asked, his face the picture of confusion. "Of course you're Wentworth's daughter. The sisters said as much."

"The sisters were wrong. Wentworth died before my mother got pregnant."

"How can you be so certain?"

"Because—" Over on the couch, Steffi sat watching her pony show. Oblivious to the drama playing out around her. Wanting to keep her world undisturbed, Roxy led Mike to the kitchen, where they could talk out of earshot. Her cell phone lay on the counter where she'd dropped it. Right next to the burn mark on the Formica where Wayne left a hot sauce pan and a half-finished cup of coffee. This was her reality. She should have known.

"My father explained everything." Succumbing to the unbearable heaviness that gripped her body, she slumped against the counter. Every last lousy word of their conversation had been cemented in her memory. *You ain't no Sinclair. That was just your mother's wishful thinking.* "Turns out I was born early. The real due date was too far out for me to be Wentworth's."

"Due dates can be fudged."

"Incompetent cervixes can't. Apparently the doctor

warned my mother she could go early if she didn't stay off her feet, and she kept working anyway." Why she ignored the doctor's advice, her father didn't say. Maybe they'd been pressed for money or she wanted out of the house.

Or maybe she'd wanted to go early so she could pretend. Keep the fantasy going. "Who knows what went on in that head of hers," her father had said. "She never was all there."

Hearing him speak so bluntly about something so important hurt almost as much as the story itself. Apparently, according to her father, he and her mother met in a local bar, about three weeks after Wentworth's accident. Her mother had been upset. Drinking. He bought her a drink to calm her nerves, and then a second. Next thing they were getting it on in the backseat of his Dodge Dart.

"That's exactly how my father put it, too. Getting it on." She gave a mirthless bark. "Me and my mom, two peas in a pod. Only difference is my dad lived in the same neighborhood, so when my mom found out she was knocked up, she gave him a call. Good Irish Catholic boy that he was, my dad married her."

So much for being the child of some great, unfinished love affair. She was exactly who she always thought she was. A big, unwelcome, unwanted mistake. "My father hadn't left because Fiona still loved Wentworth. He left because he didn't love us enough to stick around."

Roxy dropped her head. All her big plans, her hopes for the future. Killed by a fifteen-minute phone call and a "Sorry, kiddo, I thought you knew."

What a joke. Her gullibility made her sick to her stomach.

Mike was pacing the length of the kitchen. She watched his shoes, thinking how out of place they looked against the scuffed beige flooring. Another reminder of reality.

"This can't be happening," he was saying. His muttered words mirrored the voice in her head. "Everything was so damn certain yesterday. What the hell happened?"

"Reality happened," she murmured in reply.

A wash of his hand over his features, his voice steeled. "No need to panic. Not yet. Your father could still have his dates wrong."

If only. "He doesn't."

He stopped his pacing. "You don't know that."

"I know my luck." Why should her paternity be any different from the other bad choices and failures in her life? What on earth made her think she could possibly be an heiress?

Looking back, she realized her gut had been shooting her warning signs for weeks, telling her she was getting in so deep, but she'd been too seduced by the idea of being a Sinclair she'd ignored them.

Who was she kidding? She believed her mother's story because she *wanted* to. All these years she'd wondered what it was she did to make her parents check out. She'd grasped at her mother's love affair because the truth hurt too much. Now truth wanted to make her pay by hammering itself home. *Mistake, mistake, mistake.*

The word repeated in her head as she played with the hem of her sweater set. Her *heiress costume,* she amended bitterly. "I should have known. I failed as an actress, as a daughter, as a mother…"

Steffi. What did she have to offer her daughter now? No inheritance. No father. She didn't even have her crappy job. All she had was this lousy apartment, a world filled with lowlifes like Wayne and a family history of drunken pickups. How long before her daughter started seeing her as the mistake she was, too?

Nausea rose in her throat. She rushed to the sink, making it seconds before losing her morning coffee. Heave after acidic heave burned her throat. Mike tried to rub small soothing circles on her back, but she shoved him away. To the other side of the room. Where she couldn't see the pity that had to be in his coppery eyes. Add him to her list of mistakes. He thought he'd made love to an heiress last night. Instead he got the premakeover Roxy. The one who couldn't measure up. Why would he want her now?

"It's over." She stared at the sink drain, watching the water wash away the mess. If only she could wash the fallout from this past month as easily.

"No. It's not over. Not yet."

He was pacing again, Roxy could hear his heels hitting the linoleum. "I'll go to Florida and interview your father myself. I should have in the first place. And your mother's medical records. We'll track them down. Maybe her doctor's still alive."

"Why? What's the use? Still going to be the same outcome."

"You don't know that."

Oh, but she did. "Face it, Mike, it's a lost cause."

"So, what? That's it? You're just going to quit?"

"What else am I supposed to do?

"You can keep fighting."

"Why? So I can make a bigger fool out of myself? Hope the Sinclairs give me some money to go away?"

"Why not? A lot better than hiding in your apartment playing the victim."

Playing the vict— Roxy whirled around. "What the hell is that supposed to mean?"

"Exactly what it sounds like."

"I am not playing anything." As if he would understand anyway. When had life ever kicked him in the teeth?

"Oh, no? Sure sounds it to me. One little phone call and you're ready to quit."

"As opposed to what? Fighting a lost cause so I can get bought off? That wasn't why I did this."

"Wasn't it?"

And so it came back to her being a fortune hunter. After all they'd shared. *After she gave him her heart.* Anger ripped through her. "You know it wasn't," she hissed. It took everything not to slap his face. "I wanted to know the truth."

"You're right. I'm sorry." The apology would carry more weight if she couldn't see the wheels turning in his head. Formulating the next line of attack.

It came with a milder voice. "All I meant was you came to me wanting to give Steffi a better life. You still can."

By basically coercing a payout. "I can't," she told him. If she did lose her daughter's respect when she got older, she could at least keep some ability to look herself in the mirror.

Mike shook his head. "I can't let you quit. This case is way too important."

"Haven't you been listening? There is no case!"

"There has to be."

The ferocity with which he shouted the words shocked her. She knew he wasn't used to losing, but this… This was over-the-top. You'd think karma had played the joke on him instead of her. Surely she wasn't that important to him.

"Sorry," she told him. "Guess you'll have to win with another client."

"There is no other client."

What? She stared at him.

Mike ran a hand over his features. "I don't have any other clients," he repeated. "You're it."

"But, I don't understand. Your ad, the uptown offices…"

"Teetering on the brink of extinction." His fierceness turned sheepish. "You of all people should know things aren't always what they appear to be."

You'd think there'd be more clutter. Sophie's observation had been right. There was no clutter because there was no business.

Except for her. Her and her multimillion-dollar payday. A huge emptiness formed in the center of her chest. Roxy cut off his argument. She wasn't going to believe him anyway. No wonder he treated her like such an important client. Hanging around the bar. Doting on her.

Making love to her.

"That's all this was to you, wasn't it? A case. A way to salvage your business."

He started. Shock? Or guilt. "No. I mean, maybe things started out that way but…"

She didn't want to hear another argument. Here she thought last night meant something more, something deeper. That he felt the same emotions. But no, while she'd been making love, he'd been keeping his prized client happy.

Chalk up another bad choice.

For the first time since answering the door, she looked him straight in the eye.

"I think you should leave."

"Leave?" He looked genuinely surprised. "I'm not leaving you."

"Yeah, you are." He should be pleased. For once she wasn't the one walking away; she was making him do it. "What's that saying, fool me once, fool me twice? I'm not going to let you stick around so I can get fooled a third time."

Pushing her way past him, she marched to the front

door and flung it open. "Your job here is finished, Mr. Templeton."

Mike stared at her long and hard. "Don't do this, Roxy."

"Too late, I already have."

Took another couple of beats, but he finally got the message and walked away.

"Mommy?" From her place on the couch, Steffi broke the silence as soon as the door shut. "Mike didn't say goodbye."

Roxy kept her face to the wood, watching the lock swim in front of her eyes. "No, baby, he didn't."

Then again, she expected as much.

Damn, damn, damn!

The obscenity was the only word Mike was capable of forming. He chanted it the entire drive to his office, screaming it once or twice in the empty interior, hoping maybe, just maybe, he could make some sense of what happened in Roxy's apartment.

He had nothing.

Roxy couldn't be quitting. There was still plenty to fight. Until they had definitive, actual proof she had a case…

But no, she'd rather give up. Accept failure. He kicked over a potted plant. Dammit! Why did her father have to call this morning of all mornings? Why couldn't the miserable bastard stay missing a little while longer?

Fine. If Roxy didn't want to pursue her claim, that was her business. He didn't need her or her case. He'd figure out another way to save his firm. He was a Templeton for crying out loud. He wasn't born to fail.

His toe kicked a scrap of cloth on the way to his desk. Bending down he found his tie from last night, tangled around the wheels of one of his guest chairs. Pain shot through him, starting deep in his stomach and exploding in vast emptiness across his chest. Letting out a groan, he squeezed the silk in his fist against the rising tide of memories. Images. Feelings. This was why you didn't get involved with clients. Because they made a man start believing in long-discarded emotions again. Made him think he was a winner again.

It's over. Roxy's words hit him hard. Did she know how much she ended with those two words? It was over.

He'd failed. His eyes dropped to the tie. In more ways than he thought possible.

"That's it? You left?"

"She told me to, Grant. What was I supposed to do? Fight her?"

From the disappointed looks his brother and Sophie were shooting him from across the living room, fight was exactly what they expected.

He bristled defensively. "I don't need a client who's going to fight me every step of the way."

Sophie folded her arms, jostling the Yorkshire terrier sleeping on her lap. "Referring to Roxanne as a client? Really?"

"She was a client. What should I call her?"

"I don't know. You tell me." Challenge glittered in her blue eyes.

Mike broke the stare. They didn't know he'd slept with Roxy. Some things were none of their business.

Besides, he was trying not to think about the night they spent together. Every time he did, his chest hurt.

"I feel bad for her," Grant said. "First her mother turns her world upside down, then her father turns it the other way. And on top of everything she loses her job?"

"Terrible," Sophie agreed. "Have you tried calling her?" she asked Mike.

Had he tried calling her? "I just finished saying the woman wants nothing to do with me."

"I know what you said. But have you called her?"

Damn her. She had a whiff of the truth and she wouldn't give up. "Half a dozen times," he replied, looking to his glass of Scotch. "She's blocked my number."

"Ouch. I'm sorry."

He shrugged, feigning indifference, hoping Sophie would drop the subject. "It is what it is. Can't be helped."

"You've got it bad, don't you?"

It was Grant, not Sophie. At his brother's question, Mike looked up. "What are you talking about?"

"You and your 'client'." He quoted the word with his fingers. "She's a lot more isn't she?"

"Don't be—" He stopped. What was the sense in protesting? They'd only keep hammering until he gave up the truth. Roxanne was more. A lot more. He could barely sit in his office without picturing her there with him. Laughing. Brushing the hair from her face. The other night, he actually drove himself to the Elderion, with some foolish notion that the lounge would dredge up older memories. Stupid. Nostalgia didn't have a chance against Roxanne. He didn't even make it to his regular table before her absence slammed into him like a truck and he had to go home.

"How'd you know?" he asked.

"Personal experience," his brother replied. "I've used the nonchalant act myself. Back before Sophie and I got our act together."

"I also told him how attentive you were the other weekend," Sophie added. "Unless you stare at all your clients like a lovesick puppy."

"No, just Roxanne." He took a drink. It had been a mistake, he wanted to add, but he couldn't. Nothing about Roxanne was a mistake. Not her history, not her annoying habit of overreacting and certainly not her. Grant and Sophie were right. He had it bad. Head over heels kind of bad.

"Doesn't matter," he said, moving to their fireplace. His chest was hurting again. He realized now the ache came from a place far deeper than his body. "She told me I didn't belong in her world."

"I'm not surprised," Grant replied.

"Gee, thanks."

"Seriously. No offense, but if I were her, you'd be the last person I'd want to see, too."

His brother appeared at his shoulder. "Here she is, feeling like the world kicked her in the teeth. A guy like you would only highlight the problems."

"What do you mean, a guy like me?"

"You know what I mean, Golden Boy. I'm sure she feels lousy enough about life without her polar opposite around to remind her how low she is."

"You're saying I made her feel inferior?"

"Not on purpose. But having grown up with you, I can say it's not always easy living with Mom and Dad's clone."

If only they knew....

He was more concerned with Roxanne right now. Had he really made her feel like less of a person? The thought made him sick. "I never meant to—"

No, you only insisted she have a makeover so she'd fit in better. Made her feel less than acceptable as she was.

He slapped his glass on the mantel. "God, I'm such a hypocrite."

"I wouldn't go that far," Grant said.

"I would. I have no right making anyone feel inadequate." He stared at his empty glass, how the diamonds on the cut crystal were perfectly uniformed except for one. "Especially now," he said in a quiet voice.

"What are you talking about?"

Taking a deep breath, Mike told them the whole story. About how the firm was failing and how the money from Roxanne's case was his last hope for keeping it afloat.

When he finished, Grant simply said, "Wow."

"I knew there wasn't enough paper clutter," Sophie said. "Green office, my foot."

"I'm surprised you didn't catch on sooner," Mike told her.

The relief he hoped he would feel upon confession didn't materialize. Instead all he felt was embarrassed for not saying anything sooner. Thinking of Roxanne having to share her story over and over, he developed new respect. Took real strength to raise a child on her own, no family, no real money. When he first met her, he'd recognized the mettle in her. If only she saw it herself. Maybe they'd still be talking.

"Do Mom and Dad know?" Grant was asking.

He shook his head. "Are you kidding? Like you said, I'm the Golden Boy. The one who's supposed to do everything right." The freakin' Templeton namesake. "I was giving them what they expected." Same way he always did.

"The curse of Templeton expectations rides again."

"Excuse me?" Looking to his brother, he saw the younger man had grown intensely interested in the label on his beer bottle. "The family emphasis on super success. Screwed us all up. I got a fear of success…you developed a fear of failure. Wonder what Nicole ended up with."

"Maybe she lucked out."

"Maybe." Grant pulled a strip off the label and rolled it between his fingers. "You do realize of course, that closing shop isn't the end of the world."

"For you, maybe. I'm the one who's supposed to be better than all the rest."

"That's why you pushed Roxanne's case so hard."

"I couldn't afford to have the case drag out for years in court." The tactic worked, he had to admit that. Just not the way he intended.

"The day she told me about her father, I was shocked. I…" Remembering that final conversation, he winced. "I focused more on the case than her."

"No wonder she threw you out."

"No wonder indeed."

"What are you going to do now?" Sophie asked.

"What do I do now?" He'd messed up his career and his relationship with Roxanne. Failure wasn't a place he was used to operating from. He was lost.

"You could try talking with her," Sophie said.

"I told you, I already have. She wants nothing to do with me."

A hand clapped on his shoulder. Grant. "If you want, I can share with you a valuable piece of advice I got last summer. Something you said to me in fact."

Valuable advice? From him? "I have to hear this pearl of wisdom. What is it?"

"When's the last time a Templeton didn't go after what he wanted?"

CHAPTER THIRTEEN

"Look, Mommy. The animals made a merry-go-round!"

Roxy drew her attention away from the message on her cell phone only to wince at the plastic toys arranged in a circle on the living room floor. "That's nice. Are they having fun?"

"Uh-huh. I liked the merry-go-round we went to. Can we go back there?"

"What's wrong with the one in Central Park?"

Steffi looked up from making the horses dance. "This one has the rabbit," she said matter-of-factly.

"Oh."

"So can we go?"

Go to Bryant Park. Took her twenty-nine years to get to the place, and now it would be forever tainted with memories.

"We'll see," she said to Steffi. She hated saying no outright when she had no logical reason to give the four-year-old. What was she supposed to say? No, baby, I can't because thinking about the carousel makes Mommy cry? "Maybe someday."

"Okay. Can Mike come?"

A knife twisted in her chest. "I don't think we'll see Mike anymore."

"Why not?"

"Because we're not working together anymore. We're all done with our business."

"Why?"

Roxy sighed. Because Grandma's big deathbed confession turned out to be a deathbed fantasy, and then Mommy and Mike said some hurtful things to each other and Mommy sent Mike away, but that's okay because he would have left eventually anyway and she wanted to keep her heart from breaking. Except she didn't move fast enough and her heart ached anyway.

How was she supposed to explain that to a four-year-old?

As luck would have it, she didn't have to because someone knocked on the door. "I don't want to go see Mrs. Ortega," Steffi immediately started whining.

"We aren't going to Mrs. Ortega's," Roxy told her. "It's probably Priti from next door looking to borrow something."

But it wasn't Priti. It was Wayne. His shoulder rubbed against her as he pushed his way in. "We got any beer left?" he asked, strolling to the kitchen.

"We don't have anything," she replied sharply. "Alexis's not here. She's out with PJ." PJ, along with Wayne, had become a fixture in the apartment this week, meaning she now had two freeloaders living there. And annoying as that was, Roxy couldn't say a blessed thing. A little fact Alexis took great pleasure in. Along with all the other misfortunes that had befallen Steffi.

He came back into view, a can in each hand. "I hate cans," he said. "We gotta get more bottles."

Tell it to someone who cares. "I told you, Alexis isn't here. Wait a moment. How'd you get in the building anyway?"

"I had some business to take care of."

Business. She could imagine. "Well, you don't have any business here, so why don't you take off?"

"Relax." Wayne held up his arms. "I'm not here to cause trouble. I came by to see you. Thought maybe you might need some company."

The idea repulsed her beyond repulsion. "No, thanks. Steffi and I are fine by ourselves."

"Now don't go being like that. I know your lawyer man up and dumped you cause you ain't getting money."

"Mike didn't dump me." If anything, she dumped him, not that Wayne would believe her. "There was nothing to dump since we weren't having that kind of relationship."

"What kind of relationship is that?" Wayne suddenly appeared next to her shoulder, his breath sour from beer.

"Professional." Why was she even entertaining the guy's questions? Oh, right, because of Alexis. That reason was starting to wear thin.

Wayne smiled. "I can do professional," he said in a low voice that was supposed to sound sexy. "I can do anything you want. Like I told you. I treat my women real good. What do you say?" To illustrate his point, he ran an index finger down her arm. Roxy choked back the bile in her throat. Instead she looked over at Steffi, who was watching the entire exchange with her eyes as wide as saucers. "Steffi, baby, how about you take Dusty and go down to your room and play for a few minutes?"

As if hearing his name made her worry something would happen, the little girl grabbed her purple-and-white friend. "What about the merry-go-round?" she asked.

"Let's give the animals a break and I'll bring them in a few minutes, okay? Now please be a good girl and go to your room."

"Yeah, kid," Wayne echoed, winking in Roxy's direction. "Beat it."

The little girl rose to her feet, but wavered. Roxy gave her a nod and a smile to let her know everything would be all right. It worked, and eventually the child toddled to her bedroom and shut the door.

Roxy waited until she heard the click before whirling around and slapping Wayne's hand away. "Don't you ever talk to me or my daughter like that again, do you hear?"

The nineteen-year-old responded with a click of his piercing against his teeth. "Alexis ain't going to like you talking to me that way."

That was it. This blight of a human being had been darkening her doorstep long enough. Suggesting she would sleep with him because she hit hard times? She may have sunk low, but she would never sink that low. Ever.

She jabbed her index finger into his shoulder. "Look here, you little wannabe punk, I don't care whose baby brother you are. You so much as look at me or my little girl, and I will squeeze your private parts so hard you'll be singing soprano. Do you understand? Not one single look. Now take your beer and get out of my apartment."

Alexis would definitely not like this, but frankly she didn't care. There was only so much a woman should put up with.

Openly ignoring her threat, Wayne looked her up and down. "What if I don't want to leave?" he asked, stepping closer.

Roxy grabbed her cell phone, which thankfully, she still had in her pocket. "Then I'll call the police," she told him. "We'll see how your parole officer feels about you getting arrested. Especially since you were doing business." She pushed the first button. "Nine."

"Alexis's going to be ticked."

"I don't care. The only reason I'm giving you a countdown at all is because of Alexis." If she had actual proof of his "business," she wouldn't even give him that courtesy. She'd have his skinny butt hauled back to prison in a second. "One," she said.

"All right, all right," he said before she could repeat the last number. "Don't get all wigged out."

"You don't know wigged out, pal. Now get out."

"Uppity…" He muttered the second word but Roxy could guess it. The same oath he used before. This time he curled his lip in distaste.

"You think you're so much better than us because you did a few TV interviews and some dude bought you some fancy clothes," he said, "but I got news for you. You ain't all that."

"Maybe not," Roxy replied. "But I'm still better than you."

And she was better than this life.

"I don't like Wayne," Steffi told her when Roxy tucked her in bed a little while later. "He's mean."

Out of the mouths of babes… Roxy smoothed the sheets around her chest. "I think he is, too, but don't you worry. I won't let him bother you anymore."

"Is that why we're hiding in the bedroom? Because he's mean?"

"We're in the bedroom," Roxy said, "because it's bedtime." And yes, because she was afraid he might decide to come back, and the bedroom door had workable locks. "We can have a slumber party."

"Like the ponies?"

"Exactly."

Steffi snuggled in against her pillow, a little red-haired angel. She was a great kid, yet untouched by the Waynes in this world. So far, Roxy'd been able to keep them at bay. She intended to keep doing so. Tomorrow morning, she'd start looking for a new job and a new apartment. Maybe some place out of the city, where Steffi could have a yard. After all, when she started this Sinclair heiress business, hadn't it been to give her daughter a better life? If Wayne's little visit did anything, it told her she could sit around licking her wounds, mourning the losses she'd never get back or she could get off her duff and give her daughter the life she deserved. She chose the latter.

"I like Mike better," Steffi said, her eyes starting to blink with sleep. "He's nicer."

Speaking of losses she'd never get back. "Yes, he is. He's very nice."

"Do you like him?"

She a lot more than liked him. When he walked out, he took her heart with him. "It's complicated, baby."

"Complicated means hard. Mike told me."

"Mike's right."

"He said the same thing when I asked if he liked you."

Smart guy, thought Roxy. Notice he didn't come straight out and say yes, either.

"I don't think it is."

"What is?" She missed what her daughter was trying to say.

Steffi yawned. "Hard. Unless the person doesn't like you back. But you and Mike like each other so " she yawned again "—I don't think it's hard."

Roxy didn't know how to respond to that. How could she explain to a four-year-old that feelings weren't so black and white? There were other issues that made relationships complicated, such as being able to look the man she loved in the eye. Or look at herself.

"I love you, Mommy," Steffi said.

Heart overflowing, Roxy kissed her forehead. "I love you, too. Sweet dreams."

Giving her one last kiss, she turned out the light and laid down on her bed. For the first time since talking to her father, she felt a surge of positivity. Standing up to Wayne made her feel stronger. In control. A little bit like...

Like she had when she was doing the interviews.

At the time, she said she felt like a different person was giving those interviews. Some woman she didn't know. Capable. Confident.

Could it be that woman was still there? She certainly showed up to tell off Wayne.

Better than staying in your apartment playing victim. Mike's words came back. She'd been hurt and angry when he said them, and retaliated in kind. But now she wondered. Did she have a choice?

"Mommy?" Steffi's voice reached out through the darkness. She hoped the little girl was simply restless, and not stressed out about Wayne or other problems.

"Yes, baby?"

"I hope liking Mike stops being hard. So you won't be so sad."

Roxy felt the ache before it had fully formed. The slow winding pang of loss. "That'd be nice."

"Maybe if we took him to the merry-go-round, you could like him again. You smiled a lot that day."

"Yes, I did." How could she not? It'd been a magical day.

"Mike smiled a lot, too. We should go to the merry-go-round again." Having voiced her decision, she gave a satisfied sigh. Roxy heard the rustle of sheets and, a few seconds later, the slow, steady sound of breathing.

Could it really be so simple? Were all these obstacles things she made up? Put in her own way? Mike accused her of playing the victim. That's certainly what she'd been doing these past couple days.

She rolled on her side. In some ways, that's what her

mother did, too. She clung to her love for Wentworth so strongly, she faded away from everyone else. At least Wentworth was willing to act and make something happen. He died planning to take a stand against his father. In his mind, loving someone wasn't so complicated.

Okay, she thought folding her arms behind her head. Maybe she wasn't a Sinclair by blood. Didn't mean she couldn't steal a little of Wentworth's determination.

Without thinking, she reached for her cell phone that lay on the nightstand. Mike's text was still on the screen, undeleted, waiting for her. *You were not a mistake,* he'd written. Her case? Her? Both? The words, coupled with her newfound control couldn't help but give her hope.

When did a Templeton not go after what he wanted?

Mike remembered all too well when he posted the same question to his brother. Circumstances were different. Grant and Sophie were simply being proud and stubborn. All they needed was for one of them to make the first move. In his case, he'd tried to talk to Roxanne, and she refused.

Who could blame her? She'd been hurting and he was worried about what? A law practice? Letting down his family?

Wentworth Sinclair would be ashamed.

He slapped a file in the large cardboard box. The downside of being a small law practice was that when it came time to move, you had to do the actual moving. There were no administrative staff members or clerks to help you out.

Just as well, thought Mike as he assembled another file storage box. He wasn't fit for the company of others anyway.

Wentworth's letters lay in a stack nearby. He ran his finger over the black scrawl. Six times. Six times he'd called and not so much as a voice mail. In the end, he settled for sending her a text message, hoping the apology would help.

"So it's true."

Judge Michael Templeton, Jr. wore a Burberry trench coat and his salt-and-pepper hair was combed back, emphasizing his handsome, time-sharpened features. He entered the room as though the office was his own and sat down, opting for Mike's desk chair over one of the guest seats. "When Jim Brassard told me you inquired about a position, I thought for sure he misunderstood. What's going on?"

Mike dropped another file in the box. "Isn't it obvious?" he said. "I'm closing up shop."

"I meant why are you closing your practice? You didn't mention anything. I thought you enjoyed being your own boss."

"I also enjoy eating."

Based on the way he stiffened, his father didn't appreciate the sharp comeback. "Is that your way of saying business is a little slow?"

Mike chuckled at his father's adjective. "A little," he replied. "You may not have noticed, but we're in an economic downturn."

"If business is slow, then get out there and double your efforts. Beat the bushes for business. You don't throw in the towel, Michael. That's not how we do things."

How we do things. The phrase set Mike's teeth on edge. God, but he was so tired of hearing how "they" were raised. How he was supposed to be.

"Do you remember when you first started swimming and you couldn't keep up with the rest of your squad?" his father asked.

"What I remember is being two years younger." His father convinced the coach he needed the challenge.

"Exactly. But you dug in and by the end of the year you were beating those boys."

Of course he dug in. He was eight years old and his father was dragging him to a swimming pool every weekend for extra practice. Pushing him every step of the way till his times improved. And Mike obeyed. To win his approval. To make his father proud. On and on the cycle went. Go higher. Be better. Be the best. So many expectations, his shoulders hurt.

"We didn't raise you to be a quitter, Michael. When I was your age, I already had a thriving practice with two associates. Did I have tough times, sure, but I worked for my success. I thought we raised you the same way."

Oh, they did, all right. His father raised him to be a mirror image. The perfect namesake. "What if I don't want it?" he asked aloud.

"What are you talking about? Of course you want it. We talked about this last year. How you'd done all you could at Ashby Gannon, and should be stepping out on your own."

We discussed. *You should.* Not once did they discuss what Mike wanted. God, wasn't it time he stopped being a puppet and grew up?

"People change their minds," he told his father. "Maybe I don't want this—" he waved his arm around the room "—anymore. Maybe I want something else."

"You've wanted to be a lawyer since you were eight years old, Michael."

"Did I? Because I remember at eight years old I wanted to be a pirate." He slapped the file he was holding on the table. "In fact, that's the last time I remember wanting anything that wasn't shaped or picked for me." Until six nights ago, with Roxanne. Holding her was all his idea. Best one he'd ever had, too. "The only reason I said I wanted to be a lawyer was because that's what you were, and like any eight-year-old, I wanted to be like my father. I had no idea you would decide 'like' meant mirror image."

His father scoffed. "I did no such thing."

"Didn't you? Swimming. The debate club. Your alma maters. What was all that about then, if not to repeat your past glories?"

"To help you be the best you could be. For heaven's sake, Michael, you make it sound like we put a gun to your head."

"No gun, just a whole lot of expectations."

"If you're saying we pushed you, yes. We wanted the best for you."

"You didn't want the best." Roxanne wanted the best. She was willing to do anything, including the one thing she feared the most—losing her daughter's respect to give Steffi a better life. "You wanted us to *be* the best. Always. Because God forbid we reflect badly on the family."

"That is not true!" his father bellowed, an uncharacteristic tone of voice for him and a sign Mike had hit a nerve dead-on. He pushed further.

"If so, then why are you here?"

"Because Jim Brassard told me—"

"Told you I was closing up shop and you were afraid he was telling the truth. Well, guess what, he was. I failed. I opened my own law practice, crashed and burned. Deal with it."

Soon as Mike said the words, a thousand pounds lifted from his shoulders. He'd done it. He'd failed and the world didn't end.

Not that you could tell from the look on his father's face. Disappointment marked every line.

"Fine," the elder Templeton said. "You're closing your firm, and it's my fault. Happy?"

Mike shook his head. His father truly didn't understand,

did he? None of this was about him. Took Mike till just this moment to realize his succeeding or failing was all his. Same with the choices he made. "Why does it have to involve you at all, Dad? Sometimes bad luck happens."

He could tell his father wasn't convinced. Maybe never would be. For the first time, Mike realized there was nothing he could do about what his father thought. "So what do you plan to do? Go back to Ashby Gannon or Brassard's firm?"

"Maybe. I don't know." The uncertainty had a liberating feel. Suddenly the world was wide-open.

There was one thing he did want. Or rather, two. Question was, did they want him?

Only one way to know for sure. Forgetting all about his father and packing, Mike grabbed the stack of letters off his desk. Wentworth would be proud.

"Where are you going?" his father called after him.

"What a Templeton's supposed to do," he replied, grinning. More for himself and the world than to the man seated at his desk.

"I'm going after what I want."

First thing he'd do when he got to Roxanne's would be to apologize and ask for another chance. She'd have to talk with him eventually, right? If necessary, he'd camp out in her hallway and accost her when she stepped outside. Whatever he needed to do.

He made it as far as the lobby before his mind started playing tricks on him. Getting off the elevator he swore he saw Steffi coming through the revolving door.

"Mike!" The figment waved brightly. "Look, Mommy, it's Mike."

His wishful eyes traveled to the woman behind her. It really was Roxanne. Dressed in a pair of faded jeans and the pale blue turtleneck, she'd never looked lovelier. When she saw him, she offered a tremulous smile.

Mike's pulse skipped a couple beats. He stopped dead. "Hey!" he said.

Silence filled the gap as he struggled with what to say next, hindered by the Manhattan-size lump lodged in his throat. "I was on my way to your apartment," he finally managed to say.

"You were? Why?"

To kiss you senseless. "To return your mother's letters," he said. As if it would prove his point, he held up his briefcase.

"Oh," she replied.

Was that disappointment he caught flickering across her face? He was afraid to hope. "Why are you…?"

"Same thing."

"Oh." His heart dropped. Guess it wasn't disappointment after all.

"Where's your tie?" Steffi asked.

"My what? Oh, my tie." Automatically his hand went to the collar of his T-shirt. "I didn't wear one today. I didn't want it to get dirty while I was packing."

Roxanne frowned, hearing his answer. "Packing?" she asked. "Are you going somewhere?"

"Eventually. I hope. I'm closing my practice."

"Why?" Perhaps she didn't realize, but she rushed toward him a few steps. "Is something—? Did something—?"

Mike saved her the trouble of searching for the right question and explained. When he finished, she looked down at her shoes. "The money from my case. You needed it to stay afloat."

He always said she was quick. "I needed the case for a lot of reasons," he told her. "Notoriety, money."

"Then if I hadn't…"

"You aren't to blame for anything." He refused to pile on guilt when she had enough issues on her shoulders. "This was my doing, one hundred percent. I took the case for all the wrong reasons. That's why, when you dropped the lawsuit, I acted like such a jerk."

"You were worried."

"Not worried. Afraid." Taking a deep breath, he said aloud the truth he'd kept to himself for a long time. "I was afraid of what would happen when I failed."

"Because you never had a choice," she said quietly.

"Exactly." She understood. "I thought I'd be letting everybody down."

"And now?"

"Now I'm thinking the only person I've failed all these years is myself. Plus you."

She shook her head. "You never failed me."

He didn't? Giving in to his longing to be closer, he stepped forward, hoping when he drew near, she wouldn't back away. "I've been taking a good long look at how I see success," he said. He thought about his father, still upstairs. "Some of it in the past few minutes in fact."

"What did you decide?"

"That I need to reexamine my personal definition of success and failure. See, I've spent a good portion of my life chasing one and fearing the other. Turns out I never really knew either till I met this woman who managed to be both sweet and graceful at the same time, in spite of all the stuff life tossed her."

Of course, she'd argue that she's not very successful at all.

"That so?"

"Uh-huh." He lucked out. She didn't back away. He continued closing the gap. "In fact," he said, "she'd argue she's a complete failure, even though that couldn't be further from the truth.

"She's very feisty," he said with a smile. "Before you showed up, I was debating about going to her apartment and camping out on her doorstep till she spoke to me."

"You were going to sleep on the steps?" Steffi asked. "Do you have a sleeping bag?"

Leave it to a four-year-old to ask the important questions. "I was hoping it wouldn't come to that, but if your mother wouldn't talk to me, I would have."

"Mommy's the woman?"

Mike nodded.

"But we came here because Mommy wanted to talk to you."

He wasn't sure if he should let the hope that lodged in his chest grow or not. He decided to take a chance. "What did you want to talk with me about?"

Roxy blinked back her tears. She'd rehearsed this scene in her head a dozen times last night, but none of her versions involved Mike saying such beautiful things or his looking so breathtakingly casual. She spent all night arguing back and forth with herself over coming here. Did she take a chance and trust the sincerity that always glowed in his eyes or did she give up like her mother?

"Did you mean it?" she asked him. "What you said in your text?"

He nodded. "Every word. You were definitely not a mistake."

Relief whooshed from her lungs. Five words. Six if you added the new word, definitely. Five words that meant everything. She felt them wrap around her heart, unlocking the feelings inside and telling her that yes, this choice was worth making.

"Funny, but I had to do some reevaluating, too," she told him. "Seems this guy I know told me I was playing victim, letting all the 'stuff' life threw me convince me I'm not worthy of anything better."

"He was wrong."

"Wait!" She touched her fingers to his lips. "He was right. I was crying 'poor me,' but not anymore."

"What made you change your mind?"

She smiled, thinking of the letters in his briefcase. "My mother. I didn't want to be like her. I didn't want to find myself lying on my deathbed pining for the man I couldn't have. Especially when I had the power to get him back."

Strong arms wrapped around her waist, drawing her close. "You never lost him," he whispered.

Roxy's heart soared. "I'm so very glad," she whispered back. Rising on tiptoes, she brought her mouth to his. "I have a question. What would you have done if the successful woman didn't listen to you?"

"I would have looked her in the eye and told her I was grateful for every second I knew her. That nothing we shared was a mistake."

His words reached deep into her soul, healing its wounds. Telling her she'd made the right choice.

"And then," he said, fingers tangling in her hair, "I would have kissed her till she realized I'm crazy about her. I have been since the minute she stormed out of my office in a huff."

"Sounds perfect," Roxy whispered, her voice catching on the tears. "Because I'm pretty sure she's crazy about you, too."

In the end, it wasn't the words that convinced her, but the emotion that glowed from his eyes while he spoke. Looking deep into them, she saw love, compassion and the coppery-brown sincerity that captured her heart. For the first time, seeing them mixed together didn't frighten her, either. If anything, they made her feel more successful than she'd ever felt in her life. Because she loved and was loved.

"Just in case, though…" She touched his cheek. "You should probably kiss her senseless anyway."

"My pleasure," Mike replied. Slipping an arm around her waist, he pulled her close, his lips speaking a truth all their own. Only a small tug on her sweater stopped the moment.

"Does this mean Mike's going to come with us to the merry-go-round?" Steffi asked.

Mike laughed and scooped the little girl into his arms. "Absolutely, my little pony! There is nothing I want to do more right now." He smiled at Roxy over the little girl's head.

And Roxy, smiling back, believed every word.

* * * * *

HARD DEAL

STEFANIE LONDON

To Taryn.

For the Skype calls and hilarious GIFs, and
for always putting a smile on my face.
Thanks for being a great friend.

CHAPTER ONE

As far as Imogen Hargrove was concerned, this week could take a long walk off a short pier. Or go into space and take its helmet off. If she was a potty-mouthed kind of woman, she might've had a few more words to employ in explaining exactly how much she'd hated this week.

But alas, she could taste the soap in her mouth before any four-letter words had the chance to form.

"Breathe," she said to herself as she tidied her desk. "The day is almost over."

Most days she loved her job. Being an executive assistant to the CEO of the most respected architecture and construction firm in Australia had its perks. Like getting to work with a host of amazingly talented, smart and passionate people. Not to mention the little blue box that appeared on her employment anniversary every year.

But today had been the cherry on top of a giant pain-in-the-butt sundae. Not only had she managed to spill her morning cappuccino all over herself, but then she'd missed the start of the management meeting because she'd been frantically trying to get the stain out. Which wouldn't have been so bad, except that her arch-nemesis had swooped in and made her look disorganised by handing out the wrong agenda. Imogen was *positive* he'd done it on purpose. Then—like a sign from the gods that she really should have stayed in bed—her boss had demanded she shuffle his entire afternoon five minutes before he was due to present at the finance team's quarterly town hall.

Thank God Jason had been able to step in. Imogen bit back a smile as she thought of the CEO's son. Apart from being a total hottie, he was being groomed to take over the company. Good looking *and* ambitious, traits that went together like peanut butter and chocolate as far as she was concerned. Chances were she'd be working for him. Intimately. All the long hours and late nights trapped together in the office sounded like a scene straight out of one of those raunchy books her friend Lainey loved to read.

You could do with something a little raunchy in your life. You're one bad date away from becoming a born-again virgin.

Ugh. How was it her fault the dates she'd been on recently had less snap, crackle and pop than her morning bowl of Rice Bubbles? She'd tried to be funny and interesting and cute enough for a guy to take her to bed…but either she was picking the wrong guys, or she had no idea how to be any of those things.

She brushed her hands down the grey pencil skirt that covered her knees and matched the pearls around her neck. Her friends teased her for her "limited colour palette" but Imogen knew what worked for her. Monochrome made her mornings easier. Besides, it was important to look professional. She had a feeling Jason would appreciate that about her.

"What's got you looking so dreamy, Imogen? Wait, don't tell me." Caleb Allbrook sauntered into her office with a swagger that made Imogen's thighs automatically press together. "Daydreaming about me again?"

Then there was the CEO's *other* son. The one who managed to get her feminine hormones singing like an opera of canaries at full volume even though he was bad news in every sense of the word.

The guy was trouble enough for an entire Taylor Swift album.

"I can barely restrain myself," she said drily, not even attempting to keep the disdain out of her voice. "You should leave before I throw myself at your feet. It would be best for us both."

Caleb raised a brow. He was as handsome as his brother, without a doubt. But whereas Jason was all serious, moody glances and smooth, in-command tones, Caleb was his polar-opposite. The younger Allbrook brother was always quick with a snappy comeback, and he didn't take anything or *anyone* seriously. The guy oozed so much sex appeal he should be listed as a controlled substance. He was cocky as all get-out and most women in the office swooned whenever he walked past, which only inflated his giant ego further.

"Who am I to turn down a woman in need? Should I close the door or do you want an audience?" He wrapped a hand around the doorknob and waited for her response.

It was times like this that Imogen wondered if she *should* start swearing, because it seemed like the perfect time to use the F-word. Preferably with either a "you" or "off" following it. "What do you want, Caleb?"

His full lips curved into a wicked grin and Imogen had to tamp down the excitement zipping through her. Dammit, when was her body going to get the memo on this one?

Caleb Allbrook is not your type. It doesn't matter if you never have another date in your life, he's not for you.

"A moment of your precious time, Ms. Hargrove." He walked over to her desk and planted both palms on the smooth, wooden surface.

"*Miss* Hargrove."

"Single and loving it, huh? Good for you."

She oscillated between wanting to run her fingers through his thick, wavy hair and needing to slap him across the face with her binder. As usual. The guy was her kryptonite. In every other scenario, Imogen prided herself on her poise and level-headedness. On her ability to be the cool cucumber in a room full of ticking bombs. But around Caleb Allbrook, her brain cells packed their bags and flew on a one-way ticket to Fiji.

"Can we get to the part where you tell me what

you need so I can do it and go home?" she said, huffing.

"It's dangerous to agree before knowing what I'm going to ask." He chuckled. "Okay, fine. Enough with the death stare. I need you to help me find the marketing materials from the fifty-year anniversary campaign."

"Shouldn't someone from your team be able to assist you with that?" She raised a brow. "I assume at least one of the people you hired will have the requisite technical skills to navigate our shared folder system."

"Now, now. There's no need to be snippy, *Miss* Hargrove." He smirked. "And I need the originals, not the files."

She groaned internally. That meant a trip to the archive room in the building's basement. The CEO was paranoid about people having access to it. Something to do with a fire-related accident before her time that resulted in a ton of tax paperwork being lost. Never mind the fact that smoking was now prohibited in offices and that they had sprinklers and fire alarms in every section of the building. Oh, and technological advancements meant they had electronic copies of everything. Regardless, there were only three keys to the archive room in the whole company. The CEO's, Jason's and hers.

Caleb hadn't made the cut.

"Does it have to be done now?" she asked, glancing at her inbox. Imogen had a rule about Friday afternoons: never leave the office with outstanding tasks on the to-do list. But today she was itching to get out of there.

An image flickered in her mind—a mask hanging from her bedroom door. The white feathers, crystals and shimmering lengths of rose-gold chain were all waiting to adorn her.

"It'll take five minutes," he said, motioning for her to follow him. "If it gives you any more motivation, it's for Jason. I believe you convinced him to present to the bean counters, so he couldn't make the request himself."

She sighed and pushed up from her chair. "Fine, but make it quick. I've got somewhere to be."

"Hot date?"

Hardly. After her last few dates had ended with a "you seem like a nice person but there's no spark" conversation, she'd started to wonder if it was worth the bother. There was only so much rejection a woman could take before getting paranoid that she had some third head only other people could see. Just once she'd like a guy to get all hot and bothered over her. Just once she'd like to be the object of someone's desire. Was that too much to ask?

No, tonight was definitely not a date. But she wasn't about to tell Caleb about the sorry state of her love life. Undoubtedly, he'd laugh in her face. Because as much as he joked and teased and flirted, he'd never once asked her out. Never once made an actual move.

Why do you care? It's not like you want him to ask.

Sure. But Imogen was sick of being ignored. Unfortunately, that seemed to be her lot in life. In any case, she'd put aside worries over her own lack of love life to focus on someone *else's* love life. Her sister, Penny, was getting married in ten short weeks to Daniel the Duke of Douchetown.

It was bad enough that her future brother-in-law's stuffy old-money family had given Penny hell when they'd first gotten engaged. She'd ended up at Imogen's place in tears on more than one occasion after they'd made her feel unworthy. But now Imogen had a sneaking suspicion that her fiancé was cheating. She'd spotted him flirting with a blonde woman at a bar when he'd lied to Penny and told her he was in Sydney for work.

So, she'd hatched a plan to catch him in the act. In disguise, of course.

Caleb bit back a smile as his father's assistant walked alongside him, her pink lips set into a flat line. The woman always looked as though she'd sucked on a lemon. Logically, it wasn't a visual that should turn him on but there was something about Imogen's overly prim persona that got him all hot and bothered. And hard as a rock. Maybe it was because he suspected that beneath the boring shirt and single strand of pearls, there was a spitfire lurking.

He had a talent for seeing the reality that people tried desperately to conceal. And the fact that a woman as hot as Imogen chose to hide behind an outfit better suited to a funeral director made him curious as hell.

"Wouldn't you like to know?" she said.

"I can be your SOS. Message me if he turns out to be a foot shorter than his Tinder profile advertised." He nudged her with his elbow as they waited for the elevator. "Or if he's a close-talker. I know you hate those."

"Who doesn't hate a close-talker?" Her button nose wrinkled. "When I speak with someone, I don't want to know what they had for lunch. Let alone experience it secondhand."

The elevator opened. It was rammed, sardine-style. All his father's obedient minions were clocking out at five-thirty on the dot. That tended to happen when Gerald Allbrook went off-site. Apparently, there'd been some shit storm with contract negotiations for a new residential tower on Collins street. The big man had stepped in, which wasn't a good sign.

Not that Caleb should give a shit. He wasn't going to have a hand in this company beyond his current puff position as head of marketing. It'd been a token gesture after making Jason managing director. AKA next in line. Jason was Prince William and Caleb was the redheaded kid who'd only ever sit on the throne if everyone else kicked the bucket.

"Who's looking daydreamy now?" Imogen said as the elevator pinged at the next floor. Two more people squeezed in.

"I'm thinking about regaining my personal space," he quipped.

A smile tugged at the corner of her lips. The elevator jerked to a stop again and Imogen glanced at the sweaty-looking man standing on her other side. Her nose was unfortunately armpit-height. Her head swung to Caleb and she sighed, shuffling closer.

"Good choice," he whispered.

"You'll never be a good choice," she muttered, rolling her eyes. "Just the lesser of two evils."

Ouch. Imogen had never bothered to hide the fact that she—like everyone else—viewed him as a layabout who was riding on the coattails of his family name, never to achieve anything of his own. But the upside of that meant he could do whatever the hell he wanted without pressure to perform like his prize show-pony brother.

"I love it when you play hard to get."

"I know every other female in this office seems to be under the deluded impression that you're God's gift to cha-chas, but I'm not blinded by a pretty face." She folded her arms across her chest.

He leaned closer as people streamed past him to get out at the ground floor. For once he was grateful that the archive rooms were shoved way down in the basement. "Cha-chas? Really?"

"I'm supposed to take language advice from a guy who wears novelty socks?" She shook her head. "How am I supposed to take you seriously when you wear tacos on your feet?"

He pulled up the leg of his designer suit pants to reveal a bright red sock with a T. Rex print. The socks were his "thing." Plus, they had the added benefit of pissing off his father. The old man had strict requirements for his sons' appearances. Even on "casual days," where the whole damn company could wear denim, Caleb and Jason were supposed to suit up like penguins. So the funky socks were his way of giving the middle finger. And frankly, they were a talking point. A conversation starter. And Caleb liked talking to people.

"You know I only wear the tacos on Taco Tuesday." He grinned. "Besides, how does my sense of fashion have anything to do with your inability to correctly name your body parts?"

"What do you want me to call it?" She turned her nose up but some of the bravado had disappeared. The pink flush in her cheeks didn't match the defiant expression.

"How about you use the proper term?" They were alone in the elevator now, but Caleb continued to whisper as though there were people listening. "Pussy."

Was it his imagination or did a tremor run through her? The pink turned from a sheer tint to bright splotches on her cheeks. "That's *highly* inappropriate," she spluttered. "And the proper term is vagina, not pussy."

She blinked, as though surprised by her own words. Caleb grinned. "Did I succeed in getting the Prim Miss Hargrove to use a naughty word?"

"You're a bad influence," she said as the elevator came to its final stop. The doors slid open and she marched out ahead of him, her sensible low-heeled pumps click-clacking against the polished floor.

"You say that like it's news." He followed her, a

step behind so he could watch her hips sway as she walked.

Her skirt wasn't exactly tight fitting, but he knew for a fact that her shapely legs extended up to a pert backside. That beneath the crisp white shirt she hid a pair of perfect, bouncy breasts. That underneath all that spit and polish, the girl had a tattoo of a diamond on the side of her rib cage. He'd seen it once, during a team-building day when they'd been at a corporate retreat. She'd had on a basic black swimsuit that kept everything covered, but when she'd fallen off her paddleboard he'd caught a glimpse of it.

And ever since he'd been on a mission to find out more about Imogen Hargrove.

CHAPTER TWO

Imogen unlocked the door to the archive room and held it open for him, making a sweeping gesture with her hand as though she were leading him into a ballroom. "Now hurry up. It's home time."

Caleb chuckled to himself as he started hunting for the box of archived promotional materials. "You never did answer my question."

"Which one?"

"About whether you had a date tonight." He pulled the lid off a box and rifled through the contents. Nope, not that one.

"Why do you care about my love life?" She leaned against a steel rack that housed row after row of identical brown boxes. The way she folded her arms under her bust made the buttons strain on her shirt. "It's not as interesting as yours."

"Your love life isn't interesting because you keep turning me down."

She rolled her eyes. "I've come to the conclusion that you're all talk, Caleb. You make these pithy remarks and dirty little jokes but you haven't actually asked me out. I'm not sure I would go so far as to use the C-word, but…"

"The C-word?"

"Chicken."

Was the Prim Miss Hargrove calling his bluff? He raised a brow. "You sure I haven't asked you out?"

"Nope, not once. And I know you *have* asked out other women in the office. Tiffany from accounts. Stella from payroll." She ticked the names off with her fingers. "Bethany from the assistant pool. She was a temp, but I'm still counting it."

"I had no idea you were keeping track." That pleased him greatly. "Are you aware they all said yes?"

"I am. Seems nobody turns you down."

"Except you."

"I *haven't* turned you down." She clicked her nails against the metal shelf behind her. "Yet."

"Yet."

"You're too busy beating around the bush to ask."

"But you *would* turn me down?" He rifled through another box, acutely aware that he was being watched. "And stop staring at my ass."

"Excuse me," she spluttered. "I am *not* staring at your ass."

She totally was. He could see her in the reflection off the thick poles that stabilised the shelves. "I should have HR write you up for that."

"See, this is *exactly* what I'm talking about." She threw her hands up in the air. "You're all talk, no action. Face it, I could unbutton my shirt right now and you wouldn't do a damn thing about it."

Ka-ching! "Try me."

He turned and leaned against the shelving unit, mimicking her pose. The crappy florescent lighting of the archive room did nothing to hide the delicious flush in Imogen's cheeks. The colour spread all the way down her neck, and he imagined farther past the modest neckline of her shirt.

"It's an expression," she muttered.

"Now who's all talk?"

She narrowed her eyes at him. "You think *I'm* a chicken?"

"Free range, obviously. Possibly organic." He grinned. "Definitely one hundred percent chicken."

She licked her lips. Stalling. "There are cameras in here."

"So turn the light off. Dad's big on security but he's too tight to spring for infrared." He waited for her to back down. "No one will know."

"Doesn't that defeat the purpose of the exercise?"

Exercise. Like they were talking about a bloody fire drill. "I can see with my hands."

She sucked in a quick breath. "You're so full of it."

"Think that honour goes to you, Miss Hargrove." He laughed. "You talk a big game, but the second I try to pull the trigger you're coming up with excuse after excuse. Don't worry. I'm disappointed but I'll live."

Her nostrils flared. This was how things always were between them—simultaneously wary and oh so interested. Truth was he *hadn't* ever asked her out. Because he knew what the answer would be.

But today she'd decided to play his game. Whatever the reason, he wasn't going to question it.

"Ugh, I'm *sick* of men acting interested and then backing off the second any conversation happens." She stalked over to the door and Caleb was sure she was about to leave. But then the light went off. "Am I really that boring?"

Holy shit. Was this happening? The sound of fabric rustling in the dark got him hard as stone in an instant. He blinked, trying to force his eyes to adjust to the dark. But the archive room was like an underground cell. Not even a crack of light slipped in from the hallway outside.

"Stay by the door," he said. He walked around the perimeter of the room, his hands trailing along the edge of the shelves so he knew where he was. "And don't turn that light back on."

Silence. For a second there was nothing. Then his hands brushed something warm. Bare skin.

"Found you," he said, his voice low and gravelly. "My, my. The Prim Miss Hargrove knows how to play a game of truth or dare."

"Just dare," she said. He stepped closer, his hand brushing her bare skin again. The area felt flat, possibly her stomach. God, he wanted to touch all of her. "And I play to win."

She stayed stock still as his hand travelled up. There was a curve, something hard beneath her soft skin. Rib cage. Then his fingertips brushed over something soft and textured. Lace. The swell of her breast filled his palm perfectly—firm and round.

His thumb grazed over a hard nipple and his cock shifted in response.

Imogen made a soft, strangled sound and it was like an arrow of excitement straight through him. How many times had he thought about doing this with her? How many times had he wondered what her soft, curvy body would feel like under his hungry grasp? It would be so easy to back her up against the door and lift her leg over his hip.

"See," she said, though her voice trembled as his thumb brushed her nipple again. "Told you I'm not all talk."

Caleb opened his mouth to respond when a loud knock came down on the other side of the door. The thud was so hard it seemed to rattle the door in its hinges. "Hello? This is Jim from security. Everything okay in there? We saw the lights go out on the security monitor."

Fuck. He hadn't thought anyone would be watching them.

"We're fine!" Imogen's shrill voice made Caleb wince. Then she shoved him away from her with one hand. "Just testing some new glow-in-the-dark promo items."

A second later the light flicked back on and Imogen was buttoned up as if their game had never taken place. She yanked the door open and gave the security guard a charming smile. "Sorry, we should have warned you. We needed to test that the items glowed properly and the rooms upstairs don't get dark enough."

The security guard raised a brow as though he didn't really believe the story, but she didn't give him a chance to ask any more questions before marching out of the room, leaving both Caleb and the security guard in her dust.

Caleb pulled into the sweeping driveway of his parents' Albert Park mansion with his head still spinning from the incident in the archive room. He needed to put it out of his mind, though, because it was family dinner night. And that meant being on his A-game.

It looked as though Jason had already arrived, since his brother's black BMW was parked out front. It sat next to his mother's gunmetal Mercedes and his father's silver Audi. God, it was like someone had done a photo shoot of the world's most boring vehicles.

He pulled his candy-apple-red Alfa Romeo into the empty spot next to the Merc. Like most things about Caleb's life, it didn't fit in with the rest of his family. In his world, he wasn't the black sheep. More like lime green with purple polka dots.

"About time," his brother called from the front door. "I thought we'd have to start without you."

"That would make a change. Since when am *I* the last to arrive?"

Caleb and his mother often jokingly made bets about who would be later to dinner—Gerald or Jason. They were two peas in a pod, unable to tear themselves away from work even with the promise of a home-cooked meal. Well, a meal cooked *in* their home, anyway. No one had cooked in that house but their personal chef, Luis, since they moved in a decade ago.

"I went to the finance town hall and it finished up a little early. So, I stayed for a drink and then came straight over." His brother slapped Caleb on the back as he entered the house. "Thought it might be nice not to hold up the show, for once."

"And Dad's here already?" They walked through the foyer and into the open-plan dining and living room. His parents were already seated, a bottle of wine open between them.

"Yeah, the negotiations turned out fine."

Of course they did. There weren't many people who could face down Gerald Allbrook and come out on top. His father had intimidation down to a fine art. The only difference between him and a mob boss was that he didn't need henchmen. Or a gun.

"What held you up?" Jason asked.

"Had to get something from the archive room." Caleb grinned at the memory. "Since you and Dad were gone, I had to get a key from Imogen."

"You *still* don't have a key?" Jason raised a brow. "Get Imogen to cut one for you."

The whole key issue was representative of Caleb's relationship with his father. Gerald had made a big song and dance about only wanting three keys and it turned out the old man trusted his assistant more than his youngest son.

"All good, mate," he said loud enough for his

father to hear. "It's never a hardship to visit Dad's lovely assistant."

Gerald grunted from the table. His mother jumped up and enveloped Caleb into a hug—her earrings made jingling sounds as she squeezed him tight. The familiar scent of her perfume immediately lifted his mood.

"What's that about Imogen?" she said. "Oh, we should have invited her for dinner."

The Allbrooks were big fans of Imogen Hargrove. There'd been some chatter among staff that when Gerald had promoted her from the general assistant pool to be his dedicated executive assistant that it'd been due to her pretty face and shiny blond hair. But that rumour was quickly dispelled when it became evident that Imogen ran a tight ship and, despite being younger than almost everyone who worked at the company, she didn't take shit from anyone. Not even Gerald himself. A fact that endeared her to Caleb greatly.

"I'm sure she's got friends to hang out with." Jason shook his head and pulled two beers from the fridge. He popped the caps and handed one bottle to Caleb. "Or her own family."

"Oh, I know. But it would be nice to see her." She waved a hand in the air, a stack of gold bracelets clinking with the movement. Caleb smiled. His mother was like a one-woman band with all the noise she made—she was always humming or wearing something that chimed when she walked. "Maybe we'd see her more often if you asked her out on a date."

"Not sure how Dad would feel about that." Jason's eyes shifted to their father, who grunted. "Good assistants don't grow on trees."

Caleb's stomach revolted against the idea. It was stupid. Outside their quick grope in a darkened room, they were hardly an item. And Jason and Imogen were about as perfectly matched as two people could be. They were both driven, serious types set on conquering the world. But the moment he even thought about his brother's hands on her, it was like Caleb's brain went into meltdown mode. An unfamiliar roar of jealousy surged through his body, squeezing his muscles and tightening his hands into fists.

"If either of you do anything to make her leave, I'll have your hides," Gerald replied, his gaze drifting purposefully toward Caleb.

"What the hell did I do?" He took a swig of his beer, the taste bitter on his tongue.

"Don't think I've forgotten what happened with Neila." Gerald pierced him with a gloomy stare. He and Jason had the same irises—light, nearly colourless. Eyes that gave nothing away. "She was a valued member of our team until you interfered."

And by "interfered" he meant having a relationship with the woman, one that was supposed to be meaningful until he found out that she was using him to climb the ranks at work.

The memory shot through him like a bullet. He'd come back to the office to surprise her with flowers and a fancy dinner reservation. Neila's voice had floated down the empty office corridor, her snide tone cutting him to the bone as she told someone he was her second choice. She'd wanted Jason because he would have given her a more solid foothold within the company. But at least Caleb was a good fuck. The way she'd laughed had shredded him into a million jagged little pieces.

Rather than admit that humiliation to anyone, he'd let his family assume he'd dumped her because he'd gotten bored.

"She didn't have to leave," Caleb drawled as he dropped into a seat next to his mother. "That was her call."

As usual, his mother averted her eyes. Such was her role in every family argument. That was where she differed from Caleb. *She'd* let his father's domineering personality water her down over the years. The boring car out front wasn't her style, nor was their sleek modern mansion. His mother was a free spirit who loved colour and texture and clutter. But Gerald had pressed down on her until he'd squeezed the vibrancy out, until he'd moulded her into a version of his first wife—Jason's mother.

But Caleb wouldn't ever let that happen to him. He'd continue to bug the shit out of his father with his flashy car and too-loud socks and his refusal to be a carbon copy of Jason.

"You know what," he said, leaning back and taking another long pull on his beer. "Maybe I *will* ask

Imogen out. Practice makes perfect, right? Let's see if I can get this one to last a whole month."

His father glared at him. "If you don't take anything seriously, how do you expect anyone to take *you* seriously?"

He'd wanted that at one point—willed it to happen by working as hard as he could in everything from soccer to biology to Scouts. But nothing had ever been good enough. He'd always be tarnished with the label of "unwanted." Unplanned. He was the son who wasn't supposed to exist. A product of the trophy wife who'd stepped outside of the bounds of their agreement by refusing to terminate her pregnancy.

"I take myself seriously, Dad. That's good enough for me."

An awkward quiet settled over the table as Luis delivered the food. The clack of cutlery against porcelain echoed against the house's high ceiling, highlighting how little they all had to say. Caleb kept his expression neutral, even as his mother patted his arm out of sight of her husband.

Show no weakness, that was his motto. People like his father would only win if they got to see how much their words stung. And no matter what happened, Caleb would rot in hell before he gave them such satisfaction.

CHAPTER THREE

IF IMOGEN WAS going to do something as outrageous as gate-crashing the Carmina Masquerade Ball, then she was going to make sure she'd thought of everything. Each step of her plan had been meticulously combed through. Including how she'd convinced the head of the catering company to let her and her best friend, Lainey, pose as staff members to gain entry, in exchange for putting the company on the "preferred suppliers list" at work. She'd even studied the venue, Patterson House, by taking the online virtual tour to better understand the layout of the heritage-listed estate and ensure that she and Lainey would have a place to slip out of their catering uniforms and into their ball gowns without getting caught.

This was how she'd come to be walking along a secluded path, wearing a borrowed gown with a mask covering her face.

Tonight was exactly the distraction she needed after the incident with Caleb in the archive room. Any time her mind veered in the direction of what might've happened if they weren't interrupted, she'd bring her focus back to "Operation Catch a Cheater."

Everything was in place. Her dress was dark and vampy with panels of black lace and glossy black silk, allowing glimpses of bare legs, arms and back. It was sexy with a capital *S* and impossibly removed from her usual style, which was exactly why she'd chosen this dress over the dozens of others that were more muted or quietly elegant.

Her jewelled mask disguised her identity by covering the top half of her face from hairline to nose, and she'd opted for a dark plummy stain on her lips. Even her nails—which she always wore bare—were painted in an inky polish that shifted from navy to onyx in the light.

The devil is in the details.

Imogen walked carefully along the path that ran the length of Patterson House, where the Carmina Ball was hosted each year. The stately old building was something that would have made her stop and stare on any other day. But this evening was a different story.

Pausing at the corner which would lead her to the courtyard, she turned to look back at her friend. Lainey's disguise was perfect—she'd recently dyed her hair a bright flame red. That coupled with her mask made her look like a totally new person. She had her own reasons for wanting to sneak into the ball, and had begged Imogen to let her tag along. Trouble loved company, right? Or was that misery?

Imogen flashed Lainey a thumbs-up and got one in return. This was it. Time to get the show on the road.

Imogen fussed with the front of her dress, checking all the areas she'd stuck down to her skin with special skin-safe adhesive tape. The last thing she wanted was to accidentally flash anyone.

In fact, despite the sexier-than-sin dress she didn't want to stand out at all. There were two reasons for that. One, she didn't want to talk too much and risk Daniel catching her out. Two, she didn't technically have an invite.

Okay, so that wasn't a technicality. She didn't—and would likely never—receive an invite to this event. The Carmina Ball was for rich people who could afford the five grand ticket price. For people like her future brother-in-law and his family, who enjoyed attending events which excluded the average person, like Imogen and her sister.

Penny hadn't received an invite, either, and yet Daniel was going to be here. Why? That was what she was going to find out.

The thought of catching Daniel cheating on Penny made her stomach churn. It was one of those cases where finding out she was right wouldn't make her feel any better. But for her sister's sake, she had to know. There was no way in hell she'd let Penny go through that experience.

Imogen cringed as the memories assaulted her—the ghosts of old feelings like shame and despair that came back to life whenever she thought of her ex.

Not now. This isn't the time for pity.

Sucking in a breath, she walked into the courtyard with her shoulders squared and her head held high, like there was no question of her belonging.

"Relax," she said to herself. "All you have to do is blend in with the crowd. You're good at that."

A group of men in tuxedos stood at the edge of the courtyard, drinking and laughing. Some had white jackets and others were dressed all in black. Their masks ranged from simple Zorro-style bands, with cutouts for the eyes, to more elaborate designs. Though none of them compared to the artistry adorning most of the female guests.

Imogen had asked Daniel if she could see his mask earlier that week—feigning curiosity about the event. He'd been only too pleased to show her the "one of a kind" gold creation that looked like it belonged in the Roman Empire. The design had a crest with two horses and some elaborate scrollwork, making it far more interesting than what most of the men were wearing. Which would also make it easy to spot in the crowd.

Imogen hovered at the double doors which opened into the ballroom. The scene was like something out of a movie—the old estate was grand and richly decorated, the people elaborately dressed. It was like being transported back in time to a royal kingdom where princes and princesses held fancy parties.

"Remember why you're here," she said to herself. "It's time to catch a cheater."

* * *

Caleb had never thought it possible for a human's head to pop from sheer frustration, but he had a feeling he might be about to witness it.

"But he said it was one of a kind," Daniel Godfrey spluttered.

"I assume things that are handmade *are* one of a kind, because they can't be exactly replicated. But that doesn't mean the design won't be reused," Jason replied. "And there *are* slight differences."

"They're basically the same." Daniel jabbed a finger in Caleb's direction. "From a distance, you wouldn't even be able to tell them apart."

"Oh, I don't know." Caleb tilted his head, touching his fingertip to the gold mask covering his face. "I think mine's a bit bigger."

Jason shot him a look.

Daniel had been livid to discover that the designer who'd created his "one of a kind" masquerade mask had sold similar designs to other people attending the Carmina Ball, Caleb included. Since men's masks tended to run on the boring side, Caleb had been immediately attracted to the outlandish style of this artist's creations. It suited his anti-wallflower personality. But Daniel wasn't as amused by the whole thing, since he'd banked on being the only one with such a unique design.

Which was Daniel in a nutshell. He made snowflakes look hardy.

"Look at this bit," Jason pointed out. "The scrollwork along the edge is different as is the shape here."

Caleb stifled a laugh. The masks were pretty much the same, and his brother was only placating his friend. Typical Jase, always trying to keep everyone happy. He had no idea why his brother chose to hang out with someone like Daniel. The guy was a spoiled brat.

"I guess it is slightly different," Daniel conceded with a sour tone. "But I won't be going back to that place. It's highway robbery what they charge considering the designs aren't exclusive. I'll take my business elsewhere."

Caleb turned to face the crowded ballroom as he rolled his eyes. At this rate, he'd die of boredom before anything interesting happened. The Carmina Ball was supposed to be a big deal, but Caleb had come every year since his eighteenth birthday and had yet to understand why people were foaming at the mouth to get an invite. It was nothing but a bunch of stuffy old blue bloods standing around in expensive outfits while they talked about the same shit they discussed every other day of the week. Golf, investing, who bought a bigger yacht. *Yawn.*

"Where's Penny?" Jason asked.

"Oh, she decided not to come," Daniel replied. "I was hoping to show her off but I guess that'll have to wait for the wedding."

Daniel Godfrey was getting married? Caleb buried his surprise by rubbing a hand over his jaw. It wasn't the fact that he was entering into a marriage that'd shocked him, but rather the fact that someone out there was willing to put up with his droning voice and constant complaints. He had to assume that the poor woman was also unaware off the fact that he wanted to "show her off" like a bloody trophy. The more he hung around this guy the less he liked him—and there hadn't been a lot of positive feelings to begin with.

"Have you got a photo?" Caleb asked, curiosity getting the better of him.

"Sure." Daniel pulled out his phone and produced a photo of himself next to a petite woman with light brown hair. She looked vaguely familiar. Sweet face with a cute smile and bright eyes. Pretty. But no further recognition sprang to mind. "This is my darling Penny. We're getting married in two months."

"Congratulations." Caleb nodded.

"Weddings are such funny occasions," Daniel said. "We had this quite extraordinary experience with choosing our menu…"

Kill me now.

Caleb flagged down a passing waiter and swapped his empty glass for a full one. In his experience, there was only one way to get through an event like this without completely climbing the walls. Make a drinking game of it.

"They suggested the chicken for the first course," Daniel continued. "Can you believe it? Chicken! We already had that planned for the main. There was no way we could serve the same protein in two courses."

Outrage over the most first world issue imaginable? Check.

Caleb took a swig of his drink. "Amateurs."

"Oh, don't even get me started." Daniel huffed. "Then they wanted to use gold ribbons on the chairs when we'd specifically requested silver for the centrepieces. I mean, I'm no interior designer but even *I* know gold and silver don't go together."

Humble bragging. Check.

Stifling a laugh, Caleb took another sip. At this rate, he was going to be hammered before Daniel even finished his story. "I'm surprised you haven't taken your business elsewhere," he said, mimicking Daniel's words from earlier.

"I should, but Penny really wants this venue. Apparently, it has special meaning to her." He rolled his eyes. "And you know what they say about the old ball and chain—happy wife, happy life."

Referring to his partner as a burden. Check. And that, ladies and gentlemen, is the douchebag trifecta!

Before Caleb could raise the glass to his lips again, Daniel groaned suddenly.

"Oh God, my stomach." He clutched his midsection. "My irritable bowel syndrome always acts up when I get stressed."

Before anyone could comment, he darted off toward the ballroom's exit. Jason sighed. "Did you have to wind him up?"

"He missed his calling in standup. Truly, the man is a comedic genius." Caleb stifled a laugh. "How on earth *are* you friends with him?"

Jason shook his head. "Don't start."

"Do you not see what a pompous prima donna he is?" He raised a brow at his brother. "Let me reiterate so it's clear." He cleared his throat and puffed out his chest. "Oh, Jason, you simply have *no idea* how difficult the wedding folks are. The silver and gold clashes, my good chum. It clashes *terribly*."

Jason's lip twitched but he cleared his throat instead of laughing. "Stop it."

"But, Jason, you don't understand." He'd gotten the "plum in the mouth" voice spot on. He even threw in a little of Daniel's mannerisms to complete the picture—the rolling of his hand for emphasis, the jut of his chin into the air. Even the little head shake that punctuated his sentences. "Penny and I are *delighted* to be married and everything must be perfect for my darling ball and chain."

This time Jason snorted. "Enough. I have to go to that wedding and I don't want to be envisaging your performance during the ceremony, thank you very much."

"Fine," he said. "But you owe me big-time. If I have to spend another three hours with that man I'll go certifiably crazy."

"He might not make it back. Once the stomach troubles start he's usually out for the night." Jason sighed. "You pushed him too far."

"By asking about his wedding?" Caleb rolled his hands around again. "But the silver and gold, Jason. Silver and gold!"

"I'm going to find Dad." His brother laid a hand on his shoulder. "Want to come?"

Caleb knocked back the rest of his drink. "Hard pass."

"Fine. But try not to make anyone else sick, okay?"

"No promises." Caleb scanned the room as Jason walked away, a restless itch burrowing under his skin and causing him to shift from one foot to the other.

Next year he was going to find a concrete excuse not to come to this bloody thing. Nothing was worth standing around being bored out of his skull to keep his father happy. Why bother? It wasn't like it would make a difference in the long run, anyway.

Out of the corner of his eye, he caught a woman looking at him. Putting on his most charming smile, he headed toward her. If the company wasn't up to scratch, all he had to do was find new company.

CHAPTER FOUR

Imogen moved through the crowded ballroom, looking for the man with the golden mask. Was this how a glamorous spy in an old-school Bond movie felt? It was the most excitement she'd had for some time.

Excitement isn't what you're looking for, remember? You want reliability, security. Comfort.

She rolled her eyes behind her mask. It was a little disconcerting that her ideal life situation sounded like an ad for a Maxi Pad. Or a nursing home.

But she'd had excitement before. She'd had the wild thrill of an electric, charismatic man sweeping her off her feet and filling her head with false promises. A guy who flew in and out of her life as he pleased, drama and chaos nipping at his heels. It was exhilarating to be wanted by a man who could have anyone, sure. But it was also exhausting, stressful and left her heart shattered into a billion jagged pieces.

In other words, excitement was not all it was cracked up to be. Which was why she needed to focus on her mission.

Then she spotted him. The gold mask gleamed

under the twinkling light of the grand chandelier. The design left part of his jaw free, and showed some of the styled hair at the back of his head. Imogen squinted. She hadn't remembered Daniel's hair being quite so fair, but he could have dyed it. It wouldn't surprise her—the guy *did* get weekly manicures after all. He was also looking more trim than usual, but her sister had mentioned something about them being on a prewedding diet. No carbs or some such craziness.

She made her way forward, heading toward a waiter who was standing near Daniel and the man he was talking to. Smiling, she accepted a flute of champagne and took a delicate sip. Up close, the masked man looked broader and more athletic than she remembered of her future brother-in-law. Imogen bit down on her lip. He *had* said his mask was one of a kind, so this must be him. But something didn't seem quite right.

"Oh my, I *love* your dress." A woman in a long blue ball gown came over to get a closer look at Imogen's borrowed outfit.

Grateful for the chance to better blend in, Imogen positioned herself so she was in earshot of the man in the golden mask. As the other woman started talking about designers and ball gowns, Imogen strained to listen to the conversation between the two men beside her.

"...you simply have *no idea* how difficult the wedding folks are. The silver and gold clashes, my good chum. It clashes *terribly*." The man made a gesture with his hands, rolling them at the wrists. She'd recognise it anywhere. It was hard to hear what Daniel's companion was saying, as he was farther away. "Penny and I are *delighted* to be married and everything must be perfect for my darling ball and chain."

Penny. Imogen breathed a sigh of relief. She'd let it slide that he'd referred to her sister as a "ball and chain" for the moment. At least she knew she had her man.

"Don't you think?" the woman in the blue ball gown asked. Oops! She'd been too busy eavesdropping to know how to respond. "I mean," the woman continued, "I know they predicted last year that cerulean was going to be all the rage, but I rather prefer navy. It's much more elegant."

"I totally agree." Imogen bobbed her head and took a sip of her champagne.

By the time she turned her head back to Daniel, he'd started walking away. Imogen smiled and made an interested *mmm-hmm* sound so the woman in the blue dress would keep talking.

"But we decided to go with this shade because it's in the middle. Fashionable but still elegant, because I don't want to be *completely* off-trend…"

Daniel stopped in front of a woman in a full-skirted dress in a vibrant pattern that looked like it could have been lifted directly from an Impressionist painting. Her mask was elaborately designed, with lace and ribbon in shades of soft pink, purple and yellow.

"But I mean this *is* the biggest event of the year. One must step out of their comfort zone."

"Absolutely," Imogen said, her eyes fixed on her brother-in-law as he chatted to the woman in the stunning dress.

Perhaps this was the blonde she'd seen him with at the bar a few weeks back. Between the mask and full-skirted gown, it was impossible to tell. But then he reached down and grabbed her hand, slipping his fingers between hers. It was an intimate gesture. Definitely not the kind of thing two strangers did.

Bile rushed up the back of her throat. Poor Penny. She was so in love with Daniel and here he was acting like she meant nothing at all—and after talking about her moments earlier, no less. Imogen drained the rest of her champagne and excused herself from the conversation with the woman in the blue dress.

Daniel might think he could keep someone on the side, but Imogen wouldn't allow it. The memories rushed back—of finding her husband's dating profile on a site specially for people wanting extramarital affairs. Counting the women he'd agreed to meet with…one, two, ten. Fifteen. More. He hadn't even tried to deny it.

That one time she *had* used the F-word.

Daniel and the mystery woman made their way to the courtyard, heads bowed. His companion smiled, her perfect white teeth practically sparkling like in those cheesy toothpaste ads. Imogen could almost hear the *ping* sound-effect. Ugh.

Her stomach churned and a wave of uneasiness

washed over her. How was she going to break the news to her big sister? Penny was so optimistic and caring and kind. The wedding was her whole world right now and this would shatter everything.

But what was the alternative? Letting her sister walk down the aisle with a guy who didn't deserve her? Letting her have that sickening moment of discovering betrayal?

No. That couldn't happen.

Imogen flagged down another waiter and snagged a glass of champagne. She hovered at the edge of the ballroom and kept her eyes on Daniel. It wouldn't do to get too close in case they spotted her. If she spooked him now, there might not be another chance. Holding her champagne flute in one hand, she used her other hand to fish her phone out of her evening bag. Photographic evidence, that was what she needed.

Once he and the mystery woman walked into the courtyard and rounded a corner, Imogen set off again. The string quartet played a lively piece of music and people flocked to the dance floor. Judging by all the giggling and the unsteady way some women tottered in their heels, the circulating drinks were doing their job. Hopefully it would mean Imogen's actions would go unnoticed.

She headed outside and made sure her steps were slow and easy. Like she had all the time in the world. Balmy air brushed her bare arms and caused the panels of her skirt to flutter around her ankles. The scent of white flowers enveloped her in a heady, intoxicating hug. Every detail of this ball had been meticulously thought through—from the white roses and gardenia trees dotting the courtyard to the tiny white cakes sitting pretty on silver trays. It was impossibly romantic. Like a grown-up version of Alice's Wonderland.

For a moment Imogen stood there, sucking it all in. If only she was here for fun and frivolity, rather than amateur sleuthing—all because Daniel couldn't keep it in his pants.

Draining the rest of the champagne, Imogen set the flute down on a table. Liquid courage acquired.

Refocusing, she scanned the courtyard. No gold mask or Impressionist dress. They must have snuck off for some privacy. Imogen followed a path that led deeper into the mansion's gardens, all the way to the stables at the back of the property.

She toyed with her phone. How on earth was she supposed to get a picture of them without being completely obvious?

You're a master of improvisation. You'll think of something.

Flying by the seat of her pants—or in this case, by the skirt of her sexy lace gown—was so *not* her style. But she had to go with the flow, no matter how uncomfortable it made her.

The stables were set back on the property, away from the main building. But against the brown tones of wood and trees, the mystery woman's dress was easily visible. From this angle, Imogen couldn't see Daniel and she *definitely* couldn't get a photo.

The zoom on her iPhone camera wasn't exactly paparazzi-worthy.

"Shoot," she muttered. If she walked too much farther along the path she'd come into their view. There was only one option.

Sighing, Imogen hiked up her dress and bundled the length in one hand as she stepped onto the grass.

"I can't believe you picked me out right away," Caleb said.

Karolina made a snorting sound. "You're wearing literally the most ostentatious mask I've ever seen, and I would know that cocky swagger anywhere."

He chuckled. "Subtly isn't one of my strong suits, huh?"

Karolina Petrov-Wells was a longtime friend of both his and Jason's. She had a fun-loving, vibrant and vivacious personality and could make anyone smile. Which was why Caleb had crushed on her hard all through high school. But after sharing an awkward kiss in their university days, it was clear the romantic chemistry wasn't there. They'd decided to remain friends and Caleb was happy it had turned out that way. She was the sister he'd never had.

"So, are you going to tell me why you dragged me out to the stables so we could 'talk'? This doesn't seem like the place where a lot of talking happens." He waggled his brows in an exaggerated fashion that was about as far from sexy as he could possibly get. "Are you going to seduce me?"

"You wish." She grinned. "Seriously though, I needed to escape for a minute. I swear, if my mother drags me over to one more 'suitor'—"

"Suitor?"

"Yeah." Karolina snorted. "She actually said that. Pretty sure she thinks we're living in a Jane Austen novel."

He shook his head. "I don't see what the big rush is."

"Well, I'll be thirty next year, Caleb," she said, rolling her eyes. "Apparently that means my uterus is about to shrivel up and die. I told her I didn't need to get married in order to have a baby."

Caleb stifled a laugh. "How did that go down?"

"Uh, not well." She bobbed her head. "Not well at all. I don't suppose you want to marry me?"

He raised a brow and Karolina burst into a laugh a second later. "Can you not even keep a straight face through your phony marriage proposal?"

"Sorry." She pressed a hand to her stomach and shook her head. "The thought of it... We'd drive each other crazy."

"We certainly would." He raked a hand through his hair. "Besides, one sham marriage is enough for my family."

Karolina made a tutting sound. "Stop that. Your parents are *not* in a sham marriage."

"Okay, a one-sided marriage."

"Not even that." She placed a hand on his arm and squeezed. "Look, I know what they have isn't perfect. But that doesn't make it fake. Jase was telling me things have been tense between you and Gerald. You're projecting. I bet he's different when it's the two of them."

He made a noncommittal noise. "You sound like Jase."

"That's because he's the smart one," she said with a wink. She was winding him up now, the little minx.

"I'm not going to bite."

"Damn, you're getting too good for me." She grinned. "I used to be able to tug on your strings a lot easier than that."

"Not anymore, I'm afraid." He slung an arm around her shoulder. "I'm awake to your tricks."

"I guess we should go, huh? God, these things are such a drag." Grinning, she turned her face up to his and planted a kiss on his jaw below his mask. She looked at him as if waiting for something, then she pressed her lips together. "Nope, nothing. Not even a little zing."

He chuckled and wiped at his face where there was no doubt an imprint of Karolina's bright pink lipstick. "Some people are meant to be friends, Karo."

She sighed. "It would be easier if that wasn't the case. Then we could get married and everyone would leave us alone."

"No way," he said. "You deserve the real deal. Hearts and flowers and all that shit."

"And all that shit, huh?" She rested her head against his shoulder. "Yeah, I guess you're right. I wouldn't object to having the perfect person land in my lap so I could skip the whole dating thing."

At that moment there was a loud thud outside the stables followed by a high-pitched squeak. What the hell? Was someone spying on them?

CHAPTER FIVE

"Just freaking great." Imogen planted a hand on the ground and tried to stand. She could already tell there'd be a grapefruit-size bruise on her butt.

But bruises were the least of her problems. Her dress was stuck on a bush and her shaking hands couldn't free it.

Everything had been going along smoothly, too. She'd found a window to peer through that was clear enough for her phone camera to get a decent shot of what was going on inside the stables. It was a trade-off—she couldn't hear what either person was saying, but she had more places to hide than if she'd approached the entrance.

When Daniel had put his arm around the woman and she'd kissed him, Imogen had taken a perfect shot. But in trying to get the best angle, her sandal had slipped on a loose rock and she'd gone down like a sack of potatoes.

"Graceful as a baby freaking elephant," she muttered.

All she had to do was get her dress free, then she

could slip back into the ball with her phone in hand. Hopefully Daniel and the mystery woman hadn't heard her. She strained to listen, but the only thing her ears picked up were the distant notes of the string quartet.

She located the offending pieces of shrubbery holding her captive and carefully extracted the lace. There was a hole but it was tiny. The dress was a loaner, and Imogen couldn't afford to drain her bank account because of a stupid bush. Breathing a sigh of relief, Imogen got to her feet and tried to see where her phone had landed.

"Fudge nuggets," she muttered, glancing up at the window. Thankfully there wasn't a face peering down at her, but she *needed* to find her phone. Now.

Hoisting her dress up, so it wouldn't catch on the bush again, she searched the ground. The phone had bounced close to where she landed, so the blasted thing couldn't have gone too far. Maybe it was on the grass behind her. The second Imogen turned her stomach plummeted.

Daniel stood in front of her, lips pressed into a hard line as he held her phone in one hand. Even though his face was mostly covered, he still managed to effectively radiate a "peeved as hell" vibe.

"I can explain," she said, her mind kicking into overdrive. Which wasn't a good thing—she tended to word-vomit when she got nervous.

"Go on," he said, folding his arms across his chest and keeping her phone out of reach.

Out of the corner of her eye Imogen saw the

mystery woman approaching, but Daniel waved her away. Once they were alone, Imogen sucked in a deep breath and pressed her hands to her stomach to quell the butterflies flapping up a storm.

"I don't know how to say this, but I was following you." Her mouth was drier than desert dust, but she forged on. "I know it was wrong, but I thought you'd lie if I confronted you. You have to understand, I'm looking out for Penny. I can't have her marrying someone who's cheating on her."

Her words were met with a wall of silence, which only served to irritate her further. She balled her hands into fists as fury filtered through her veins. How could he stand there and not say a freaking thing? He wasn't even defending himself.

"Seriously, did you think you could cheat and no one would ever find out? She *loves* you and you're treating her like...like..." She shook her head. "Shite."

"Shite?" The amusement in his voice made her see red.

"Yes, shite. And I'm not going to allow it." She stuck her hand out. "Give me back my phone. Now."

Silence.

She could rush him and hope that their size differential would be negated by the element of surprise. *That* might get her kicked out of the ball. Not that it mattered, now she had the evidence. But she needed to get her phone back...by any means necessary.

"If you don't say something, this is going to end badly for you." Her voice had taken on a shaky quality now. Adrenaline pumped through her body, preparing her fight response. Because she sure as hell wasn't going to pick flight now. "Hand over the phone."

"Who do you think I am?" he asked.

"Oh come on, Daniel," she scoffed. "You're really going to play that card? I *heard* you talking about Penny before. Ball and chain, huh? That's real charming."

Caleb wasn't sure what kind of twilight zone fantasy land he'd ended up in, but this was a hell of a lot more interesting than what was going on inside the ballroom. After hearing the thud outside the stables, he'd gone to investigate only to find a woman in the sexiest black dress he'd ever seen on hands and knees, trying to disentangle herself from a bush. It wasn't until he'd spotted the shiny silver case of a phone that he figured out what she'd been up to.

The mystery woman was an amateur paparazzo. He'd fully intended on handing the phone over. After all, it was clearly a case of mistaken identity. There wasn't a person in the world who would care that he was having a "secret" meeting with Karolina Petrov-Wells. And the fact that she'd now called him "Daniel" was proof of that.

But the mistaken identity wasn't the bit that interested him most about this situation. Oh no. What had his whole body buzzing was the glimpse of the diamond tattoo on this woman's rib cage. It was clear she'd used that weird tape girls loved to keep her dress in place, but it must have come unstuck when she'd fallen and now the dress gaped enough to reveal the edge of some sexy, minimalist ink.

Prim Miss Imogen Hargrove.

If the tattoo hadn't given her away, the self-righteous tone and use of *shite* would have done it. What the hell was *she* doing here?

And damn, her body was like a fucking midnight fantasy in that dress. The glossy black panels of silk and lace hugged her curvy figure, the plunging neckline giving him a good look at her gorgeous, full breasts.

The only problem was, if he said too much he'd give his identity away. And he wasn't done with this bizarre exchange yet. So he bit his tongue, stifling a laugh as she got angrier and angrier at him.

"Seriously, what man refers to his future wife as a ball and chain?" She planted her hands on her hips and huffed when she didn't get a response. "You have nothing to say for yourself?"

Ball and chain? Suddenly the penny dropped. No pun intended. She thought he was Jase's friend Daniel. That would explain the identity mix-up. She must have seen the mask and overheard their conversation. He wanted to rub his hands together in glee. Anything that gave him leverage to stir up trouble with Imogen was a treat and today he'd hit the goddamn jackpot.

Never mind the fact that all he could think about was that moment in the archive room. With each move, her breasts shifted beneath the silky dress, stirring his memories and sending his blood south.

Caleb shrugged and steam practically rose out of Imogen's ears. He pocketed her phone and stood there, curious as to what she'd do next.

You're a horrible person, Caleb Allbrook. A despicable, no-good, dirty rotten scoundrel.

And fuck yeah did he love it.

"You…" Her lips were so pursed Caleb genuinely feared she'd cut off blood supply. "Smurfing smurf-face!"

Caleb couldn't hold it in a second longer, a huge belly-deep laugh burst out of his lips. The woman was ridiculous in the best, most appealing way possible. Even now, she wouldn't swear because people might hear. Not that there was much chance of it, since they were hiding behind the stables, where the garden turned into a lush bushland area, dense with trees and shrubs.

"Oh my God." He bent forward, one hand braced on his knee as he laughed. "That's brilliant. Smurfing—oof!"

Caleb jolted as his back hit the ground, the darkening evening sky now in his field of vision. Imogen was on top of him. What the hell? Had his favourite goodie two-shoes tackled a full-grown man to the ground? Colour him impressed.

He'd fantasised about getting her in this position many times. Admittedly, the circumstances had been a little different in his head.

"Give it back," she demanded, wriggling on top of

him as he tried to fend her off. She had him pinned down, one small hand braced on the ground next to his head and the other trying to worm into the inner pocket of his jacket.

Caleb grabbed her wrists and pulled them up by his head, forcing her to lean closer. Behind the elaborate mask, her olive green eyes were wide. Her ragged breathing caused her chest to rise and fall deeply, moving her breasts up and down against him. She straddled him, the full length of her dress bunched around her legs. Every last bit of blood in his body rushed south as she shifted, the sweet heat between her thighs brushing deliciously over his cock.

Truly despicable.

"Give me back my phone this second or I will scream blue murder," she threatened. "Daniel—"

He yanked her hands higher, bringing her face even closer. They were nose to nose or, in this case, mask to mask. Her breath puffed over his cheek, and the scent of her perfume—something vanilla-like and softly feminine—wound through him like a drug.

He leaned forward, bringing his lips next to her ear. "Stop calling me that."

"What?"

"My name isn't Daniel." With each word, his lips brushed over the shell of her ear. She stilled against him, her arms and legs going as rigid as steel. "You've got the wrong guy."

"You're lying." But her words were tinged with

doubt. "Don't think you can bluff your way out of this."

"Do I sound like Daniel?" he asked. Would she place his voice or figure out that she'd made a mistake?

Part of him wanted her to know who he was, to see if she'd push him away or if she'd lean in farther. Had she been stewing on the way he'd touched her in the dark? Had she gotten hot and horny thinking about it?

"I…" She bit down on her lip. "I don't know."

"So you were spying on me, taking photos of a private meeting between two friends, and now you've tackled me to the ground, and yet you don't know if I sound like the man you're after?" He let his voice take on a growl and a tiny shudder ran through her. She shifted, her body rubbing against his erection so perfectly Caleb had to stifle a moan.

"But you're wearing his mask," she squeaked. "It's one of a kind."

"Apparently not. Daniel was pretty pissed about it, too." He grinned. "Said it was highway robbery what they charged considering the designs weren't exclusive."

"Oh no," she groaned. "That *does* sound like something he'd say."

She looked at him dead on, confusion flashing in her eyes. He probably should clear up the mystery, hand her phone over and send her on her way. But she *had* both spied on him and knocked him over. In the grand scheme of things, his sins were matched by hers.

"She started it." Really? Great justification, Allbrook. Totally solid.

He ignored the sarcastic voice in his head and met her stare.

"Do I know you?" she asked.

Damn it. He obviously hadn't been doing a good enough job of disguising his voice. "I don't know. Do you?" He spoke slowly, trying to use a gravelly tone to throw her off.

She huffed. "You're impossible. Now let me go and give me back my phone. This is ridiculous."

"Ridiculous? You attacked *me*."

"I didn't attack you." She tried to pull her hands back, but he held her tight. "I attempted to retrieve stolen property. You're a thief."

"And you're a spy. Do you even have a ticket to this event?"

Her olive green eyes blinked and she sucked in a sharp breath. "Well…of course I do."

Did Prim Miss Hargrove sneak into the Carmina Ball? The night was getting more and more interesting by the second. Her skin flushed pink and she stopped wriggling against him.

"I call bullshit," he said. "And there's a quick way to find out if you're telling the truth."

She swallowed, the delicate muscles in her neck pressing momentarily against her fair skin. "If you hand over my phone, I'll leave now."

"I'm not so sure I want you to leave. I could get used to being manhandled by a gorgeous woman."

She rolled her eyes. "You can't even see my face. Your flattery means nothing."

But she was no longer struggling against him—her arms were soft in his, not straining or pulling. Her lips were parted and her tongue darted out to moisten them. Caleb had to force himself not to rub up against her.

"I don't need to see your face," he said. "Besides, it's the whole package. I find feisty women incredibly attractive."

"You think I'm feisty?" She cocked her head.

"Feisty, sexy. I bet you have men beating down your door."

She snorted. "You'd be surprised."

He would. Imogen might be a little—okay, *a lot*—tightly wound, but that didn't mean she wasn't hotter than the gates of hell. Besides, today had proven there was a whole lot more to her than met the eye. And he was going to make it his mission to get to the bottom of this new side of her.

"Still want your phone back?" he asked.

"I do."

"What do I get out of it, huh?"

She narrowed her eyes. "How about the opportunity to keep your man parts intact?"

"Always appreciated." He nodded. "But you've put me in a tight spot. I'm pretty confident that you've snuck into this ball, which isn't allowed. People pay a lot of money to be here and if I let you go, I'm aiding and abetting a criminal."

"I am *not* a criminal."

"Just amateur paparazzi, then? You know there's a strict no-press policy for this event. Privacy is a huge concern for the attendees."

"I wasn't planning to sell the photos, for what it's worth. Can't we go our separate ways and forget this ever happened? You don't have to hand me over to the masquerade police and I won't tell anyone you kept me hostage."

She was hardly being held hostage. Sure, Caleb had her wrists in his hands but if she'd showed any signs of distress he would have let her go. Besides, her knees were nestled next to his "man parts" so if she'd intended on doing any damage, it would have happened already.

This was a game of cat and mouse, and Caleb intended to win.

Now Imogen had messed things up. Big-time. What were the odds that two men would have the same "one of a kind" mask? Where was the artistic integrity?

Although, if she was being totally honest, this wasn't the most unpleasant situation she could have landed herself in. Held captive by a man with a deep, sexy voice and hands that were made to roam a woman's curves? Not bad at all. But she had the niggling sense that something was off—there was something about the man that had her intuition all fired up. He sounded familiar, and also like he was trying to disguise his voice by using that growly, cha-cha-melting whisper.

Focus, Hargrove. This isn't a mission to reclaim your mojo. Priority number one is escaping without getting arrested.

But she couldn't leave without her phone because it would give her identity away. If she could convince the man to hand it over, she could hightail it out of the ball without anyone knowing her name.

"My arms are getting tired," she said. "And we appear to be at an impasse. I have nothing to offer other than a promise to delete the photos I took."

"That goes without saying," he said. "Not that anyone would be interested in them."

"Then what's with the indignant act? Are you trying to see what you can get out of me?" She huffed. "Don't even answer that. I already know what you're going to say."

He grinned. But Mr. Sexy Mask Man wasn't budging an inch. And speaking of inches…

Every little movement made her acutely aware of his rock-hard erection rubbing against her inner thigh. Holy smokes. Either the guy was hung like a donkey or he kept a zucchini in his pants. And thanks to prolonged involuntary celibacy, Imogen's body was celebrating the sexual contact. How long had it been? Twelve months? More? She absolutely could have pulled free of his grip, but there wasn't a cell in her body that wanted to.

That's pathetic. You know that, right?

True. But it had been too smurfing long since she'd felt the spark of physical excitement, or that delicious throb of arousal between her legs. Sure, she was a serious, career-focused woman. And sure, she wasn't going to jump into bed with any random guy for the sake of satisfying carnal need. But man, was this guy hitting all her hot buttons right now.

It wouldn't hurt to revel in the friction a little more. She shifted her hips, brushing her sex along the hard ridge of him as subtly as she could. But she had to dent her bottom lip with her teeth to keep a moan of pleasure in. Every nerve ending in her body was sparking like New Year's Eve fireworks.

"What if I gave you a kiss in exchange for my phone?" The words tumbled out before she could stop them. But it wasn't a terrible idea—a kiss in exchange for walking away free of consequence.

A kiss she would most absolutely enjoy.

"A kiss, huh?" His smile turned wolfish. Hungry. "Sounds fair to me."

"You have to let me go first. I don't kiss men who've got a hold on me—literally or figuratively."

The masked man immediately released her. He'd been holding her so gently there wasn't even a sign that his fingers had been wrapped around her wrists. She'd be able to pretend it never happened. Though something told her she wouldn't forget it anytime soon.

"Okay, ground rules for this kiss." She sucked in a breath. "It's a kiss, nothing more. You try to pin me down again and I'll knee you where it hurts. Got it?"

"Got it."

Adrenaline pumped through Imogen's veins, giving her body a jittery, overstimulated feel. Everything was sensitive—from her nose sucking in the scent of his cologne mixed with the grass beneath them to her palms pressing against his muscled chest. Even the cotton beneath her fingertips was sublime.

"Do you want a countdown?" he asked. "I'll start with three."

She placed one hand by his head, the blades of grass tickling her skin. Music floated softly from the ball, the garden otherwise peaceful and quiet. Luckily for Imogen, no one could hear the blood fizzing in her veins.

"Two."

Leaning forward, she angled her head over his, her lips parting in anticipation. There was a slight scent of alcohol on his breath, but it was richly pleasant. His lips were curved and full, and his jaw was freshly shaven and smooth.

"One."

She closed the remaining distance and pressed against him, fusing them from the lips all the way down. Heat enveloped her as she melted into him, her thighs softening as she rested on her forearms. His tongue greeted hers, gently at first, probing and tentative. But it only took a second for the kiss to turn wild.

Then his hands were at her back—one sliding up to cup her head and the other sliding down to press her hard against him. The kiss was confident, possessive. She groaned into him, eyes fluttering. He flexed beneath her, rolling his hips up to meet the tender space between her legs. Rubbing…no, grinding. It was sensual and basal and more than a little dirty. The kind of kiss that a girl like her never seemed to get.

"Christ," he muttered, his lips at her neck. Nipping. Scraping.

He was marking her and it was the hottest thing she'd ever experienced. He'd turned her body into a live flame and she was burning, consuming. Turning to ash.

"You're so fucking hot," he growled against her neck.

His words were like a drug. She revelled in the contradiction of it all—in the hard ridge of him pressing against her and the soft glide of his tongue over her skin. In the delicate brush of his lips and the firm grip of his hand sliding up her thigh. In his hard groan and subtle swish of her dress as he shoved it to one side. He was stripping her defences down, peeling back the protective layer she wore like permanent armour, and whipping her into a frenzy.

Imogen ached. Her whole body pulsed with electric energy and she wanted nothing more than to let him roll her onto her back so he could shove her skirt higher and bury himself between her legs.

A kiss. Nothing more.

She forced herself to pull back, terrified if she didn't put the brakes on she'd be drunk on lust and unable to stop. Unable to resist turning a kiss into something more. Into *every*thing more. Without a word, she slipped her hand into his jacket and pulled out her phone.

Rocking back on her heels, she grabbed a fistful of her dress and carefully got to her feet. She might have been happy to crash tackle the man, but she didn't want to accidentally impale him with a heel. He didn't move. His lips were slack, chest rising and falling with quickened breath.

I know how you feel, buddy.

Oh boy. That was a kiss to render all other kisses useless. Poor specimens of kisses. Sorry excuses for kisses. So pale in comparison to this kiss that she felt like she'd never been kissed before.

Imogen scooped up her bag from where it had fallen and stashed her phone safely away. But what now? Was she supposed to say something? She resisted the urge to ask for his name and number. The quicker she got out of the ball the better, and the less risk of her getting in trouble.

Then she could get back to what mattered—finding out whether Daniel was cheating on her sister. Staying at the ball would be too risky now. For all she knew, this man would go back on his word and turn her in. Or use her weakened position to blackmail something more than a kiss…which actually didn't sound so terrible. And that meant it was *definitely* time to go.

"Well…" she said, her voice ragged and frayed as the ends of her nerves. "That was…"

"Fucking brilliant?" he offered. "Or would that be smurfing brilliant in your case?"

A smile tugged at her lips. "Yes, smurfing brilliant."

She slipped the chain strap of her evening bag over one shoulder and turned to leave, but something compelled her to look back. A piece of information had set off an alarm in her head—but through the thick haze of arousal she couldn't quite process it. Something was wrong, and her mind whirred.

Then she saw it.

The blood drained from her face so quickly the world swayed beneath her heels. She pressed a hand to her stomach, hoping to hell the champagne she'd downed wouldn't come rushing back up. But this was bad...very bad.

Colossally, insurmountably, cataclysmically bad.

The masked man rose to a sitting position, causing his tuxedo pants to pull a few inches farther up his leg. Dinosaur socks. T. Rexes to be precise. Almost identical to the red ones she'd seen that day of the archive room incident. But this time they had a blue background.

Maybe it's a coincidence? Cheesy novelty socks might be some high-fashion menswear trend that you're unaware of?

However, the stone sitting in the pit of her stomach would not be relieved. His voice had stirred something in her, but he'd definitely been disguising it. Tricking her. She knew the socks and she knew the man. And now she knew that he tasted like heaven and was as well-endowed as the rumours had indicated.

Oh my God, oh my God, oh my God...

She opened her mouth to speak, but her voice had turned to dust. Instead, she spun around and raced back toward the ball.

CHAPTER SIX

IMOGEN SPENT THE remainder of the weekend trying to determine the best way to prevent Monday from rolling around. But Monday was a tricky beast. No matter how hard you hung on to Sunday, Monday would always make an appearance.

She arrived at work early, hoping to make it to the executive floor undetected so she could hide out in her office. Would Domino's deliver directly to her desk? She could acquire a blanket and make a fort. Or push some furniture against the door and barricade herself in.

"You're an adult. You can handle this." She dropped into her desk chair and emptied her lungs in a long, slow *whoosh*. "It's not like he knows it was you."

Her disguise had been perfect, and all he knew was that she was after someone named Daniel.

What if he recognised your voice?

That had to be a long shot...right?

And the kiss, while wild and reckless, shouldn't bear any consequences. Outwardly, anyway. Inwardly... well, her brain had turned into Pornhub overnight. That was two strikes now. Two instances of crossing a line previously marked "No. Nope. No way in Hell. Do not proceed under any circumstances." If she made one more wrong move, who knew where that might lead?

"Let's be real. You *know* where you want it to lead," she muttered to herself.

And that was a big smurfing problem.

Falling for a guy like Caleb wasn't inviting trouble—it was courting it, seducing it and taking it to bed. And Imogen wasn't about to take trouble to bed, no matter what her lady parts were saying.

"Stop thinking about beds." She sipped her flat white. Nothing. Her taste buds had tapped out and not even a coffee from her favourite café could help.

Caleb had officially broken her.

Shaking off the stressful thoughts, she ran through the CEO's calendar and started compiling all the documents, briefing notes and travel arrangements that he needed. The process calmed her. When there was order, Imogen's mind wasn't such a chaotic mess.

After printing and binding Gerald's "day book," she headed to his office. His receptionist, Mary, waved her through.

Gerald was the kind of CEO who picked his team with great care—which was a nice way of saying that he had zero tolerance for idiots. Mary was the "face" of the CEO's office, playing gatekeeper for him and the boardroom. Imogen worked more on the business side of things, organising his documents and taking minutes during his leadership meetings. The three of them made a tight-knit, effective team.

It was everything she'd hoped for when she started out as a temp. Hard work and keeping her nose clean had helped her rise to the top. She couldn't ruin that now by getting entangled with the CEO's least favourite son.

Imogen knocked softly before pushing the door open to find Gerald discussing business with Jason and Caleb. He waved her in but continued talking. She sat at the table by the window and waited for them to finish. It gave her a moment to observe the three men; the Allbrook family had an interesting dynamic.

"We need to consider the cost of such events," Gerald said. "The reason we've been able to weather these hard times is because we've kept a firm grip on unnecessary spending."

"A leadership retreat isn't unnecessary," Caleb said. "If we don't invest in our team we'll keep losing people. It looks bad to have *another* executive leave so soon after Joe."

Gerald stood at his desk, his hands linked behind his back. He wore a dark navy double-breasted suit and a light blue tie. Jason's outfit was identical except his suit had a more modern cut and the blue tie was shot through with white stripes. They were every bit the successful father and son duo, practically ready for a *Forbes* cover shoot.

In contrast, Caleb wore a light grey suit with a blue windowpane check, a hot-pink tie and a silver polka-dot pocket square that should have looked hideous, but somehow managed to appear stylish and bold. His blond hair was loosely styled, but she could tell it'd been a rough morning. He tended to run his hands through his hair a lot when he was stressed and the telltale flop of the lock at the front said he'd already played with it too much.

"Shouldn't this be covered by our People and Culture budget?" Caleb asked. "We don't have to go crazy, but we do need to show them we reward loyalty."

"It sounds like we're pandering to their egos," Gerald scoffed.

"No, you're valuing them. How is that a difficult concept? Doesn't our HR team collect talent retention data? If we're doing that with entry-level staff, why not with the people we're paying five times as much?"

"They should stay with the company because this is the best place to work, not because we're funding these wasteful events."

"It's worth considering," Jason interjected. It wasn't the first time Imogen had seen the elder Allbrook son playing peacemaker between his conservative father and creative younger brother—he was definitely the buffer in that relationship. "The cost to onboard one or two executives far outweighs what we would spend on a retreat. You might see it as pandering, but we can tie it to our new strategy rollout. Get them on board with where we want to take the company, give them ownership of the new direction."

Gerald thought for a moment. "You have a point, Jason."

Imogen cringed. It was like anything that came out of Caleb's mouth was disregarded as fluff, but the second Jason chimed in the idea suddenly had merit. Given Caleb looked like he wanted to set fire to the office, he must have thought it, too.

"Put together a page with rough costs and benefits." Gerald took a seat behind his desk. "I want it on my desk by the end of the day."

Jason nodded and headed out of the office, his head bowed as he tapped at his phone. Caleb walked over to Imogen. The frustration he'd been exuding a moment ago had vanished, replaced by a wolfish smile.

"Come past my office when you're done with the old man," he said, his voice low.

"I'm busy. What do you need?" She pretended to inspect her compendium. "I'll find one of the roaming assistants to help you."

"I'm afraid you're the only one who can help with this," he said. His hand came to her shoulder and she bit down on her lip to keep from reacting. "And please don't crash tackle me to the ground this time."

Well, fudge.

Caleb popped the cufflinks on his shirt and rolled his sleeves back as he slumped into his leather desk chair. It felt like he'd been split in two.

On one hand he was livid at his father…again. His idea, which apparently had been a "waste of money," was suddenly worthy of attention the second Jason got involved. No doubt the retreat would turn into another success for the golden child, while Caleb sat on the sidelines. Story of his fucking life.

But the other half of him was running on electric excitement. All weekend he'd thought about how to handle today—should he give Imogen the chance to fess up on her own? He hadn't planned to drop it on her like that, but watching her sit at his father's table in her prim grey suit, pearls around her neck, was a temptation impossible to ignore.

Besides, he needed something to focus on or else he'd storm back into the old man's office and have it out with him once and for all.

There's no point—nothing is going to change. You've tried and failed to make things right, so set yourself on cruise control and get back to enjoying the good things in life.

For years he'd assumed his relationship with his father would level out at some point. Become a little less…prickly. But time had the opposite effect and they'd drifted further apart. These days they swung from arguing to not talking, without any of the pleasant middle ground. His mother was constantly trying to bring them together—but Gerald never seemed interested, and so Caleb decided he wasn't, either.

"Caleb?" His assistant, Mina, poked her head into his office. "Imogen is here to see you. She said you asked her to stop by."

"Send her in."

"Will do. Remember you've got a meeting with

our advertising consultant at ten." She gave him a pointed look.

Shit. He'd been putting this meeting off for weeks, because the guy had been trying to poach him. Apparently, Caleb had "an eye" for design, which was odd considering he'd only landed this marketing role as a consolation prize from Dear Old Dad. But the ad agency probably thought his business contacts would be worth something. Right now, though, he didn't need that kind of temptation. Because as much as relations were strained with his father, this was *still* the family company.

"I need to move it."

"Again?" She sighed. "He'll think you want to drop the agency."

"I don't. Tell him something came up and I'll shout him a drink on Friday." He gave her a lopsided grin and she laughed, shaking her head. "Thank you."

Mina disappeared and a second later Imogen walked through. "Door open or closed?" she asked.

Her movements appeared stiff—though it was possible that her overly starched white shirt was inhibiting joint mobility. Or maybe it was because her hair was so tightly scraped back that her brain was under a lot of pressure. That was Imogen's go-to look.

But not this past weekend.

"Closed," he said. "Thanks for coming to see me."

"What do you want?" Usually when she asked him that her tone was sharp enough to slice bone.

Today, however, her voice was uncertain. Had she been thinking about that kiss all weekend as he had? Was she distracted in her meeting earlier because she couldn't forget how his hands felt on her body?

"I want to talk." He leaned back in his chair and interlocked his fingers behind his head. "How was your weekend?"

She swallowed, the delicate muscles working in her neck as she stood statue-still by his door. "It was good."

Yeah, she was definitely rattled. No way in hell would she have normally given him the time for idle chatter. The last time he'd tried to make small talk she'd walked away midsentence.

He raised an eyebrow. "Get up to anything interesting?"

Her face was a kaleidoscope of wariness and confusion as her fingertips danced along the edge of her necklace. "Just the usual."

"No hot date?"

"No."

"You didn't, say…kiss anyone?" Ideally, he would have kept a straight face, but he was enjoying himself far too much. "Say, perhaps…me?"

Her jaw tightened. "How did you know it was me?"

"No denial, then? Hmm, interesting." He pushed up from his chair and came around to the front of his desk. She was skittish as a rabbit caught in the stare of a fox. "I saw your tattoo."

"Wait, how...?" She shook her head. "My dress covered it."

"When you fell. Apparently, that sticky tape stuff doesn't withstand everything. Also, you called me a 'smurfing smurf-face,' so that was kind of a dead giveaway."

She'd looked pale before, but now the colour rose through her, a flush impressing itself on her skin. Behind the stiff white collar of her shirt, her neck was rosy pink. "Wait, you knew it was me from the second you picked up my phone?"

"Blondie, I'd recognise you anywhere."

"Then you tricked me into kissing you," she spluttered. "I have no idea why I'm surprised. That seems like *exactly* something you would do."

"Let's get one thing straight. You rushed me, you pushed *me* to the ground and you kissed me. I simply lay back and enjoyed." He grinned. "Who knew you were hiding a siren under all those pearls."

"You were stringing me along and holding my phone hostage." She sucked in a breath. "I did what I had to do."

"Bullshit."

"It's true." She sounded far from confident.

"Then tell me you didn't enjoy it." He sauntered closer and she backed up, lining her back against the office door. Silence. "All you have to do is say, 'Caleb, it was all an act. I didn't enjoy kissing that disgusting mouth of yours one little bit.'"

She tipped her nose up at him. "Okay fine, I

kissed you. I may have enjoyed it, but that was *only* because I didn't know it was you."

"Uh-huh. Sure." He planted a hand next to her head, penning her in. "You know you're the world's worst liar, right?"

"Ugh." She speared him with a glare. "Fine. You got me. I kissed you and I liked it. Now I need to have a million showers to wash this dirty feeling off me. Happy?"

He chuckled. "Very."

"Now what? Are you going to hold this over me for the rest of my life?"

Now what, indeed. Caleb had no idea why he'd called her in to have this conversation, other than getting some perverse pleasure from seeing her squirm. "I wanted to hear you say it. But I pity your future brother-in-law. Hell hath no fury like a Hargrove scorned."

"Damn straight."

"I'll do you a favour. I won't even mention it to him *or* Jase. You can continue your mission in peace."

Imogen baulked. "You *know* him?"

"Sadly, yes. He's a friend of Jason's."

"Then you can help me." Her tense expression melted into one of elation.

"After you said you'd need 'a million showers' from kissing me?" He cocked his head. "Not real great at this manipulation thing, are you?"

She rolled her eyes and slipped out from between him and the door. "I'm not a master like you, that's for sure."

Caleb scratched his head. "Still not hitting the mark for asking a favour."

"You *have* to help me." She knotted her hands in front of her. "My sister is the kindest, sweetest, most loving person on the planet."

"Your total opposite, then?"

Irritation flashed across her face. "I think he's cheating on her and they're due to get married in two months. I can't have that."

"Does *she* think he's cheating?" Caleb asked.

"Well, no…but I saw something." A dark cloud filtered over her face. "He goes to Sydney for work a few days each month. But last month when he was away my sister decided to take a trip. Remember that night we were at The Boatbuilders Yard for Pete's going-away drinks?"

Caleb nodded. "How could I forget? He got so wasted he made out with the crook of his elbow."

"Well, I'd spoken to Penny that afternoon. As far as she knew, Daniel was in Sydney until the following night." She gritted her teeth. "But he was there, at the bar. And he was with this blonde woman."

"Did you tell your sister?"

Imogen sighed. "I tried to and she accused me of hating him from day one. Which is true, but that's beside the point. I've got this feeling in my gut that he's cheating on her. I'm *sure* of it."

"All because you saw him at a bar with a woman?"

"Firstly, they looked like they were flirting. Secondly, he'd lied about where he was. Doesn't that seem suspicious to you?"

It did. Though Caleb found it hard enough to believe that Daniel had found one woman to marry him, let alone another with whom to have an affair. But once a person's mind was made up, the facts couldn't do much to change it. He knew that better than anyone else.

"Perhaps he got his dates mixed up and he wanted to go for a drink," Caleb said. "You know, like a normal person."

"I can't explain it but…" Imogen sighed. "But I know the signs. Trust me."

The pain in her voice ricocheted around his chest. Apparently, there was more to Imogen's standoffish behaviour than met the eye.

"Okay, you think he's cheating. How am I supposed to help with that?"

"By getting the dirt. Don't guys brag about that kind of stuff?" She shrugged. "Like how much sex you have?"

Now it was Caleb's turn to roll his eyes. "I don't know what cave troll has given you such a poor opinion of men, but we're not all knuckle-draggers who boast about the women we sleep with."

"Women, as in plural?" She raised a brow.

"I never said I was a saint, but I don't kiss and tell, either." He raked a hand through his hair. "I get that you seem to think I'm some unabashed fuckboy, but I'm not."

Imogen's mouth opened and closed as if she wasn't sure how to respond. She looked like a goldfish—an adorable, blonde goldfish. "I don't think you're a...one of those."

"Again, you're a terrible liar," he said. "And if your future brother-in-law *is* cheating then why would he tell the whole world about it?"

"He wouldn't, but you seem to be able to talk to anyone. Give him a few drinks and see what comes out." She pressed her hands together and shot him the most deadly puppy-dog face he'd ever seen. "Please, Caleb. This is my sister. I don't want her to marry a cheater. It'll destroy her."

He tilted his face to the ceiling. "Fine. But if I go for drinks with Daniel you owe me *big*-time. Like, the favour to end all favours."

"Anything." The second the word popped out of her mouth she mashed her lips together.

Colour him interested. "Anything?"

"Within reason."

Reason wasn't something he hung on to around her. And her promise lodged in his mind, making him spin through the list of all he wanted to do with her. *To* her.

"A date," he said. "In exchange for the pain and torture of getting your future brother-in-law drunk."

Her tongue darted out to swipe across her lips, hesitation making her eyes flick back and forth. "Just a date," she said, eventually. "I'm not sleeping with you for a favour."

He stuck his hand out and when she accepted it, he pulled her in close. "Just a date. But if the night ends in my bed I won't be complaining."

"Keep dreaming," she said, but her voice wavered.

And that little wager was going to keep him going all week. He wanted Imogen, and now he had the opportunity to show her exactly how much.

CHAPTER SEVEN

IMOGEN WAS PRETTY sure that every romantic comedy Lainey had forced her to watch featured a scene where the female lead stood in front of a mirror, trying to decide on the perfect dress. Imogen didn't have that problem. She had a dress. Well, *the* dress.

It was her "date" outfit. A simple black shift which finished on the knee and had cute, fluttery sleeves made of sheer black chiffon. It was *Breakfast at Tiffany's* meets *Rear Window*. And since she almost never made it past the first date, she only needed one dress.

One dress to rule them all. How Tolkien of you.

But the real issue was what should go *under* the dress.

"If he's not getting up your skirt then why do you need fancy underwear?" Imogen stared at the options sitting on her bed.

She didn't own a lot of lingerie, but she kept a few nice pairs "just in case." Black lace, cream silk with pearl details and, if she was feeling extra confident, va-va-voom red with a cheeky little heart-shaped cut-out at the back. But she wouldn't be sleeping with Caleb, because his tat-for-tat date would end at midnight. Then poof! Pumpkin time.

Frilly things weren't necessary. In fact, a pair of ugly beige knickers might be the insurance she needed to fight temptation. If things got out of control she'd only need to think of how badly Caleb would rib her for wearing Bridget Jones–style granny undies on a date.

"Good thinking," she said to her reflection.

Caleb had insisted on picking her up because, in his words, if they were going on a date then he wanted to do it properly. The sentiment made her smile—it was a little old-fashioned and...unexpected. But now that meant waiting on pins and needles until he arrived. Grabbing her bag, she headed into the living room.

"Oh la *la*." Her roommate and friend, Lainey, grinned. "You're getting your mileage out of that dress."

"This is the only time I know for sure a first date won't turn into a second." She sat on the couch, careful to smooth the fabric so it wouldn't wrinkle.

"Is that why you won't let me do your hair?" Lainey pouted. "You won't be able to take advantage of my skills for much longer."

"Ugh, don't remind me that you're abandoning us," she said with a huff. Lainey was about to head to London for her dream job working for a celebrity hair stylist, meaning Imogen would have to find a new roommate soon. "I'm still dark on you for leaving. Even though I hope the move is everything you want and all your dreams still come true."

Lainey chuckled. "You can't even jokingly say something mean to me."

"That's because I use up all my 'mean' at work."

"And yet you're going on a date with a colleague." Lainey tapped a red lacquered nail to her chin. "Interesting."

"I'm trading a date for information." She shot her friend a serious look. "That's why I'm not doing my hair and I'm not wearing fancy underwear. Because I'll be coming home nice and early."

"Why even bother wearing the date dress at all? Why not wear your work clothes?"

That was a good point. "I like this dress."

"And don't think I haven't noticed that you're wearing my shoes," Lainey said in a smug tone. "You argued black and blue last time I tried to lend them to you."

"They make my legs look good." Imogen inspected the slender gold stilettos. They were tame by Lainey's standards, but not by hers. "What's wrong with wanting to feel confident?"

"Nothing, but I think it's less about self-confidence and more that you want him to think you're hot."

Dammit. How did Lainey manage to see through her like that? She'd purposely avoided asking her hairdresser friend for help because she didn't want to seem like she was putting in too much effort.

"A pair of nice shoes won't do that. You should

see all the women in his team." Imogen rolled her eyes. "I'm pretty sure it's a Victoria's Secret pre-screening zone."

"You don't give yourself enough credit."

Before Imogen could respond, the rumbling of a car engine sounded in the driveway. Much to her surprise, Caleb's ridiculous retina-searing Alfa was right on time. Lainey rushed to the window and peered out, making no move to hide her curiosity.

"He's gorgeous." Lainey gaped at her. "How the hell are you *not* interested in him?"

"He's not my type." She lifted one shoulder into a shrug. "He's too…"

"Chiselled? Stylish? Mouth-wateringly handsome?"

"He's too much like Mike."

Even now, five years after her marriage had ended, saying his name was like taking a cleaver to her heart. She'd never admitted it aloud before, but the inkling had been there for too long. Caleb had way too much in common with her ex—that magnetic charisma that drew people in, being surrounded by beautiful women all the time, that slick way of getting what he wanted.

The difference was, Caleb never tried to hide the fact that he dated around. It was part of his persona.

"Oh, Immie." Lainey pulled her in for a hug. "Not all men are like Mike, okay? You know that."

"Yeah, I do. But I also know when I can objectively see similarities." She sucked in a breath. "I'm protecting myself."

A loud knock on the front door echoed through the apartment, and Imogen squared her shoulders. She was going to enjoy tonight and use it as an opportunity to make sure Caleb was prepared for his side of the deal. Then she would come home, granny undies intact, and forget that it ever happened.

"If you nurse that drink any longer you'll have to file adoption papers," Caleb said.

Imogen sat across the intimate table at *Samantha*. The restaurant had opened a few weeks ago and boasted a three-month wait list. Not to mention all the hoop-jumping required to even get on the list in the first place. But Caleb had pulled a few strings and secured a reservation. Perks of having the Allbrook name.

"I'm pacing myself," she said. "No point chugging a good wine."

"Worried you'll get drunk and become susceptible to my charms?"

She scoffed. "I'd *need* to be drunk."

"You know, some women do find me charming," he said, his lip quirked. "I still haven't figured out why you're so impervious."

"High standards." This time she couldn't keep a straight face. "It's nothing personal, but you're not my type. And I get the impression you have plenty of choice, so why do you care what I think?"

That was a bloody good question. Maybe it was because the second Imogen had walked into the Allbrook office he'd been permanently distracted. His attraction to her didn't stop at the physical. She put him in his place on a regular basis, never sugar-coated her opinions and didn't treat him any different despite him being related to Gerald. She'd risen up on her own merits, without any of the sucking up or politicking that most people used, and that was genuinely fucking refreshing. Plus, he enjoyed the chase. And Imogen gave it to him in spades.

"I respect your opinion," he said.

Their dessert arrived and Imogen fussed with her napkin. "I didn't know that."

"I also figured you hated all men," he joked.

"Why? Because if I don't fall at your feet I must hate all men? Give me a break." She spooned some of the cream into her mouth and sighed. "I date. I just don't date *you*."

"Current circumstances might argue that."

"You blackmailed me."

"No, I traded my services." He reached for the bottle of wine and topped her glass up, not caring if it took her another two hours to drink it. For once, he wasn't itching to get on with the evening. "Totally different."

"This isn't a real date."

"No? You're certainly dressed like it's a date. No starchy white shirts in sight." He cracked the top of his crème brûlée with the back of his spoon. "The most important question is, what did you put under the dress?"

Her cheeks flared a bright shade of pink, making

her eyes look even greener by comparison. "None of your business."

"Boring beige, then? Interesting."

She looked like she wanted to say something, but held her tongue. Instead, she reached for her wine and took a long gulp. Liquid courage, perhaps?

"We should talk about the information you're going to extract from Daniel," she said.

Ah, change of conversation. An obvious diversion tactic, but he'd let it slide. For now.

"I need to find out if he's got someone on the side. What else do you want to know?"

She thought for a moment. "Who it is or how many women he's seeing."

Caleb raised a brow. "Why does *that* matter? Isn't it cheating, regardless of whether it's with one person or ten?"

"There's a big difference between one person and ten…or nineteen."

Caleb's body revolted at though he'd been sucker punched. Nineteen? That was far too specific a number to have been plucked from thin air. Of course, it had been obvious that Imogen herself had been a victim of cheating, given her determination to catch her brother-in-law. But she was right, there *was* a big difference between one and nineteen.

"How did you find out?" he asked.

He wouldn't have been surprised if she'd thrown up the shutters and locked him out. It wasn't any of his business and it was obviously painful for her to talk about. But she rested her dessert spoon against the porcelain dish and sucked in a breath.

"I got a call," she said. "He'd given an STD to one of the women he was sleeping with and she was furious because he'd told her he was clean. So her 'revenge' was alerting me to his affairs."

Fucking hell. What a way to find out.

"I was gobsmacked. I knew our marriage wasn't all sunshine and roses, and we weren't having the amount of sex that newlyweds were supposed to be having…or any sex at all, really. But I didn't think we were doing *that* badly."

"I had no idea you were married," he said.

"I was nineteen and he was thirty. The marriage only lasted a year, so it's not exactly something I put on my résumé." She attempted to smile but it came off as more of a grimace. "The woman who called told me he was using that affair site, the one where married people go to cheat on their partners. So not only was he cheating on me but it was with multiple women, and he was paying for the privilege. I managed to find the messages of all the women he'd agreed to meet with, but there could have been more that he met off the site. He was away at conferences a lot."

Caleb blinked. It wasn't often that he was rendered speechless, but this had thrown him for a loop. No wonder Imogen was so standoffish when he'd teased and flirted with her. She obviously guarded her heart closely.

"And then I spent an agonizing few weeks getting tested to make sure he hadn't passed anything on to me. I'd never thought I would be so grateful that he lost interest in sleeping with me the second we got married."

"Oh God, Imogen. I'm so sorry." He raked a hand through his hair and shook his head. "What a bastard."

"I was young and naive." She shrugged. "I thought he loved me, but he proved that everyone had been right. I *was* too young, I didn't know what I was doing and I shouldn't have gotten married."

"Your parents gave you a hard time?"

"They were supportive considering they'd warned me off him. But a few of my aunts and uncles were quite vocal. They baulked at the age difference and thought I should have waited longer. It was kind of a whirlwind." She sighed. "But you think you're invincible at that age."

"It certainly explains why you're going to such extremes to find out about Daniel."

"I know it seems over the top, but I've tried to talk to Penny and she won't listen. I was *exactly* the same before I got married. Wouldn't even consider that I might be wrong about my future husband." She sighed. "But now I have hindsight, and if I can save Penny from getting her heart broken then it's worth being a little crazy."

They ate their desserts in silence for a moment before she looked at him with a sheepish grin. "See, this isn't a real date. I've already veered into inappropriate conversation."

He chuckled. "I'm quite fond of inappropriate things."

"Why doesn't that surprise me?" She cocked her head, studying him for a moment. Her intensity stirred his blood in all the right places. Normally Imogen glossed over him, her eyes always darting away or focusing on something else. But now she looked at him like she could really see him, for the first time. "Why aren't you in a relationship?"

"I haven't found the right person. And, contrary to popular belief, I also have high standards."

"And yet here you are with me," Imogen joked.

But he wasn't about to let her hide behind self-deprecating humour.

"The only way I could convince you to come on a date was to swap a favour. If I wasn't interested, why would I have bothered? I'll be honest, I'm not hard up for dates but I'd never say yes if I didn't feel any attraction."

"Are you saying you're attracted to me?" Her brows shot up.

Was she *that* blind?

"You want me to spell it out? You're far sexier than you give yourself credit for. All those jokes I've made about us getting together weren't really jokes and I think you have a kick-ass personality. I appreciate that you're smart and hardworking, and it gets me quite hot and bothered that you have this prim and proper thing going on when I get the distinct impression it's nothing but an act."

Imogen's mouth hung open. "Okay, wow."

"Too much?"

"I..." She took a gulp of her wine. "Well, like I said when we were in the archive room, you'd only ever teased me. So I assumed it was because you were joking."

"For such a smart woman you're pretty terrible at picking up on signals."

"Lack of experience," she said. "I guess when men don't throw many signals in your direction it's difficult to decipher them."

That was an easy fix. Caleb dropped his spoon down next to the unfinished dessert and stood.

"Come on," he said, holding out a hand. "Let's get you some signal practice."

CHAPTER EIGHT

IMOGEN HAD EXPERIENCED a few key types of dates since forcing herself to get back into the scene a year ago. There was the "bad match" date where conversation halted more than it flowed. Awkward, and usually done by 9:00 p.m.

There was the "oh dear God this is so bad someone is probably live-tweeting us right now" date, which she'd experienced twice. The first time with a guy who'd quizzed her like it was a job interview, and the second with a doctor who thought it important to tell her that they should skip dessert for "the sake of her health."

Lastly, there were the dates that seemed positive until it came to the end of the night, when it was clear things wouldn't be going further. She liked to think of these as Gandalf dates. *You shall not pass.*

They were the most disappointing ones of all, because Imogen usually saw potential. Unfortunately, she wasn't good at holding people's interest.

Until tonight.

After cutting dessert short, Caleb dragged her

to a club that managed to avoid all the things she hated about regular clubs. There was no questionably sticky carpet, no jostling at the bar, no beefcakes invading her personal space. It was classy, fun...and sexy.

The people in this club were impossibly attractive. The entry line snaked down the street, but Caleb sailed past it with her by his side. After a quick joke with the bouncer they were in. A stone settled in the back of her throat. This was *exactly* how things had started with her ex—the fancy venues, being swept away and treated like a princess...

"So, signal practice." Caleb took their drinks from the bartender and they found a secluded spot in the corner of the room to people watch. "What do you think is going on there?"

He nodded to a couple at a stand-up table. It looked like they were on a date, and the guy was talking animatedly while the girl smiled on. "It's going well?"

"Are you asking or telling?"

Imogen wrinkled her nose. "Telling. She's smiling and they're talking a lot, which is a good sign."

Caleb made a buzzer sound. "Wrong. *He's* talking. Watch his mouth—he barely takes a breath. She's bored but trying to be polite. The smile is fake, though. She's tapping her nail against her leg. I give this date one star, would not reach date two."

"You don't know that." Imogen sipped her drink. She hated to admit it, but Caleb could read people like no one else she'd ever met. Maybe that was why he was so effective in winding her up?

They watched as the woman's phone started ringing. A second later, she gathered her things and headed out of the club in short, hurried steps. Once her back was to the table, her serious expression melted into relief.

"Oh no, family emergency. What bad timing," Caleb said with a smug smile as he drew a checkmark in the air. "Score one for me. That was most definitely a *get out of jail* call."

"Okay, fine, smarty-pants. What about them?" As subtly as she could, she nodded to a couple seated at a booth a few feet away. They looked blissfully unaware of the world around them.

"She's pregnant."

"Huh? But we're in a club."

He leaned closer so it wasn't obvious they were talking about the people around them. The scent of his aftershave, which was faded and warm, coiled inside Imogen's belly. It stirred her butterflies and kicked her pulse up a few notches.

"She's not drinking. That glass of wine hasn't been touched, and she keeps reaching for her water. Plus, that dress she's wearing is very loose."

"So? Lots of women like loose dresses."

Then the woman cradled her stomach under the table. She didn't have much of a bump at all, but that protective, maternal gesture could not be mistaken.

"Maybe he doesn't know it yet…or maybe the baby isn't his," Caleb mused.

A second later the man excused himself from the table, and the woman stealthily tipped some of her drink into his. Then she pressed the glass against her lip so some of her lipstick transferred.

Caleb made a motion of drawing another mark in the air. "Convinced yet?"

"Let's try one more. Two could be a fluke." She scanned the room.

Usually Imogen's black dress was perfect on a date—it was one of those clothing items that fit well, was comfortable and still looked pretty and put-together. But gazing out over the fashionable Melbourne crowd made her LBD look a little… frumpy. The women here were diamonds and she was a cubic zirconia in need of a clean.

Swallowing her insecurities, Imogen found a couple for Caleb to assess. "Those three. The guy in the blue shirt with the two women."

A brunette in a floaty green dress stood to one side of the man, and a redhead in a silver mini skirt was on the other. The dynamic was unusual—the man appeared to be in his element and the other two women seemed a little…off.

"Good one." He slung his arm around her shoulder, and pulled her farther along the bar. "Let's get a closer look."

"This is what you do on a Saturday night, huh? Stalk unsuspecting people while you pick apart their personal lives?"

"A guy's got to have fun."

The man chuckled and sipped his drink. There

was definitely tension there. Even Imogen could see that.

"He's dating the brunette, but he wants to fuck the redhead," Caleb said.

"You don't think they're having an affair already?"

The brunette sidled up to the man and slung her arm around his waist, but her fingers were digging in. Possessive. A stamp of ownership. The redhead continued to bat her lashes, however.

"No, I don't think so. If they'd gotten to that stage already he would be more subtle." He turned to Imogen. "Maybe he's trying to convince them to have a threesome."

"What? Out in the open?"

"Well, they might be doing negotiations out in the open but I'm sure they'd get a room. I doubt it'll happen, though—the girlfriend is *not* feeling it."

"She's probably jealous. Who wants to share the attention with someone else?" Imogen snapped her mouth shut, suddenly aware that she'd revealed something of herself. Saying too much around a guy like Caleb was dangerous. "How did you get to be so good at reading people?"

"Don't think I missed that little statement, Miss I Want to Be the Centre of Attention." His arm was still around her shoulders and it took all of her willpower not to melt against him. "And people reading is a necessary skill in my family. When no one wants to say what's really going on, you have to read between the lines."

"I'm not very good at that." She frowned.

"True. But then I always know where I stand with you."

Did he, though? Did he know that she willed herself not to be attracted to him? That she'd thought about him every night since they'd kissed? That she tried to convince herself it would be better to lust after his brother instead?

"So why the fake jokes about us going out?" she asked. "Why not come out and ask me seriously?"

"I knew you'd say no."

He was right, she *would* have said no. "Then you got lucky at the masquerade ball."

Grinning, he took the cocktail glass from her hand and placed it on the bar with his. The brush of his fingertips made her insides turn to goo. It was soft and subtle, but undoubtedly intentional. He knew every string to tug, every button to push, every bell to ring. Her body was an instrument for him to play. Her desire his to shape.

The breath stuck in the back of her throat as he pulled her closer, his hand snaking around her. Memories of the ball flashed in her mind—of his sharp jaw beneath that incredible mask, his lips firm and demanding on hers. His body hard between her legs.

"If I'd gotten lucky at the ball then I wouldn't have felt the need to touch myself every night while thinking about what I would do to you, given the chance." The words were like sparks, like little flares of energy threatening to start a fire. Threatening to burn her to the ground. "About how many different ways I could make you scream my name."

"There's more than one way?" The question popped out before Imogen could think about how juvenile and inexperienced it made her sound. She cringed. "Forget that."

"Not on your life." His hand stroked up and down her back, not going low or high enough to frighten her into pulling away. But rather, creating a soothing, sensual burn at the base of her spine that radiated all through her body, melting her slowly, but steadily, into his arms. "That's one thing I've realised about you, Imogen. I couldn't forget, even if I tried."

Slipping his hand into hers, he pulled her toward the dance floor. The music playing overhead wasn't the typical bass-heavy club thump. It was more relaxed, a slower grind but no less sensual. Caleb pulled her to the middle of the floor, into the heart of the crush.

Oh God, no. Not dancing.

While she'd been blessed with her father's eye for detail and a sharp memory, she'd also inherited his two left feet.

"I don't dance," she said, trying to raise her voice above the music, but Caleb tapped his ear and shrugged as though he couldn't hear her. Bastard.

People pressed in from all sides, pushing her closer to Caleb. He moved easily, as though he conducted the music and allowed it to flow through him. It was sexy as hell and when he pulled her against him, his hips brushing against hers, a tremor ran through her. The pulsing flicker of strobe lights made his hair flash gold. A lock curled forward, stubbornly brushing his forehead no matter how many times he tried to push it back. The desire to reach up and tug at it ripped through her.

Maybe it was due to the shelter of the dim lighting, the inhibition-loosening effects of the alcohol, or the fact that he'd finally gained an ounce of her trust…but she melted. It was hard to worry about consequences in the middle of a dance floor where the crowd granted anonymity.

He dipped his head, forehead pressing against hers, and she sucked it all in. Cologne and sweat on his skin, the scent of whisky on his breath, the wicked curve of his lips. He reached behind her, finding the elastic band holding her ponytail and tugging until it came loose. Her hair spilled over her shoulders and into his hands. He ran his fingers through it, gently pulling so her face angled up. He pressed his lips to her neck, holding her captive, and she fisted her hands in his shirt. Was this what it was like to fall?

Because she was inches from the edge of the cliff, ready to tumble into the deep abyss below.

"Don't dance, huh?" he growled into her ear. "We'll see about that."

He nudged her legs apart with his thigh as they moved. The crush closed in, people crowding from all directions but the second that Imogen's mouth popped open, a silent moan causing her eyes to flutter shut, everything dissolved around them.

The bass from the dance music created a rhythm

in her blood. There was nothing tangible left, only sensation. The flicker of lights, the tightening grip of his hands at her waist, the rub of his thigh against her sex, the vibration of a moan in the back of her throat. The club was warm, the scent of booze permeating the air, intoxicating her. Imogen wrapped her arms around Caleb's neck and followed his lead, swinging her hips and losing herself in the music.

She rubbed against him, letting her body revel in their mismatched state. While she was languid, liquid softness, he was hard. Everywhere. His teeth scraped her neck, stubble roughing up her skin. His hands were full of her, tugging, pulling, biting. She'd never thought dancing was like this—that it was a precursor to sex. Foreplay.

Caleb Allbrook's seduction had begun.

Watching Imogen's outer layer dissolve was truly fascinating. The difference between now and the night of the ball was that before she'd been fuelled by frustration. Anger. Lust. Things squarely in the defensive category.

But now, with her olive green eyes turning slowly black with excitement and her body softening under his touch, this was raw Imogen. The real Imogen. The woman she tried so damn hard to hide away. *That* was the woman he wanted. And he was certain with every cell in his body that she wanted him, too.

Her face tipped up to his, eyes wide as her lips moved. But he could only hear snatches of what she said—something about not being the dancing type.

Something told him there were a lot of things in her "not my type" list. He was going to shred that list to pieces.

His hands found her waist, drawing her closer. Her body was perfectly soft and rounded with a sexy dent at her waist followed by the flare of her hips. Like an hourglass. Touching her was like being on a roller coaster—each smooth curve made his heart thump as he chased the next high. The next stomach-summersaulting dip.

It wasn't enough. Nothing would be enough until he dragged her to some dark corner and got between those soft, curvy thighs.

"You're so fucking sexy," he growled into her ear. "Why have you been hiding from me all this time?"

She rested her cheek against his, her lips brushing his skin. "I'm not hiding now."

They moved together, the stiffness leeching out of her limbs as she followed his lead. Mimicking him. Finding the beat for herself. Her dress had ridden up her legs, tempting him to brush his hand along the inside of her thigh. Everything about her was a trip for his senses—all that smooth skin and silky hair. She was a goddess.

"I want to touch you," he said, pulling her earlobe between his teeth.

"But the people..." Her words faded into a gasp as he brushed his knuckles over her sex. Her underwear was already damp. Fuck, the woman was a firecracker. His cock twitched, pressing hard against the fly of his dress pants. "They might see us."

"It's dark, baby. No one cares." He continued to stroke her through the thin cotton, rubbing his fingertips between the lips of her pussy. Her nails dug into his skin with a sharp bite as he nudged her clit. "I want to feel how wet you are."

Imogen's eyes were wild—her pupils black and wide, lashes fluttering as he stroked her. She squeezed her thighs, trapping his hand there. But when he thought she was going to pull away, she rocked against him.

"Fucking hell," he groaned. "You're killing me."

He breached the elastic band around her leg and brushed the back of his finger along her sex. Christ. The smooth, slick skin had him foaming at the mouth. He wanted her orgasm and he wanted it now.

"We should go somewhere private," she said, dragging his head down to hers. Her lips landed on his, so soft and sweet—positively chaste, all things considered.

"Not yet." He pushed the fabric aside and ran his fingertip along her seam. She was dripping wet, so ready for him. "I've got this fantasy, Imogen, and it won't let go."

She bit down on her bottom lip, stifling a moan as he pushed against her entrance. "What fantasy?"

"Of getting you off in a roomful of people." He kissed the tender spot behind her ear. "Originally it was in the middle of a board meeting, but this will have to do."

"A board meeting?" she squeaked. "Caleb, you're... Uh!"

He ground the heel of his palm against her clit, teasing her for a moment before backing the pressure off. There was no way he was rushing this. Someone bumped against Imogen and she pushed harder against him. "Disgusting? Exciting? Thrilling?"

"Yes," she breathed.

He brought his mouth down to hers, coaxing her lips open so he could taste her better. His free hand pressed into her lower back, shielding their activities as best he could. Her tongue swiped along his lip, leaving the taste of orange liquor in its wake. When he pushed a finger inside her, Imogen's moan vibrated on his lips.

"That's it, baby. I want to feel you shake on my hand."

Imogen was holding on tight, her fingers thrusting up into his hair as she kissed him back with brute force. The chaste kiss was long gone—this was raw and desperate. Her breath quickened and her forehead dropped to his shoulder. A second later she shattered, the inner muscles of her sex squeezing him rhythmically as she shuddered against his chest.

Caleb cradled her, his cock impossibly hard and the voice in his head screaming at him to push her up against a wall. Or down to the ground. Or fuck it, maybe he should pick her up and wrap her legs around his waist right here. Anything to sate the beast she'd unleashed.

No. He couldn't waste this moment—the perfect, dirty, sexy moment.

The DJ shouted something over the music and

a whooping cheer rose from the dance floor. The crush surged and Caleb tucked Imogen under his arm. Time to move the party to a new location.

The club was enormous. Much bigger than it looked from the sedate bar area where they'd shared a drink. There were several more rooms depending on your music taste—chill R&B, hard-core dance music and a lounge area that was better suited to talking. But none of those interested Caleb.

He dragged Imogen toward a set of stairs leading up to a walkway that ringed the main room. It was mostly used by bouncers, since their staff room was located on this floor. He'd been to this club several times and often came up here to people watch. But tonight, he had different plans.

"Where are you taking me?" It was easier to hear as they moved away from the speakers, although the bass still rumbled through his veins.

"Somewhere we can finish what we started."

CHAPTER NINE

Holy freaking poodles. Had she really done that? Had an orgasm in the middle of a nightclub surrounded by, oh, at least a few hundred people?

Imogen's knees wobbled as she climbed a flight of stairs tucked around a deserted corner of the club, her hand nestled in Caleb's. The waves of post-orgasm bliss continued to roll through her, leaving her foggy in the most delicious, endorphin-drenched way. It was like he'd filled her veins full of cotton candy and glitter, coaxed her eyes open to a world of pleasure she hadn't known existed.

"Whoa there." He steadied her as they took the last few steps up to a black balcony overlooking the dance floor. Frowning, he cupped her face in his hands and looked closer. "You haven't had too much to drink, have you?"

"Nope." She giggled.

Imogen was as sober as a judge. The two wines at dinner had been soaked up by their delicious meal and she hadn't even finished her cocktail at the bar downstairs. She was floating on a cloud made of pure desire. No alcohol required.

"I might not be a perfect gentleman but I want my partners in crime to be willing accomplices," he said, staring her down. "I don't want you waking up tomorrow and regretting anything."

"I'm not sure I even know what regret is at the moment." Her voice sounded softly distorted, like her brain hadn't quite caught up. "Wait, 'willing accomplice'? What are we doing up here?"

"Getting you ready for round two." He nuzzled her neck and led her farther along the walkway.

Bright lights swung from a contraption on the roof, flicking on and off in time with the beat. Beams of green, blue and purple light changed direction with mechanical ease, bathing the floor below in supernatural colours. From above, the dance floor didn't look as though it was filled with people, rather it was some kind of mythical heaving mass. A place where people ceased to exist as individuals, and became absorbed by the crowd.

Imogen had never thought that kind of feeling was a positive one. But now the anonymity of the darkened club was...freeing. She could leave her uptight, type A persona at the door. No questions asked.

Caleb wedged her against the balcony railing, his chest lining her back as he gripped the black metal rail. Penning her in. Her hips dug into the metal as he pressed against her backside, lips at her neck. He was hard as stone and knowing that she'd gotten him so worked up only fuelled her euphoric haze.

"What does round two involve?" she asked, turning to look over her shoulder.

Caleb's thumb traced the line from her jaw down to her collarbone. "Another orgasm for you. One for me."

"Here?"

Despite being more alone here than they were downstairs, she felt exposed. Anyone below them would be able to look up and see what was going on. Not to mention the fact that the stairs were open. What if a group of people stumbled across them screwing around?

Literally or figuratively.

But she didn't want to put the brakes on. Instead, her body temperature shot up a few hundred degrees. Excitement scraped along her nerve endings. She wanted this.

"Yes, here." His breath blew hot against the back of her neck.

His hand was still at her throat, pressing lightly but possessively. In that moment, he owned her—owned her pleasure, owned her fear, owned the words before they came out of her mouth.

"Do you want me inside you, Imogen?"

"Yes," she whispered. Her agreement came without hesitation.

"Louder," he growled.

"Yes."

"I want everyone to know it."

"Yes!" she shouted into the abyss, but the rising pulse of the music swallowed it. "I want you inside me."

Caleb yanked the hem of her dress up and his hand searched for her underwear. "Bloody hell, how high up do these things go?"

Crap. She'd totally forgotten about her granny knickers and now Caleb would be getting an eyeful of them in all their stodgy, beige glory. She wriggled, humiliation overriding her lust as she tried to get out of his grip. But Caleb had her trapped.

"Let me go," she said, cringing. Dear Lord, could she not get through one date—even a sort of fake one—without making a fool of herself? She could already imagine the story he'd tell. Hot and heavy night ruined by underwear big enough to carry your groceries in.

Maybe she could flip them inside out and use them to hang-glide off the balcony and escape her bad decisions.

"Stop. Moving." The words were short and sharp—more commanding than she'd ever heard from Caleb before. There was a seriousness in his tone, a presence that swelled in the air around them. "I don't give a fuck about your underwear. Because as far as I'm concerned, it's a barrier to me getting my cock inside you. And that is unacceptable in any form."

Sweet. Baby. Jesus.

Imogen curled her hands around the railing, panting with need as he finally got a grip on the top of her underwear. Then he yanked them down all the way to her ankles. Strong hands guided her feet, helping to free her. The soft, floaty fabric of her dress smoothed over her bare backside and the sensation was startlingly erotic. It was like he'd sensitised her skin, so that even the gentlest brush felt like a thousand-volt shock.

He hadn't asked her to stay still, but Imogen couldn't bring herself to move. There was something about playing a passive role that eased the concerns in her mind. That quietened the shrieking doubts telling her she wasn't going to be good enough for someone as experienced as Caleb.

"Spread your legs."

Imogen gingerly moved her feet farther apart, unstable on jelly-like limbs. His hand slid up the back of her thigh, curving over her butt and squeezing hard.

"Perfect," he growled into her ear.

Her dress swished as he moved behind her, the sounds lost in the thumping techno beat. Then his hands were back and the blunt head of his erection pressed against her entrance. His fingertips danced up her inner thigh, teasing her by inching forward and then retreating. Dancing in a way that had her begging.

"Please. More."

The words evaporated into a hiss the second Caleb's fingers parted her. Shutting her eyes, she let the sensation wash over her. There was nothing but flashing lights, the beat of the music and the pain-pleasure snap of being stretched by him as he entered her. The music swallowed her words and that meant she could say whatever she wanted without fear of repercussion or judgement or humiliation. She let the words fly—every four-letter word under the sun, and a few that probably came from another universe, as well.

Caleb's front lined her back, his hips pressing into her backside with each stroke. His hands were everywhere—plucking her nipples, tugging her hair, holding the railing in front of her for extra leverage. It was dirty and hot and nothing she'd ever experienced before.

"Anyone could see us." His lips were at her ear, his free hand snaking over her hip to dip between her legs.

Imogen's dress bunched around her waist and she fisted the fabric in one hand to give him access. Sighing, she leaned back and let her head rest against his shoulder. He wasn't rushing things, wasn't mindlessly pounding away like her ex used to. No, Caleb had rhythm. His moves on the dance floor totally translated—he wasn't too quick nor too slow, he balanced the perfect line between forceful and gentle. The man was the goldilocks of fucking.

She giggled at the thought. It was like he'd pulled the stopper out and all the naughty words she'd bottled up for the last twenty-something years had come flying out.

"Can you see all those people down there, Imogen?"

She nodded. "Yes."

"Are you watching them while I fuck you?"

A tremor ran through her. "Yes."

"What are you going to do if someone looks up and sees me playing with this perfect little pussy of yours?"

Her eyes fluttered shut as his fingers circled her clit. "Nothing."

"Are you going to let them watch?"

She nodded, mostly out of her mind with lust and the pressure of the orgasm welling inside her.

"What if they want to come up here and get a better look?"

She knew it was bad to want this. What if someone she knew came up those stairs? What if it was someone from work? She'd be caught with her legs spread, half-undressed while the guy she was supposed to avoid screwed her senseless.

But she was all in with this fantasy—hook, line and sinker.

It was entirely possible that Caleb was in a coma right now and this was a drug-induced dream. Because how else was he lucky enough to get the girl of his literal dreams writhing beneath his hands while they fucked in the middle of a nightclub? The thrill of knowing they could be caught made his cock hard enough to hammer nails.

Imogen's blond hair tumbled over his chest, her head resting against him. She was wet and hot as a summer storm, and a tight fit. Her muscles clamped down on him as he thrust in and out, keeping his pace steady so he didn't reach the finish line too quickly. But everything about this was his catnip—

the semipublic location, the spontaneity of it. And Imogen.

"The thought of having an audience gets you all hot and bothered, doesn't it, baby?" He curled his fingers over her damp sex, teasing her. "Who would have known you were such a sexy little minx? You hid it so well."

He continued playing with her clit while his other hand came up to her throat, tipping her head back so he could see her face. Her mouth was slack, her eyes hooded.

"I think you're ready to orgasm again. Your sweet little pussy is feeling very needy right now." He dragged a finger between her lips, coating himself in her. "I want those sexy thighs to shake for me."

She was so close to the edge it barely took any pressure at all and within seconds she was shuddering around his cock, crying out something hoarse and incoherent. It sounded like his name repeating on loops so close together the syllables blurred into one another.

"Yes, baby." He nipped at her ear lobe. "Let everyone know how good it feels."

He was calm and in control until the second Imogen let go of the balcony and her nails bit into his skin. She sagged back against him—giving herself over completely. That trust was more than he could have asked for and—along with everything else she was doing out of her comfort zone—it fuelled the primal side of him. Instinct took over, turning his smooth words into a garbled mess. He thrust into her harder, wedging her against the railing as he stretched the last waves of her orgasm out while chasing his own.

She turned her head, and he bent forward, capturing her mouth as best he could at the awkward angle. But it wasn't enough. He wanted that pouty mouth in all its glory—the way a mouth like that was meant to be taken.

Caleb pulled out so he could spin her around and drag her thigh up over his hip. "I need to see that beautiful face of yours."

Her cheeks were pink, as if she'd spent a day in the sun. A drop of red clung to her glistening lower lip where she'd bitten down, and Caleb swiped it away with his thumb. "Kiss me," she said.

"Gladly." He angled his mouth over hers, fisting one hand in her hair and curving the other over her sexy, rounded butt as he drove them toward the edge. In this new position, his pubic bone brushed over her clit and soon she was shaking with need again.

"It's too much," she gasped. "Too sensitive."

"You want me to stop?" His lips were at her neck, teeth marking her skin. Claiming her. She tasted like honey with the faintest salty tang of sweat.

He wondered if she would taste so sweet between her legs. The visual of him going down on Imogen rocketed through him, causing his hips to jerk as he ground into her.

"No. Don't stop." She buried her face against his shoulder. "Just don't let me fall."

"Never." Determined to get as deep into her as

possible, he lifted her other leg so she could wrap them around his waist. Fucking hell, she was tight. He buried himself to the hilt, and encircled her with his arms. "You're safe with me, baby."

"I know," she whispered.

The sincerity in her eyes was the final straw. This was all he could take. With a deep groan, he thrust into her one last time, letting the release barrel through him as he clung to her like she was the most precious thing in his life.

CHAPTER TEN

Reality was a big, fat B-word. Mondays were bad enough, but the beginning of a new week after terrible life decisions was downright cruel and unusual. Imogen took the stairs, climbing eight flights rather than risking being trapped in an elevator with Caleb.

She took the long way to her office, avoiding his, and slammed her door shut the second she got inside.

Okay, so you slept with him. It's not a big deal.

Except it was. She'd totally lost her head. Lost all control of what she believed about sex and dating and *him*. She'd slept with him in public, where hundreds of people could have seen what they were doing, and she had no idea where her underwear had ended up. And then there was the kicker, the biggest moment of idiocy… She hadn't even checked if he'd used a condom.

Imogen wasn't on the pill because, frankly, she didn't need to be. What was the point of taking medication for something that wasn't an issue? Caleb was the first guy she'd slept with in over a year. What if she got pregnant? What if he had an STD?

"Oh God, oh God, oh God." She dropped her head into her hands. How could she have been so stupid?

This wasn't like her at all. She never lost her cool. She never let her feelings take over the rational part of her brain. And yet, he slipped one hand beneath her dress and she turned into a brainless idiot.

That was why she'd stayed away from Caleb previously.

"What's done is done," she said to herself. "Woman up and deal with it."

Despite wanting to avoid it, they needed to have that awkward conversation about whether or not she'd need to see her doctor. Then it would be waiting a week or two before peeing on a stick. She could only hope that the powers above wouldn't punish her too harshly for one ill-advised indiscretion.

Her phone vibrated against her desk, a message flashing up.

Caleb: Are you in yet?

Smurf. It wasn't even 9:00 a.m. and he was already looking for her? After he'd dropped her home on Saturday night—at her insistence—with a very *un*gentlemanly kiss, she hadn't heard from him. And for once, a day of silence was a welcome relief. She needed time to process what'd happened.

Imogen: Yes.

Caleb: I didn't see you walk past. I hope you're not avoiding me.

Busted. Caleb might seem like he was as chill as an ocean breeze, but the guy didn't miss a trick.

Imogen: I took the long way around. My Fitbit says I gotta get those steps in!

Caleb: Take a few more and come to my office.

She wasn't ready to confront him yet. Would he act like nothing had happened? Or would he make it clear that once had been enough? What if she was going around thinking it was the best sex of planet Earth's history and he thought it was average?

Imogen: I'm busy.

Caleb: I have something of yours.

Her dignity? Her ability to think clearly? Her underwear? She'd lost all three on Saturday night.

Imogen: Later.

Caleb:…

The three little dots ticked over and over. When Imogen reread what she'd written, she cringed. This day definitely needed coffee. Without waiting for his response, she stuffed her phone into her bag and headed out of the office, taking the long way back to the elevator.

Caleb leaned back in his chair and interlaced his fingers behind his head, giving his back a deep stretch. Every muscle in his body ached. He'd spent all of Sunday in "distraction" mode—going for a run, rearranging all the furniture in his apartment, taking his neighbour's dog for a walk. He'd been certain that if he didn't keep himself busy there was a high likelihood of him landing on Imogen's doorstep ready for a repeat of Saturday night.

But he knew rushing into things would only make Imogen more skittish than she already was. And fair enough, too. It wasn't every day that one had spontaneous public sex…unfortunately.

"Yo." Jason walked into Caleb's office and shut the door behind him. "Where were you all weekend? I thought we were going to grab a parma."

Caleb smacked his head. "I got caught up. Sorry, man."

He hadn't, really. But something had stopped Caleb from heading out to see his brother. Perhaps it was the fear that Jase would take one look at him and know what'd happened. Or maybe it was the fact that their father's words were still niggling at him— the idea that Jason was a better match for Imogen. That he'd treat her properly whereas Caleb would chew her up and spit her out.

"Got caught up, huh?" His brother raised a brow.

"Not much comes between you and the pub. She must have been good."

Caleb wasn't sure if that was jealousy or disapproval tinging his brother's words.

"If she rendered you speechless, I *have* to meet her." Jason chuckled. "I ended up catching the game with Daniel, anyway, but I shouldn't have bothered. St. Kilda got us ninety to forty-eight. Bloody disgraceful."

Caleb's ears pricked up. "I didn't think Daniel was into the footy."

"He's not. But he and Penny were having a blue over something." Jason shrugged. "He was happy to be out of the house."

"Is there a wedding cancellation on the horizon?"

"I don't think so. Just petty stuff." Jason shot him a look. "Why do you care?"

"I was hard on him at the ball." Caleb got out of his chair and wandered around to the front of his desk, doing his best to look as casual as possible. This was the perfect time to dig up some dirt for Imogen. Because Caleb might be a joker, but he *always* upheld a promise. "I was thinking the three of us should grab a drink."

His brother looked at him like he'd suddenly sprouted a second head. "A drink?"

"Yeah, you know, one of those liquid things humans consume to relax after work." He grinned. "I was a bastard for riling him up about the mask and I want to make amends."

"Will wonders never cease?" Jason muttered.

"You were the one telling me to cut him some slack," Caleb reminded his brother. "And I can admit when I've gone too far."

"We're going to Riverland after work on Friday if you want to join us." Jason speared him with a serious look. "No funny business."

"Done." He clapped a hand down on his brother's shoulder. "Looking forward to it."

"Now, we need to talk about the executive retreat since you decided to skip the family dinner on Thursday."

Cue older sibling judgement. Caleb looked up. Yep, Jase was giving him the "big brother" face. "What? I was busy."

"We could have rescheduled. You didn't have to no-show."

Caleb shrugged. "I don't see what the big deal is. They give all the leftovers to the dogs anyway."

Truth was, after their meeting last week he'd needed a break from the family drama. Normally he was better at brushing off his father's antics, but lately they'd gotten under his skin and stayed there.

Jason sighed. "In any case, Dad went over the one pager and I've convinced him that we should proceed. We need a team to take care of the event management side of things, so I've got the HR team onto it."

Caleb's cheery mood soured in an instant. His father had laughed the idea off as "pandering" and now all of a sudden Jase had the tick of approval. What a fucking surprise. *This* was why he didn't bother turning up to dinner. "When was that decided?"

"We talked about it on Thursday but we finalised it this morning." Jason shifted on the spot. "I would have invited you to the meeting but you weren't in yet."

"I wasn't in because we didn't have a meeting booked. If I'd known we were going to discuss *my* idea then I would have come in early." Tension pulled at the muscles in his jaw and he bit back the rest of what he wanted to say, which was that he was sick of being left out of Gerald and Jason's little club.

"Does it matter whose idea it was? It's a great thing for the company, regardless of who delivers it."

Says the son who always gets a pat on the head.

"I'm not trying to shut you out," Jason added. "But you know what Dad's like. Sometimes it takes hearing things from a few people before he sees the value."

"You mean it takes him hearing it from *you*." Caleb shook his head. "Fuck it. I'm over it, anyway. I'm quite happy not to carry the mantle of golden child."

"Don't be like that." Jason frowned. "Anyway, I'm not stealing your idea. We got it over the line, that's all that matters. You can run point with HR to get it organised."

"Trying to palm work off to me now," Caleb teased.

Jason punched him in the arm. "You can't have it both ways."

"Watch me," he said with a grin as he picked up

his laptop and headed to the door. "Being difficult is my superpower."

He sauntered through the office as though he didn't have a care in the world, but all the while his blood was beginning to boil. It wasn't about the retreat, exactly. Rather, what it stood for. For Caleb's entire life his father had criticised his work, torn down his ideas and generally made him feel worthless. Why? Because he'd never wanted him to be born? Because his mother was supposed to be another decoration on Gerald's mantel?

Part of him wished that he could be as "zero fucks given" on the inside as he projected on the outside… but he wasn't. The key, however, was not to *ever* let anyone know.

It was bad enough to be the unwanted son—he wasn't about to let people pity him on top of it.

"Caleb!" Mary trotted up behind him. "I know you're supposed to be in a meeting, but Mr. Allbrook has called a management team meeting. Now."

Caleb bristled. "Am I supposed to keep the ad team waiting?"

"I'll ask Mina to send an apology on your behalf and reschedule. I was told to…" She bit down on her lip. "I was told everyone had to be there. No excuses."

He could only imagine what his father had actually said. Caleb sucked in a breath and changed direction, heading toward the boardroom. There was no point getting shitty with Mary. It wasn't her fault. But the idea that everything should be dropped because the old man bellowed got under Caleb's skin.

Like everything else he does. Calm blue fucking ocean.

By the time he got the elevator to the executive floor, the room was already full. There were two spots remaining at the long, glossy black table and one of them was next to Imogen. His bad mood dissolved as her gaze connected with his, eyes widening as she figured out he was going to take the spot next to her.

"Thanks for saving me a seat." He dragged the chair away from the table and sat. "Very kind of you."

"No problem." She appeared to study her notepad...her *blank* notepad.

Gerald was at the front of the room, fussing with some papers and talking quietly with Jason. It appeared like they were waiting for someone—whoever was supposed to fill that last empty seat.

"Busy day, huh?" he asked. "You still need to come by my office."

"Yes, I'm busy. I'm not sure if I'll have time." She didn't meet his eyes.

He scooted his chair closer until their knees touched under the table. Her hair was slicked back into one of those brain-tugging ponytails and tiny pearl studs dotted her ears. So prim.

"Make time," he whispered. "Or do you want me to leave your soaking wet panties in your mail slot instead?"

Her head snapped up and she glared at him. "Stop it," she mouthed.

"I can't. I've been running it through my mind all weekend." He pulled a Montblanc pen from the inside pocket of his suit jacket and pretended to make notes on her notepad.

I get hard thinking about it.

Between the small font and his naturally scratchy handwriting, no one would be able to see what he'd written. But she could. The muscles in her neck worked as she swallowed.

You need to hold up your end of the bargain, she wrote.

Friday night. Catching up with Dan and Jase. I'll meet you after.

She smiled and nodded, her expression relieved.

Drinks at mine or yours?

She shook her head. *No drinks. Just talking.*

Fine. I'll call you when I'm done. You can come over.

Something flickered in her eyes, an uncertainty, but then she nodded and dutifully scribbled over all their text, erasing the evidence.

His father started the meeting, droning on about their recent engagement scores and some challenges they were facing with staff retention. Caleb watched with a tightening in his jaw as his father unveiled the plans for the executive retreat, giving all credit to Jason. He brother stood cool and calm at the front of the room, but he avoided Caleb's angry stare. No doubt Gerald was behind the surprise announcement, but his brother should've had the balls to say something. Give credit where credit was due.

The room nodded along while Gerald ran through the purpose of the event, and outlined all the benefits they were hoping to achieve. Caleb scratched his pen back and forth along the notepad in front of him, bearing down on the paper until the nib pushed through sheet after sheet. Fuck both of them for stealing his work and passing it off as their own. All the positive noises and comments from the management team were like a swarm of beetles over his skin.

He replaced the cap on his pen and tucked it into his jacket, about to shove back his chair and get the hell out of the room. But a hand stopped him. Imogen's palm came to his thigh, a gentle command to sit still. The gesture was completely shielded by the large wooden table. They were sitting close, since the room was packed, so unless someone looked under the table, they wouldn't notice a thing. Caleb looked over at her, and the sympathetic gaze socked him in the chest. She'd been in Gerald's office that morning. She'd heard the argument and *knew* it was his work.

"Don't go," she mouthed.

Her palm burned through the wool of his suit pants—though he wasn't sure whether it was because she cared enough to stop him storming out or simply because she was touching him. As Gerald droned on about how they were committed to increasing staff retention at all levels—giving no mention to his concern about pandering—Caleb grew increasingly frustrated.

Imogen's fingers bit into his thigh when he moved, so he stayed. She wanted to distract him? Fine. He curled his hand over hers and pulled her palm farther up his leg. She didn't resist. Her fingers burned a trail up the seam in his pants and his cock hardened in an instant.

Caleb let Imogen's hand go, wanting to see what she would do. She swivelled in her chair, angling herself toward him as if wanting to discuss something.

She pushed her notepad toward his, moving her body closer and sliding her hand farther up his thigh. The tip of one of her fingers brushed the edge of his cock and he was filled with electric excitement. Was she really going to touch him like that in the middle of a management meeting?

"I think the retreat is a wonderful idea," she said, her voice smooth and calm. The discussion going on in the room almost swallowed her softly spoken words and her fingers brushed over the aching head of his cock again, this time more boldly. "It's so important to show people how much they're appreciated."

"You don't think it sounds like a waste of money?" he asked.

She shot him a look. "Not at all. In fact, I think getting out of the office really helps people to connect."

This time she squeezed him and he had to stifle a moan. What kind of awesome, kinky alternate universe had he landed in?

"That's quite a *stroke* of genius," he said, gritting his teeth.

"Sometimes you have to coax people out of their shells." Her cheeks had flushed pink and she worked him up and down through his pants, the strokes short and subtle so it wouldn't be obvious to anyone who looked in their direction. But her grip was firm and he was so hard he risked busting his fly.

"That only works if things are out in the open," he said. "Easier to address the issue that way rather than trying to do things behind closed doors."

Would she accept his challenge?

"We're currently exploring venues for the retreat, but we'll be putting together a team to create a schedule for the three days," Jason said from the front of the room. "If you're interested in being part of this team, please email Mary and we'll schedule a meeting for later this week to get things started."

Imogen bit down on her lip, making a note of Jason's instructions on her notepad all while her other hand found the tab of his zipper and slowly pulled down. Caleb thanked his lucky stars that he hadn't bothered with underwear today. Her soft, warm palm enveloped his cock and he gripped the edge of his seat to keep himself from thrusting into her hand.

Holy fucking hell, this was the hottest thing he'd ever done. Imogen was an utter surprise, and if he'd been hot for her before then he was downright burning up now. Her fingers formed a tight ring around him and she paused to squeeze his head before sliding her hand back down. His balls drew up tight against him. He couldn't let himself come…but *damn* her hand was working magic.

"And we have one more announcement to make," Gerald said from the front of the room. "It's with a heavy heart that I announce my intent to step down from the position of CEO within the next three months."

Caleb froze and Imogen snatched her hand away. All eyes were glued to the front of the room. Tucking himself back into his pants, Caleb tried to figure out what the hell had happened.

"I know many of you will not be surprised that I'm announcing Jason as my successor. He's been shadowing me for some time and I am confident he will take this company in an exciting new direction while holding on to the values that we at Allbrook hold dear." He held up his hand when questions started to fly. "This is earlier than intended, but I have some health issues which I have kept private. However, for the sake of my family, it's time for me to take a step back and let someone else have the spotlight."

Health issues? Since when?

Imogen looked at Caleb, her mouth agape, but he could only shrug. Jason, however, didn't look surprised in the slightest. He *did* look guilty when Caleb speared him with a look.

How could they not have told him what was going on?

"This transition will take some time, but in the interim we have decided to appoint someone to fill Jason's role while he shadows me more intensely." Gerald cleared his throat. "We'd like to thank our current head of projects, Matthew Donaldson, for agreeing to step up and help out."

The wind was totally knocked out of Caleb's lungs. So, not only was his father sick and hadn't told him about the changes to the family company, but he hadn't even given Caleb the opportunity to take up the position of general manager.

If it had ever been foggy before, the message was crystal-fucking-clear now: Caleb was totally on his own.

CHAPTER ELEVEN

Imogen walked, shell-shocked, from the ladies' room where she'd gone to wash her hands and splash her face with cold water in the hope it might pull her out of her stunned state. Prostate cancer. Totally treatable. But Gerald's doctor had indicated the need for rest and a reduction of stress. That meant reducing his role to board-level involvement in the Allbrook family business.

Oh, and she'd given her boss's son a hand job under the boardroom table.

What the ever-loving smurf were you thinking? Have you lost your freaking mind?

Thoughts buzzed around in her head like bees, each one fighting to be the loudest until all she could hear was an incessant, ear-splitting whine. Her job was safe, Gerald had stressed that when he'd called her into his office after the management meeting. She would be working for Jason.

Let's make sure you don't get fired for performing a sex act in the middle of a team meeting.

She headed into her office and shut the door, sagging back against it for a moment to catch her breath. But that's when she saw Caleb leaning against the wall beside her desk, arms and ankles crossed, his pants pulled up just enough to reveal a pair of electric-blue socks patterned with yellow polka dots.

"Did you know?" he asked.

His hair—which had been perfect in the meeting—now flopped over his forehead. That coupled with the dark expression and narrowed eyes gave him a wild, dangerous look. But even then, Imogen could only see him through a veil of lust. Her body remembered too much—the demanding grip of his hands at her hips, the velvety hard erection in her palm. How he'd tasted on Saturday night—like whiskey and sex and sinfulness.

"Not until now," she said. "I… I'm so sorry."

"Sorry that my father has cancer or that I found out along with the rest of the company?" His lips took on a cruel edge as he smirked. "Don't answer that."

"I wasn't going to," she whispered.

She couldn't imagine what that must be like—to have a father who so coldly cut you out of his affection, out of his business. Out of his life, from what she could tell. Her own father was a tough, hard-working man of few words. And even though he never mustered the vulnerability to say "I love you" outright, he always managed to show it by coming over to repair her light fixtures or tighten the decrepit pipes under her kitchen sink.

But Gerald—a man she'd once admired with all

her being—was rapidly losing her respect for how he treated his youngest son.

Sure, Caleb wasn't an ambitious self-starter like his brother…but had he ever been given a chance? She'd always thought of him as a party guy, a social butterfly who didn't really care too much about work. But she'd seen what he was like in Gerald's office talking about the leadership retreat, she'd heard the passion in his voice. And now she'd seen the devastation in his face when his father and brother took credit for his idea.

What if his lack of ambition had nothing to do with his personal goals and everything to do with being forced to live in the shadows?

"Do you want to talk?" she asked.

He shook his head. "There's nothing to say."

His eyes were ablaze with fury and lust. She'd never experienced something so volatile and exciting before—something so…exhilarating. Caleb turned her into a different woman; he dragged out a new side of her, a side she hadn't even known existed.

"Then why are you here?" Her voice disappeared like steam curling up into the air.

"I told you," he said. "I have something of yours."

He pulled her beige underwear out of his suit jacket and flung them onto her desk. She swallowed, her palms flattened behind her against the office door. Outside, the sound of heels against the marble floor tracked back and forth. People coming and going, all potential opportunities for her to be caught.

Caught? You're not doing anything wrong...
Yet. The word hovered on her tongue because she knew where this was going. He'd come to finish what she'd started. Imogen shook her head, trying to find the words to return everything to normal. To regain control of the situation.

"Thanks for returning them," she said. "I have a meeting now that—"

"Cancel it." His voice was like ice.

"I can't, Caleb. It's important…uh, I…" Oh God, what was wrong with her? He'd reduced her to a babbling mess with nothing more than a simple command and that powerful, intense stare. "I really need to get back to work."

"Leave it." He stalked over to her. "Work can wait."

"We can't do this here. Not after…" Her head swam as he placed one hand on either side of her head, hemming her in. "Saturday was unexpected and unplanned. I don't even know if…"

His brow furrowed. "You don't know what?"

"I didn't even tell you to use protection." She clamped her eyes shut, the shame of her stupidity washing over her. "I'm not on the pill and I didn't even say anything and I'm not ready for kids yet. It's too early and I—"

"Shh." A warm hand cupped her cheek, the gesture shocking her with tenderness. "I used a condom."

"You did?" She sagged with relief. "Oh thank God."

"Imogen, you might think I'm a selfish brute, but I wouldn't put you in danger like that." His expression softened. "I promise."

"Everything happened so fast."

"I know, baby." He lowered his forehead to hers, his eyes holding her captive. "Now lock this fucking door and clear your schedule."

She swallowed. Her stomach was a circus performer doing summersault after summersault, but there was no denying the soul-deep *yes* that rang loud and clear in her head. She wanted this. She wanted *him*.

"This is so unprofessional," she said, her mind grappling for an excuse to walk away. She couldn't come up with one. "What if someone hears?"

"If you can't be quiet, you can stuff those panties in your mouth." He smirked.

Holy guacamole.

She reached behind herself and flicked the lock on the door handle. The quiet *snick* shot through her body, making her hands tremble in anticipation.

Caleb stepped back. "Sit on your desk."

On shaking legs, she walked to her desk. It wasn't anything fancy like they had in the executive offices—a plain white desk that housed her laptop, diary and a potted plant. It was uncluttered, simple. Like how she wanted her life to be…or so she'd thought.

She rose up on her tiptoes and slid her backside onto the desk. The fabric of her pencil skirt bunched at the tops of her thighs and she automatically pushed it down. Which seemed a little pointless, but Imogen was far out of her depth.

"Cancel the meeting."

He unplugged her laptop and handed it to her, waiting while she rescheduled her catch up with Mary. The second she sent the notification, her phone rang, but Caleb was already sinking to his knees in front of her.

"Answer it," he said.

She brought the receiver up to her ear. "Hello. Imogen Hargrove speaking."

Caleb's hands smoothed up her thighs, breaching the hem of her skirt until his fingertips found the waistband of her underwear. A gentle hand pushed her back against the desk until she was lying flat, her legs dangling over the edge. He worked the underwear down over her hips, past her knees and removed them completely.

The voice on the other end of the phone prattled on. It was the assistant of one of Gerald's business contacts wanting to arrange delivery of some important documents.

"Courier is fine," she said in the calmest tone she could muster while Caleb snaked back up her body, pushing her skirt higher and nudging her legs apart. "Address them to the CEO but send them care of me."

Warm breath skated over her skin, teasing her. Caleb's hands were braced on her inner thighs, his thumbs delicately brushing against her sex. A hint of what was to come.

No pun intended.

The woman went over the documents in frustrating detail, and Imogen wanted to scream at her to hurry up. She clamped her lips down and squeezed her eyes shut, her hands white-knuckling the phone receiver, as Caleb dragged his tongue over her sex.

Holy guacamole, indeed.

"Yes, that's right," she said. "We're on level eight. Bourke Street. No, Bourke with an *e* on the end. Yes."

His tongue flicked over her clit, dragging a moan from deep inside her. She pressed her hand over her mouth to stop it flying out, but the energy spent on trying to keep quiet only made the sensation of him lapping at her even more intense.

"No, there's no *e* at the end of Allbrook." She gritted her teeth. "It's fine. If the company name is correct, then we'll get the documents."

When the woman on the other end of the phone said she wanted to go over the address one more time Imogen sucked in a breath. "I'm sorry to cut you off but I'm in the middle of something. I'll call you back."

She slammed the phone down and arched her back as Caleb sucked on her. Reaching down blindly, her fingers searched for his head and found purchase in the thick waves of his golden hair.

"Tsk tsk," he said, looking up. "That was very rude."

"It would have been ruder to scream your name in that poor woman's ear."

"Do I need to gag you?" he asked with a grin. "I thought you'd have a little more control than that."

Her cheeks burned. "Does it look like I have any control right now?"

"Good point."

He dipped his head back between her legs and worshiped her with his mouth. This time he didn't hold back—he gave her the pressure she wanted, the right level of friction. It was like he knew exactly how to push her straight to the edge of need.

"Caleb," she whispered, her body writhing against the desk. "That's so good."

"How good?" he growled.

She didn't have the words to tell him, so she tightened her grip on his hair, raking her nails over his scalp in an effort to show him. He nipped at the inside of her thigh in response. *This* was how they could communicate openly. With their bodies. Without any fear that words might not adequately do the job.

She rolled her hips, grinding himself against her face until the tremors started. Behind closed lids there was a pinpoint of pleasure and she chased it, her body tripping over itself to get to that blissful feeling of release.

"Oh God." She bit down on her lip, stifling all the things she wanted to say—dirty, naughty, bad things. Instead she curled her hands around the edge of the desk and held on while he consumed her and she chanted his name over and over in her mind.

When her tremors stopped, he placed a chaste kiss at the top of her sex and stood. His self-satisfied grin made her laugh—he looked truly pleased with himself.

"It's a shame we had to be so quiet," he said. "I still haven't been able to hear you properly when you come."

Imogen pushed up into a sitting position. "That's because you keep accosting me in public."

"Accosting?" He laughed. "Yeah, you look like you thoroughly hated that. And there's a locked door—this hardly counts as public."

Imogen caught a glimpse of herself in the mirror on the wall. Her ponytail looked like something a kookaburra might nest in and her pink lipstick was smudged up onto her cheek. If the dictionary had pictures, this would be sitting under "dishevelled."

"I have to go," he said.

"We're not going to finish this?" she asked.

Even though the orgasm was great, she had a distinct feeling of being cheated. Her sex still pulsed and throbbed, desperate to be filled. But Caleb was going to leave her hanging.

"If you want it Friday night, I'm all yours." He planted a kiss on her lips and she caught a brief taste of something unfamiliar and earthy. *Her.* "Until then…looks like I've ruined two of these now."

He gestured at the two pairs of underwear sitting on her desk. Neither one was wearable.

"See you on Friday." He sauntered toward the door and let himself out as she scrambled off her desk, pulling her skirt down and wondering how the hell she was going to be able to concentrate on work for the rest of the day.

You've got to put a stop to this. He's running

rings around you already. You'll get chewed up and spat out.

The plan had been to approach the dating scene carefully. Regain her confidence. Start paving the road to feeling sexy and attractive again. Her ex-husband had left scars so deep that whenever she looked in the mirror all she could see was a flashing neon sign that said Not Good Enough. If she'd been prettier/funnier/smarter she could have kept her husband from straying.

Imogen knew thinking like that was a slippery slope to despair. His inability to stay faithful wasn't anything to do with her, in the end. He was addicted to the attention, to the thrill of the chase. But finding out that he'd never had any intention of being monogamous had cut deep.

Reentering the dating scene only to be met with a whole lot of reinforcing messages that she still wasn't pretty/funny/smart enough had unpicked that wound stitch by stitch.

That was why she was intoxicated by Caleb's attention. He gave her what she needed, what she craved—that feeling of being beautiful and attractive and wanted. Of being enough.

It wasn't because she thought they had a future together…was it?

No. Caleb would grow bored of her like he had with the other women he'd dated. She was a challenge for him, since she'd rebuffed his advances. He, like her ex, enjoyed the chase. So now that he'd caught her it would be over soon. And the quicker she got that into her head, the better.

After she got the information about Daniel on Friday night, she would go back to looking for a nice, safe, sensible man who wouldn't use and discard her.

Unfortunately, the glorious pride at bringing Imogen to her knees—or in this case, her back—in the middle of the workday had worn off the second Caleb left her office. The dark cloud hanging over him thickened as the week progressed, causing him to crack with frustration and resentment at any mention of his father. The kind words, while well-meaning, fuelled the fire in his heart.

He'd been avoiding his family like the plague, knowing full well that if they tried to talk to him he was liable to blow a fuse. His mother and Jason had made contact. Gerald, as usual, had stayed silent.

But Caleb had a promise to keep, and that meant having drinks with his brother and Daniel after work on Friday. And, given Imogen was the only person he wanted to see right now, he wasn't about to break that promise.

"Hey." Jason looked up from packing a bunch of files into his satchel as Caleb walked into his office. "I had a feeling you were going to cancel on me tonight."

"Why, because our father decided to tell his employees and his son that he had cancer at the same time? Was that supposed to upset me?" He ladled the sarcasm on thickly. "Nice try, old man, but I guess he forgot I'm immune to giving a shit."

"I *know* you don't mean that." Jason sighed. "Look, this situation is royally fucked up. I get it. But what am I supposed to do? Neither one of you is willing to give an inch, and I'm not a miracle worker."

Caleb swallowed back the resentment burning a hole inside him. "Maybe you could have given me the heads-up so I wasn't blindsided."

"It wasn't my news to share. At first he told me he wasn't going to tell anyone." Jason raked a hand through his hair. "He wanted to announce my new role and be done with it, but I told him the staff would ask questions if it happened suddenly. We don't want the company suffering from a lack of confidence because of his secret-keeping."

"It's always about the company, isn't it?" he said bitterly.

"It'll be different when I'm in charge."

"Thank God. Big brother to the rescue again." He held up his hand when Jason went to retort. "Just tell me, did he go to you first or did he go to Mum?"

His brother eyed him warily. "Why does that matter?"

"Because *I* can take it when he treats me like shit, but she can't." He'd seen his mother cry too many times over the way Gerald held her at an arm's length, even after all these years. The sad thing was, she genuinely loved him. It was the reason she never argued or stood up for herself. "I know she's not your mother, so you don't have to care. But she's his *wife*. That should mean something."

"Let's cut that bullshit out right now. I *do* care about her. You know that. More importantly, *she* knows that." He cleared his throat. "But yes, he came to me first. It was only so we could work out how I was going to transition into the role quickly enough for him to start chemo."

Chemo. As much as he hated himself for feeling anything at all, the word was a sucker punch. It was easy to be angry at Gerald in principle, because he had every right to be goddamn furious at the old man, but cancer was serious. Cancer that required timelines for chemo was…next level.

It would be easier if Caleb could hate him. But he didn't.

There was still a part of him—albeit a worn-out, broken-down part—that clung to his childhood hope of one day making his father proud. Of finally feeling like he was every bit as legitimate as his brother.

Caleb shoved the thoughts aside. There wasn't any point rehashing those old desires. Logically, he knew nothing would ever change. "When did he find out?"

"Last Thursday."

The night Caleb was supposed to go for dinner. But instead he'd blown it off because he was still pissed about their meeting. It was a petty thing to do, because Caleb was punishing his mother by not showing up. But he'd wanted to avoid yet another fight with his dad, and sometimes the only way to achieve that was to stay away.

Clearly Gerald had swung back by keeping him out of the loop.

"Are you going to let this grudge go?" Jason asked. He motioned for Caleb to follow him and they headed out toward the elevators.

"Because he's sick?" That was the million-dollar question, wasn't it?

Should Gerald get a free pass for all the years he'd committed the ultimate parenting sin by favouring one child over another? Should he be forgiven for doing everything to advance one child in life while acting as though the other was a burden?

"The doctor is confident that he'll beat it." Jason jabbed at the elevator's down button.

"But?"

"There are always people that fall into the unlucky five percent." His brother sighed. "All I'm saying is, he won't be around forever. It might not be now or even in ten years, but one day he'll be gone."

"I know that."

"Then I would think long and hard about what you do next. Because once he's gone, you don't get a chance to do things over."

A memory flashed in Caleb's mind. He was seven years old, lying in a hospital bed after being hit by a cyclist. He'd broken his arm and had been knocked out for a few seconds, but it could have been worse. All he'd wanted was to impress his dad by walking on his hands.

Dad, Dad! Look at me!

He'd slipped and stumbled into the street outside

their house. The cyclist had tried to avoid him, but it had been too late. He remembered waking up in the hospital, his mother's face streaked with tears. Jason and their friend from next door both looking on with worried eyes.

Gerald hadn't been there. He'd been called away to work.

"Don't make a decision now," Jase said, cutting into his thoughts. "But think about it."

"I will." He nodded.

For some reason, his mind strayed to Imogen and the way she'd touched him under the boardroom table. Not after things got heated—though that *definitely* played on his mind—but the way she'd stopped him from storming out of his father's meeting, the gentle pressure of her palm against his leg soothing him. She made him feel grounded, wanted. She restored his balance and helped him feel in control even when the rest of his life was a shit show.

Why was she different?

She cared. About her job, about her boss, about her sister. She cared about things so intently and so outwardly, it made him wonder if he was cutting his life short by bottling everything up and pretending it didn't matter.

But did she care about him? Why else would she have stopped him leaving the meeting? It would make no difference to her if Caleb's relationship with his father imploded. There was no reason for her to intervene unless it was because she felt something for him.

For the first time in days the dark cloud lifted off Caleb's shoulders and hope took its place. No one else had succeeded in making the shitty things in life more bearable. Most women he dated were a welcome distraction from it all—good company, a way to keep his mind off his problems. But Imogen was something more. It was like she saw through his cheeky, happy-go-lucky persona to the guy underneath. The one who wanted desperately to be a valued member of his family. The one who was at his wits' end.

And she hadn't turned away.

You sure it's not simply because she's hanging around to get the dirt on Daniel?

It was a good thing they were catching up tonight, because he wanted to know if his suspicions were true.

CHAPTER TWELVE

IMOGEN WANTED DRINKS with her colleagues as much as she wanted a hole in the head. The knowledge that she would be seeing Caleb later tonight—at his place, no less—weighed on her in that confusing and exciting yes/no way she'd come to associate with him. Her brain and her body were at a disconnect, and her heart refused to take sides.

She shouldn't want him. But she did…so very much.

"I've barely seen you all week." Mina, Caleb's executive assistant, handed a drink over. It was tall and colourful in a way that indicated it would go down far too easily. "How are you holding up? The news about Gerald was quite a shock, right?"

Imogen sipped her drink. "Yeah, it was. I know he's been out of the office more than usual lately, but I had no idea."

Three sets of eyes peered at her curiously. Did they think she was lying? Imogen was friendly with the other executive assistants, but she mostly stayed out of gossip, which left her a little on the outside.

Mina waded a swizzle stick through her drink and then tapped off the excess before setting it neatly down on a napkin in front of her. She was flanked by Dave—their CFO's executive assistant—and Petra, who'd been with the company since its inception. The latter was a goldmine of information and Imogen often wondered if she had compromising pictures of someone stashed away, since no one *ever* crossed her.

"Do you think Mary knew?" Dave asked.

"Mary knows everything," Mina replied, running a hand through her chin-length black hair. "Not that she'd ever give anyone the heads-up."

"It's certainly possible," Imogen agreed. "She books most of his personal appointments, and he probably asked her not to say anything."

"Apparently Gerald didn't even tell Caleb," Petra said. "Shay heard someone talking about it after the big meeting, said apparently he looked like he was about to storm out."

"He's been in a foul mood all week." Mina drummed her fingers against her desk. "That would certainly explain it."

Petra shot a sly grin in Imogen's direction. "I'm sure he can find someone to cheer him up."

Imogen almost choked on her drink. What on earth was *that* supposed to mean? She tried to play it cool by swirling her straw through the chopped-up pieces of fruit and coral liquid like she hadn't even noticed Petra's expression.

Oh God, what if someone had seen them at the club? Or heard them in her office? Or worse, what if someone had noticed her touching him under the boardroom table?

You're two consenting adults. It's no one else's business what you do with your body.

Except that only worked in theory. In practice, she'd broken at least one HR policy, a handful of personal rules and had compromised her reputation at work. For what? The thrill of a man wanting her?

Not just any man.

Caleb made her feel so…alive. So desired and powerful and deliciously out of control. But it was a slippery slope, and she still had the bruises from when she'd landed hard on her butt the last time.

"No comment, Imogen?" Mina asked.

"Why would I have something to say about that?"

"Come on." Petra winked. "Don't be coy, you can tell us."

A dull throb started at the base of her skull. Stress headache, a sure sign things were going south. Fast. "Tell you what?"

"She's not going to admit it." Dave patted Imogen on the arm. "I'm afraid your cover's already blown, girl. Shay saw you at *Samantha* having dinner with Caleb."

"Dinner." Imogen nodded, relief filtering through her bloodstream. "Yeah. It was nothing. Business."

"Bullshit." Mina dug an elbow into Imogen's ribs. "You do *not* go to the hottest restaurant in the city for a business dinner unless you're a CEO or a celebrity. And what the hell would you two be discussing there that couldn't be done at work?"

They weren't buying her lame excuse. Not even a little bit.

"I…" *Think! How are you going to explain this?* "I won a bet."

Her colleagues raised their eyebrows, but this time there wasn't any protest. "A bet?" Dave asked.

"Yeah. Caleb bet me that he could…crack my laptop password." Oh God. *So* lame. "And the loser had to buy dinner. I won and I picked *Samantha*."

"Good taste." Petra nodded. "So he bet you for a date?"

"No." Imogen shook her head, but the instant denial did nothing but make them laugh and roll their eyes. "I picked *Samantha* because I know how hard it is to get a table there. I didn't think he'd be able to do it."

"Sneaky thing!" Petra looked on with approval. "I'm not so interested in the dinner, though. I want to know what happened afterward. Was he as good as the rumours say?"

Imogen gritted her back teeth together. The thought of Caleb sleeping with anyone else made her want to Hulk-smash the fancy cocktail glass in front of her.

That was before *you. Even if it wasn't, why should it matter? You're not in a relationship and you don't want to be, either.*

But the internal pep talk had the opposite of her intended effect. Her mind automatically spun like a rabid hamster on a wheel. *Had* he slept with anyone since her? What if she was one of a few women he had on the go? Her stomach pitched. This was exactly why she should never have let it go so far.

"I didn't sleep with him," she lied.

"Why the hell not?" Mina squeaked. "I'd give my left arm to have a night with him. One of the girls that used to work in his team said he got her off three times before they even had sex. Apparently, he's really into going down on women."

"We're colleagues. It wouldn't be appropriate." Imogen cringed. Now she sounded like the world's biggest prude. This whole situation was precisely why she stuck to business with people from the office—her best friends had been trained to laugh off her epic awkwardness, but Mina, Dave and Petra looked at her like she had a second head. "I have a rule about that," she finished lamely.

"Probably for the best," Mina said. "Don't get me wrong, I love working for him. I think he's a great guy, but I'm constantly fending off bullshit meeting invites where it's obvious the woman wants to get him alone in a room. He's hot property. I'm *way* too jealous for that."

"You think he does things in the office?" Dave raised a brow.

Mina lifted her shoulder into a delicate shrug. "I've never heard anything from his office, but that doesn't mean it's not happening elsewhere."

"That sounds like a whole lot of speculation," Imogen said, staring into her drink. "Without much substance."

"Well, I heard that he got sprung in flagrante

when he was supposed to be exclusive with someone from the office." Petra shook her head.

"You mean he cheated?" The question slipped out of Imogen's lips before she could stop it. She knew Caleb had slept around a bit, but having an active sex life and engaging in infidelity were two totally different things.

Petra nodded. "Remember Neila Anderson? She used to run the staff induction program."

Imogen remembered her, all right. Tall, long-legged, perfect platinum hair. Gorgeous. Rumour had it she'd walked away from a modelling career to finish her business degree. And not only that, she was whip-smart. The perfect package.

See? Even the perfect woman wasn't enough to hold his interest. What makes you think you'll be any different?

"Good for you, anyway," Petra said. "You don't want to get messed up in something like that. It's hard enough to be taken seriously in this industry without sleeping with the boss's son. Well, the boss's brother, now."

For a moment, Imogen thought the cocktail would come rushing back up. She clamped her lips together and forced herself to swallow the sick feeling down. How could she have let herself be lured into doing something so stupid? How could she have let herself believe that he desired her for who she was?

"Speak of the devil," Dave said with a conspiratorial look.

A few feet away, Caleb stood with Jason, Daniel

and a blonde woman. They were all laughing and drinking beers, the setting sun a perfect backdrop against the well-suited foursome. The blonde woman stood next to Daniel, her hand coming to rest on his arm. In an instant all of Imogen's worries about her own bad decisions were gone, and she squinted. Was that the same woman she'd seen with Daniel previously? It was hard to tell, but all the key points lined up. She looked to be the right height and weight, her hair cut into the same neat bob.

When her eyes landed on Caleb's appreciative stare, she wanted to cry. He looked at the woman standing next to Daniel with open admiration, as though Imogen had never even crossed his path. Let alone his mind.

"Excuse me," Imogen said, slipping her bag over one shoulder. "I need to head off."

"You're not going back to the office, are you?" Mina admonished.

"No, I'm heading home. I promised my roommate I'd help her sort through things for her move." She waved goodbye and slipped out of the bar as stealthily as she could.

Tonight she would see Caleb, but only to get the information about the blonde woman. Their fling—or whatever the hell it was—was over right now.

After a few beers, Caleb was starting to see Daniel in a different light. What he'd initially written off as pompousness was actually nerves. Turns out he'd been anxious about attending the Carmina Ball for weeks because his father was going to be there and they hadn't spoken much after he got engaged to Penny. Their relationship was severely fractured already and him deciding to marry someone "below him" had been the final straw. It was an unlikely thing to bond over, but Caleb certainly understood his pain.

And as for him calling his fiancée the old "ball and chain," that seemed to be his way of trying to fit into the nonexistent boy's club he thought Caleb and Jason had going. But now, listening to what he had planned for their wedding was kind of sweet.

Sweet? Good Lord, you've been drinking from the crazy fountain. Imogen has gotten too far under your skin.

It shocked him that instead of wanting to stick his fingers down his throat at all the mushy wedding talk, he found himself feeling happy for the other man. And perhaps a little jealous. Would wonders never cease?

"Daniel has been involved every step of the way," Emily, Daniel's friend and jeweller, said. "He came up with the design and then worked with my team to refine it. He picked the stones and the engraving message. Penny is going to love it."

"Don't you think that's risky?" Jason asked. "I mean, if she hasn't seen the ring before the wedding there's a chance it might not fit, right?"

"Oh, I'm not going to wait until the wedding day," Daniel said, pausing to take a sip of his beer. "I'm going to surprise her with the ring this weekend. We'll try it on and make sure it fits."

Caleb leaned back against the wooden railing that rimmed the bar's balcony. "How have you kept it a secret from her?"

"It hasn't been easy. We've been meeting in secret to discuss tweaks to the design and so I can pay her in cash. Penny is like a hawk with the credit card statements." He laughed. "It helps that Emily and I have known each other for years. We went to the same high school and our families have been friendly since before we were born."

"Penny is a lucky woman," Emily said.

Was it Caleb's imagination or was there a hint of sadness in Emily's voice? Daniel appeared none the wiser and he happily prattled on about the inspiration for Penny's ring. Caleb had no idea why Imogen had been so convinced that her future brother-in-law was a cheating scumbag.

"I should be going," Jason said, checking his phone. His brother had seemed preoccupied all evening, constantly looking at his watch and glancing around the bar like he was waiting for someone. It was probably the weight of their father's news and his impending promotion.

"Me, too," Emily said. "I'll walk out with you."

Caleb knew his brother was taking it all hard, even though he put on a brave face.

The two of them said their goodbyes and then wove through the crowded outdoor bar, leaving Caleb and Daniel alone.

"I've been trying to set them up," Daniel said with

a smile. "But he's not interested. Seems he's got some mystery woman in his sights."

"Really?" Caleb rolled his beer glass between his hands, watching the foamy liquid swish and dip, leaving residue around the inside. "I've been telling Jase for ages that he needs to get out more. Any idea who it is?"

"None at all. He's an enigma like that."

Caleb chuckled. "He does play his cards close to his chest."

"And he's fussy." Daniel grinned. "Not a bad thing, mind you. I'm the same, so when Penny came along I knew it was right."

Caleb didn't want to push the issue, but he'd promised Imogen he'd dig around and now was the perfect time. "And you never get tempted to go elsewhere?"

"One of the reasons I have nothing to do with my father is because he screwed someone at work and broke my mother's heart. I'm not inviting him to the wedding, either. Does that answer your question?" Daniel snorted. "It's not the only reason we don't talk, but it's certainly part of it."

"Yeah, I guess it does." Caleb bobbed his head.

"It's not saying that I don't notice a beautiful woman if she walks past. But seeing what it did to my mother… I could never do that to Pen. Or anyone."

"Families are kind of fucked up, aren't they?"

"Not all of them. Pen's lucky like that. Her parents are still married, and she's close with them and with her sister. Zero drama. It's refreshing."

It sounded as though Daniel was oblivious to Imogen's distrust of him, but Caleb wasn't about to enlighten him. And being the sort of person who prided himself on accurately reading people, Caleb was certain there was no cheating going on. He'd even probed Jason on the way to the bar and had come up with nothing. Either Daniel was good at keeping a lid on it—which meant that no amount of questioning would turn up anything—or, as was more likely the case, Imogen had let her past fuel her paranoia.

"I'd be happy with a little less drama on the family front," Caleb said. He tossed back the rest of his beer and set the glass down with a loud *thunk*. "They could make a shitty soap opera out of my family."

"Mine, too." Daniel nodded. "As they say, you can choose your friends but you can't choose your family."

"Wise words." He contemplated ordering another drink, but this whole conversation had left him itching to get home so he could see Imogen. And that had nothing to do with the current company. "We should do this again. Drinks, I mean."

"Absolutely." Daniel beamed and stuck out his hand in an awkward, overly formal way that made Caleb smile. "Name the date."

Caleb bid him farewell and headed out of the bar. Jogging down a short flight of stairs, he came to the path that flanked the Yarra River. It was still light and bright, the sky tinged with orange and gold on the horizon. Two men ran past him, and a group of teenage girls walked in the other direction, laughing and playing with their phones.

Despite all the issues with his family, Caleb was strangely at peace. Daniel's words had struck him deeply.

You can pick your friends but you can't pick your family.

It was time to let go of his anger over his father's actions. Nothing would ever change the old man's views; nothing would ever elevate Caleb's status from the lowly rung of unwanted second son. But what he *could* control was the people he surrounded himself with. And right now, he wanted to surround himself with Imogen. Wholly and completely.

CHAPTER THIRTEEN

CALEB ROUNDED THE corner and headed up the path to his apartment building when he spotted the best thing he'd seen all day: Imogen in a pair of faded jeans with a rip over one knee and a black top that clung to her sexy curves.

"I don't think I've ever seen you in jeans before, Ms. Hargrove," he teased.

"*Miss* Hargrove." She fiddled with the end of her long gold braid. "Single and loving it, remember?"

This time he couldn't smirk at the joke. He didn't want Imogen to be single and loving it—he wanted her to be his.

His.

The word hissed in his mind, like a warning. Seeing her here—dressed down and bare-faced and looking more beautiful than ever—waiting for him, ready to come upstairs, had his body buzzing. Normally he'd blame it on the beers, allow himself to think that something else was responsible for that addictive feeling. But it was all her.

You can choose your friends...

He could choose more than that. He could choose her. And he didn't want to stop at friendship.

"Welcome to Casa Allbrook." He swiped his key card over the security pad and led her inside.

The building was one of his father's earlier creations—it wasn't sleekly modern like the newer towers, but Caleb enjoyed the slightly outdated charm. Plus, the apartments were bigger and he liked the fact that he was less likely to bump into any of his father's cronies here. They'd all taken up residence in the fancier buildings.

They headed to the elevator and Caleb hit the button for the top floor.

"Penthouse, huh?" Imogen said with a nod. "I should have guessed."

It didn't sound like a compliment. Without responding, he observed her. Imogen wasn't the greatest at hiding her feelings, no matter how hard she tried. But he enjoyed that—her body was responsive and communicative, and she spoke clearly through her actions and inactions. It was comforting to know where he stood.

But now the language wasn't positive. She picked at a frayed patch on her jeans, her pale pink nail polish chipped around the jagged edge of her thumb where she'd no doubt been chewing on it. He got the impression her lack of makeup and the plain clothes were meant to be a signal, too. A warning. Her appearance told him this wasn't a date.

When the elevator stopped and the doors slid

open, she practically leaped out. "You're awfully skittish tonight," he said.

The plush carpeted hallway muffled their footsteps as they walked to his front door, which was one of only two on the top floor. The silence amplified the tension between them.

"I'm not skittish," she said. "But I don't want to make any mistakes."

Ah, so he was on the money. She *definitely* didn't want him to think this was a date. Caleb shoved his key into the lock and let them in. Usually he felt a sense of relief in coming home—because this was a space where he didn't have to worry about what anyone else thought. He could be himself. But now he'd caught Imogen's tension, and the feeling sat uncomfortably on him.

"Any mistakes or any *more* mistakes?" He shrugged out of his suit jacket and walked through to the bedroom so he could hang it up. Imogen's footsteps sounded cautious and slow behind him. She stopped at the edge of his bedroom, not daring to set foot inside.

"Any more." She cleared her throat. "The other day in the office, we shouldn't have... It was unprofessional."

"Life's more exciting when you're a bit unprofessional." He slid open the mirror door to his wardrobe and hung his jacket up.

"Is everything organised by colour?" she asked. "I'm not sure why that surprises me so much."

Caleb's image was the one area where he could

exercise control. The wardrobe was custom fit to cater to his every need. Shirts hung in a gradient from white through blue through bolder patterns all the way to the dark shades. His suits were hung in a similar manner from the palest grey to the inkiest black. A lone navy suit—which he'd barely worn since it made him look too much like this brother—hung at the end next to his tuxedo. Even his shoes were arranged by colour and style, all housed with shoe trees so they'd keep their shape.

Not a single item was ever out of place.

"You should see my sock drawer," he quipped.

Suddenly, having Imogen in his space was like being part of an exhibition. He'd never thought about how much his place showed the real him—the guy who was organised, who lined his books up alphabetically, who liked order and was neat as a pin. It was the part of him he'd hidden in the office, preferring a charmingly chaotic front, with clashing colours and a sly grin because it was a better mask than anything else at his disposal.

He did everything he could not to be like his brother and father. To divert people from understanding the real reason he was a black sheep in his own family. He made it look like he was a playboy and a party animal and a natural born charmer. It was the perfect disguise and the reason he'd never be respected while he worked for his dad.

A double-edged sword.

"We should talk about your meeting with Daniel,"

she said, folding her arms across her chest. "That's why I'm here."

More barriers. Imogen was working overtime to draw a line between them, to push him away. Was she scared her willpower wouldn't hold up?

"Sure." He nodded. "What would you like to drink?"

"Water, please."

After he'd poured her a glass and made a gin for himself, they settled on the soft, worn-in leather couch that faced the windows running the length of the apartment. Outside, the city shimmered. Imogen seated herself as far away from his as the furniture would allow.

"This is the best spot in the whole house." He took a sip of his drink.

"Should I be afraid to sit on this couch?" she asked drily. "You clean it between women, right?"

The barb stuck hard in his chest. Maybe it was because his guard was down, maybe it was because of his chat with Daniel, or maybe it was the deep regret that her poor opinion of him was partially his fault...and he was done taking it on the chin.

"Actually, I prefer to fuck on the balcony. I've got a thing for voyeurism in case you hadn't noticed." His tone was granite-hard.

Imogen blinked, her bottom lip rolling between her teeth. "That was unnecessary."

He swirled the liquid in his glass, watching the ice cubes and wedge of lime bob up and down. "I'm not the guy you think I am," he said eventually. "Just like I know you're not the uptight, Prim Miss Hargrove you try to be in the office."

"It's not a front."

"Isn't it? The night we went out I saw something different. I saw it in your office, too." He rubbed his thumb over a chip in the rim of his glass, feeling the sharp edge catch his skin. "You change when you stop trying to hold on to that image. All the hardness and the sarcasm and the walls melt away. You… transform."

Her eyes were wide, the olive green irises made even more vivid by the tinge of red around them. How did he miss that earlier?

"I'm not pretending to be someone else. This is me. I'm sorry if you find it boring, but there's no treasure waiting to be discovered." She swallowed. "No matter what you thought you saw that night."

"I *know* what I saw." He set his glass onto a coaster on the coffee table. "You might not think you're hiding, but you are. And you've done such a good job that you've even fooled yourself."

"No, you're right." She rolled her eyes. "You absolutely know more about me than I know about myself. How silly of me."

"This is what I'm talking about. The second anything gets real you shut down."

"The second anything gets real," she scoffed. "Spare me. I know what this is, Caleb. I'm not some deluded bimbo who thinks you'll change thanks to the magical powers of my cha-cha."

"Pussy," he corrected.

She gritted her teeth. "This isn't a game."

"Then why are you turning it into one?"

"I'm not!" She threw her hand in the air. "You were the one who took what was supposed to be a simple date and turned it into…"

"The best sex of your life?"

She rubbed a hand over her face. A groove deepened in the middle of her forehead. "Yes."

He raised a brow. "I'm sorry?"

"No, *I'm* sorry. I should have known better than to put myself in a position to be tempted." She huffed. "You're like a really good pizza. I know I shouldn't want it and I know it's really freaking bad for me. But does that stop me wanting to nibble on a slice? No, because I'm an idiot with no willpower."

That was a lot to take in. She wanted him but didn't think she should—why? Because of his reputation? Because she was worried it might affect her career? Because she thought he'd hurt her?

"I've never met anyone who tries so hard to resist their feelings before."

"Yes, I know everyone falls all over themselves to get in your pants…or to get you into their pants." She scrunched up her nose. "You know what I mean."

"People tend to either love me or hate me. There isn't a lot of in-between." His lip pulled up on one side. "I'm polarising like that."

Was it possible to be on both sides at once? Her body was wholly in the *oh God, yes, yes, yes!* side of things, while her brain was already detailing an exit strategy. Being pulled in two directions at once wasn't a comfortable situation. But the worst thing of all was that her heart was starting to side with her lady bits. Which was a problem.

That was how her heart got battered and bruised and broken last time.

Caleb sat on the other side of the couch, his arm slung along the back like he was about to be photographed for a magazine. The sleeves of his baby blue shirt were rolled up and his open collar revealed a slim triangle of skin. His suit pants perfectly hugged his thighs, the hems pulled up enough that she could see which socks he'd put on that day. Sky blue with majestic-looking ducks. Business mallards.

She had to stop the manic giggle rising up the back of her throat. What the hell was she even doing here? This was supposed to be the conclusion to a transaction. She'd fulfilled her end of the deal, now it was his turn to hand over the goods.

But the longer he stared at her with those incredible blue eyes—which perfectly matched his shirt, of course—the more pressure built behind her sternum. It was like a growing fireball—the larger it got, the more it consumed her. Despite her efforts, Caleb saw past her defenses. Like the fade-into-the-background monochrome outfits she wore to work, the sensible ponytail and boring shoes… Prim Miss Hargrove. It was no less a mask than the one she'd worn to the Carmina Ball, as much as she denied it out loud.

That way, if anyone rejected her they weren't rejecting the *real* her. The Imogen who'd thrown caution to the wind by marrying the guy everyone warned her off, the same girl who'd gate-crashed an important event for the sake of her sister. The woman who let lust sweep her down a road of scorching-hot, semipublic sex.

"We're supposed to be talking about Daniel," she said. Her voice came out squeaky and unnatural.

"Getting too real again?" He raked a hand through his hair, his fingers driving rows through the thick strands. "I want to figure this out, Imogen. I want to know where we stand."

"Where we stand?" She set the glass down for fear that she'd drop it with how her hands trembled. This was not what they were supposed to be discussing. "There is no *we*, Caleb."

"Yes, there is. *We* are colleagues." His stare burned right through her. "We are friends. We are incredibly attracted to one another."

"We are?" Her breath hitched.

He knows all the right things to say—he knows your weaknesses and your sore spots. He knows how to press on them until you do what he wants. Don't fall for it.

But she'd already started to fall—she had done the moment she'd crossed his path on her first day in the Allbrook office. The attraction had hit her like a bolt of lightning, frying her insides and hollowing her out so that she'd never ever be the same again. For the last five years she'd put on her armour, to shield against him. Against herself. Against anyone who might want to see her bleed.

Caleb shifted, closing the gap on the couch until he was next to her. The small distance between them crackled with electricity. The need to press her palms to his chest, to run her fingers along his jaw and trace the curve of his lips was like a lion's roar in her head.

"We are." He reached out and rubbed his finger along the strap of her top. "I know you're fighting it, but your body tells me. Your eyes get dark, your lips get all pouty and kissable, and this bit—" he traced the line of her chest from her collarbone to the valley of her cleavage "—goes up and down, quicker and quicker. It's exciting to see you come undone, Imogen. It makes me so fucking hard to see you stripped bare like that."

But bare was bad. Bare meant vulnerable, and vulnerable was a hop, skip and jump away from broken.

"You're just saying that," she whispered. "You want something and you know all the right things to say. That's not real."

"Do you think I would have persisted after you shut me down if I only wanted a warm body?"

God, she wanted to believe him. She wanted to fall headfirst into this fantasy and stop doubting herself. Caleb slipped the strap off her shoulder. The drag of the fabric over skin caused her to shiver, anticipation building. Pressing. Demanding.

"I only shut you down because I thought you were teasing me," she admitted. "I don't seem like your type."

"And what's my type, huh?" His lips came to her

skin, sucking until blood rushed to the surface, sending goose bumps rippling across her arms and chest. They'd done so much more than this, but the talking combined with the gentle touches was a new level of intimacy.

She shivered. "Fun, sexy women."

"Why do you think you're not fun or sexy?"

It was impossible to keep the blood pumping up to her brain while he marked her neck with his lips and teeth. "You told me once I would fit in with the Golden Girls."

He laughed. "To be fair, that was after you said I had the mental capacity of a drunk Teletubby."

"I stand by it." Her lip twitched.

"I don't know how to appease you other than to say you've ruined me. I've wanted to find out what was under the suit and pearls from the second you set foot in the office and the deeper I dig, the more I want you." He kissed along the top of her shoulder, his face burying into the crook of her neck. "I'm addicted. So don't sell yourself short, because it's bullshit and I'm not buying it."

Her eyes fluttered shut and she concentrated on the feel of his lips against her hairline, on the hot whisper of breath along her skin, on the sneaky crawl of his fingertips along her thigh. Her boiling point was close and restraint fell through her fingers like water.

"It's bordering on disgusting how you know exactly what to say." Imogen shook her head. "You're dangerous, Caleb Allbrook. And it scares me."

"Don't be scared." His hand was higher now, sliding up the inside of her thigh. "I'm doing this because I want *you* in whatever form I can get. You want to toss a smile in my direction, I'll take it. You want a verbal throw-down? I'm in."

His fingers inched higher and she gasped. The slow build of anticipation amplified everything—from the sensation skittering over her skin like a pebble skipping across a pond, to the rush of need in her veins, to the chant of *higher, higher, higher* as she willed his hand to cup her sex.

"You're really happy to stop at a verbal throw-down?" she asked.

"It would be a great challenge to see if I could get you to come with only words." He nipped at her earlobe. "I'd be up for it."

"You *do* have a filthy mouth."

"Baby, when it comes to you I haven't got an ice cube's chance in hell of being anything *but* filthy." He grinned. "You bring out the best in me."

"So you haven't taken other women to that club?"

He drew her into his lap and without thinking, she straddled him and slung her arms around his neck. Instead of trying to distract her from the question as she'd assumed he might, he cupped the back of her head and brought her forehead down to his. "There have been other women before you. But right now, I'd be perfectly fucking happy if this was it."

What was that supposed to mean? He wanted her…permanently? He thought they had more than physical chemistry? It was a lot to take in and considering she'd been ready to hightail it out of his apartment tonight, she wasn't equipped to deal with this turn of events.

"Enough words," she whispered, her lips grazing his.

"You want me to show you?" He wrapped his arms around her waist and stood. "Fine."

Instinctively, she locked her ankles behind his back and let him carry her to the wall of glass that separated them from the night sky. When the door opened a breeze whipped along her skin, the crescendo of nightlife lifted into the air around her—the rush of tires over bitumen, the distant throb of club music and laughter from somewhere below.

"I wasn't joking about the balcony," he said. "And I've thought about bringing you here so many times. I wanted to the feel the contrast of your hot skin and the cool air. I wanted to know if you'd scream for me, let everyone know how good I make you feel."

Swallowing, Imogen turned and saw Melbourne stretched out before them like a postcard. The Arts Centre spire glowed in the distance, the coloured lights melting from blue to green to red. Flinders Street Station and the whole of Southbank glimmered, reflections shifting in the river below. It was the closest she'd ever get to being able to fly and instead of feeling scared, she felt…free.

"Don't you dare drop me," she said with a smile. They weren't anywhere near the edge of the balcony, but that wasn't the kind of falling she was really worried about. The wind pulled strands of her hair free and sent them whipping around her face. "I'm trusting you with my life right now."

"I've got you." He pressed his lips to hers. "And I'm rock solid. You're not going anywhere."

"Good," she whispered. "I want to be right here. With you."

He set her feet on the ground and brought his hands to her face, leaning in for a long, searching kiss. It wasn't like the others they'd shared—hungry, needy, desperate kisses. The type you had to grab with both hands before they burned to ash. This was slow seduction. A kiss meant for learning and discovery.

His lips were soft and coaxing, his hands gliding under her top to trace the contours of her waist, the swell of her rib cage and the little dip at her back. So she did the same—she ran her fingers over the gentle stubble along his jaw, over the corded muscles in his neck and the broad expanse of his chest. She counted his shirt buttons all the way down to his belt.

Before she knew it, she was yanking at the leather. Tugging at his zip. Dipping her hand into the soft fabric of his suit pants until she found him hard and pulsing in her palm. But even that thin layer of cotton was too much—she wanted all of him. Only him.

She found the slit in his boxer briefs and wrapped her fingers around him. But this time she wasn't content to stop here. Sinking her to knees, she ran her fist up and down his length. This was the first time she'd seen him like this—unrestrained and uninhibited. Not hidden by the darkness of the club or the flat, solid wood of the boardroom table. Not fully clothed while he took charge of the seduction. Now it was her turn.

"I want to taste you," she said.

His hand came to her head, brushing back the loose strands of hair from her forehead. "Which bit do you want to taste?"

"Here." She pressed a chaste kiss to the tip of his erection. "All down here." She drew her fingertip along the length of him. "Here." She gave his balls a gentle squeeze and almost melted when he groaned, long and loud, into the night.

"And you think you're not sexy," he growled. "Bullshit, Imogen. Absolute bullshit."

Stifling a smile, she swiped her tongue along the head of him, enjoying the taste. He was earthy, with a hint of salt. She'd forgotten how powerful it made her feel to have a man under her control like this—to have him surrender to her mouth.

Caleb grunted as she drew him along her tongue, sealing her lips into a tight ring around his shaft. "Fuck me, that feels good."

"Does it?" She swirled her tongue around the head, growing more confident by the second. "Tell me."

The grip on her hair tightened, and he slowly thrust his hips back and forth. The movement was so primal, so instinctual. He wasn't the kind of guy to sit back and take—he wanted to be an active partner in their sex. Each and every time he was in it for her pleasure as much as his, and that was a first for Imogen.

"You have no idea, baby. Your lips are like heaven."

She drew back. "What about the rest of me?"

"Perfection." His hand curved around her head and he tugged lightly on her ponytail to tilt her face up. "You've ruined me. You know that, right? I'm damaged goods now."

The words turned her bones to goo and she braced one palm against his thigh. "You're not damaged goods."

"Yeah, I am." He pulled her up and started working on her jeans, popping the button and drawing the zipper down so slowly she wanted to shove his hand out of the way to get the job done faster. "Nothing else will ever feel as good as this."

"You keep saying these things…" She swallowed. "Like you're trying to make me feel special."

"Is it working?" He pulled her jeans down over her hips. The air had started to chill and Imogen was acutely aware of how exposed she was. Her backside was facing the balcony's edge—her boring, beige undies bared for the world to see.

You've got to stop doing that. It's clear the boring undies trick doesn't work around him.

"Yes, but you don't need to romance me." A lump swelled in the back of her throat. Hope filtered through her veins, her heart pumping the stupid feeling all around her body. She might be agreeing to sex, but that was it. If she started to care about Caleb then she was really going to be at risk. "You don't have to say that stuff to get into my pants."

"I know." He hooked a finger into the waistband

of her underwear and slowly dragged the fabric over her hips and thighs. She wriggled and stepped out of them so she was naked from the waist down.

"Then why do you keep saying those things?"

"Because your body isn't enough. I want to get in here." He tapped the side of her head and then he tapped the spot over her heart. "And here."

It was too much—the words, the feeling of drowning in her own desire, the fact that she wanted the same thing from him. His body was great, the sex was great, but that was secondary to the fact that she never felt invisible to him. He'd brought her out into the open—literally and figuratively—shown her it was possible to indulge in her sexuality. To break her boundaries and to try again. To let herself fall for someone.

That's how you got so messed up last time. You fell for a guy even when your head said it wasn't right—and what happened? You should have learned your lesson.

"I don't want you in there," she said. Tears pricked at the backs of her eyes. Maybe he was right—every time something started to feel too real she pulled away.

It was why her dates always fell flat—she never shared anything of herself. Instead, she blamed the lack of chemistry on her not being sexy enough when in reality she didn't make the effort. Turning up wasn't enough. She needed to engage.

But that was too freaking scary.

"I'll wait," he said. "And I'll be patient, but I *will* keep trying."

"Why? It's not like I'm making it easy for you." She tried to twist away but he held her fast, forcing her to look at him. "Why would you keep trying?"

"Because I like you. I've always liked you."

The simple sincerity undid her. Whatever remaining ties held the last walls in place around her heart were sliced through. "I like you, too."

Against her better judgement, the lessons of her past and what she thought she *should* want…it was true. She liked Caleb Allbrook. A lot.

"Does that mean you agree I'm God's gift to cha-chas?"

"Pussies," she corrected with a grin.

He threw his head back and laughed. "Let's get inside. I want that glorious butt of yours all to myself."

"No sharing with the great wide world tonight?"

"No way." He cupped her face with his hands. "Tonight, you belong to me."

CHAPTER FOURTEEN

Imogen woke with her face mushed into Caleb's pillow, one arm totally numb from being tucked underneath her. His bed sheets were knotted around her legs and it took her a good minute to disentangle herself. She spotted a drool mark on the pillow and decided to flip it over to hide the evidence.

Post-sex in real life wasn't quite as glamorous as the movies made it out to be, but that was fine by her. In fact, she kind of liked the imperfect little details because it made everything so much more real…and she wasn't running away from that anymore.

A stupid, unbreakable grin stretched across her lips and Imogen buried her face into her palms to muffle a fizzy laugh. Who the hell was she right now? Her limbs ached from a night of pure unadulterated bliss, each muscle group telling its own story, from the tightness in her forearms from when she'd gripped Caleb's headboard, to the tenderness in her butt from where she'd fallen off the bed after he'd chased her across the room. To the ache between her legs from where he'd pushed her to come over and over, their need driving and insatiable.

The room had taken a hit, too. They'd knocked over a lamp, caused the fitted sheet to ping off one corner of the bed and there was a slight splatter on the carpet from where they'd opened a bottle of chocolate sauce and Caleb had gotten a little too excited about licking it off her body.

This *wasn't* how she did sex. With her ex it'd been good, albeit a little bland. Missionary mostly, lights off. That was how she'd thought he liked it until she'd discovered that it wasn't. It'd bothered her for years after whether he preferred it like that so he could imagine she was one of his mistresses—if he could superimpose someone else's face over hers in the dark?

But with Caleb everything was full colour, surround sound. Nothing got hidden or glossed over. Every part of her body had been worshiped.

The bed still bore an impression of his frame. He was in the kitchen, judging by the noises that filtered under the crack at the bedroom door. An empty champagne bottle sat next to his alarm clock, late-morning light glinting off the gold foil around the neck. It was almost lunchtime.

Smoothing her hands over her legs, she contemplated what to do next. She feared that leaving his room might burst this wonderful fantasy bubble. But reality had to be faced at some point. As if sensing her indecision, Caleb walked through the door.

"I'm going to do a coffee run." He looked even

better the morning after with his blond hair rumpled and his muscled torso bare above black boxer briefs that left nothing to the imagination. "And stop staring at my junk. It's not cool to objectify someone when they're about to procure your breakfast."

"Can I do it *after* you procure breakfast?" She grinned. "And I'll have a latte, soy—"

"Soy milk, no sugar. Extra hot." He winked. "Yeah, I know."

A warm, fuzzy feeling settled in her chest. "Thanks."

"Anything for you." He pressed a kiss to her forehead and pulled the bedside drawer open. Rows and rows of patterned socks were neatly folded, organised by colour like his wardrobe. He pulled out a pair that were black with little green Martians. "What are you looking at?"

"Your socks. That's quite a collection."

"The world needs more colour." He dressed quickly and kissed her again before he fished his wallet out of his suit pants, which were still in a heap on the floor. "I'll be back. If you want a shower, clean towels are in the cupboard in the bathroom. I won't be long."

"I'll wait," she said. "We should save water and do it together. You know, for the planet."

"Hot *and* environmentally friendly. I like it."

Imogen didn't move until the front door slammed shut. It was strange being alone in his space and yet totally at ease. His apartment was far from the slick, overly styled image she'd imagined. It was cosy and lived-in. *Real*.

There was that word again.

She grabbed a towel from the bathroom and wrapped it around herself before heading into the lounge room. A set of four framed photos hung on one wall. They were all black and white but each one had a slim, coloured frame. Red, blue, green and yellow.

Rising up onto her tiptoes, she inspected the photos. One showed a mother and baby—which she assumed was Caleb. Then there was another photo of the two of them, years later. Caleb looked about ten and he had a huge grin on his face. His fair hair was spiked up and his mother smiled dotingly at him. One photo was of him and his brother as teenagers. Jason wore a serious expression and Caleb was smirking. The last one was the two brothers standing in front of the newly built Allbrook office, which would make the photo about six years old. A ribbon stretched across the front door behind them and Jason held a pair of ceremonial scissors. This time Caleb wasn't smiling.

Imogen touched her fingertip to the photo, brushing over his expressionless face. It made her chest ache to see his smile missing. Why would he put this photo on his wall? It didn't look like a happy memory. Maybe it was a reminder? But of what?

There were no photos of Gerald, which she suspected wasn't an accident. Theirs was a relationship so fractured Imogen couldn't even begin to comprehend it. At least when her ex had broken her heart she'd been able to walk away. Cut ties. Heal—well, kind of. But Caleb didn't have that luxury. He had to face the person who tore him down every single day. He had to experience that pain over and over.

No wonder the guy hid behind a charming smile, slick suits and snappy comebacks.

"I see you," she said to the photo. "I see who you are underneath."

A knock at the door broke through her thoughts and Imogen headed over to answer it. She hadn't expected Caleb to go out and fetch them breakfast, but his gentlemanly morning-after approach was super sweet and very much appreciated. He knew that she needed a coffee to function, and it proved he'd been paying much closer attention than she'd given him credit for.

"Hey." She pulled the door open and the smile died on her lips.

It wasn't Caleb. The woman standing in the hallway looked as shocked as she felt—and her gaze slid over Imogen's bare legs and arms, over the fluffy white towel keeping the important bits covered, but not much else.

"I'm sorry." The woman shook her head. "I wasn't expecting… I didn't know he was seeing anyone."

Up until those last few words, Imogen might have been able to brush off the awkward encounter as a neighbour looking to borrow a cup of sugar or whatever the hell was the generic reason one person knocked on another's door. But on closer inspection, the woman wasn't dressed like she needed a simple favour. Her hair was done, her face perfectly made-up in that way that made guys think you weren't wearing any makeup at all. The breezy summer dress was short and left miles of tanned skin free.

"Grace?" Caleb's voice made both women whip their heads around.

He strode down the hallway, a tray with two coffee cups in one hand and a paper bag in the other. He was every bit the dashing, dishevelled playboy—light hair mussed from a night of passionate sex, a hint of a shadow beneath his eyes, one darker along his jaw.

"I, um…" The woman took a step back. Her expression was tight, her jaw ticking like she was trying damn hard to keep herself together. "I didn't mean to interrupt."

"What's wrong? Do you need something?" He seemed genuinely concerned, but otherwise emotionally detached.

Had they slept together? Was this how he got after he moved on? Polite but cold. Distant.

Bile rushed up the back of Imogen's throat. Was she staring down the barrel of their breakup? This would be her, soon. Stumbling across him with another woman, being asked if she "needed anything" like there was nothing between them. Like there had *been* nothing.

"I know you," Grace said suddenly, her eyes squinting. "You're Gerald Allbrook's assistant, right?"

Mother frogging shazbot. Of all the places to get caught. Of course she had to be dressed in a towel, too, so there was no denying what was going on.

"Grace Henry." The woman bit down on her lip. "My firm pitched an advertising campaign to Gerald a few months back."

Imogen didn't have the faintest recollection of the woman, but Gerald had hundreds of people in and out of his office each week. Admitting that wasn't going to smooth over this nightmarish situation, however. "Of course." She nodded.

"Anyway, well…" The woman pressed her hand to her chest and turned on her heel, ducking her head as she walked past Caleb. But Imogen hadn't missed the tears shimmering in her eyes.

Caleb ushered Imogen back into his apartment. But his expression had changed—the happy glow from earlier had been stripped away, replaced by something akin to wariness. "Grace is my neighbour, nothing more," he said as he set the coffees down on the table.

He pulled out two plates and set the bag on top. The scent of freshly baked croissants wafted into the air, but instead of making her mouth water, they turned her stomach.

Imogen folded her arms across her chest, suddenly wishing she'd gotten dressed instead of putting on a towel. "I didn't ask."

He raised a brow. "I know, but since you look like you want to murder me with a pickaxe in my sleep, I'm telling you."

"You don't have to be sleeping," she muttered.

"Sit." He pulled a chair out for her and gestured to the breakfast. "You can grill me over pastries."

"I don't want to grill you, Caleb." She shook her head. "That would imply there's been some kind of agreement between us…and there hasn't. I don't have any right to demand an explanation."

"This is a woman trap, isn't it? Like where you say you're 'fine' but you're testing me to see if I'll give you the 'right' response." He reached for his coffee. "It's not my first rodeo, Imogen."

"Yes, I'm well aware you've had *many* rodeos to hone your skills." The words popped out of her mouth before she could stop them, but Caleb simply nodded. Well, now she'd done it. If he wasn't certain she was a raging ball of jealously before then he would be now.

It was stupid, really. She *didn't* have any claim on him and she certainly didn't want to end up like poor Grace, who was clearly still smitten with him and was probably nursing a rather nasty bruise on her ego right now.

"If you want to ask something, then do it," he said. He sipped his coffee, trying to act as cool as a cucumber, but the muscles around his jaw were tight, his lips pulled into a flat line. "I would hope after what we've done that you could at least talk to me about what's upsetting you."

"Did you sleep with her?" It was shameful that she wanted so badly to know. She shouldn't care… but she did.

"No." He sighed. "I kissed her once after we had a few too many drinks, but that was it. A kiss, nothing more."

"Was that after me?" All the old feelings came rushing back—the confusing mélange of hope that she was wrong, with fear that she was right. The tight fist of anger and despair closing around her heart and squeezing hard.

"After that night at the club, you mean?" His blue eyes grew darker, stormier. The muscles in his neck corded, like he was holding his whole body tight as a wire. "No. It was before that. Months ago."

"So why was she here looking like she expected you to be alone?" Her voice wobbled and she wanted to pound her fist into something. Was she so pathetic that she couldn't even keep herself together long enough to get through this conversation?

"I don't know." He raked a hand through his hair. "Do you expect me to account for other people's actions?"

"No, but you should account for your own. If you weren't interested in her…"

"What? I should've shut her down harder, is that what you're saying? Because that would make me an asshole." He slammed his coffee cup down on the table and some of the brown liquid splashed out of the drinking spout and pooled on the plastic lid. "But then if I let her down gently I'm leading her on? I can't fucking win."

"I'm not saying that—"

"Yes, you are. You're acting like it's my fault that

she turned up here when I told her that I'm not interested in pursuing a relationship with her." His nostrils flared. "I kissed her and it was a mistake. I apologised and tried to let her down as best I could. But I knew she was coming into the office the following week to present to Dad and I didn't want to shoot her down so hard that she lost her nerve. I tried to do the right thing."

It sounded so plausible. She *wanted* to believe it. She wanted to trust that he was the kind of guy who didn't sleep around or lead people on. But what about the woman from the office, the one they were discussing last night?

"What about Neila?"

His expression turned to stone. "What about her?"

"I heard…" She swallowed and clutched the towel tight to her chest. "One of the girls said…"

Crud. That wasn't right either, and with each false start he grew increasingly distant. Caleb was shutting down. But she *had* to know. If this went any further—like she'd started to hope it might—then she needed reassurance he wasn't a cheater.

"You were talking about me?" he said. "Gossiping."

How could she possibly deny it? She wrung her hands. "I usually try to stay out of that stuff. You know that."

"And yet you're still asking me to explain myself." She'd expected him to look angry but instead he was cold. Expressionless. "Fine. Ask if you need to know so badly."

This was her fork in the road—if she asked the question, it would be as good as admitting she didn't trust him. But if she didn't, she'd always wonder. And then their relationship would be certain to fail because she'd let the uncertainty eat away at her like she'd done last time. The scars were still too raw and too fresh.

And the fact was, she didn't trust him because she didn't trust anyone. Ever.

"Did you cheat on her?"

"I say no, she says yes." His eyes bore right into hers—unwavering and unyielding. It was like being physically flattened, like being a butterfly stretched out and pinned down. Trapped behind glass. "We were dating. I found out that she told people in the office that she wanted to be with Jason but when he wasn't interested, she came after me. Neila was a social climber, and she wanted to find a way into my family."

Imogen cringed. "Oh."

"I sent her a message saying it was over and that I didn't want to hear any excuses. I went out and got hammered and did some stupid things because I was hurt." He paused. "She claims she didn't get the message and that she never said any such things about me."

"And you don't believe her?"

"I find it convenient that a serial texter who always carried a spare battery for her phone didn't get the message that one time." He shrugged. "But I overheard her. And when I asked Jason he admitted that she'd come onto him a few times before we started dating. I *won't* be someone's consolation prize. But she decided that I cheated on her and so that's what she told everyone."

"It wasn't that you got bored with her?"

Caleb laughed but the sound had none of the warm baritone she'd grown to crave. This time it was flat and metallic, like an imitation of the real thing. "Would it be better for you to think of me as some asshole who chews women up and spits them out? Would that make it easier for you to walk away? Because I'm not going to make it easy, Imogen. I'm not going to tell you what you want to hear so that you can keep living in the past."

"I'm *not* living in the past."

"No? So why were you chasing your sister's fiancé all over town, thinking that he cheated on her?"

"I saw him with a woman," she protested.

"Doing what? Having a drink?" He threw his hands in the air. "You've sent yourself on a wild-goose chase for nothing. He's madly in love with your sister and I would be surprised if he'd *ever* cheated on her."

"But what about the blonde woman, the one from the bar last night?"

The second Caleb's expression changed, she knew she'd stepped over a line. "You were there?"

"The assistants wanted to grab a drink after work. I didn't know you'd be there."

"You didn't come over and say hello." He frowned.

"But you were watching long enough to see who I was with. Were you spying on me or Daniel?"

She gulped. "It's a public space. I wasn't spying."

"No? Because that would be twice now."

This conversation was going downhill, fast. And Imogen had a feeling it was going to hurt when she landed.

Would he be so angry if he had nothing to hide? How can you trust him? How can you trust anyone ever again?

"I wasn't spying," she repeated through gritted teeth.

"But you don't trust me. You were here all night and you never once mentioned that you saw me—were you waiting to see if I'd tell the truth that there was a woman with us?"

"No… I don't know." She pressed her fingers to her temple. "I don't know what I'm doing anymore."

"For the record, the woman's name is Emily. She's a jeweller and a friend of Daniel's. He commissioned her to design a wedding band for your sister. They've been meeting in secret for months because he wanted to be involved in the whole process, but he didn't want Penny to find out."

"Oh."

That wasn't what she'd expected. And the more she thought about it, the more she was *sure* it'd been the same women from that night she'd first grown suspicious of Daniel.

"So, you've concocted the whole plan to catch him in the act and all because he wanted to do something nice for your sister. You snuck into a ball for chrissake." He held up a hand. "Now, that's not to deny that I'm pretty fucking impressed you did that—because I am—but what the hell was it all built on? Just because your husband cheated on you does not mean that every man is out to get some on the side."

"I never said that." Tears pricked the backs of her eyes—shame and embarrassment and humiliation trickling through her like poison. She'd let Caleb get too close, get under her skin. He was starting to see the ugly truth beneath her carefully polished veneer and she didn't like it one bit.

"You sure as hell acted like it." He raked a hand through his hair. "Imogen, I get it. You were hurt in a brutal way. But Daniel isn't your ex. *I'm* not your ex. You need to move on."

"I have."

"No, you haven't. You're clinging to this bad thing that happened like it's your life raft, but it's really a weight around your feet and it's going to drag you to the bottom of the ocean." He sighed. "How long has it been? You need to live your life and let your sister live hers."

"Don't tell me what to do." She turned away from him—the bright light streaming in through the floor-to-ceiling windows almost blinding her. He was right, but how could she move on when she still woke up in a sweat after having nightmares of the shame? Of the humiliation?

How could she trust someone like him, who had a reputation like he did, to be the one to help her get past it all? She needed someone safe, someone boring who didn't push her or challenge her. Not this man who turned her world upside down and threatened everything she thought she knew about herself.

She liked Caleb, a lot. But she wasn't ready to be shoved to one side like Grace or Neila. She wasn't ready to be on the receiving end of a "you're dumped" message or that cold, polite "what do you need?" when she passed him in the hallway at work.

"I don't want to tell you what to do." His hand landed soft and reassuring on her shoulder. "But I meant what I said last night. I like you."

"For now?" She turned, blinking back the tears because she couldn't shame herself further by crying. "But what happens when you get bored, when you move on to someone else?"

"What if I don't?"

God, she wanted to believe it so freaking bad.

"You have done with all these women." What on earth made *her* any different? "I can't take that risk. I need someone…safe."

"It's a shame you think so little of me, because I really do think you're pretty damn amazing." He took a step back, his head bobbing. "But right now, I think you should go."

She nodded and walked into his bedroom, this time unable to blink the tears away. They fell hot and fast onto her cheeks as she stumbled around his room looking for her clothes, trying to ignore the rumpled bed and overturned lamp that stood as evidence of what had fizzled out as quickly as it started.

By the time she walked back into his living room, Caleb was standing on the balcony, coffee in hand. The rest of their untouched breakfast sat cold on his kitchen table. She left without a word.

CHAPTER FIFTEEN

IF CALEB HAD a raincloud above his head the previous week, now it was a typhoon. His anger had morphed into something larger than himself and he carried it like a noose around his neck. The worst thing of all, however, was that he could only blame himself.

After trying every trick in the book to get a positive word or a pat on the head from his father—to get some semblance of love or legitimacy—and failing, he'd thrown all his energy into covering up how he felt by putting on a mask every day until he'd lost himself in the process.

And the mask had become his reality.

The weekend's events had given him a new perspective, however. Having Imogen confirm his fears that he'd always be burdened by his persona was something he needed to hear. And, in a strange turn of events, Daniel's wisdom over beers had been the glass-shattering moment he'd been waiting for.

You can choose your friends but you can't choose your family.

It was simple, really. But he'd spent so long thinking his family and his work were one and the same when they could easily be separated. It was clear he'd never get what he wanted working in the family business—Jase would always be number one, and Caleb would always resent it. Eventually it would ruin their relationship, too. And he didn't want that.

But he did have the power to change his circumstances.

While Gerald Allbrook might not think much of his son's skills, Caleb had a degree and years of experience. And, despite failing hard with the one relationship he'd truly wanted in life, he was talented at building relationships with *other* people. Which meant the calls he'd made this past week were already starting to pay off.

Caleb waited until the office was mostly cleared out, and then he made the long walk down to the big corner office. Mary waved him through and Gerald barely glanced up when she announced his son had come for an impromptu chat—something that *never* happened.

"We need to talk," he said, planting his hands on the back of the chair facing his father's desk. The buttery-soft leather caved under his grip, clearly marking the indentations of his fingers.

"So talk." Gerald looked up then, his expression impassive. If it was possible for the old man to say *you're wasting my time* with a facial expression, then the message was coming through loud and clear.

"Why didn't you tell me you were sick?"

Okay, so that wasn't the question he'd planned

on asking. But when the words slipped out, and the pressure in Caleb's chest swelled and swelled until it pushed on his ribs and lungs and on his heart. Leaving wasn't enough—anyone could resign. He wanted answers…and the truth.

He deserved it.

"You weren't home." Gerald's ice-cold eyes stared right through him. "If we can't rely on you to attend a dinner when you say you're going to attend, then why should I go out of my way?"

"Because I'm your son. So what if I didn't come to dinner? That pales in comparison to the fact that you have fucking cancer and didn't tell me." His hackles rose but he tightened his grip on the chair to give the tension a way out. Losing his cool in front of the old man would only shift the power balance away from him, and he couldn't have that right now. "And it's not like you ever seem to give a shit if I turn up to family things, anyway."

Gerald put his Montblanc pen down with great effort, as though it seriously pained him to interrupt his work. "Is this because I named Jason my successor? I'm sorry, Caleb, but he *is* more qualified. I've been grooming him for years for this moment."

"Honestly, I couldn't care less what you do with this company anymore. But if you think this is about career jealousy then you're deluded." He sucked in a breath. "And you know even less about me than I thought."

"I have no idea why I assumed you'd give a second thought to your career." Gerald huffed. "I doubt that topic has ever risen above what car you're going to buy next or what woman you're going to take into your bed."

The words stung like an open-palmed slap across his face. "What's the point in caring about my career when the glass ceiling is barely an inch from the floor?"

"I've given you plenty of chances, Caleb." The impassivity started to crack and crumble, giving way to a raw anger underneath that most definitely wasn't something new. Old wounds were a bitch like that. "I gave you a job that, frankly, you were underqualified for. I then promoted you to try and give you some incentive to care. Nothing works with you."

"You think making me feel like a charity case was motivating?" Caleb spat the words out. "You made it clear from the start that you thought I would fail. It felt more like a social experiment than a favour. Be honest with yourself—with me—you don't want me here any more than I want to be here."

"It's no longer my problem." Gerald stood and folded his arms across his barrel of a chest. "Jason will have to keep you in line now."

"No, he won't." Caleb shook his head. "I'm done."

"Really, Caleb. Don't be melodramatic—"

"Dad, I quit." He said it as calmly as he could. Because he wanted this move to be a positive step for him—proactive rather than reactive. And while he couldn't deny that his dying relationship with his father had a lot to do with it, Caleb knew it was time. He'd never find his place here. "I'm giving notice right now. I'll be out of the office intermittently to take interviews. Margot will help out during the transition, but I've told her it'll be Jason's decision as to who replaces me permanently."

For once in Caleb's almost thirty years of life, his father looked truly gobsmacked. Oh, they'd argued over Caleb leaving before. But deep down he'd never had any plans to pull the trigger and his father knew that.

But making a mess of things with Imogen had solidified something: he was done shortchanging himself. And that meant the old way of doing things—the false persona, the denial and living without committing to anything or anyone—was over. He was pissed off at how things had gone with Imogen, but mostly at himself. That would have to be dealt with later. For now, going out on his own was priority number one.

"And where are you going to work, huh?" Gerald cocked his head, but the scoffing tone had vanished. It struck Caleb, then, that him continuing to work for the family company had given Gerald the control he craved. It kept him in the position of power. And now, Caleb was taking that from him.

"I've got an interview with one of the banks and with a consulting firm." He paused. "So far."

"You're not bluffing?"

"No." Caleb shook his head. "I've got a resignation letter typed up but I wanted to do you the courtesy of telling you in person. Regardless of what issues we have, I *do* want to salvage our relationship and I think it'll be better for everyone if I leave the company for a while."

The muscles in his father's jaw tightened. "For a while?"

"Until I'm the best marketing executive Australia has ever seen." A smirk twitched on his lips. "I may come back then...if you can afford me."

His father laughed, and the sound was loud, foreign and unanticipated. It eased the pressure in the room enough that Caleb could breathe easier.

"I know I'm hard on you." Gerald swallowed. "It pains me to see you skate through life when you could be so much more."

That was a first. Normally his dad would have stopped at the "you skate through life" bit, instead of adding an acknowledgement of potential. The thing was, he didn't need to hear it anymore. Caleb *knew* he had it in him to do something productive with his life, and that was what mattered. Not everyone else's opinion.

"Your brother was always easy, you know." Gerald turned and let his gaze drift to the enormous window gleaming with the early-evening view of the city. "Slept well, ate whatever we put in front of him. Never had trouble in school."

"Tell me something I don't know." He rolled his eyes.

"And you came out kicking and screaming like you were already fighting a battle. Every night you'd yell and yell until I seriously thought the house was going to come apart at the seams. Your mother was exhausted from taking care of you and your brother, and I wasn't ready to do it again." He squared his shoulders and looked Caleb dead in the eye. "I had wanted her to terminate the pregnancy."

"I know that." Caleb nodded. "She told me once."

"I put a lot of pressure on her and I regret that every day. But I wasn't ready for you, for how…all-encompassing you would be." He sighed. "For how much like me you were."

"Are you kidding me?" Caleb raised a brow. "Everybody knows Jason is your carbon copy."

"On the outside, maybe. But you're me through and through, Caleb. You fight, you're proud and stubborn and hot-headed like me." He came around the desk and Caleb stood rooted to the spot. They'd never spoken like this. Not with such honesty and vulnerability. "I was certain you were my punishment for the hell I put your grandparents through. And unfortunately, I did about as good a job with you as they did with me."

Caleb's grandparents had passed away over ten years ago, but they'd always had a strained relationship with the family. His grandfather had been a formidable man who'd run the company with an iron fist, much like Gerald.

"I wanted Jason to take over the company because it's time they had a leader with a different approach. He's going to be an amazing CEO, and I stand by my decision."

"Like I said, it's not about that. I know Jase will be great and I'm still leaving regardless of anything you have to say." He sucked in a breath and finally released the chair that he'd been gripping like it was his only tether to earth. "But I *do* want to know why you didn't tell me you were sick. Do you think that I care so little that I could brush that off?"

"It crossed my mind." He hung his head for a second, before the stoic expression was back in place. "The doctor tells me the survival rate is high. Your mother is making sure we see the best oncologist in the country. She's taking good care of me."

"Then you should take good care of her, and I don't mean with money."

Gerald nodded. "I'm looking at things…differently now. I know what it's like to be in her position."

He never talked much about his first wife, but Caleb's mother had told him once that the woman had experienced a very drawn out and painful passing. And it was obviously playing on Gerald's mind now.

"Mum really loves you."

His father cleared his throat, the rough noise sparking something deep in Caleb's chest. It stirred memories, not all of them good. But this was a step forward. The right step forward.

"I can put a good word out for you," his father said. "I have some contacts—"

"I'd prefer if you didn't."

Gerald nodded. "I accept your resignation, then."

"Good, because you don't have a choice." Caleb stuck his hand out and his father took it. For a moment, he wondered if the older man might pull him into a hug. But instead they stood stiffly. Awkward. Like always.

Baby steps.

"You *what*?"

Imogen cringed at the eardrum-shattering pitch of her sister's voice. It took a lot to rattle Penny. The woman wrangled a classroom of six-year-olds on a daily basis, so she knew how to deal with drama. She hadn't even gotten annoyed that one time Imogen borrowed her fanciest dress without telling her and then proceeded to spill red wine all over it.

But this...this was something else.

"Pen, if your head starts to spin around I'm going to call a time-out, okay?" She tried to laugh but the sound came out like more of a croak. "I'm sorry. I messed up and I see that now. It's why I'm coming clean."

"Coming clean does not immediately absolve you." Her sister's face pixelated on the screen for a moment as the internet stalled. Spilling the beans via FaceTime wasn't exactly ideal, but Daniel had whisked her away for a surprise getaway since it was school holidays. Imogen hadn't been able to hold on to the guilt any longer. "I can't believe you did that. Actually I can, you're like...like... Bridesmaid-zilla!"

"I know it's not an excuse, but I wanted to protect you. And I totally went about it the wrong way."

"No sugar, Sherlock." Penny sighed. "I asked you at the beginning if being involved in the wedding would tear open all those old wounds, and you said you'd be fine."

"I know." She rubbed a hand over her face. "I guess it was more difficult than I thought it would be... I didn't want you to go through what I did."

"All because you saw Daniel have a drink with someone?"

She wasn't going to tell Penny that she thought they'd been flirting, because in hindsight she wasn't as sure as she'd been at the time. Was it her past overlaying this lens of distrust like Caleb had said? Perhaps. Maybe he *had* been flirting and it was nothing but harmless fun? In any case, it was none of her business. Penny and Daniel didn't need her intruding on their relationship. She knew that now.

"And then when he didn't invite you to the ball... I was suspicious."

"His father was going to be there. You *know* how difficult he's been." Penny frowned. "Daniel and I discussed it and we decided it would be best if I didn't go. *I* wasn't up to dealing with it, but I didn't want to discuss Daniel's family problems behind his back."

"I guess I should strike 'jumping to conclusions' off my extracurricular activities list, huh?"

"Don't be cute while I'm trying to be angry at you." A smile tugged at her sister's lip. "And you owe Daniel the apology, rather than me."

"I do."

Penny's eyes darted to something offscreen. "I

don't want to do it while we're here, though. He's worked so hard lately and he needs the time to relax."

"When you get back, we can do dinner and I'll talk to him. I want to make it right."

"I know, Immie. You're a good person." Penny laughed. "When you get a bee in your bonnet about something, though...you're like a bulldog."

"Does that mean you forgive me?"

"Always." Penny narrowed her eyes. "And why are you calling me from the car? I thought you had another month left on your lease. You're not living out of the Corolla, are you?"

Ever since Lainey had moved out to pursue her dream career—and to nurse a broken heart in London—Imogen was more alone than ever. She missed Lainey's ceaseless chatter and the way she always had the music turned up loud. But the silence had given her a lot of time to think and reflect. Being left alone with her thoughts had given her the space to see how bad she'd messed up with Caleb.

You're getting too good at that. There's no gold star for being a screw-up.

"I needed to get some air." She pulled the keys out of the ignition and pushed the car door open, trying to hold her phone steady with her free hand. "Figured if you were getting to sun it up all week, then so should I."

"It's good for the soul," Penny agreed.

The St. Kilda boardwalk was Imogen's happy place. There was something about the combination of sand and gentle waves rolling in, the warm planks of wood beneath her feet and the insistent squawk of seagulls that made all her problems seem less formidable. The breeze brushed against her legs, blowing sand particles around.

"I made a mistake, Pen," she said with a sigh as she squinted out into the distance. The sun was low, but still bright like a ball of fire on the horizon. It bathed everything in amber light, making the water twinkle as it moved.

"Another one?" Penny made a tsk-ing sound. "Work related?"

"Love related. Well…" She swallowed. "Maybe not love, yet. But something that's heading in that direction."

Love was a hell of a word, and Imogen wasn't sure she was ready for that. What she did know, however, was that the second she'd found out about Caleb's resignation her whole world flipped upside down. Rumours were rife about his father firing him, but when she'd asked Gerald outright—ready to defend Caleb to her own undoing—her boss had denied it and seemed genuine.

There was a parcel sitting on the passenger seat of her car, wrapped in blue-and-yellow paper. A going-away gift. She'd bought it on her lunch break earlier that day with every intention of going to Caleb's office after her work day wrapped up. But the second she'd made it to his door, doubt had kicked her butt and she'd turned tail like a coward.

"A man. Wow." Her sister let out a low whistle. "I didn't know you were seeing anyone."

"I'm not… I wasn't." She found an empty spot along the boardwalk and dropped down, letting her feet go over the edge so she could bury her toes in the sand. "I don't know what to call it."

"Ah, so it's friends with benefits, then?" her sister teased.

"No." Imogen shook her head.

It wasn't like that. Sure there were plenty of benefits, if that was what Penny wanted to call them, but what she shared with Caleb was so much more. Around him, she could be free of her own restrictions. Free of the boundaries she'd set up so tight around herself they felt like a cage. And those feelings might have come about through sex, but they weren't because of it.

"We never labelled it." She wriggled her toes back and forth, watching the sand rise and fall. "I kept giving myself reasons why it wouldn't work. He's, uhh…got a bit of a reputation."

Penny nodded. "And you thought history would repeat itself?"

"Something like that. I try not to get involved in all the gossip at work, but you hear things. He's charming and funny and I thought he'd eat me alive."

"Did he?" Penny shifted and Imogen caught a glimpse of the hotel's view—a strip of blue water, greenery and palm trees. "Or did you pull the pin because you were scared?"

"The latter," she admitted. "I heard that he'd cheated on one of his previous girlfriends and I confronted him about it."

"What did he say?"

"That it was complicated. He overheard her telling someone that she was only after him for his connections. He dumped her via text and she claims she never got the message."

"Let me guess, he then went out, got drunk and decided to screw his way through his problems."

"Got it in one."

Penny laughed. "Sounds like both parties were to blame. Although, if it's true what he overheard then I question how much of a relationship they had to begin with. Daniel dated a woman like that, before me. I think it hurts them a lot more than they let on. He didn't tell me about it until we'd been together for over a year."

She suspected Caleb held a lot of his pain in—pain about the way his father treated him, pain about being second to his brother. Maybe there was even more beneath the surface.

Imogen ran her fingertips over the smooth wooden planks, her fingers catching on the imperfections. "It would be easier if everything was black and white."

Penny laughed. "Tell me about it. But then I guess we'd all be bored if we knew exactly how everything would turn out. Thing is, you *might* get hurt again one day. There's no way to prevent it unless you never have another relationship."

The finality of her sister's statement echoed through her. It made her feel heavy and…sad. She'd put herself out into the dating world because she missed having someone in her life. She *wanted* the companionship and fun and affection that Caleb had shown her.

She wanted him.

And in a perfect world he'd sign a contract to say he'd never do anything wrong. But that wasn't life.

"I guess if no one ever did anything wrong then we'd never learn how to trust," Imogen mused.

"That's deep, baby sis." Penny chuckled. "Who knew Little Miss Practicality could get all philosophical like that."

"Shut up," she mumbled. "It's the sunset. It makes me all mushy."

She was only half joking. Red, gold and yellow streaked the horizon like a painter had dragged their brush along the water's edge. Two children stood where the bay lapped at the sand, kites sailing above them, one yellow and one purple. Both had rainbow streamers flickering in the breeze.

This place was so...colourful. Imogen looked down at her work clothes. Grey pencil skirt, black-and-white blouse, white pearls. Silver watch. Monochrome. Like always.

Perhaps along with losing her ability to trust—both others and herself—she'd also forgotten what it was like to live with colour. Going to the masquerade ball and putting on that sexy dress, the pink and rose gold mask, and the dark, vampy lipstick had been thrilling. It had been like unlocking the old Imogen and letting her out to play. The old version of her who liked to take risks, and be daring, and make decisions without overthinking everything.

She missed that Imogen.

"Immie?" Penny waved from the screen. "I have to go. Daniel's back from golf and we're going to grab a drink. It's tiki night!"

She waved at her sister. "Have fun. I want to talk more when you get back, and I'll apologise to Daniel like I promised."

"Pinkie swear?" Penny held up her little finger and Imogen copied the gesture.

"Pinkie swear."

She ended the call, pushed up from the boardwalk and headed back to the car. The blue-and-yellow parcel was still sitting on the seat, with Caleb's name in her neat handwriting printed across a gift tag. What would the old Imogen do in this situation?

She slid into the driver's seat, her hands wrapping around the steering wheel as her brain whirred. The old Imogen wouldn't sit around worrying about what to do next, that was for smurfing sure. She'd act.

Imogen glanced at the parcel again. It was time to pay Caleb a visit. But first, she had to make a quick detour.

CHAPTER SIXTEEN

CALEB STOOD OVER his bed and looked at the clothing he'd picked out for his interview tomorrow. Charcoal suit, white shirt, red-and-blue-striped tie, black socks. It was a bit more conservative than what he normally favoured—okay, a *lot* more conservative—but he wanted to make a good impression. The Wentworth Group was a predominantly retail company and a household name across Australia. Their department stores were in every major city and a lot of minor ones, too. The role would allow him to mix creativity with business, and they were keen.

Tomorrow was an important moment. He was meeting with Parker Wentworth, the CEO, and his siblings, who sat on the board. The three-person panel would likely be the most intense interview of Caleb's career, and in the last week he'd had a few. Jase had helped him prep—firing questions and scenarios at him like bullets. And Gerald had mercifully stayed silent. No critiques, no advice, no criticisms. Perhaps it was sad that the best thing his father could do was to keep his distance from the whole thing, but Caleb knew it was a small step in the right direction. He'd gone over for dinner even more than usual lately and while he and Gerald hadn't said much to one another yet, the animosity had eased. Even his mother had commented on it.

Caleb picked up the tie and flipped it over in his hands. It wasn't his—he'd borrowed it from his brother for a formal event where Gerald had determined Caleb's usual wardrobe to be too outlandish. It seemed right for an interview, but God it was boring. Sighing, he threw it back down onto the bed and headed into the living room.

The intercom buzzer sounded and he raised a brow. He wasn't expecting anyone tonight, but the small black-and-white screen revealed a woman in a floaty dress standing by the front door on ground level. Did she have the wrong apartment? He picked up the receiver.

"Hello?"

"Caleb?"

His throat tightened. Imogen. "Yes?"

"It's me…uh, Imogen. Imogen Hargrove." More words followed, like she was chastising herself under her breath. "Can I come up?"

"Sure." He hit the access button and hung up the receiver.

What the hell was she doing here? He'd been giving her distance since their fight, focusing on finding a new job because he couldn't figure out what to do about her. He wanted her—that much was damn sure. Wanted to be with her, in more than the physical sense. But she didn't believe in him and right now he needed all the belief he could get. There was no denying that his feelings for her ran deep—he simply didn't know if now was the right time to act on them.

A soft knock caught his attention and he went to the front door. "Wow."

The black-and-white intercom screen hadn't prepared him for what she looked like in person. Her long gold hair sat fluffy and soft around her shoulders, her curvy body encased in a dress that would make fire engines blend into the background.

"Good wow, or bad wow?" she asked. Her hands gripped a small present and the paper crinkled beneath her white-knuckled grip.

"Definitely a good wow." He stepped back and motioned for her to come into his apartment.

The dress hung past her knees and swished as she walked, but the rear view was the cherry on top of an incredibly sexy sundae. The dress dipped into a point at her midback, and was trimmed with a soft bit of fabric that fluttered with each step. The straps were thin enough that he could snap them with his teeth. And *boy* did he want to.

"I'm glad you let me know that you were Imogen *Hargrove*, so I didn't get you confused with any of the other Imogens I know," he said drily. "Very thoughtful."

"My social awkwardness knows no bounds, apparently." She rocked on her heels. "I heard you quit."

He nodded. "It was time."

"I hope it was nothing to do with what I said about...you know."

"About Neila? No, it wasn't that. Well, not that alone." He watched her closely. "I waited until I had every possible sign that I should leave, instead of going with my gut from the start."

She sucked on the inside of her cheek. It was hard not to be overwhelmed by how much he wanted to haul her into his arms and act like their whole blowup had never happened. But sweeping things under the rug was what had gotten him into trouble the first three hundred times.

"I contributed to that," she said. "And I feel terrible. I judged you because of what happened to me in the past, and that's not fair."

"Everyone has baggage, Imogen. You don't have to apologise for that."

"Not for having baggage, but because I let it get between us." She toyed with the parcel in her hand and then held it out to him. "Anyway, I wanted to get you a little something to say good luck with the job hunting. And to say goodbye, I guess. It's been good working with you."

Her voice was stiff and proper, a far cry from the wild dress and loose hair and her turning up unannounced. She was caught between the old and new, stuck in the limbo of wanting to change but not being sure how to do it. Just like he was. For two people who seemed to be polar opposites, they definitely had a lot in common.

"Thank you. I'll be around for a few more weeks,

though." His fingertips grazed hers as he took the package. It was soft beneath the thick paper wrapping. "Is this what I think it is?"

A tentative smile played on her lips. "Maybe."

She'd folded and stuck the edges down so perfectly that he avoided tearing into the paper like he usually would have. Inside was a pair of socks with a yellow background and little black llamas printed all over.

"I thought my socks made it hard for you to take me seriously." He raised a brow.

"These are business llamas. Can't you see? They're all going to their important corporate jobs." She pointed at one of the llamas. "That one's a lawyer. And that one works on spreadsheets all day."

How could he ever have thought this woman was stuffy and serious? Perhaps because she was an expert in hiding herself.

"Totally interview appropriate." Her eyes glimmered with mischief. "*Much* more professional than the tacos."

"Well, I was going with plain black."

Imogen's brows shot up. "I didn't even know you owned plain black socks."

"I had to dig them out. I keep a pair for funerals." As he said it, he realised how ridiculous it sounded. He was going to an interview in funeral socks and a borrowed tie that was basically a cure for insomnia.

"You're serious?" She shook her head, the light bouncing off the fine gold hairs framing her face like a halo.

"What? Black is entirely professional. Seems to be a mainstay in your wardrobe, though I'm a big fan of the red."

"You are?"

"Fuck yeah. You look…" He swallowed. "Luminous."

"Thanks," she said with a shy smile. It was like watching the compliment warm her from the inside out. "It would be a terrible idea for you to go for an interview in such boring socks."

"How so?"

"It's false advertising." She cocked her head. "They'll be expecting a serious, upstanding gentleman who will toe the company line and play buzzword bingo every day."

"And what are they really getting, huh?" He leaned against the dining table, crossing his legs at the ankles. The relaxed pose hid the tension and anticipation roiling inside him.

We've been over this already. Her opinion of you is based on what you've presented her—and it isn't good.

But then why was she here? Why not wait until they were back in the office to come and see him. She could have easily given him the "good luck" present earlier that day. He'd seen her walking toward his office then making an about-face at the last minute.

"They're getting someone vibrant and interesting and creative. Someone who's ready to stop living in the shadows and make their own success." She took a step toward him. "Someone who's smart and sexy and has a lot to say."

"You calling me a big mouth?" He suppressed a smile.

"What I'm trying to say—and doing a crappy job of it—is that you should go in there being you. Because who you are is pretty freaking great." Her eyes dropped to the floor and her shoulders rose and fell with deep breaths. "I know we haven't done things the conventional way and when I left here the other day I told myself I wouldn't be back…"

"Then why are you here?"

"I couldn't stay away." Her voice trembled as she looked back up. "And I realised that you'd only ever seen me in granny knickers."

"What?" he growled.

For once his mind hadn't moved past her outer layer of clothing. The red dress was enough to keep the imagination whirring—how it clung to her rounded hips and exposed the delicate shadow of her cleavage in a way that told him she most definitely wasn't wearing a bra. But now all he could think about was what she had on underneath.

"You know, I wore them that first night as a deterrent," she said. She bent down to undo the buckles on her sandals, giving him a fine view in the process. Her hair slipped over her shoulders and she craned her head up, the sharp angle making her olive green eyes look wide and round. "I told myself that if I put on those hideous things there was no way I'd let you get under my dress. That the potential embarrassment would keep me from letting you get too close."

She slipped the strap through the buckle and stepped her bare foot onto the floor. Then she started on the second one.

"I told myself that it would be a terrible idea to get involved with you at all. That the date was only part of the deal because you were trying to get some kind of hold over me. Because you wanted the woman who said no."

She stepped out of the second sandal and gently nudged them to the side with her foot. Without shoes, she was more than a head shorter than him but her presence filled the room as though she were eight feet tall. He'd never seen her like this before—shining and radiating emotion. Raw and vulnerable... and owning it.

"I told myself it was a game for you. A challenge. Just to see if you could do it." She slipped one of the straps over her bare shoulder. The slide of satin over skin was like an electric shock, it vibrated through Caleb's body—stealing his breath, halting his heart. Tightening and hardening and tensing him. She slipped the other strap down. "That maybe you were laughing at me on the inside."

"I was never laughing at you, Imogen. Only with you."

His brain wanted to shut this down—tell her to stop. There wasn't a chance in hell he'd be able to think straight once she shimmied out of that dress. But there was more to this than baring skin. She was baring her soul to him. Stripping back everything that she used to hide herself away.

"The second you took me up those stairs I knew I had underestimated you." She reached behind herself, her chest thrusting out as the sound of a zipper being lowered sliced through the air. "I had *seriously* underestimated you."

"How?"

"Because in a room full of people you made me feel like I was the only one there."

The dress sagged and she let the material slip down her body like a caress. Her breasts were bare, her nipples pink and pointed. The world's tiniest scrap of red lace covered her sex. It was studded with stones that winked at him, taunting him.

"To me, you *were* the only one." His hands twitched by his sides. But he couldn't reach out to her—not yet. Sure, it filled him with pride to know he'd rocked her world, made her feel special, but what he wanted from Imogen wasn't limited to the physical. He wanted more. "I wasn't proud that I had to resort to blackmailing you for a date."

"Trading services, I believe you called it." Her fingertips toyed with the edge of her underwear. The damn woman would short-circuit his brain if he wasn't careful. "And I'm glad you did. You opened my eyes, Caleb. I think I was sleep-living before that—each day was the same and I kept failing to move on from what'd happened. I had bad date after bad date and then there was you... I've never had sex like that before."

"Glad I could be of service," he said, unable to keep the bitter tone out of his voice.

If she was here because she wanted to sleep with him again, then he would do everything in his power to resist. He'd help her back into that gorgeous dress and send her packing. Because, as much as he wanted those sweet legs wrapped around his waist and her hands tangled in his hair, he wanted everything else, too.

And he was done with settling.

Imogen sucked in a breath, her mind moving so fast she was seriously concerned that it might zoom right out of her head. She'd assumed that once she got out of the dress the talking would stop…at least for a little bit. But now she was standing almost butt-naked in front of the man she cared deeply for, her nipples growing hard with a combination of excitement, fear and air-conditioning, feeling like she was in one of those weird public nudity nightmares.

"I'm doing a terrible job of this." She bent down to grab the fabric of her dress, adrenaline pumping through her veins so hard it made her head spin.

But Caleb was in front of her in an instant, his hand wrapped around her wrist. "Stop."

"I shouldn't have done that." Tears pricked the backs of her eyes, shame filtering through her system. She'd wanted so bad to break out of her shell, to be the seductive, confident one.

Why did you think you could come here and strip off and that would be enough? You think your boobs are going to make up for what happened?

"I..." Oh God, now the tears weren't only pricking. They were spilling onto her cheeks.

She was naked and sniffling, struggling against his grip so she could attempt to regain some of her dignity. She pulled the dress up over her, slipping her arms into the straps so that even if she couldn't get her trembling hands to deal with the zipper, all the important stuff was covered.

"You what?" His other hand came to her jaw as he tipped her face up to his.

"I thought..." She squeezed her eyes shut. It was now or never. "I'm sorry I talked about you behind your back and that I questioned you about the Neila thing. And... I'm sorry I didn't trust you. That I *haven't* trusted you."

"I understand why that's hard for you."

"The thing is, instead of letting people start at zero and giving them a chance to win or lose my trust, I start them way down at negative fifty." She swallowed. "It's not fair to judge you on someone else's actions."

"Imogen, I accept your apology. But I'm not exactly blameless, either. I let people think the worst of me. Hell, I've played into it time and time again. I've set people up to have a low opinion. You can't take all the responsibility."

"Is that why you're leaving?" she asked.

"Part of it. I need to do my own thing, be my own person. I can't untangle all the shit at Allbrook—people's perceptions of me and all that. It's fine. I've made my bed, so now I'm going to find a new one."

A lopsided smile drifted across his lips. "Fresh start will do me good."

She nodded and wrapped her arms around herself. Was that supposed to mean he wanted a clean break altogether, including from her? Was she part of the stuff he couldn't untangle?

"That sounds good." She bobbed her head. "Any chance I can get in on that? I'd like a fresh start, too."

He raised a brow. "You want to leave Allbrook?"

"No." She sucked in a breath, the pressure of all she wanted to say crowding her heart and her lungs. If she walked away now she'd always regret not going all in. Not giving this "new her" a fighting chance to have the man who'd made her see how much she held herself back. The man who'd opened her eyes and stolen her heart. It was because of him that she could even be here now, saying these words. Wearing this dress—well, half wearing it. "I want a fresh start with you."

"Do you like me, Imogen Hargrove? Even though I wear taco socks and tease you mercilessly and give you fake excuses to trudge down to the storage room?"

"I knew you didn't really need those files!" She swatted at him and he laughed.

"What can I say? I was smitten and I wanted an excuse to talk to you." The lopsided grin morphed into full-fledged megawatt goodness.

"You could have told me that."

"You wouldn't have believed me," he pointed out.

"True." She nodded. "Okay, confession time.

Every time you came into my office I would have to remind myself not to drool all over you."

"That explains the strange face you used to make." He threw his head back and laughed, and the soul-deep rumbling sound soothed her.

"The truth was, I was smitten, too. And the more I got to know you…" She steeled herself. "The more I realised you were so much more than I thought. And I want to explore it. I want to get to know everything about the real you. I want to have wild, kinky, semipublic sex with you. I want to wear colour with you. I want to have it all with you. I do like you, a heck of a lot. And I know I'd regret not telling you now even if you turn me down."

His eyes sparkled. "How could I possibly turn you down? You said the magic words."

"'Kinky, semipublic sex'?" She grinned, hope and something deep and strong blooming inside her. Something more than "like," but she wasn't ready to say it yet. They had a lot of baggage to wade through. But deep down she knew they were already past like, they just didn't know how to label it yet.

"Exactly." He leaned down and nuzzled her neck, nipping at her skin. "You're putting ideas in my head."

"So that's a yes?" She gasped as he sucked on her skin, heat flaring inside her like a struck match. "We can start afresh?"

"Yes." His kissed his way up to her mouth, capturing her lips. His tongue stroked against hers while his arms wound around her. Claiming her. "Fresh start begins in three—" he cupped her backside "—two—" he pressed her hard against him "—one."

"Why hello, Mr. Allbrook. It's lovely to meet you." She cupped his hands with her face. "I have a feeling we're going to get on famously."

EPILOGUE

One year later...

"Does it feel any different being here with an actual invite?" Imogen fiddled with her mask—the same one she'd worn last year—as she surveyed the Carmina Ball's crowded ballroom.

"To be honest, I missed the thrill of getting changed outdoors." Lainey grinned. "But when I mentioned it to Damian, he didn't seem too keen."

"Not up for a roll in that hay, then?"

"Not all of us like to get our kit off in public."

Imogen's cheeks grew hot. Though whether it was from embarrassment at her friend's comment or from all the scorching memories she'd made with Caleb in the last twelve months, she wasn't sure.

"I should never have told you about that," she muttered.

"No judgement, I promise. But you should know that after a glass or two of bubbly you open up like a fountain." Lainey slung an arm around Imogen's shoulders. "It's a truth serum."

Frowning, Imogen offloaded her half-finished glass to a passing waiter. Given she and Caleb were planning to get up to trouble soon, it was probably best to keep a clear head. A little ball of excitement zipped through her, and she bunched her hands in the thick, frothy layers of her gown.

Her eyes darted to the grand old clock that hung on one wall. Five minutes before she had to sneak away to their meeting spot. The stables. Caleb wanted to re-create the moment that had changed everything last year, only this time they weren't going to stop at kissing.

"What's wrong, Immie?" Penny squeezed her arm. "You seem fidgety."

"I'm fine. I should be asking you that question." She shot a look at her sister. "How's the dress?"

"Tight," Penny grumbled, placing a hand over her stomach. Her bump was fully visible now, but she hadn't wanted to wear a maternity dress to the ball. So they'd found one that made her look like an earth goddess, but she'd "popped" a little more than expected in the last week. "I feel like a human sausage."

"I'm sure Daniel will take you home early if you've had enough," Lainey said. "We should probably find the guys, anyway. They were supposed to be back with drinks."

Imogen glanced at the clock. The minutes were ticking down far slower than she wanted them to. Her whole body buzzed with anticipation, like a million butterflies had been set free in her stomach. "I'm going to head to the ladies' room. I'll catch up with you in a bit."

She didn't wait for her sister or her friend to reply, and instead darted out of the ballroom and took the long way around to the courtyard, hoping to hell that neither of the women chose to follow. Outside the air was warm and the scent of jasmine drifted on the breeze. This year they'd set a theme for the ball—summer blooms. Many of the women had dresses with beautiful bold floral patterns and romantic shades of pink and red.

Imogen's dress was lush and dramatic. The navy background was offset by huge red and white roses and vivid green leaves. It was cut shorter in the front, hovering around her knees and dipping into a slight train behind her. It showed off her shoes—a pair of strappy, sexy red heels that Caleb had surprised her with earlier that day—to perfection.

Coupling that with her mask and sneaking around to find her lover, she felt like a supersexy spy.

Making sure no one was looking in her direction, she slipped into the garden and followed the path around the side of the building. The stables stood proud and quiet, with no sign of her mischievous boyfriend. The mere sight of the charming old structure brought back a rush of memories. The thrill of kissing the masked man, the burn of lust that hadn't left her body since.

She walked carefully over the grass, keeping her weight forward so her heels didn't sink into the earth.

The past year had been a roller coaster. Once she

and Caleb had started dating properly, things had moved quickly. He'd gotten the job with the Wentworth Group and was working harder than ever. They'd grown tired of schlepping back and forth between each other's places with overnight bags, so she'd moved into his apartment after only two months, much to the dismay of her family.

They thought she was rushing into commitment again, setting herself up to make the same mistakes. Setting herself up to have her heart crushed. But she knew it was different. And while there had been some adjusting to do, Imogen had no doubt in her mind that it was the right move.

"Hey, sexy lady."

Imogen jumped and pressed her hand to her chest. "You scared me. I thought I was early."

A lazy grin spread over Caleb's lips, curving up toward the black leather mask covering the top half of his face. His broad shoulders were encased in a fitted tuxedo jacket, the satin lapels gleaming in the early evening light. "Baby, you're right on time."

He held a hand out and she took it without hesitation, need and desire rocketing through her at the touch. It was incredible how quickly he could fire up her body these days. It was like he'd found the key to her pleasure centre and could punch the code in with lightning speed.

"What are we going to do if we get caught?" she said with excitement, rather than fear. His desire was catching and she'd found herself becoming addicted to the thrill.

"Don't you worry about that," he said, squeezing her hand as he led her into the stables. "I'll keep you covered."

"You never know who might be spying." She nudged him with her elbow. "What if some sticky beak is trying to take our photo?"

"I'm not sharing," he growled.

He twirled her around and backed her up against the wall, hands hard at her hips. She loved that he was demanding and in charge when it came to sex. He pushed her boundaries and managed to make each time feel like the first. It was exhilarating, and despite some initial fears that they might burn out as quickly as they'd started, she lusted after him even more now than she had a year ago.

But it was more than lust. The nights they spent on the couch eating pizza and watching Netflix were just as enjoyable. He cooked for her often, frequently surprised her with dinner reservations or plans for a weekend away—but more important, he never held back in telling her how much he adored her, how much he wanted her.

There were no secrets between them. His laptop was always open and had no password—not that she'd ever snooped. She didn't need to. Because secrecy didn't lurk in the shadows of their house, and doubt didn't linger like a poison in her mind. She trusted him with all her heart.

"I love you," she blurted out.

Oh God, oh God, oh God.

Were they ready for that? They hadn't talked

about it yet, but the word had been bouncing around in her head for a few months now. Saying it felt right, like kicking off a pair of heels that had been restrictive and painful. It relieved the tension inside her, released a wave of warmth that penetrated her all the way down to the marrow of her bones. Honestly and completely.

Maybe he wasn't ready, but she was.

"I know we haven't talked about where this is going or anything yet, and I don't know if you agree but I guess I needed to say it out loud because I've been thinking it for a while now," she babbled.

Caleb didn't move, didn't flinch. His bright blue eyes burned intently into hers—like he was looking right into the heart of her. Stripping her back, breaking her apart.

"Don't stay silent," she whispered. "Please."

"I think you dropped something." He pointed to the ground.

"What?" She shook her head, her eyes searching around their feet but all she could see was dirt. "If that's your way of distracting me it's—oh."

Caleb held a ring in front of him. The simple white gold band held a diamond that looked almost too big to be real, but the way the light fractured inside it told her it was as real as the earth beneath her feet.

"Imogen Melanie Hargrove—" He dropped down to one knee. "I love you, too. And thanks very much for stealing my thunder."

Tears pricked her eyes, making her vision swim.

A wet drop fell onto her cheek and rolled toward her chin.

"Great, and now you're crying. This is *not* how I thought it would go down." His tone was warm and teasing. "We don't do anything the right way, do we?"

"I'm sorry, I didn't know!" She brushed the tears away with the backs of her hands. "I thought you were bringing me out here so we could get busy."

"That's my girl," he chuckled. "Always thinking about sex."

"Thanks to you." She grinned. "Now ask me the freaking question."

"Imogen Melanie Hargrove," he tried again, pausing to clear his throat. "It would make me the happiest man alive if you would spend the rest of your life getting busy with me."

She laughed through the tears and shook her head. "Really? That's what you want out of this relationship?"

"I want it all, baby. I want to have you in every position. I want to wake up every morning next to you so I can see how adorable you look with your face smooshed into the pillow. I want to sit on the couch and yell at the footy with you." He grinned. "I want to see you wear every colour of the rainbow. And I want to do it until we're old and grey."

"Yes," she said, her voice tripping on all the emotion clogging her throat. "I want that, too."

He slipped the diamond onto her finger and the cheer of a crowd startled Imogen. She hadn't even noticed the people gathering at the entrance to the stable—Penny, Daniel, Lainey, Damian, Jason and his soon-to-be fiancée, Anna. Their friends and family.

Caleb stood, still holding her hand, which suddenly felt so perfect with the ring on it, and drew her into his arms. "I can't believe you cut my grass like that."

She threw her head back and laughed. "I can't believe you invited an audience. I was promised sex and you haven't delivered, my dear fiancé."

"Just you wait." He lowered his head to hers, the intense stare reflecting all the love and desire she had swirling inside her. "I've got plans for us, Imogen. Big plans. And we're going to need a lifetime."

"Good." She tilted her face up to his, parting her lips in anticipation and not caring at all if everyone watched them kiss. "Let's get this party started, shall we?"

* * * * *

COMING SOON!

We really hope you enjoyed reading this book.
If you're looking for more romance
be sure to head to the shops when
new books are available on

Thursday 17th July

To see which titles are coming soon, please visit
millsandboon.co.uk/nextmonth

MILLS & BOON

MILLS & BOON

THE HEART OF ROMANCE

A ROMANCE FOR EVERY READER

MODERN — Prepare to be swept off your feet by sophisticated, sexy and seductive heroes, in some of the world's most glamourous and romantic locations, where power and passion collide.

HISTORICAL — Escape with historical heroes from time gone by. Whether your passion is for wicked Regency Rakes, muscled Vikings or rugged Highlanders, awaken the romance of the past.

MEDICAL — Set your pulse racing with dedicated, delectable doctors in the high-pressure world of medicine, where emotions run high and passion, comfort and love are the best medicine.

True Love — Celebrate true love with tender stories of heartfelt romance, from the rush of falling in love to the joy a new baby can bring, and a focus on the emotional heart of a relationship.

HEROES — The excitement of a gripping thriller, with intense romance at its heart. Resourceful, true-to-life women and strong, fearless men face danger and desire - a killer combination!

afterglow BOOKS — From showing up to glowing up, these characters are on the path to leading their best lives and finding romance along the way – with plenty of sizzling spice!

To see which titles are coming soon, please visit

millsandboon.co.uk/nextmonth

LET'S TALK
Romance

For exclusive extracts, competitions and special offers, find us online:

- **f** MillsandBoon
- **X** @MillsandBoon
- **O** @MillsandBoonUK
- **d** @MillsandBoonUK

Get in touch on 01413 063 232

For all the latest titles coming soon, visit
millsandboon.co.uk/nextmonth

FOUR BRAND NEW BOOKS FROM
MILLS & BOON MODERN

The same great stories you love, a stylish new look!

OUT NOW

Eight Modern stories published every month, find them all at:

millsandboon.co.uk

afterglow BOOKS

Afterglow Books is a trend-led, trope-filled list of books with diverse, authentic and relatable characters, a wide array of voices and representations, plus real world trials and tribulations. Featuring all the tropes you could possibly want (think small-town settings, fake relationships, grumpy vs sunshine, enemies to lovers) and all with a generous dose of spice in every story.

♪ @millsandboonuk
◎ @millsandboonuk
afterglowbooks.co.uk
#AfterglowBooks

For all the latest book news, exclusive content and giveaways scan the QR code below to sign up to the Afterglow newsletter:

afterglow BOOKS

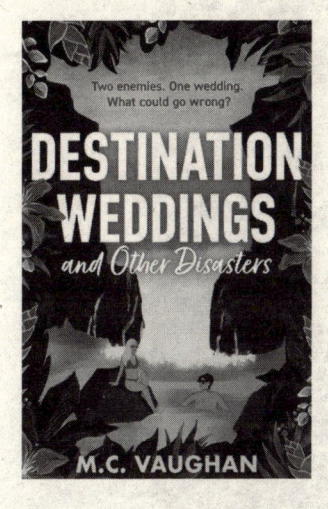

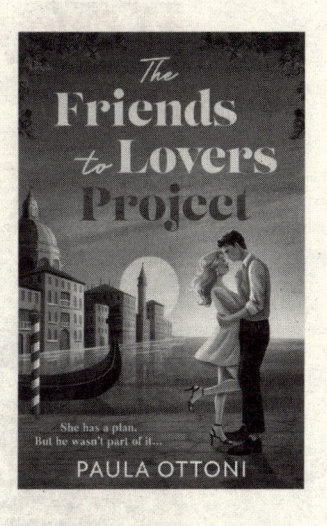

DESTINATION WEDDINGS and Other Disasters
Two enemies. One wedding. What could go wrong?
M.C. VAUGHAN

The Friends to Lovers Project
She has a plan. But he wasn't part of it...
PAULA OTTONI

- ✈ International
- 🔥 Enemies to lovers
- 📻 Forced proximity

- 👬 Friends to lovers
- ✈ International
- ▲ Love triangle

OUT NOW

Two stories published every month. Discover more at:
Afterglowbooks.co.uk

OUT NOW!

SECOND Chance

HIS UNEXPECTED HEIR

3 BOOKS IN ONE

LOUISE FULLER · AMANDA CINELLI · HEIDI RICE

Available at
millsandboon.co.uk

MILLS & BOON

OUT NOW!

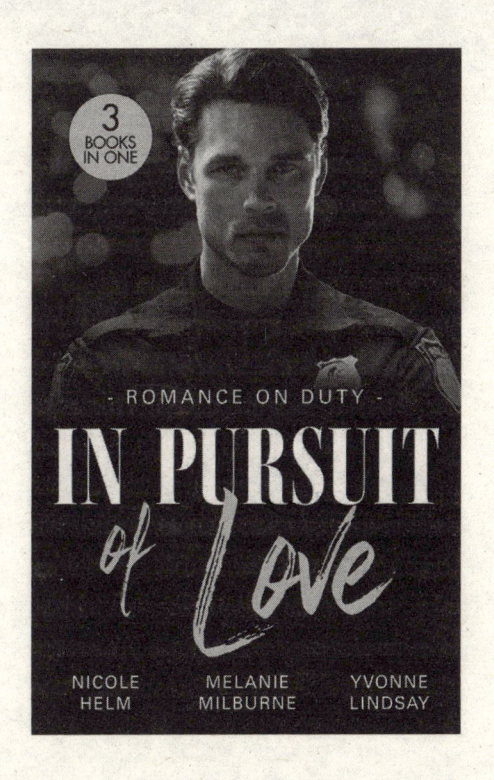

3 BOOKS IN ONE

- ROMANCE ON DUTY -

IN PURSUIT of Love

NICOLE HELM · MELANIE MILBURNE · YVONNE LINDSAY

Available at
millsandboon.co.uk

MILLS & BOON

OUT NOW!

A DARK ROMANCE SERIES

Veil of Deception

CLARE CONNELLY FAYE AVALON JENNIE LUCAS

Available at
millsandboon.co.uk

MILLS & BOON

MILLS & BOON
MODERN
Power and Passion

Prepare to be swept off your feet by sophisticated, sexy and seductive heroes, in some of the world's most glamorous and romantic locations, where power and passion collide.

Eight Modern stories published every month, find them all at:

millsandboon.co.uk

MILLS & BOON
HEROES
At Your Service

Experience all the excitement of a gripping thriller, with an intense romance at its heart that will keep you on the edge of your seat. Resourceful, true-to-life women and strong, fearless men face danger and desire – a killer combination!

SHADOWING HER STALKER
MAGGIE WELLS

COLTON'S LAST RESORT
AMBER LEIGH WILLIAMS

KILLER IN SHELLVIEW COUNTY
R. BARRI FLOWERS

COLTON'S DEADLY TRAP
PATRICIA SARGEANT

FUGITIVE HARBOR
CASSIE MILES

MISTAKEN IDENTITIES
TARA TAYLOR QUINN

Eight Heroes stories published every month, find them all at:

millsandboon.co.uk